A Book Of

STUDY OF
GLOBAL ECONOMICS

For BBM Semester - VI
As Per Revised Syllabus w.e.f. 2015

Mr. Himanshu Mehta
M.B.A. (International Business)
From Victoria University, Australia and North Carolina, USA

NIRALI
PRAKASHAN
ADVANCEMENT OF KNOWLEDGE

N3478

Study of Global Economics　　　　　　　　　　　　**ISBN 978-93-5164-848-2**

Second Edition : January 2017

Published By :　　　　　　　　　　　　**Polyplet**
NIRALI PRAKASHAN
Abhyudaya Pragati, 1312, Shivaji Nagar,
Off J.M. Road, PUNE – 411005
Tel - (020) 25512336/37/39, Fax - (020) 25511379
Email : niralipune@pragationline.com

☞ DISTRIBUTION CENTRES

PUNE
Nirali Prakashan　　　: 119, Budhwar Peth, Jogeshwari Mandir Lane, Pune 411002, Maharashtra
Tel : (020) 2445 2044, 66022708, Fax : (020) 2445 1538
Email : bookorder@pragationline.com, niralilocal@pragationline.com
Nirali Prakashan　　　: S. No. 28/27, Dhyari, Near Pari Company, Pune 411041
Tel : (020) 24690204 Fax : (020) 24690316
Email : dhyari@pragationline.com, bookorder@pragationline.com
MUMBAI
Nirali Prakashan　　　: 385, S.V.P. Road, Rasdhara Co-op. Hsg. Society Ltd.,
Girgaum, Mumbai 400004, Maharashtra
Tel : (022) 2385 6339 / 2386 9976, Fax : (022) 2386 9976
Email : niralimumbai@pragationline.com

☞ DISTRIBUTION BRANCHES

JALGAON
Nirali Prakashan　　　: 34, V. V. Golani Market, Navi Peth, Jalgaon 425001,
Maharashtra, Tel : (0257) 222 0395, Mob : 94234 91860
KOLHAPUR
Nirali Prakashan　　　: New Mahadvar Road, Kedar Plaza, 1st Floor Opp. IDBI Bank
Kolhapur 416 012, Maharashtra. Mob : 9850046155
NAGPUR
Pratibha Book Distributors　　　: Above Maratha Mandir, Shop No. 3, First Floor,
Rani Jhanshi Square, Sitabuldi, Nagpur 440012, Maharashtra
Tel : (0712) 254 7129
DELHI
Nirali Prakashan　　　: 4593/21, Basement, Aggarwal Lane 15, Ansari Road, Daryaganj
Near Times of India Building, New Delhi 110002
Mob : 08505972553
BENGALURU
Pragati Book House　　　: House No. 1, Sanjeevappa Lane, Avenue Road Cross,
Opp. Rice Church, Bengaluru – 560002.
Tel : (080) 64513344, 64513355,Mob : 9880582331, 9845021552
Email:bharatsavla@yahoo.com
CHENNAI
Pragati Books　　　: 9/1, Montieth Road, Behind Taas Mahal, Egmore,
Chennai 600008 Tamil Nadu, Tel : (044) 6518 3535,
Mob : 94440 01782 / 98450 21552 / 98805 82331,
Email : bharatsavla@yahoo.com

niralipune@pragationline.com　|　www.pragationline.com
Also find us on 🟦 www.facebook.com/niralibooks

DEDICATION

I dedicate this book to my family, especially my wife who has been my pillar of strength in all my endeaveours.

Preface ...

In today's globalised world, it is important to understand the nuances of various international economies and the manner in which each economy affects the globe. Until now, the western powers have directly and indirectly controlled the economy of the world. However, today world order is changing rapidly and has become so dynamic, that within a matter of just one decade almost all the aspects of a given economy change.

India is at the cusp of staging a big change in its economy and history is in the making as reflected in the BRIC report. The whole world is undergoing a change which would affect the dynamics of the world. Another developing country, China, has already undergone a transformation which has given it a place amongst the best rankings in the world. Countries like India and Russia are following closely and it is only a matter of time when other countries like South Africa and Brazil, etc. will also knock at the doors of becoming recognised as developed countries.

This book briefly outlines the salient aspects of international economies, and describes how these affect the global businesses and global relations. This book also provides an insight into the modalities of managing international businesses through a thorough understanding of international economies.

The book has been written strictly according to the syllabus. All attempts have been made to fulfill the objective of familiarising the students with the emerging issues in business at the international level with special focus on the policies of liberalisation and globalisation. This will help the students to recognise the status of Indian economy as one of the most important emerging economies in the global scenario.

I am thankful to NIRALI PRAKASHAN, especially Jignesh bhai and Dinesh bhai, for allowing me to write this book. Without their support, it would have been impossible for me to write with the freedom that any author would cherish. I am also thankful to my students who have taught me so much during my interaction with them.

As far as I am aware, this book does not have any errors. If the readers of this book come across any errors or mistakes, please feel free to inform me about the same. I will make the necessary changes to give updated and accurate information of the topic in more detail in the new editions.

***

Syllabus ...

1. **Introduction** [09]

   1.1 Globalisation

       1.1.1 Drivers of Globalisation

       1.1.2 The Globalisation Debate

   1.2 The Changing World Order

   1.3 Global Economy of the 21st Century

2. **Study of International Monetary Fund [IMF] and World Bank with reference to :**

   2.1 Nature of Global Financial Markets [08]

   2.2 Emerging Markets

   2.3 Poverty Aid

3. **Global Human Resource Management** [08]

   3.1 International Labour Relations – Concern and Strategy of Organised Labour

   3.2 Mobilising Talent for Global Development with respect to International Migration of Skilled and Unskilled Labour

4. **Challenges Confronting the Global Economy with reference to:** [05]

   4.1 Energy and Commodity Crisis

   4.2 Financial Turmoil

5. **India in the Global Setting** [08]

   5.1 India – An Emerging Market

   5.2 India in Global Trade

   5.3 Liberalisation and Integration with the Global Economy

10. **Case Studies in Economic and Business Environment in the Global Economy** [10]

    6.1 India and Europe

    6.2 India and Association of South East Asian Nations [ASEAN]

    6.3 India and North America

***

Contents ...

1. Introduction to Global Economics 1.1 - 1.42

2. Study of International Monetary Fund [IMF] and World Bank 2.1 - 2.34

3. Global Human Resource Management 3.1 - 3.38

4. Challenges Confronting the Global Economy 4.1 - 4.30

5. India in the Global Setting 5.1 - 5.48

6. Case Studies in Economic and

   Business Environment in the Global Economy 6.1 - 6.38

• Question Paper P.1 - P.1

***

Chapter **1**...

Introduction to Global Economics

Contents ...

1.1   Globalisation

    1.1.1   Introduction

    1.1.2   Meaning and Definitions of Globalisation

    1.1.3   Different Waves of Globalisation

    1.1.4   Drivers of Globalisation

1.2   The Globalisation Debate

    1.2.1   Introduction

    1.2.2   Arguments in Favour of Globalisation

    1.2.3   Arguments against Globalisation

1.3   The Changing World Order

    1.3.1   Introduction

    1.3.2   Factors Accountable for Changing World Order

1.4   Global Economy of the 21st Century

•   Points to Remember

•   Questions for Discussion

Learning Objectives ...

- To define globalisation
- To understand the different waves of globalisation
- To identify the drivers of globalisation
- To illustrate the debate on globalisation
- To highlight the changing of world order in terms of globalisation
- To describe the global economy of the 21st century

1.1 Globalisation

1.1.1 Introduction

Today, the global economy is in a state of dynamic flux – one that is, both rapidly undergoing and alternately triggering tremendous changes in its wake across societies and nations. This, juxtaposed with revolutionary changes in technology, attitudes of peoples, opening up of markets, production and trading and investment patterns is proving to be a game-changer insofar as conducting businesses go. That apart, the phenomena of faster information flows coupled with falling transport costs are increasingly breaking down geographical barriers to economic activity. As a result, the boundary between what can and cannot be traded is being steadily eroded. This is more so in the scenario wherein the global market is encompassing ever-greater numbers of goods and services. In a nutshell, the whole paradigm of doing business is being redefined, with the developing countries like India, China at the crux of the system.

Globalisation is a process of developing deeper economic integration among countries as well as regions of the world. It is a trend of increasing the mutual association of different markets by investing funds and businesses to progress beyond domestic and national markets to other markets across the globe. Globalisation has the tendency of not only increasing international trade but also cultural exchange. It is a method of communication and integration between people, companies, and governments of various nations. It is a course which focuses on international trade and investment supported by information technology. Globalisation creates an impact on the environment, culture, political systems, and economic development as well as on human physical well-being in societies around the globe. A perfect example for early globalisation is the Silk Route across Central Asia that connected China and Europe during the Middle Ages for trade.

1.1.2 Meaning and Definitions of Globalisation

Globalisation is the free movement of goods, services and individuals across the globe in a seamless and integrated style. Globalisation is the outcome of the emerging global economy and the simultaneous increase in trade amid nations. In other words, the nations those were up till now closed to trade and foreign investment, are going global by opening up their economies. The consequence is a growing interconnectedness and integration of the world economy. It also indicates that countries liberalise their import protocol and welcome foreign investment into sectors that are the basis of its economy. In short, nations attract global capital by opening up their economies to multinational corporations. Globalisation is an ongoing and a complex process, which has several layers and dimensions. Since its scope is constantly stretching and its pace continues to quicken up its meaning is undergoing changes.

Globalisation can also be defined as the growth and acceleration of economic and cultural networks that function on an international level that have far-reaching consequences for individuals and civilisations in distant parts of the world. According to critics, globalisation has economic, political, technological and cultural aspects that are strongly intertwined. In the economic domain, it is a systematic process of integration of national economies with the aim of making the global economy widen the capacity to work as a unit. Globalisation needs to be distinguished from internationalisation. Since global networks have become instant, globalisation transcends the nation's frontiers and acquires a super-territorial and trans-world character.

Globalisation *"is the closer integration of the countries and peoples of the world... brought about by the enormous reduction of costs of transportation and communication, and the breaking down of artificial barriers to the flows of goods, services, capital, knowledge, and people across borders".*

A useful definition of globalisation is that offered by Gibson-Graham (2006) – *"A set of processes by which the world is rapidly being integrated into one economic space via increased international trade, the internationalisation of production and financial markets, the internationalisation of a commodity culture promoted by an increasingly networked global telecommunications system".*

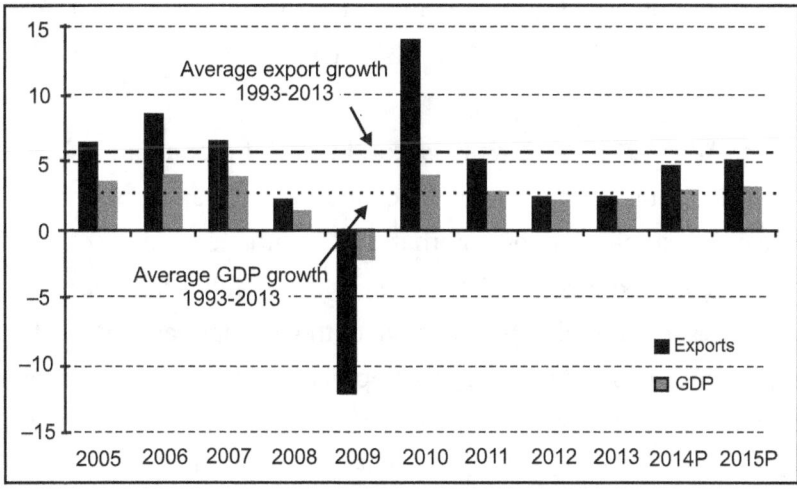

Fig. 1.1

Many factors contributed to the weakness of trade and output in 2013, including the lingering impact of the EU recession, high unemployment in euro area economies (Germany being a notable exception), and uncertainty about the timing of the Federal Reserve's winding down of its monetary stimulus in the United States. The latter contributed to financial instability in developing economies in the second half of 2013, mainly in certain "emerging" economies with large current account imbalances.

The preliminary estimate of 2.1 percent for world trade growth in 2013 refers to the average of merchandise exports and imports in volume terms; that is, adjusted to account for differences in inflation and exchange rates across countries. This figure is slightly lower than the WTO's most recent forecast of 2.5 percent for 2013. The main reason for the divergence was a stronger than expected decline in developing economies' trade flows in the second half of last year. For the second consecutive year, world trade has grown at roughly the same rate as world GDP (gross domestic product, a measure of countries' economic output) at market exchange rates, rather than twice as fast, as is normally the case.

1.1.3 Different Waves of Globalisation

1. Wave One: It began around 1870 and ended with a descent into global protectionism during the inter-war period of the 1920s and 1930s. This period was, on the one hand, marked by a rapid growth in international trade, driven by economic policies that sought to liberalise the flows of goods and people, and, on the other, which persisted for over a century, of developing countries specialising in primary commodities which they export to the developed countries in return for manufactures. During this wave of globalisation, the level of world trade (defined by the ratio of world exports to GDP) increased from 2 percent of GDP in 1800 to 10 percent in 1870, 17 percent in 1900 and 21 percent in 1913.

2. Wave Two: After 1945, there was a second wave of globalisation built on a surge in world trade and reconstruction of the world economy. The rapid expansion of trade was supported by the establishment of new international economic institutions. The International Monetary Fund (IMF) was created in 1944 to promote a stable monetary system so as to provide a sound basis for multilateral trade, and the World Bank (WB) (founded as the International Bank for Reconstruction and Development) to help restore economic activity in the devastated countries of Europe and Asia. Their aim was to promote lasting multilateral economic co-operation between nations. The General Agreement on Tariffs and Trade (GATT) signed in 1947 provided a framework for progressive mutual reduction in import tariffs.

3. Wave Three: The current wave of globalisation which is demonstrated, for example, by a sharp rise in the ratio of trade to GDP for many countries and, secondly, a sustained increase in capital flows between countries and trade in goods and services.

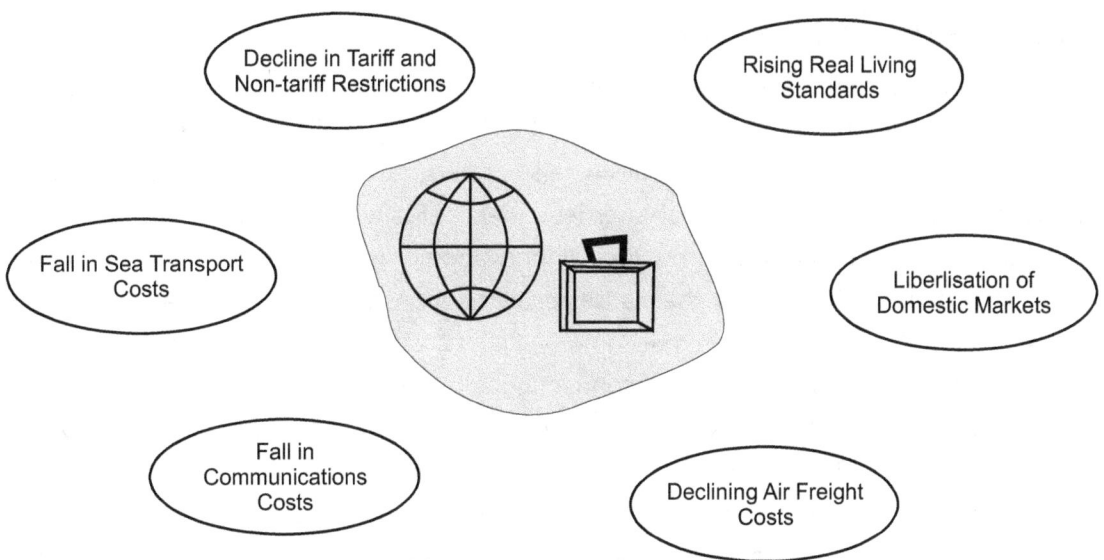

Fig. 1.2: Different Waves of Globalisation

Table 1.1

	The First Wave	**The Second Wave**	**The Third Wave**
Time period	1860-1914	1944-1971	1989-
Technology	Steam engine Telegraph Electricity Internal combustion engine	Jet planes Television Communication satellites Container traffic	Microprocessor PC Internet Mobile telephones
Political Leadership	Great Britain economic leader Colonialism	USA economic leader Cold War	Multi-polar (USA, EU, China). Global democratic processes
Commerce	Initially free trade, but increasing protectionism	Gradually reduced industrial tariffs	More and more countries adopt free trade
Trade in Services	Limited scale Shipping industry most important	Limited scale Shipping industry most important	Increased scale in more and more branches
Capital movement	Free	Regulated	Free
Migration	Free movement Emigration	Regulated (excluding Nordic countries) Labour migration	Regulated (excluding EU) Political migration

1.1.4 Drivers of Globalisation

On the whole, the presence of globalisation suggests that it is driven by some strong environmental issue. 'The technology revolution' or 'techno globalism' are the terms used to refer to globalisation. Techno globalism also refers to the role that technological advancement plays in building global interdependence. Many a times it is difficult to make out whether globalisation drives technological innovation or its technological innovation that drives globalisation. This makes the cause-result relationship very vague and uncertain. However, without doubt, modern telecommunications systems aid the establishment of subsidiaries or the effective interaction connecting alliance business partners – for instance, when mutual access to electronic booking details facilitates code-sharing between Qantas and British Airways. Telecommunications also solves the time and space barriers for communication that earlier made it very difficult to execute business. For instance, the usage of the Internet, makes a message available to the receiver the moment the sender sends it. It has helped the world big-time right from a student getting a course done till clients booking airline tickets at any time of the day or night irrespective of location. This reality allows people to communicate across vast distances, at a very low cost, and with dramatically reduced time cost.

Other drivers that aid globalisation are related to a specific environment in which a business functions. These drivers can be grouped as **market drivers, cost drivers, government and economic drivers, and competitive drivers**. These environmental drivers are listed below:

1) Globalisation market drivers

Market globalisation drivers are the forces and factors that influence the pace of globalisation of an industry. Market drivers are essential for understanding the customer demand pattern of consumption. If many customers demand similar products, the pace of globalisation is accelerated. There is a "convergence" in demand, when there are sufficient channels of distribution for supplying products and services to customers globally. For instance, semiconductors have similar demands across the world. PC manufacturers in Europe, Asia, or the United States would seek a common 1-megabyte memory chip. In comparison, the local regulations still governs publishing and has less of a uniform demand across different parts of the planet. There are five market globalisation drivers.

(a) Common Customer Needs and Tastes

Common customer needs and tastes "represent the extent to which customers in different countries want the same things in the product or service category that defines an industry". Many factors like culture, climate, and infrastructure affect the tastes and preferences of consumers. The higher the level of commonalities among consumer groups, the more likely that product will be accepted by them. Today, teenagers all over the world wear Nike athletic shoes and Levi's jeans. As compared to thirty years ago, bottled water which is now consumed around the world is no longer a luxury item confined to only the most exclusive cafes in Paris. The pace of globalisation becomes much faster with consumer needs converging or become more common.

(b) Global Customers

Global customers are generally companies that purchase certain items in bulk on behalf of an entire organisation and distribute them to subsidiaries. They create a demand of standardised products for large batches. For example when Wal-Mart and IKEA, the furniture retailers, source items they purchase in bulk. By doing so, they are also able to secure cost economies, which can leverage into low prices. This reflects Wal-Mart's role as a global consumer. The presence of such global consumers in an industry tends to accelerate the pace of globalisation.

(c) Global Channels

A global channel indicates the distribution of a particular type of products on a large scale in a universal way. This lessens the cost of managing various distribution requirements. Across the world, supply chains have been cautiously crafted to benefit the sourcing opportunities and to open up means of distribution. IKEA found channels to be closed to them—a form of retaliation from the traditional furniture retailers. These channels were opened up to enable it to become the world's leading, low-cost furniture retailer. With the employment and development of global channels, the industrial globalisation flourishes with a fast pace.

(d) Transferrable Marketing

Transferable means the degree of adaptation that has to be made for brands that are to be transferred for international trading. The pace of globalisation will be easier and faster, if the marketing schemes, models or strategies can be transferred from country to country with very little adjustment. A good example is the leading world supplier of laundry detergents, Procter & Gamble (P&G) is able to use marketing developed in Europe in its Asian markets, thus reducing the cost of redesigning them for promotional and advertising schemes.

(e) Lead Countries

The globalisation of industry goes down with the infrequency of trade. Lead countries are where innovation is concentrated in a few countries, which ultimately leads the development of new products. Non-lead country customers tend to look at lead countries for latest trends. By using their reputation in lead countries, the existence of lead countries permits companies to endorse a product in other countries. The popularity of the United States products reflects its lead-country status in many industries, notably financial services, entertainment, information technology, biotechnology, and nanotechnology. Japan's strengths lie in optic design and materials management, while Korea's Samsung is beginning to excel in photo-plasma technology. As more lead countries emerge and as more firms participate in these lead countries to lie exposed to sources of innovation, the faster would be the pace of industrial globalisation.

(f) Lead companies (MNCs)

MNCs (Multi National Corporations) form a very important constituent of increasing globalisation in today's world. The MNCs try to increase their footprint throughout the world and in te process, increase the exports and imports of the countries. These MNCs are predominantly from USA and other western countries but in recent times, developing countries like Mexico, China, India, etc. are fast catching up. Some of these companies are so large that their turnover is larger than the GDP of many countries.

2) Cost Globalisation Drivers

Cost globalisation drivers are the cost factors and forces that can transform the pace of globalisation. The pace of globalisation enhances when costs are reduced to the point that products become affordable. The main advantage of global strategy is cost reduction which results from scale and scope economies. Cost globalisation drivers are medium that helps cost reduction. As their cost of production has sharply decreased, semiconductors and VCRs have become global industries. However, the pace of globalisation is relatively slower with the high process and differing standards for HDTV. There are basically seven cost globalisation drivers.

(a) Global Scale Economies

Economics of scale (cost efficiencies that are realised when the volume of an activity is increased) are essential for cost reduction. Global strategy demands economies of scale at the global level to attain cost benefits that value global strategies. This takes place when a single market is not big enough for competitors to optimise economics of scale. In some cases, economies of scope (cost efficiencies that are realised by spreading activities across different product lines and multiple plants), which permits a firm to trade multiple products in multiple countries, become a part of a global strategy which aims at reducing costs. Chemicals, steel, petroleum, and automobile industries with large fixed costs tend to utilise expansion strategies in which economies of scale and scope can be realised. In fact, steel and consumer electronics world markets have resulted from cost reductions emanating from scale. In case of automobiles, multinational firms have gained from efficiencies in scope arising from several plants and locations.

(b) Steep Experience Effects

By repetitively performing an activity an experience (learning) curve representing cost efficiency is gained. In a chain of studies conducted by the BCG (Boston Consulting Group) researchers, many products including bottle caps, refrigerators, and long-distance calls, observed a remarkable regularity in which costs were lessened with cumulative production. Doubling of cumulative production typically reduced unit costs by 20 to 30 percent (defined now, as 80 percent and 70 percent experience curves, respectfully). The greater the reduction in unit costs with increased production, the steeper the experience curve. In case of global strategy, this means that experience effects should be relevant to many locations and that experience effects achieved from one place can be applied and utilised in other locations to boost the overall global-level effects. For instance, in case of semiconductors, the cost per unit over reduces by 30 percent every time experience is doubled.

(c) Global Sourcing Efficiencies

This is related to economies of scale from the supply side. In order to attain global sourcing efficiencies, a firm should be capable enough to obtain inputs on a large scale and at a low cost through well-established coordination among suppliers globally. Wal-Mart serves as a best example of it which excels in worldwide sourcing efficiencies, particularly in China. McDonald's which specifically uses local supplies for its basic food ingredients, also benefits from its global sourcing.

(d) Favourable Logistics

This refers to the economies in transporting products against the value of the products. The usage of standardised products across multiple consumer groups is discouraged, when products are low in value but have high transportation costs. A favourable situation takes place when cost benefits and logistical convenience are available in many countries globally. Cisco, with a ramped-up supply chain can move quickly around the world in search of its best source of supplies. The capacity of Starbucks to secure vital partnerships with suppliers in Latin America and Africa has helped its global strategy.

(e) Differences in Country Costs

Global firms, generally tend to approach the lowest-cost suppliers, designers or skilled labour. In order for to the global strategy to be successfully applied, different cost levels in different countries should exist. There will be minimal or no cost benefits if there are insignificant or no differences. Due to their lower labour cost, Vietnam, India, and China have become desirable. A lot of North American publishers have started to produce software in India where they are able to pay programmers a much lower wage along with comparable quality in the products.

(f) High Product Development Costs

High product development costs virtual to the size of the national market can be a driver of globalisation, but two considerations apply. Firstly, when the costs of product development are high, to reduce total costs firms are motivated to promote mere products in various markets so as to reduce the average cost of development per unit. Secondly, high product development costs discourage some less resourceful firms to contribute in the competition. Semiconductor costs are significant, with a new plant costing over $1.5 billion. This has led to various consortia, SEMATECH being one example, which shares developmental costs across competitors.

(g) Fast-Changing Technology

For products that depend on rapidly-changing technology, firms have to spread out the cost of the product through multiple, large markets before the product becomes outdated or imitated. Thus, industries characterised by fast-changing technologies (for example, semiconductors) tend to have a greater globalisation potential and a faster pace of globalisation. As new semiconductor plants are costly and have a three-to-five-year lifespan, Samsung and Hyundai rely on large markets to meet their returns on investment which in turn, accelerates the pace of semiconductor globalisation.

3) Government Globalisation Drivers

Government globalisation drivers are policies that can enhance or impair the pace of globalisation. Globalisation is enhanced when policies favour free trade and relatively open access. The pace of globalisation is much slower if the policies deter market entry. These policies' existence depends on the overall friendly or unfriendly environment that the government makes available for business. There are generally five government globalisation drivers.

(a) Favourable Trade Policies

Favourable trade policies consist of trade liberalisation for foreign investment and user-friendly business policies, which create possibilities for global firms. For instance, lower tariff rates for the semiconductor industry have improved its pace of globalisation. In contrast, if tariffs were reduced, the worldwide market for agrarian products would be much more developed. The lowering of rates aids the globalisation of production.

(b) Compatible technical standards

Sometimes for the sake of protecting home markets and consumers, countries adopt different technical standards for products. This makes it difficult to transfer and standardise products. Compatible technical standards among countries offer a platform for facilitating product transfer and standardisation. For instance, inconsistent standards prevent HDTV from being widely adopted around the globe. In contrast, when DVD standards were openly adopted, DVD sales soared to become a universal product.

(c) Common Market Regulations

Common marketing regulations refer to the uniformity of the marketing environment in different countries. The more uniform they are, the easier it is for standardised products to be marketed across multiple consumer groups.

(d) Government-Owned Competitors and Customers

Government-owned competitors, if they have the support from their governments, tend to be more aggressive in entering foreign markets. Such firms are more capable of following foreign markets. In the case of government-owned customers, with their preference for buying from local suppliers, the opposite is true. In such a case, government-owned customers become an obstacle to globalisation. The preference on the part of European customers to source from local suppliers, instead of buying much cheaper semiconductors with comparable quality from Japan, impeded the development of the European PC industry. Nonetheless, government-owned corporations are not essentially successful in their global activities. One source of debate is China's hold on its SOEs (state-owned enterprises), which comprise about 60 percent of China's GDP. They are encouraged by the Chinese government in spite of their poor performance, as SOEs tend to be the primary source of employment.

(e) Host Government Concerns

Some aspects of a foreign firm's global strategies cause legal worry that discourages host governments from being open-minded towards it. Some of these issues consist of tax avoidance by the firm and the possibility that the firm may regularly relocate its subsidiaries from nation to nation.

4) Competitive Globalisation Drivers

Competitive globalisation drivers are the competitive forces that can modify the pace of globalisation. By bringing in different rivals, products and services, the pace of globalisation is encouraged. There are five competitive globalisation drivers.

(a) High Exports and Imports

A high volume in the export and import of certain goods is a sign that potential standardised products exist. Manufacturing the products near their markets will reduce the transportation cost reduction. Moreover, trade between countries spurs the pace of globalisation.

(b) Competitors from Different Continents

The competition tends to be more severe, if rivals in a particular industry come from various backgrounds. Hence, it is vital for firms to pursue global strategies to fight competition. The entry of the Chinese and the Vietnamese into telecommunications signals different strategies that will only intensify competition and increase the pace of globalisation. Reflecting on the entry strategies used by Japanese firms it is not unusual for new competitors from different countries to initiate new strategies, thereby changing the rules of competition.

(c) Interdependence of Countries

Interdependence among foreign subsidiaries permits firms to reimburse for one subsidiary's weaknesses by sharing resources among all subsidiaries. It also spurs competitors to pursue like strategies to offset rivals. Firms can subsidise attacks on competitors in other countries along with interdependent countries. Komatsu's success against Caterpillar in the United States stemmed in part from Komatsu's success in Eastern Europe, which allowed the company to drive down cost through experience. Komatsu was able to prepare itself when it battled Caterpillar in the United States without having to compete openly with Caterpillar in Eastern Europe.

(d) Globalised Competition

The competitive factor is transformed and other firms are pressured to become global when globalised competitors actively engage in global activities. Consequently, more firms turn global and the industry itself transforms into being global. Citibank, which found competition in Asia to be quite intense with the established presence of Chase Manhattan, J. P. Morgan and HSBC, become more multinational in their operations.

(e) Transferable Competitive Advantage

If a firm's competitive advantage can be transferred from market to market, then it is encouraged to keep going abroad and to duplicate its success from country to country. The successful application of its Direct System by Dell Computers in London and China will certainly leverage its entry into new markets that are receptive to this system. The same holds for Starbucks, which has successfully made a way into Latin America, Asia and parts of Europe using its strategy of creating a superior coffee experience for targeted consumers.

In short, all four globalisation drivers dictate the globalisation potential of an industry, that is, its pace of globalisation. If the pace of globalisation is high, it quickly develops global strategies. There is growing pressure for companies to develop an international market presence if the globalisation of the competitive landscape intensifies. Nevertheless, having a global presence does not guarantee that a firm will sustain its competitive advantage. Its ability to learn quickly from experiences and develop dynamic capabilities becomes important considerations in forging a successful endgame.

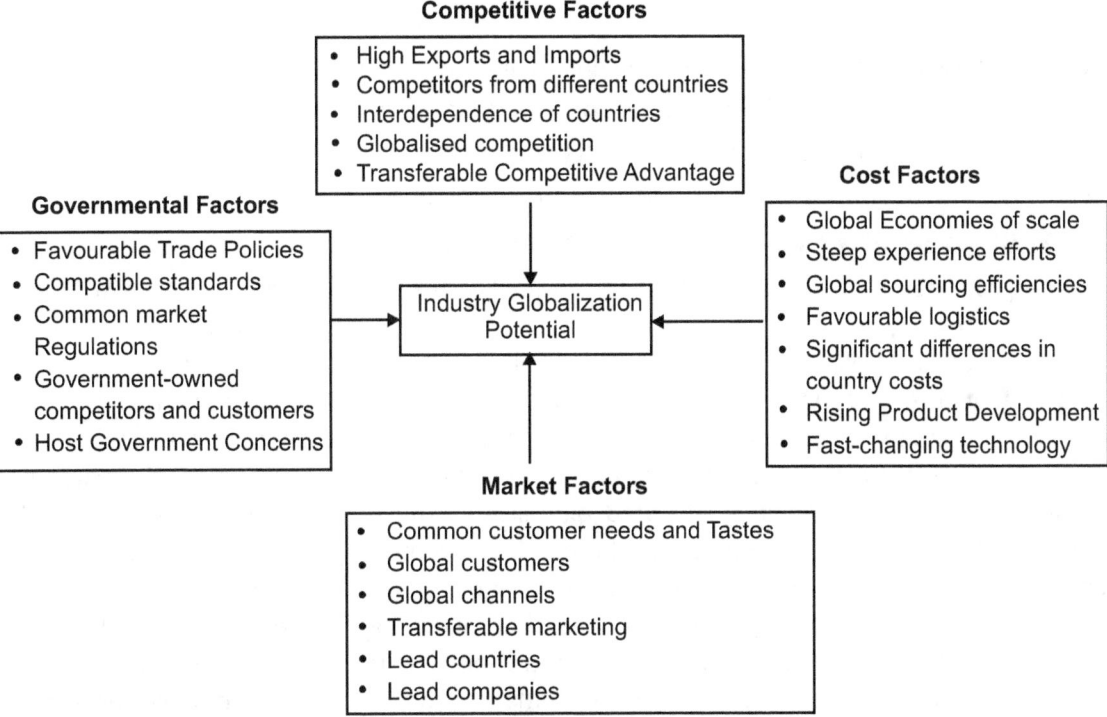

Fig. 1.3

1.2 The Globalisation Debate

1.2.1 Introduction

There are seemingly conflicting reactions from the two sides on the ongoing debate on globalisation and inequality. On one side, the website of a prominent NGO in the anti-globalisation movement, the International Forum on Globalisation, confidently claims that "globalisation policies have increased inequality among and within nations. This stands in marked contrast to the claims made by those more favourable to globalisation".

It must be accredited that the available data on poverty and inequality are imperfect which neither side of this debate has paid much attention to. There are also potentially important differences in the types of data used. The "pro-globalisation" side has tended to prefer "hard" quantitative data while the other side has drawn more eclectically on various types of evidence, both systematic and anecdotal or subjective. Differences in the data used no doubt account in part for the differing positions taken.

One reason now such different views persist is that it is difficult to detach effects of globalisation from the many other factors imposing on how the distribution of income is evolving in the world. The processes of global economic integration are so persistent that it is hard to say what the world would be like without them. These complications of attribution offer ample fuel for debate though they also leave one suspicious of the confident claims made by both sides.

Conflicting assessments can also stem from hidden contextual factors. Diverse impacts of the same growth-promoting policies on inequality can he expected. Policy reforms shift distribution of income in different directions in different countries. Yet both sides make generalisations about distributional impacts without specifying the context. In a given country setting, there may well be much less to disagree about.

1.2.2 Arguments in Favour of Globalisation

The proponents of free trade claim that globalisation increases economic prosperity as well as opportunity, especially amongst developing nations, enhances civil liberties and leads to a more efficient allocation of resources. Economic theories of comparative advantage suggest that free trade leads to a more efficient allocation of resources, with all countries involved in it standing to benefit. In general, this leads to lower prices, more employment, higher output and a higher standard of living for those in developing countries. Research has proved that countries that have accepted globalisation have grown faster than those who have not. The GDP of the countries and the real income of the people have increased much faster than those countries that have yet not opened their markets to foreign companies. Proponents of capitalism say that countries that allow higher degrees of political and economic freedom in the form of democracy and capitalism in the developed world are ends in themselves and also produce higher levels of material wealth. They see globalisation as the beneficial spread of liberty and capitalism. The supporters of globalisation argue that the anti-globalisation movement uses anecdotal evidence to support their protectionist view, whereas worldwide statistics strongly support globalisation.

The benefits of globalisation are mentioned in the points below. They are as under –

1. Life expectancy has almost doubled in the developing world since World War II and is starting to close the gap between itself and the developed world where the improvement has been smaller. Even in Sub-Saharan Africa, the least developed region, life expectancy increased from 30 years before World War II to about a peak of about 50 years before the AIDS pandemic and other diseases started to force it down to the current level of 47 years. Infant mortality has decreased in every developing region of the world.

2. Democracy has increased dramatically from there being almost no nations with universal suffrage in 1900 to 62.5 percent of all nations having it in 2000. Feminism has made advances in areas, such as Bangladesh through providing women with jobs and economic safety.

3. The proportion of the world's population living in countries where per capita food supplies are less than 2,200 calories (9,200 kilojoules) per day decreased from 56 percent in the mid-1960s to below 10 percent by the 1990s.

4. Between 1950 and 1999, global literacy increased from 52 percent to 81 percent of the world. Women made up much of the gap; female literacy as a percentage of male literacy has increased from 59 percent in 1970 to 80 percent in 2000.

5. The percentage of children in the labour force has fallen from 24 percent in 1960 to 10 percent in 2000.

6. There are similar increasing trends toward electric power, cars, radios, and telephones per capita, as well as a growing proportion of the population with access to clean water.

7. The book *'The Improving State of the World'* also finds evidence that these and other measures of human well-being have improved and that globalisation is part of the explanation. It also responds to arguments that environmental impact will limit the progress.

8. Although critics of globalisation complain of westernisation, a 2005 UNESCO report showed that cultural exchange is becoming mutual. In 2002, China was the third largest exporter of cultural goods, after the UK and US. Between 1994 and 2002, both North America's and the European Union's shares of cultural exports declined, while Asia's cultural exports grew to surpass North America.

9. The percentage of people living on less than $2 a day has decreased greatly in areas affected by globalisation whereas poverty rates in other areas have remained largely stagnant. In East-Asia, including China, the percentage has decreased by 50.1 percent as compared to a 2.2 percent increase in Sub-Saharan Africa.

10. Income inequality for the world as a whole is diminishing in the countries that have opened up their markets for the world. Due to definitional issues and data availability, there is disagreement with regards to the pace of the decline in extreme poverty. As noted below, there are others disputing this. The economist Xavier Sala-i-Martin in a 2007 analysis argues that this is incorrect, income inequality for the world as a whole has not diminished. Regardless of who is right about the past trend in income inequality, it has been argued that improving absolute poverty is more important than relative inequality.

1.2.3 Arguments against Globalisation

Anti-globalisation is a critical term used to describe the political stance of people and groups who oppose the neoliberal version of globalisation. Anti-globalisation may involve the process or actions taken by a state in order to demonstrate its sovereignty and practice democratic decision-making. Anti-globalisation may occur in order to put brakes on the international transfer of people, goods and ideology, particularly those determined by the organisations, such as, the **IMF** or the **WTO** in imposing the radical deregulation programme of free market fundamentalism on local governments and populations. Anti-globalism can denote either a single social movement or an umbrella term that encompasses a number of separate social movements, such as, nationalists and socialists. In either case, participants stand in opposition to the unregulated political power of large, multi-national corporations, as the corporations exercise power through leveraging trade agreements which damage in some instances the democratic rights of citizens, the environment particularly air quality index and rain forests, as well as national governments' sovereignty to determine labour rights including the right to unionise for better pay, and better working conditions, or laws as they may otherwise infringe on cultural practices and traditions of developing countries.

The critiques of the current wave of economic globalisation typically look at both the damage to the planet, in terms of the perceived unsustainable harm done to the biosphere, as well as the perceived human costs, such as, increased poverty, inequality, miscegenation, injustice and the erosion of traditional culture which, the critics contend, all occur as a result of the economic transformations related to globalisation. They point to a multitude of interconnected fatal consequences – social disintegration, a breakdown of democracy, more rapid and extensive deterioration of the environment, the spread of new diseases, increasing poverty and alienation which they claim are the unintended but very real consequences of globalisation.

The harmful effects of globalisation are mentioned in the points below. They are as under –

(1) Poorer countries are sometimes at a disadvantage. While it is true that globalisation encourages free trade among countries on an international level, there are also negative consequences because some countries try to save their national markets. The main export of poorer countries is usually agricultural goods. It is difficult for these countries to compete with stronger countries that subsidise their own farmers. Because the farmers in the poorer countries cannot compete, they are forced to sell their crops at a much lower price than what the market is paying.

(2) The MNCs exploit the environment of the poorer countries which cannot fight against the might of the larger companies and have to bear with the exploitation or risk losing the companies which may go to other countries for their productions and operations. Organisations, like the WTO, IMF etc. have been working under the influence of the developed world and thus they are not sympathetic and supportive of the developing countries which lead to the developing countries being victims of unfair practices.

(3) The deterioration of protections for weaker nations by stronger industrialised powers has resulted in the exploitation of the people in those nations to become cheap labour. Due to lack of adequate protections, the companies from powerful industrialised nations are able to offer workers enough salary to entice them to endure extremely long hours and unsafe working conditions. The abundance of

cheap labour is giving the countries in power incentive not to rectify the inequality between nations. If these nations developed into industrialised nations, the army of cheap labour would slowly disappear alongside development.

(4) With the world in this current state, it is impossible for the exploited workers to escape poverty. It is true that the workers are free to leave their jobs, but in many poorer countries, this would mean starvation for the worker and, possibly even his/her family.

(5) The low cost of offshore workers have enticed corporations to move production to foreign countries. The laid-off unskilled workers are forced into the service sector where wages and benefits are low, but turnover is high. This has contributed to the widening economic gap between skilled and unskilled workers. The loss of these jobs has also contributed greatly to the slow decline of the middle class which is a major factor in the increasing economic inequality in the United States. The families that were once part of the middle class are forced into lower positions by massive layoffs and outsourcing to another country. This also means that people in the lower class have a much harder time climbing out of poverty because of the absence of the middle class as a stepping stone.

(6) The surplus cheap labour coupled with an ever-growing number of companies in transition has caused a weakening of labour unions in the United States. The unions lose their effectiveness when their membership begins to decline. As a result, the unions hold less power over corporations that are able to easily replace workers, often for lower wages, and have the option to not offer unionised jobs anymore.

The critics of globalisation typically emphasise that globalisation is a process that is mediated according to corporate interests, and typically raise the possibility of alternative global institutions and policies, which they believe address the moral claims of poor and working classes throughout the globe, as well as environmental concerns in a more equitable way. The movement is very broad, including church groups, national liberation factions, peasant unionists, intellectuals, artists, protectionists, anarchists, those in support of relocalisation and others. Some are reformist (arguing for a more humane form of capitalism), while others are more revolutionary (arguing for what they believe is a more humane system than capitalism) and others are reactionary, believing globalisation destroys national industry and jobs.

Table 1.2: Distribution of World GDP

Quintile of Population Income	
Richest 20%	82.7%
Second 20%	11.7%
Third 20%	2.3%
Fourth 20%	2.4%
Poorest 20%	0.2%

1.3 The Changing World Order

1.3.1 Introduction

In the global economy, wide changes are afoot. As the second decade of the 21st century unfolds and the world exits financial crisis, the growing influence of emerging markets is paving the way for a world economy with an increasingly multi-polar character. The distribution of global growth will become more diffuse, with no single country dominating the global economic scene. The world has witnessed emerging economies rise to become a powerful force in international production, trade, and finance, over the past two decades. Developing countries' share of international trade flows has increased steadily. Financial holdings and wealth of emerging economies have also improved. Emerging and developing countries now hold two-thirds of all official foreign exchange reserves, and sovereign wealth funds and other pools of capital in developing countries have become key sources of international investment. Multinational companies increase their exposure to fast-growing emerging economies as investors. Thus, international demand for emerging-economy currencies would grow, making way for a global monetary system with more than one dominant currency. The growing strength of emerging economies also affects the policy environment necessitating more inclusive global economic policy-making in the future.

The world is increasingly moving toward a single currency. In due course of time, we will see a currency that is accepted all over the world. Also, the creation of a financial stability seems to be the prelude towards a global financial regulator, or, simply put, a global central bank is likely to be created. It is important to take a closer look at these 'solutions' being proposed and implemented in the midst of the current global financial crisis. However, the larger economies have fast-tracked their agenda of forging a New World Order in finance. It is important to address the background to these proposed and imposed 'solutions' as to what effects they are likely to have on the International Monetary System (IMS) and the global political economy as a whole. We have to try and understand which countries have the potential to be the superpower in the future. There are many reports which give an insight into what are the important aspects of the potential countries that may have a larger impact in the world in the future.

1.3.2 Factors Accountable for Changing World Order

1. The Financial New World Order

Today, the world is trying to integrate as much as possible. Many organisations, like, the WTO, IMF, IBRD etc. are operating since a long time with efficiency and effectiveness. These organisations are facilitating trade, commerce and investment and thus international business has increased by more than 6 percent today as compared to the increase in the GDP of countries, which has increased only by 3 percent. Many more such organisations are coming forward to control a larger part of the global economy that will facilitate trade to a much larger extent thereby making the world a much smaller place. A common currency, a common bank etc. throughout the world is something that is being tried and tested in today's environment. The world is increasingly moving toward a single currency. In due course of time, we will see a   currency that is accepted all over the world. Also, the creation of a Financial Stability seems to be the prelude towards a global financial regulator, or, simply put, a global central bank is likely to be created.

We should bring transparency, sound banking, responsibility, integrity and global governance. We agreed that urgent decisions implementing these principles should be made to root out the irresponsible and often undisclosed lending at the heart of our problems. To do this, we need cross-border supervision of financial institutions; shared global standards for accounting and regulation; a more responsible approach to executive remuneration that rewards hard work, effort and enterprise but not irresponsible risk-taking; and the renewal of our international institutions to make them effective early-warning systems for the world economy.

2. Emergence of Regional Currencies

On January 1, 1999, the European Union established the Euro as its regional currency. The Euro has grown in prominence since then. However, it is not to be the only regional currency in the world. There are moves and calls for other regional currencies throughout the world. Many regions around the world are in the process of starting their own currencies. We already have the Euro, which is likely to be followed by the other regional currencies, like, The Union of South American Nations (UNASUR) in South America, The Gulf Cooperation Council (GCC) and a Regional Currency in the Middle East, an Asian Monetary Union (AMU) in Asia, the North American Monetary Union (NAMU) and the Amero in North America and the African Monetary Union (AMU) in Africa. A lot of work is being done to bring these currencies into being.

National currencies and global markets simply do not mix; together they make for a deadly brew of currency crises and geopolitical tensions and create ready pretexts for damaging protectionism. In order to globalise safely, the countries concerned should abandon monetary nationalism and abolish unwanted currencies, the source of much of today's instability. In October, 2008, European Central Bank council member Ewald Nowotny said a tri-polar global currency system is developing between Asia, Europe and the U.S.

3. A Global Currency

In 1988, The Economist ran an article in which he wrote, "Thirty years from now, Americans, Japanese, Europeans, and people in many other rich countries and some relatively poor ones will probably be paying for their shopping with the same currency. Prices will be quoted not in dollars, yen or but in a common currency which will be favoured by companies and shoppers because it will be more convenient than today's national currencies, which by then will seem a quaint cause of much disruption to economic life in the late twentieth century."

The market crash has taught the governments that the pretence of policy co-operation can be worse than nothing, and that until real co-operation is feasible (that is, until governments surrender some economic sovereignty) further attempts to peg currencies will flounder. Several bigger exchange rate upsets, a few more stock market crashes and probably a slump or two will be needed before politicians face squarely up to that choice. These point to a muddled sequence of emergency followed by patch-up followed again by emergency, stretching out far beyond 2018 – except for two things. As time passes, the damage caused by currency instability is gradually going to mount; and the very trends that will make it mount are making the utopia of monetary union feasible.

As seen in Europe, the sequence of development is (1) building a common market, and (2) establishing a common currency. Indeed, until one has a common currency, one does not truly have an efficient common market. Ideally, every nation should stand willing to convert its currency at a fixed rate into a universal reserve asset. That would automatically create a global monetary union based on a common unit of account. The alternative path to a stable monetary order is to forge a common currency anchored to an asset of intrinsic value. While the current momentum for dollarisation should be encouraged, especially, for Mexico and Canada, in the end the stability of the global monetary order should not rest on any single nation. A summary states that, "The same commercial efficiencies, economies of scale, and physical imperatives that drive regional currencies together also presumably exist on the next level – the global scale." Further, it reported that, "The smaller and more vulnerable economies of the world – those that the international community is now trying hardest to help – would have most to gain from the certainty and stability that would accompany a single world currency." Keep in mind this document was produced by the IMF, and so its recommendations for what it says would likely 'help' the smaller and more vulnerable countries of the world, should be taken with a grain or bucket of salt.

4. Renewed Calls for a Global Currency

On March 16, 2009, Russia suggested that, "The G-20 summit in London in April should start establishing a system of managing the process of globalisation and consider the possibility of creating a 'supra-national reserve currency' or a 'super-reserve currency'." Russia called for "the creation of a supra-national reserve currency that will be issued by international financial institutions," and that, "it looks expedient to reconsider the role of the IMF in that process and also to determine the possibility and need for taking measures that would allow for the SDRs (Special Drawing Rights) to become a super-reserve currency recognised by the world community."

5. Creating a World Central Bank

The world needs an institution that has a hand on the economic rudder when the seas become stormy. It needs a global central bank. Simply trying to co-ordinate the world's powerful central banks – the Federal and the new European Central Bank, for instance – would not work, and effective collaboration among finance ministries and treasuries is also unlikely to materialise. These agencies are responsible to elected legislatures, and politics in the industrial countries is more preoccupied with internal events than with international stability.

An independent central bank with responsibility for maintaining global financial stability is the only way out. No one else can do what is needed; inject more money into the system to spur growth, reduce the sky-high debts of emerging markets, and oversee the operations of shaky financial institutions. A global central bank could provide more money to the world economy when it is rapidly losing steam. Such a bank would play an oversight role for banks and other financial institutions everywhere, providing some uniform standards for prudent lending in places like China and Mexico. However, the regulation need not be heavy-handed. There are two ways – a global central bank could be financed. It could have lines of credit from all central banks, drawing on them in bad times and repaying when the markets turn up. Alternately, and admittedly more difficult to carry out, it could be financed by a very modest tariff on all trade, collected at the point of importation, or, by a tax on certain global financial transactions.

6. An Emerging Global Government

The danger in the present course is that if the world moves to a 'super sovereign' reserve currency engineered by experts, such as the UN Commission of Experts led by Nobel laureate economist Joseph Stiglitz, we would give up the possibility of a spontaneous money order and financial harmony for a centrally planned order and the politicisation of money. Such a regime change would endanger not only the future value of money but, more importantly, our freedom and prosperity.

An uncomfortable characteristic of the new world order may well turn out to be that global income gaps will widen because the rising powers such as China, India and Brazil regard those below them on the ladder as potential rivals. The new world order thus would not necessarily be any better than the old one. What is certain, though, is that global affairs are going to be considerably different from now on. In April of 2009, Robert Zoellick, President of the World Bank, said that, "If leaders are serious about creating new global responsibilities or governance, let them start by modernising multilateralism to empower the WTO, the IMF, and the World Bank Group to monitor national policies".

He further writes that, "even the international organisations and alliances we have today, flawed as they are, would have seemed impossible until recently, notably the success of the European Union – a unitary democratic state the size of India. The evolution and achievements of such entities against all odds suggest not isolated instances but an overall trend in the direction of what Tennyson called 'the Parliament of Man,' or 'universal law'." He states that he is "optimistic that progress will continue to be made," but it will be difficult, because it "undercuts many national and local power structures and cultural concepts that have foundations deep in the bedrock of human civilisation, namely, the notion of sovereignty".

Thus, the mechanisms of global governance are more achievable in today's environment, and these mechanisms are often creative with temporary solutions to urgent problems that cannot wait for the world to embrace a bigger and more controversial idea like real global government.

7. BRIC Report

The report that started this trend was the BRIC report which made the world realise that many changes are in the offing and the whole world order is going to change in due course of time. After the BRIC report, many other reports supporting and expanding on the BRIC report have come to the fore and have supplemented the fact that the world is indeed undergoing a change and the magnitude of change is going to increase all the time. To understand some details of the reports that have emerged in the past decade, we will go through them in detail.

Brazil, Russia, India and China, the so-called BRIC group of emerging powers have gained clout over the past decade as their economies grew faster than those of developed countries. BRIC leaders have held two summit meetings, one each in 2009 and 2010, to discuss the global financial crisis and reforms to the world financial and trade institutions.

Here are some facts about the BRIC countries –

a) The term 'BRIC' was coined by US investment bank Goldman Sachs to describe the four key emerging economic powers, which the bank predicted would account for an increasingly greater share of the global economy.

b) Today, the world is trying to integrate as much as possible. Many organisations like the WTO, IMF, and IBRD etc. are operating since a long time with efficiency and effectiveness. Together they accounted for about 22 percent of the world economy in 2008, up from 16 percent a decade earlier, based on the widely followed measure of purchasing power parity.

c) Real economic growth from 1999 through 2008 averaged 9.75 percent in China, 7 percent in both India and Russia, and 3.3 percent in Brazil.

d) The global financial crisis led to a sharp contraction of the Russian economy in 2009 and a small contraction in Brazil, while India and China remained on a robust growth path.

e) The Organisation for Economic Co-operation and Development (OECD) expects the four economies to power ahead in the coming years.

Some economists believe the BRICs are now at risk of overheating and asset bubbles due to heavy fund flows into high-yielding emerging markets.

a) China held USD 900 billion in US Treasuries at the end of April, according to US Treasury Department international capital data released on June 15. Bankers say China's total holdings of dollar-denominated assets are much greater, accounting for perhaps two-thirds of its official currency reserves. These came to USD 2.45 trillion at the end of March.

b) China's economy grew at 8.7 percent in 2009 thanks to a record surge in bank lending of 9.6 trillion yuan (USD 1.4 trillion) orchestrated by the government to support its 4 trillion yuan (USD 585 billion) stimulus package, which is being spent mainly on infrastructure. The average growth for 2010 will be even stronger after a brisk start to the year, though the economy is gradually losing momentum due to government steps to rein in bank lending and cool the red-hot property market.

c) Brazil, already an agricultural and mining powerhouse, could become a major player in the world energy market after finding huge deep-sea oil reserves. It is the only BRIC country without nuclear weapons but it has the capacity to enrich uranium. After a five-year run of rapid growth, its economy slipped into recession in early 2009 but has rebounded and grew at a brisk 9 percent pace in the first quarter of this year.

d) Russia, the world's largest oil and gas producer, fell into its worst recession in at least a decade last year but the economy is expected to grow by around 4 percent in 2010 helped mainly by a recovery in oil prices.

e) India's economy is expected to grow at least 8 percent this year, boosted by consumer and government spending, but it faces inflation, driven by high food prices, that exceeded 10 percent in May. It faces potential trouble from domestic militant groups and a long-running border dispute with Pakistan.

f) The BRICs want to reduce the world's reliance on a weak US dollar as a global reserve currency; among the options are a basket of currencies or a system of drawing rates. Brazil is pursuing trade in local currency with China, but analysts caution that Beijing is wary of rocking the boat because of its huge holdings of dollar-denominated assets.

g) The BRICs want more representation in the World Bank and the International Monetary Fund. Discussions to change voting power in the IMF are about to get under way in a review that has been brought forward by two years to reassure the BRICs that their concerns are being addressed.

h) India and Brazil, along with Japan and Germany, are seeking a seat on the UN Security Council but a lack of consensus among current council members has long stalled reforms. The United States wants Japan in the council, but China objects.

i)   Brazil hopes to forge a common BRIC position on global climate talks but their carbon footprints and resulting negotiating positions differ sharply. Russia, the third-largest greenhouse gas emitter after China and the United States, ratified the Kyoto protocol in 2004 while developing countries are not expected to agree to legally binding emissions targets from 2013.

8. Next Eleven

The Next Eleven (or N-11) are eleven countries, namely, Bangladesh, Egypt, Indonesia, Iran, Mexico, Nigeria, Pakistan, Philippines, South Korea, Turkey and Vietnam — identified by Goldman Sachs investment bank as having a high potential of becoming the world's largest economies in the 21st century along with the BRICs. The bank chose these states, all with promising outlooks for investment and future growth, on December 12, 2005.

Goldman Sachs used macroeconomic stability, political maturity, openness of trade and investment policies, and the quality of education as criteria. The N-11 paper is a follow-up to the bank's 2003 paper on the four emerging BRIC economies, namely, Brazil, Russia, India and China.

9. CIVETS

'CIVETS' is an acronym for favoured emerging markets coined in late 2009 by Robert Ward, Global Forecasting Director for the Economist Intelligence Unit (EIU). It stands for Colombia, Indonesia, Vietnam, Egypt, Turkey and South Africa. These countries are favoured for several reasons, such as a dynamic and diverse economy and a young growing population.

10. The G-23

The G-23 came into force to make sure that the developing countries have a say in the global affairs and now they are increasing their trade, commerce and investment within themselves to have better relations and higher growth rates in their GDPs. These countries are leading the world in terms of their growth rates which are accompanied by their high GDP sizes. Thus, this group is of a formidable size and has a bright future. It sums up the future of the world and how the world will change its dynamics in terms of economies of countries.

Currently, the group of G-23 consists of the following twenty-three nations –

a) Argentina

b) Bolivia

c) Brazil

d) Chile

e) China

f) Cuba

g) Ecuador

h) Egypt

i) Guatemala

j) India

k) Indonesia

l) Mexico

m) Nigeria

n) Pakistan

o) Paraguay

p) Peru

q) Philippines

r) South Africa

s) Tanzania

t) Thailand

u) Uruguay

v) Turkey

w) Venezuela

11. BRIC in the Future

The list of the selected countries by nominal GDP from year 2006 to 2050: BRICs, G-7 and Next Eleven. The bottom chart lists the same 22 countries by nominal GDP per capita (the rankings for this bottom chart do not reflect the GDP per capita for all the world's countries). BRIC countries are highlighted and labelled in bold. Rank 2006 – Numbers 1 to 15 are G-20 countries. Five other countries of G-20 not in the list are Argentina, Australia, Saudi Arabia, South Africa and European Union. Numbers 1 to 8 are also G-7 countries, except China. From 2027 China will surpass USA, Rank 2050.

Top 7 countries are:

a) China

b) USA

c) India

d) Brazil

e) Mexico

f) Russia and

g) Indonesia (All 4 BRIC countries plus USA, Mexico and Indonesia)

G-7 countries at 2006 which were not included in Top 7 2050 countries rank-wise are – Japan (8), Germany (10), United Kingdom (9), France (12), Italy (18) and Canada (16). So, only USA from G-7 2006 will be one of the Top 7 countries in 2050. Figures reflect data published in 2007.

Table 1.3: Gross Domestic Product

Rank 2006	Country	2010	2015	2020	2025	2030	2035	2040	2045	2050	Rank 2050
1	United States	14,535	16,194	17,978	20,087	22,817	26,097	29,823	33,904	38,514	2
2	Japan	4,604	4,861	5,224	5,570	5,814	5,886	6,042	6,300	6,677	8
3	Germany	3,083	3,326	3,519	3,631	3,761	4,048	4,388	4,714	5,024	10
4	China	4,667	8,133	12,630	18,437	25,610	34,348	45,022	57,310	70,710	1
5	United Kingdom	2,546	2,835	3,101	3,333	3,595	3,937	4,344	4,744	5,133	9
6	France	2,366	2,577	2,815	3,055	3,306	3,567	3,892	4,227	4,592	12
7	Italy	1,914	2,072	2,224	2,326	2,391	2,444	2,559	2,737	2,950	18
8	Canada	1,389	1,549	1,700	1,856	2,061	2,302	2,569	2,849	3,149	16
9	Brazil	1,346	1,720	2,194	2,831	3,720	4,963	6,631	8,740	11,366	4
10	Russia	1,371	1,900	2,554	3,341	4,265	5,265	6,320	7,420	8,560	6
11	India	1,256	1,900	2,848	4,316	6,683	10,514	16,510	25,278	37,668	3

Rank 2006	Country	2010	2015	2020	2025	2030	2035	2040	2045	2050	Rank 2050
12	South Korea	1,071	1,305	1,508	1,861	2,241	2,644	3,089	3,562	4,083	13
13	Mexico	1,009	1,327	1,742	2,303	3,068	4,102	5,471	7,204	9,340	5
14	Turkey	440	572	740	965	1,279	1,716	2,300	3,033	3,943	14
15	Indonesia	419	562	752	1,033	1,479	2,192	3,286	4,846	7,010	7
16	Iran	312	415	544	716	953	1,273	1,673	2,133	2,663	19
17	Pakistan	161	206	268	359	497	709	1,026	1,472	2,085	21
18	Nigeria	158	218	306	445	680	1,083	1,765	2,870	4,640	11
19	Philippines	162	215	289	400	582	882	1,353	2,040	3,010	17
20	Egypt	129	171	229	318	467	718	1,124	1,728	2,602	20
21	Bangladesh	81	110	150	210	304	451	676	1,001	1,466	22
22	Vietnam	88	157	273	458	745	1,169	1,768	2,569	3,607	15

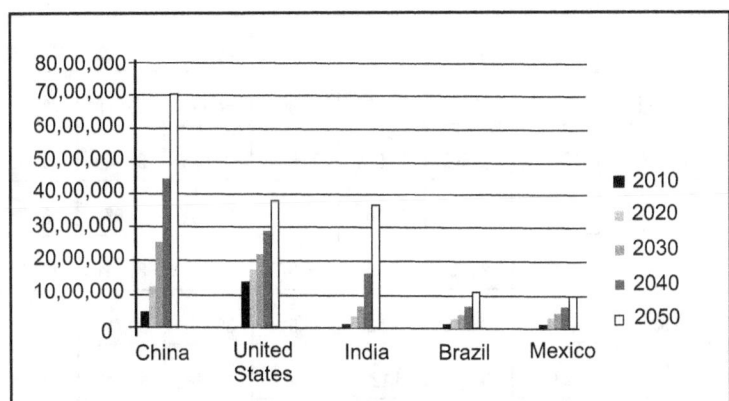

Fig. 1.4

As can be seen from the figure, the world order will change dramatically in the next few decades. This is only an approximation and can change with course of time. There are many hiccups for this report to materialise. For example, India has to build on its infrastructure and provide uninterrupted power and water supply to industries all around the country if it has to achieve the growth that is shown in the table. Another example is that Pakistan has to improve its political and legal system to become a part of the faster growing countries list.

We can choose either the above or below figures. The difference between them lies in the ranking.

Table 1.4: Gross Domestic Product per capita (nominal)

Rank 2006	Country	2015	2020	2025	2030	2035	2040	2045	2050	Rank 2050	2050/ 2006
1	United States	50,200	53,502	57,446	62,717	69,019	76,044	83,489	91,683	1	2.06
2	United Kingdom	45,591	49,173	52,220	55,904	61,049	67,391	73,807	80,234	3	2.10
3	Canada	43,449	45,961	48,621	52,663	57,728	63,464	69,531	76,002	5	1.99
4	France	41,332	44,811	48,429	52,327	56,562	62,136	68,252	75,253	6	2.08
5	Germany	40,589	43,223	45,033	47,263	51,710	57,118	62,658	68,253	7	1.97
6	Japan	38,650	42,385	46,419	49,975	52,345	55,756	60,492	66,846	8	1.96
7	Italy	35,908	38,990	41,358	43,195	44,948	48,070	52,760	58,545	10	1.88
8	South Korea	26,012	29,868	36,813	44,602	53,449	63,924	75,979	90,294	2	4.97
9	Mexico	11,176	13,979	17,685	22,694	29,417	38,255	49,393	63,149	9	7.97
10	Russia	13,971	19,311	26,061	34,368	43,800	54,221	65,708	78,576	4	11.37
11	Brazil	8,427	10,375	12,996	16,694	21,924	29,026	38,149	49,759	11	8.79
12	Turkey	7,460	9,291	11,743	15,188	20,046	26,602	34,971	45,595	13	8.22
13	Iran	5,888	7,345	9,328	12,139	15,979	20,746	26,231	32,676	15	8.67
14	China	5,837	8,829	12,688	17,522	23,511	30,951	39,719	49,650	12	24.32
15	Indonesia	2,197	2,813	3,711	5,123	7,365	10,784	15,642	22,395	16	14.85
16	Philippines	2,075	2,591	3,372	4,635	6,678	9,815	14,260	20,388	19	15.53
17	Egypt	1,880	2,352	3,080	4,287	6,287	9,443	14,025	20,500	18	16.00
18	Nigeria	1,332	1,665	2,161	2,944	4,191	6,117	8,934	13,014	20	14.16
19	India	1,492	2,091	2,979	4,360	6,524	9,802	14,446	20,836	17	25.50
20	Pakistan	1,050	1,260	1,568	2,035	2,744	3,775	5,183	7,066	21	9.08
21	Vietnam	1,707	2,834	4,583	7,245	11,148	16,623	23,932	33,472	14	51.10
22	Bangladesh	627	790	1,027	1,384	1,917	2,698	3,767	5,235	22	12.25

Table 1.5: Gross Domestic Product

Rank 2006	Country	2015	2020	2025	2030	2035	2040	2045	2050	Rank 2050
4	China	8,133	12,630	18,437	25,610	34,348	45,022	57,310	70,710	1
1	United States	16,194	17,978	20,087	22,817	26,097	29,823	33,904	38,514	2
11	India	1,900	2,848	4,316	6,683	10,514	16,510	25,278	37,668	3
9	Brazil	1,720	2,194	2,831	3,720	4,963	6,631	8,740	11,366	4
13	Mexico	1,327	1,742	2,303	3,068	4,102	5,471	7,204	9,340	5
10	Russia	1,900	2,554	3,341	4,265	5,265	6,320	7,420	8,560	6
15	Indonesia	562	752	1,033	1,479	2,192	3,286	4,846	7,010	7
2	Japan	4,861	5,224	5,570	5,814	5,886	6,042	6,300	6,677	8
5	United Kingdom	2,835	3,101	3,333	3,595	3,937	4,344	4,744	5,133	9
3	Germany	3,326	3,519	3,631	3,761	4,048	4,388	4,714	5,024	10
18	Nigeria	218	306	445	680	1,083	1,765	2,870	4,640	11
6	France	2,577	2,815	3,055	3,306	3,567	3,892	4,227	4,592	12
12	South Korea	1,305	1,508	1,861	2,241	2,644	3,089	3,562	4,083	13
14	Turkey	572	740	965	1,279	1,716	2,300	3,033	3,943	14
22	Vietnam	157	273	458	745	1,169	1,768	2,569	3,607	15
8	Canada	1,549	1,700	1,856	2,061	2,302	2,569	2,849	3,149	16
19	Philippines	215	289	400	582	882	1,353	2,040	3,010	17
7	Italy	2,072	2,224	2,326	2,391	2,444	2,559	2,737	2,950	18
16	Iran	415	544	716	953	1,273	1,673	2,133	2,663	19
20	Egypt	171	229	318	467	718	1,124	1,728	2,602	20
17	Pakistan	206	268	359	497	709	1,026	1,472	2,085	21
21	Bangladesh	110	150	210	304	451	676	1,001	1,466	22

There are many other economic groupings in the world which are very important in today's world. They are namely:

12. Other economic groupings in the world are:

- Arab Maghreb Union (UMA)
- Common Market for Eastern and Southern Africa (COMESA)
- Council of Arab Economic Unity (CAEU)
- East African Community (EAC)
- Economic Community of Central African States (ECCAS)
- Economic Community of West African States (ECOWAS)
- Intergovernmental Authority on Development (IGAD)
- Southern Africa Development Community (SADC)
- Union for the Mediterranean (UfM)
- New partnership for Africa Development (NEPAD)
- Andean Community of Nations (CAN)
- Caribbean Single Market and Economy (CSME)
- Central American Integration System (SICA)
- Latin American Integration Association (LAIA)
- Mesoamerica Project
- North American Free Trade Agreement (NAFTA)
- Southern Common Market (Mercosur)
- Asia-Pacific Trade Agreement (APTA)
- Association of Southeast Asian Nations (ASEAN)
- Cooperation Council for the Arab States of the Gulf (CCASG)
- Economic Cooperation Organization (ECO)
- Eurasian Economic Community (EAEC)
- Shanghai Cooperation Organisation (SCO)
- South Asian Association for Regional Cooperation (SAARC)
- Eurasian Economic Community (EAEC)
- European Economic Area (EEA)
- European Economic Community (EEC)
- European Union (EU)
- Regional Cooperation Council (RCC)
- Union for the Mediterranean (UfM)
- Cooperation Council for the Arab States of the Gulf (CCASG)
- Council of Arab Economic Unity (CAEU)
- Euro-Mediterranean Free Trade Area (EU-MED FTA)
- Union for the Mediterranean (UfM)
- U.S.–Middle East Free Trade Area (U.S. MEFTA)
- Melanesian Spearhead Group (MSG)
- Pacific Islands Forum (PIF)

13. The World Economic Forum

Another important forum is the world economic forum. The world economic forum is the International Organization for Public-Private Cooperation. The Forum engages the foremost political, business and other leaders of society to shape global, regional and industry agendas. It was established in 1971 as a not-for-profit foundation and is headquartered in Geneva, Switzerland. It is independent, impartial and not tied to any special interests, working in close cooperation with all major international organisations.

It engages political, business, academic and other leaders of society in collaborative efforts to improve the state of the world. Together with other stakeholders, it works to define challenges, solutions and actions, always in the spirit of global citizenship and serves and builds sustained communities through an integrated concept of high-level meetings, research networks, task forces and digital collaboration.

1.4 Global Economy of the 21ˢᵗ Century

Since World War II, the world economy enjoyed its best 10-year growth performance. The huge post-war reconstruction effort of the earlier decade led to vibrant growth in Europe and Asia. Some incredible changes where observed in the world economy during the following half century. Some low-income nations while struggling with constant development problems started flourishing much faster and ultimately became major contributors to global expansion. The world economic order went through a tectonic transformation, accompanied by groundbreaking advances in science and technology and the rise of globalisation. The world economy experienced an impressive progress during this period. There is still a glaring need for progress in many areas, but there is also cause for optimism. Some of the factors are listed below –

1. Rise of globalisation

"We live in a global world." This sentence has become a cliché, especially with the rise of globalisation over the past two decades—the growing trade and financial integration of the world economy (see Fig 1.5). Improvement in communication and transportation technologies coincided with and promoted accelerated globalisation while countries became more interdependent through a rapid increase in cross-border movement of goods, services, capital, and labour—and led to much faster diffusion of ideas and cultural products.

Aided by the liberalisation of trade policies the world over, the past 50 years has witnessed profound changes in the volume, direction, and nature of international trade. Global trade in goods and services has risen rapidly. With the proliferation of regional trade agreements, intraregional trade flows have also become more important. Trade in manufacturing goods has grown quickly, leading to cross-border supply chains—companies can now trace different stages of the production process in several countries.

Even more dramatic is the change in international financial flow. Over the past 50 years, the portion of countries with a liberalised financial system has risen threefold. Since more countries have embraced the benefits of permitting the free movement of capital, international financial flows have increased noticeably. The composition of international financial flows has also transformed; the share of portfolio equity investments is much larger. Even though the extent of integration of labour markets across countries is much lesser than that of trade and financial markets, cross-border movements of labour have also registered a considerable increase over the past 50 years. Regional migration between developing economies now exceeds migration to developed economies.

The World Grows Closer

Global trade and financial links increased dramatically in the past 50 years.

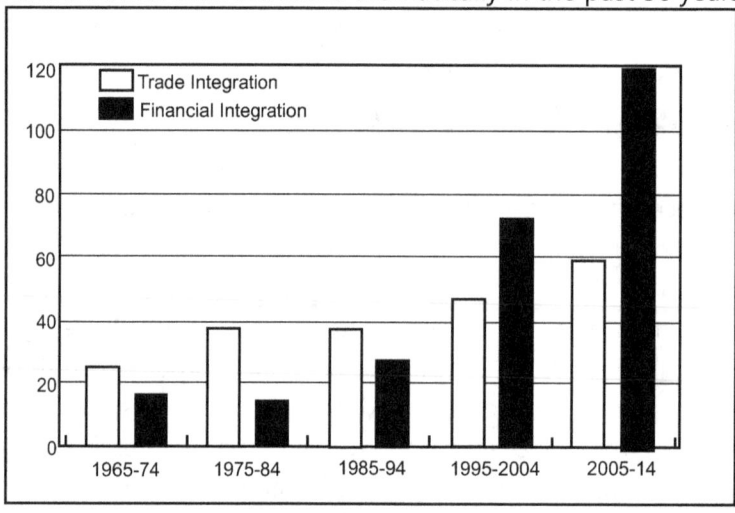

Fig. 1.5

Source: Lane, Phillip R., and Gian Maria Milesi-Ferretti, 2007, "The External Wealth of Nations Mark III: Revised and Extended Estimates of Foreign Assets and Liabilities, 1970-2004, Journal of International Economics, Vol. 73, No. 2, pp. 223-50; and IMF, World Economic Outlook Database

Note: Trade integration is measured by the ratio of total imports and exports to global GDP. Financial integration is the ratio of total financial inflows and outflows (including bank loans, direct investment, bonds, and equities) to global GDP.

New countries, new members

Wars, political and social conflicts, and the dissolution of the Soviet Union increased the number of independent countries from 139 in 1965 to 204 in 2014. These new countries quickly assumed their roles in international policy forums. For example, at the end of 1965, International Monetary Fund and the World Bank each had slightly more than 100 members. Over past 50 years, they have added about 85 members – first from newly independent African countries and more recently from former states of the Soviet Union. Each institution now has 188 members.

Growing bigger

The number of countries that are members of the IMF and the World Bank has grown from less than 40 in 1946 to 188 today.

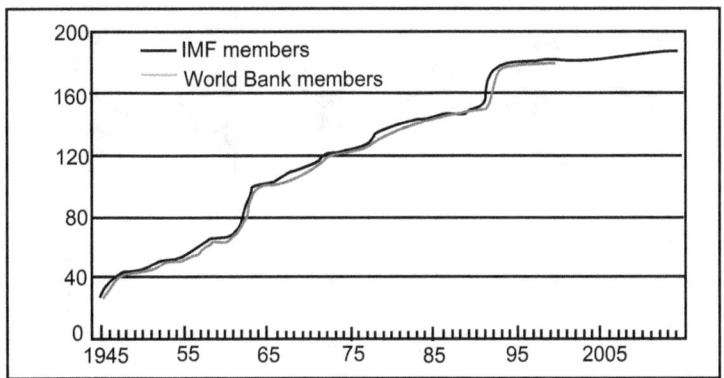

Fig. 1.6

2. New global actors

Through the past 50 years, a number of countries became independent (see Fig 1.6). On the other hand, during this period a bipolar world economy—composed of developing countries in the South and developed countries in the North—was the norm. The South consisted of mostly poor and labour-abundant economies that supplied agricultural products and raw materials to the North while the countries of the North were richer and more developed. They created manufactured goods and accounted for the bulk of global trade and financial flows.

However, some of the countries of the South, the so-called emerging market economies, grew at an extraordinary pace while rapidly integrating into the global economy. They have also expanded their production base and exports away from agricultural products and towards manufactured goods and services. The emerging market economies have established a growing presence in every economic dimension, while their shares of world population and labour force have remained relatively stable over the past 50 years. Their share of global GDP as a group nearly doubled (see Fig 1.7). During the past decade, they accounted for more than 70 percent of global expansion, while advanced economies' share fell to about 17 percent (see Fig 1.8). Emerging market economies have also become the main engine of global trade while rapidly establishing stronger banking and other financial links with the rest of the world.

Some emerging market economies have performed even better. For example, the BRIC countries Brazil, Russia, India, and China, accounted for half of global growth over the past decade. China is now the world's 2nd and Brazil the 7th largest economy, up from the 8th and the 16th, respectively. The list of the 20 largest economies now includes South Korea and Indonesia, which were nowhere close a few decades ago.

Rise of emerging markets

Emerging market economies' share of global GDP has risen steadily.

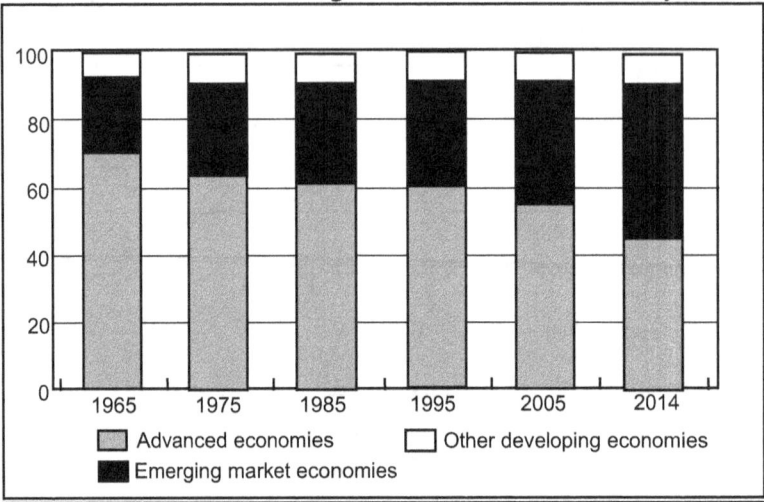

Source: IMF, World Economic Outlook Database

Note: Data are measured in purchasing power partly - the rate at which currencies would be converted if they were to buy the same quantity of goods and services in each country. Data for 2014 are forecasts.

Fig. 1.7

Growing up

Emerging market economies account for a growing share of world GDP growth.

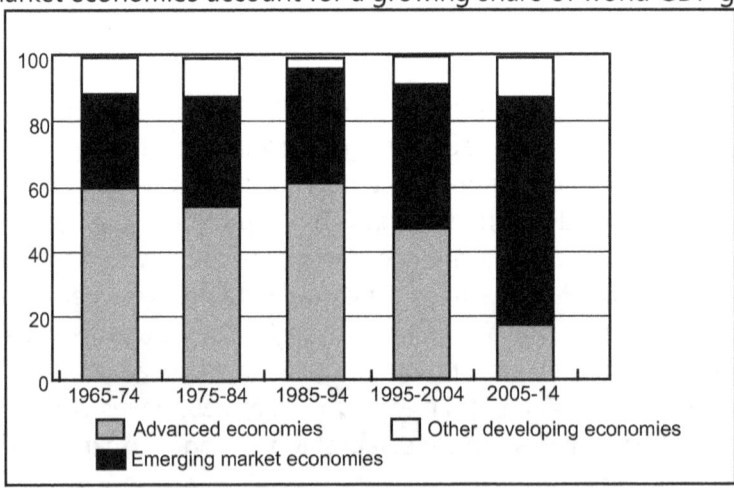

Source: IMF, World Economic Outlook database
Note: The data for 2014 are forecasts
Fig. 1.8

3. Disturbance

At an annual growth rate of 4 percent, the world economy is six times larger than it was half a century ago. Innovative and new technologies have paved the way for more proficient production systems in a wide range of industries and encouraged economic growth. The global per capita GDP more than doubled between 1965 and 2013 despite a major increase in population (see Fig. 1.9). But the global growth process itself has never been smooth. Many nations faced financial crises that led to significant declines in their growth during the past half century (see Fig. 1.10).

Also, the global economy went through periods of severe interruptions in growth. In every decade after the 1960s there was a global recession (see Fig 1.11). In 1975, 1982, 1991, and 2009, world per capita output declined and various other measures of global activity fell simultaneously. Each of these global recessions corresponded with severe economic and financial disruptions in many nations around the world. A quick increase in oil prices triggered the 1975 recession. A chain of global and national shocks—including another jump in oil prices in 1979, the U.S. Federal Reserve's battle against high inflation in 1979 and 1980, and the Latin American debt crisis—played significant roles in the 1982 recession.

Though the 1991 recession coincided with several adverse global and national developments, it became a worldwide event since various domestic difficulties were transmitted to other countries – financial disruptions in the United States, Japan, and several Scandinavian countries; exchange rate crises in many advanced European economies; German unification; and the collapse of the Soviet Union.

Each global recession lasted only a year, but left deep and long-lasting human and social costs – millions lost their jobs, businesses closed, and financial markets fell. Worldwide, the number of unemployed people rose by almost 20 percent. 83 million young people were unemployed. The global economy, especially labour markets, still suffers the effects of the 2009 recession.

Sharing prosperity?

Although, today the average person is richer, those in advanced economies have done far better than those in emerging market and other developing economies.

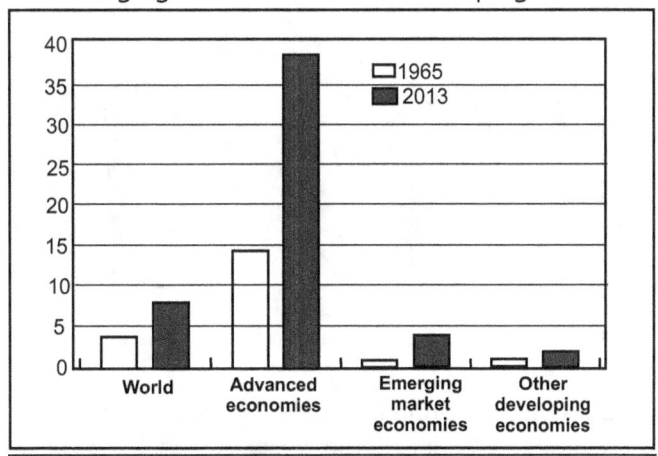

Source: World Bank, World Development Indicators database.

Fig. 1.9

Recurrent Financial Crises

Financial crises have interrupted economic growth around the world. Roughly 400 of them took place between 1970 and 2013. Advanced economies experienced only 35 crises, half of them after 2007. Emerging market economies had 218 financial crises, most of them in the 1980s and 1990s, especially during the 1997 Asian financial crisis. Currency crises were the most prevalent, accounting for half of all crisis episodes. Banking and debt crises accounted for half of all crisis episodes. Banking and debt crises accounted for the rest. It is still impossible to predict the location and time of the next financial crisis.

Financial crises are widespread

Between 1970 and 2013 there were more than 400 banking currency or debt crisis.

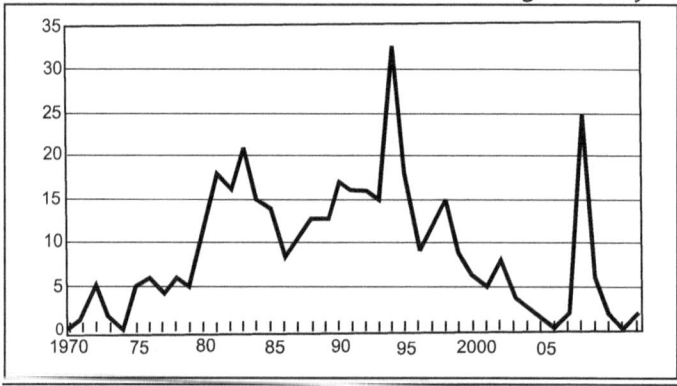

Source: Laeven and Valencia (2013)

Note: The shaded bars represent the three years surrounding global recessions which occurred in 1975, 1882, 1991 and 2009.

Fig. 1.10

Up and Down

Global GDP per capita grew at an average 2 percent a year in the past half century, but that average masks years of strong growth and years of recession.

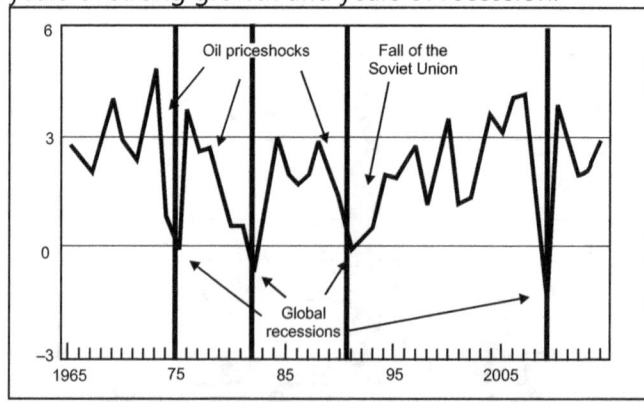

Source: IMF, World Economic Outlook database.

Note: Data are for 163 countries. Red bars indicate years of global recession. Purchasing power partly is the rate at which currencies would be converted if they were to buy the same quantity of goods and services in each country.

Fig. 1.11

4. New technologies

Due to the several technological developments over the past half century, nowadays we have immediate access to a vast array of information sources and are able to share new knowledge with the rest of the world in seconds. Rapid growth in communication and transportation technologies has facilitated major inventions in several fields. It drastically changed the work environment, raised productivity, and led to stronger international trade and financial links.

Communication has changed the most, since advances in computers and mobile technologies have revolutionised all mediums of communication. In 1965, the first commercially successful minicomputer had an inflation-adjusted price tag of $135,470. It was able to undertake basic computations, such as addition and multiplication. Its capacity was about 4,000 words of 12 bits. Today's typical smartphone has a capacity 3 million times larger and costs less than $600.

The introduction of the Internet to the public in 1991 started a new era in communication. The incredible boost in Internet access has brought people, businesses, and countries nearer, while mobile communication has become cheaper and more accessible. In 1965, the first commercial communications satellite was launched from the United States, providing 240 two-way telephone circuits. Today, there are about 400 commercial communication satellites processing and transmitting information across the world. In 1980, there were five mobile phone subscriptions for every million people; today there are more than 90 for every 100 people (see Fig 1.12). New technologies have been making earlier modes of communication outdated. With a quick increase in wireless communication, landlines have declined during the past decade.

Over the past 50 years, the transportation sector has also gone through a major change. Today, we can travel and ship goods much faster and more cheaply than a half century ago. Small businesses have access to overseas markets, with the availability of cheaper and faster communication and declining shipping costs.

Even though, over the past half century, annual global energy consumption from primary resources (fossil fuel, natural energy, nuclear power) has more than tripled, technological improvements in the energy sector made production more efficient than ever. To generate $1,000 in output, the mankind used the equivalent of 137 kilos of oil in 2011, 50 fewer than 20 years earlier. The global oil supply as a percent of total primary energy supply has also declined with increased supplies of natural gas, nuclear power, and renewable energy sources such as geothermal, solar, and wind.

New ways to communicate

Internet and mobile phone use has grown radically, while some customers are ditching landlines.

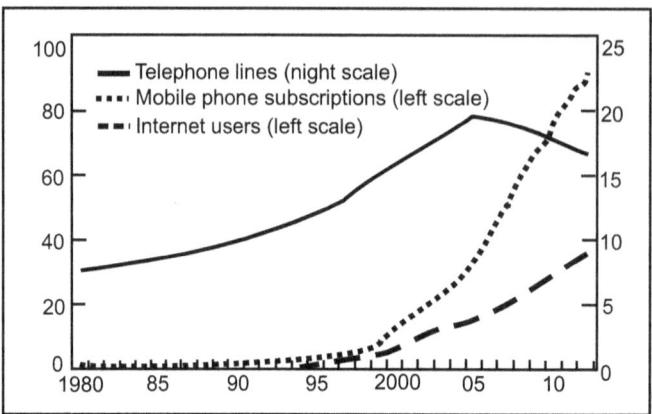

Source: World Bank, World Development Indicators database

Fig. 1.12

5. Poverty and inequality

In spite of the world population growing from 3 billion in 1965 to about 7 billion in 2013, the global economy grew faster than the world population, leading to a better standard of living for the average world citizen.

Progress in medical technology, sanitation, and vaccination helped decrease the death rate and despite declining birth rates, the world population has kept rising as people enjoy longer lives. In the mid-1960s, life expectancy at birth was about 55 years; today a newborn is expected to live about 70 years (see table 1.6).

Table 1.6: Population growth slows but people live longer

Life expectancy has grown steadily over the past half century.

	1965-74	1975-84	1985-94	1995-2004	2005-14
Population growth (percent change)	2.1	1.7	1.7	1.3	1.2
Life expectancy at birth (years)	59.0	63.0	65.5	67.6	69.9
Birth rate (per 1,000 people)	32.1	27.6	25.7	21.7	19.8
Death rate (per 1,000 people)	12.0	10.2	9.2	8.6	8.1
Output growth (percent change)	5.0	3.3	3.1	3.6	3.7
Per capita output growth (percent change)	2.9	1.5	1.4	2.2	2.5

Source: World Bank, World Development Indicators; IMF, World Economic Outlook database
Note: Output is GDP weighted by purchasing power parity for individual countries. Purchasing power parity is the rate at which currencies would be converted if they were to buy the same quantity of goods and services in each country. Data for 2014 for output growth and per capita output growth are forecasts from the World Economic Outlook; population-related data are through 2013.

There has been progress in education too. The number of children undertaking primary education increased from 80 percent of the global school-age population to 92 percent. This change has been more dramatic in low-income countries, from 45 percent to more than 70 percent in the past three decades. Owing to the growth the global economy has enjoyed over the past 50 years. The average world citizen is richer than ever. However, the benefits of this growth have not been equally distributed—the result is enduring poverty and inequality.

One of the Millennium Development Goals the United Nations agreed to in 2000 was to reduce extreme poverty by half between 1990 and 2015. The goal was however achieved five years ahead of schedule. Extreme poverty remains widespread in a number of low-income countries. In 1981, the percent of people living on less than $1.25 a day, the extreme poverty line, was about half in both upper-middle and low-income countries (see Fig 1.13). Thirty years later, upper-middle income countries have achieved a considerable decline in poverty due to rapid growth in emerging market economies. Nearly half of the population still lives in extreme poverty in low-income countries.

Inequality has also increased in many countries. Cross-country inequality reached its highest level in the late 1990s and then started declining, but is still higher than in the early 1980s. Moreover, the share of income earned by the top 1 percent of the population has risen in most of the major advanced and emerging market economies (see Fig 1.14).

Poverty endures

Extreme poverty fell across the globe, but it fell the least in low-income countries and the most in upper-middle income countries.

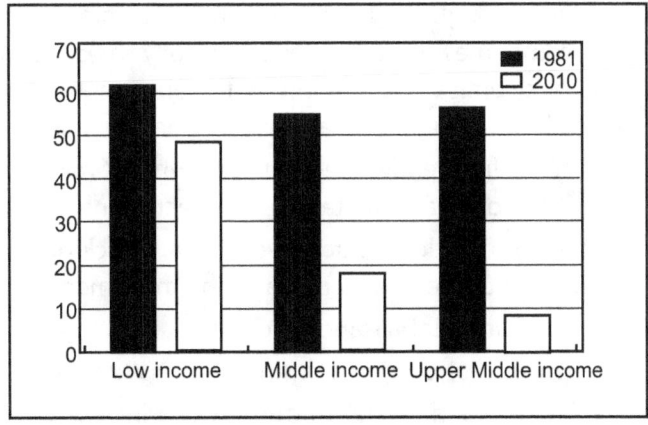

Source: World Bank Development Indicators database

Fig. 1.13

Rise of inequality

The share of income earned by the top 1 percent of the population rose in most countries over the past 50 years.

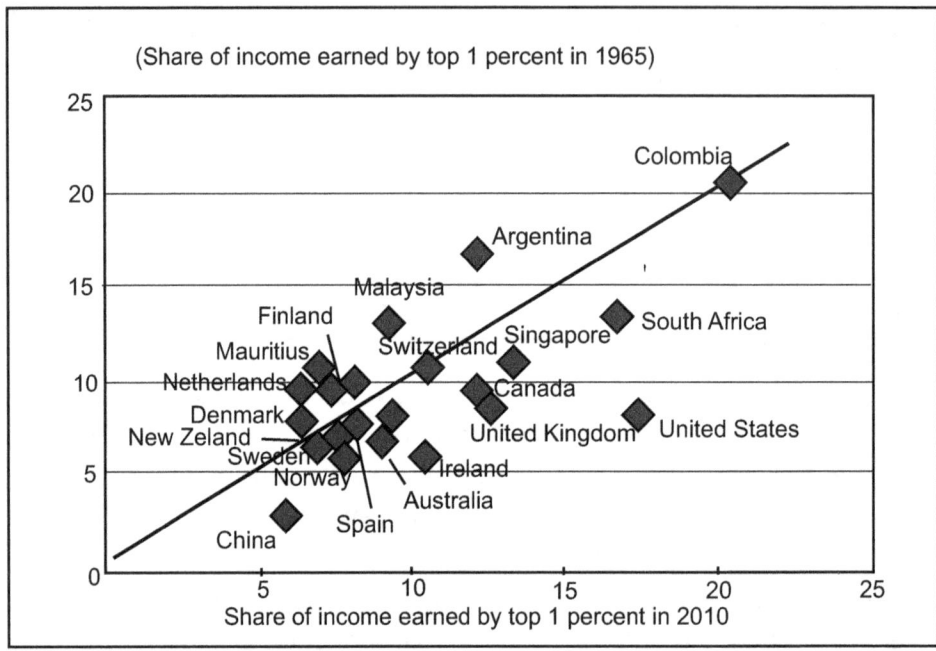

Source: Alvaedo and others (2014)
Fig. 1.14

Points to Remember

- Globalisation describes the process by which regional economies, societies, and cultures have become integrated through a global network of communication, transportation, and trade. The term is sometimes used to refer specifically to economic globalisation; the integration of national economies into the international economy through trade, foreign direct investment, capital flows, migration, and the spread of technology.

- The term "globalisation" is frequently used but seldom defined. It refers to the rapid increase in the share of economic activity taking place across national boundaries.

- This goes beyond just the international trade in goods and includes the way those goods are produced, the delivery and sale of services, and the movement of capital.

- A number of key players driving globalisation include –

   1. Multinational enterprises that carry out business across national boundaries.

   2. The World Trade Organisation (WTO) through which international trade agreements are negotiated and enforced.

   3. The World Bank and the International Monetary Fund (IMF) which are meant to assist governments in achieving development aims through the provision of loans and technical assistance; and national governments, who together with these international institutions, are instrumental in determining the outcomes of globalisation.

- Market globalisation drivers are the forces and factors that affect the pace of globalisation of an industry. Market drivers are essential for understanding customer demand and patterns of consumption.

- Transferable marketing refers to the degree of adaptation that has to be made for brands that are to be transferred to overseas markets. If the marketing schemes, models, or strategies can be transferred from country to country with very little adjustment, the application of global strategies will be easier and the faster the pace of globalisation. Cost globalisation drivers are the cost factors and forces that can change the pace of globalisation. When costs are reduced to the point that products become affordable, the pace of globalisation is enhanced.

- Income inequality for the world as a whole is diminishing in the countries that have opened up their markets for the world.

- Today, the world is trying to integrate as much as possible. Many organisations like the WTO, IMF, and IBRD etc. are operating since a long time with efficiency and effectiveness. 'CIVETS' is an acronym for favoured emerging markets coined by Robert Ward, Global Forecasting Director for the Economist Intelligence Unit (EIU). It stands for Colombia, Indonesia, Vietnam, Egypt, Turkey and South Africa. These countries are favoured for several reasons such as a dynamic and diverse economy and a young growing population.

- The Next Eleven (or N-11) are eleven countries, namely, Bangladesh, Egypt, Indonesia, Iran, Mexico, Nigeria, Pakistan, Philippines, South Korea, Turkey and Vietnam—identified by Goldman Sachs investment bank as having a high potential of becoming the world's largest economies in the 21st century along with the BRICs.

- The G-23 came into force to make sure that the developing countries have a say in the global affairs and now they are increasing their trade commerce and investment within themselves to have better relations and higher growth rates in their GDPs.

- Rapid progress in communication and transportation technologies has facilitated major innovation in many other fields, radically changed how we work, raised productivity, and led to stronger international trade and financial links.

Questions for Discussion

1. What is globalisation?

2. State and explain the drivers of globalisation.

3. Explain the factors of the changing order of the world economies.

4. Elaborate the pros and cons of globalisation.

5. Which are the countries that are expected to lead the growth of the world in the 21st century?

6. Describe the waves of globalisation.

7. State the factors responsible for global economy in the 21st century.

8. Write short note on:

    (a) BRIC report

    (b) G-23

    (c) BRIC in the future

Chapter **2**...

Study of International Monetary Fund [IMF] and World Bank

Contents ...

2.1   International Monetary Fund [IMF]

    2.1.1   Introduction

    2.1.2   Nature of IMF

    2.1.3   Objectives of the IMF

    2.1.4   Functions of IMF

2.2   World Bank

    2.2.1   Introduction

    2.2.2   Nature of the World Bank

    2.2.3   Functions of the World Bank

    2.2.4   Objectives of the World Bank

2.3   Global Financial Market

    2.3.1   Introduction

    2.3.2   Nature of Global Financial Markets

    2.3.3   Role of IMF and World Bank in Global Financial Market

2.4   Emerging Markets

    2.4.1   Introduction

    2.4.2   Characteristic of Emerging Markets

    2.4.3   Understanding the Sources of Development Outcomes

    2.4.4   Role of IMF and World Bank in Emerging Market

    2.4.5   Impact of World Bank and IMF on Developing Countries

2.5   Poverty Aid

    2.5.1   Introduction

    2.5.2   Factors that would help in Poverty Aid

    2.5.3   Role of IMF and World Bank in Poverty Aid

•   Points to Remember

•   Questions for Discussion

Learning Objectives ...

- To understand International Monetary Fund (IMF)
- To list the functions of IMF
- To define world bank
- To list the functions and objectives of the world bank
- To describe global financial market
- To summarise the role of IMF and world bank in global financial market
- To highlight the impact of world bank and IMF on developing countries
- To enumerate the role of IMF in poverty aid
- To describe PRSP

2.1 International Monetary Fund [IMF]

2.1.1 Introduction

The International Monetary Fund was created in July 1944 towards the end of the Second World War. The representatives of the United States, Great Britain, France, Russia, and 40 other countries met at Bretton Woods, to lay the foundation for the post-war international financial order. This was done to avoid another worldwide economic disaster like the Great Depression that had weakened some nations and had contributed to the rise of fascism and the war. Consequently, the International Monetary Fund (the IMF) and the World Bank were created by the United Nations Monetary and Financial Conference, to prevent economic crises and to re-establish economies shattered by the war. It was chiefly intended to benefit the global economy and contribute to world peace.

The aim of international monetary fund was to stabilise exchange rates and assist the reconstruction of the world's international payment system. It started off with forty-five members. The IMF describes itself as "an organisation of 187 countries (as of July 2010), working to bring about global monetary cooperation, secure financial stability, facilitate international trade, promote high employment and sustainable economic growth, and reduce poverty". The IMF is controlled by its 187 member-countries, each of whom appoints a representative to the IMF's Board of Governors. The Board of Governors, most of whom are the finance ministers or heads of the central bank of the members, meet once every year to discuss and possibly achieve consensus on major issues. With the exception of Cuba (exited in 1964), Taiwan (expelled in 1980), North Korea, Andorra, Monaco, Liechtenstein, Tuvalu and

Nauru, all UN member states participate directly in the IMF. Member states are represented on a 24-member Executive Board (five Executive Directors are appointed by the five members with the largest quotas, nineteen Executive Directors are elected by the remaining members), and all members appoint a Governor to the IMF's Board of Governors.

2.1.2 Nature of IMF

The **International Monetary Fund** (**IMF**) is the inter-governmental organisation headquartered in Washington D. C. United States, that oversees the global financial system by following the macroeconomic policies of its member countries, in particular, those with an impact on exchange rate and the balance of payments. It is an international organisation that provides financial assistance and advice to member countries. The IMF works to improve the economies of its member countries. The day-to-day operations are managed by a 24-person Executive Board. It is an organisation formed with a stated objective of stabilising international exchange rates and facilitating development through the enforcement of liberalising economic policies on other countries as a condition for loans, restructuring or aid. It also offers highly leveraged loans, mainly to poorer countries. The IMF's relatively high influence in world affairs and development has drawn heavy criticism from some quarters. The IMF was important when it was first created because it helped the world to stabilise its economic system. The IMF works to improve the economies of its member countries. The IMF is important as it was first created to help the world to stabilise its economic system.

In order to evaluate the country's economic situation, the IMF sends economists to each of its member countries. The team carefully examines the fiscal and monetary policy, exchange rate, general macroeconomic stability, and all related policies, such as labour policy, trade policy, and social policy. This process of evaluation is termed as Article IV consultation, after the section authorising it in the Articles of Agreement. Providing an outside check on national decisions that might influence the international economic system is the intention of such consultation. Assisting the national treasury departments financially is the central activity undertaken by the IMF. Member countries with balance of payments problems can be given credits and loans to pay off their debt and readjust their economic policies so as to avoid another crisis or near-crisis. Among other issues, the IMF provides technical assistance on fiscal and monetary policy, regulatory procedures, tax policy, and collection of statistics. The aim here is to strengthen the developing countries' abilities to reform and properly manage their macroeconomic policies.

2.1.3 Objectives of the IMF

The following are the objectives of the IMF.

1.   To encourage international monetary cooperation that provides the machinery for consultation and collaboration on international monetary problems.

2.   To facilitate the balanced growth of international trade. To contribute to the promotion and maintenance of high levels of employment and real income and to the expansion of the productive resources of all members as primary objectives of economic policy.

3.   To promote exchange stability, to sustain orderly exchange arrangements between members, and to avoid competitive exchange depreciation.

4.   To establish a multilateral system of payments in respect of current transactions among members and in the elimination of foreign exchange restrictions, which hamper the growth of world trade.

5.   To assure members of the general resources of the fund temporarily available to them under sufficient safeguards, consequently providing them with opportunity to correct maladjustments in their balance of payments without resorting to measures destructive of national or international prosperity.

6.   To help the liberalisation of international trade by assisting countries increase their real incomes while lowering unemployment.

7.   To facilitate stabilisation of exchange rates among countries. Especially after the global depression of the 1930s, it was considered very important to establish currencies that could hold their value, serve as mediums of international exchange, and resist any speculative attacks.

8.   To maintain a multilateral system of payments that abolishes foreign exchange restrictions. Thus, countries are free to trade with each other with no worry about the effects of interest rates and currency depreciation on their payments.

9.   To offer protection to members of the IMF against balance of payments crises, that is, when governments cannot balance the money they possess, with the money they owe to other countries.

2.1.4 Functions of IMF

1.   The IMF emerged at the end of World War II to prevent economic crises like the Great Depression.

2.   IMF along with its sister organisation, the World Bank, is the largest public lender of funds in the world. It is a specialised agency of the UN and is run by its 186 member countries. Membership is free for any country that conducts foreign policy and understands the organisation's law.

3.   The creation and maintenance of the international monetary system is the responsibility of the IMF, the system by which international payments between

countries occur. It therefore provides a systematic mechanism for foreign exchange transactions so as to foster investment and promote balanced global economic trade.

4. IMF focuses and advises on the macroeconomic policies of a country in order to achieve these goals, which ultimately affects its exchange rate and its government's budget, money, and credit management. The IMF will also evaluate a country's financial sector and its regulatory policies, as well as structural policies in the macro economy that relates to the labour market and employment. It also offers financial assistance to nations in need of correcting inconsistency of balance of payments.

5. As a result, the IMF is entrusted with fostering economic growth and maintaining high levels of employment among countries. The IMF gets its money from quota subscriptions paid by member states. The size of each quota is determined by how much each government can pay according to the size of its economy

6. The IMF offers its support in the form of surveillance, which it conducts annually for individual countries, regions and the global economy as a whole. However, if a country finds itself in an economic crisis, it may ask for financial assistance. Crisis can be anything, a sudden shock to its economy or poor macroeconomic planning.

7. The IMF lends its money by three more widely implemented facilities. A stand-by agreement, extended fund facility (EFF) and the poverty reduction and growth facility.

8. The IMF also offers technical assistance to transitional economies in the changeover from centrally planned to market run economies. The IMF also gives emergency funds to collapsed economies.

9. All facilities of the IMF intend to create sustainable development within a country and to create policies that will be received well by the local populations.

10. However, the IMF is not an aid agency, so all loans are given on the condition that the country implement the SAPs and make it a priority to pay back what it has rented. Currently, all countries that are under IMF programs are developing transitional and emerging market countries.

2.2 World Bank

2.2.1 Introduction

The World Bank Group (WBG) was established in 1944 to rebuild post-World War II Europe under the International Bank for Reconstruction and Development (IBRD). There are 184 member countries that are shareholders in the IBRD, which is the primary arm of the

WBG. To become a member, however, a country must first join the International Monetary Fund (IMF) The World Bank is one of five institutions created at the Bretton Woods Conference in 1944. The International Monetary Fund, a related institution, is the second. Delegates from many countries attended the Bretton Woods Conference. The most powerful countries in attendance were the United States and United Kingdom which dominated negotiations. Although both are based in Washington, D. C., the World Bank, by custom, is headed by an American, while the IMF is led by a European.

A member country of the World Bank is required to buy 195 World Bank shares. The president of the World Bank comes from the largest shareholder, which is the US. To encourage sustainable growth, health, education, and social development programs, the bank encourages all of its clients to implement policies that focus on governance and poverty reduction mechanisms. The system allows the largest shareholders to dominate the vote, resulting in WBG policies being implemented by the poor but decided by the rich. This can result in policies that are not in the best interests of the developing country in question, whose political, social and economic policies will often have to be moulded around WBG declaration.

2.2.2 Nature of the World Bank

World Bank is an international financial institution that provides leveraged loans to developing countries for capital programmes. The World Bank has a stated goal of reducing poverty. By law, all of its decisions must be guided by a commitment to promote foreign investment, international trade and facilitate capital investment. It is an international financial institution that provides leveraged loans to developing countries for capital programmes. The World Bank has a stated goal of reducing poverty. By law, all of its decisions must be guided by a commitment to promote foreign investment, international trade and facilitate capital investment. Today, the World Bank functions as an international organisation that fights poverty by offering developmental assistance to middle-income and low-income countries. By giving loans and offering advice and training in both the private and public sectors, the World Bank aims to eliminate poverty by helping people help themselves. Under the World Bank Group, there are complimentary institutions that aid in its goals to provide assistance.

The bank provides training, assistance, information and other means that lead to sustainable development. But it has been observed that developing countries often have to put health, education and other social programs on hold in order to pay back their loans. Despite having similarities with IMF, the World Bank remains distinct. The basic difference is that the World Bank is primarily a development institution, whereas, the IMF is a cooperative institution that seeks to maintain an orderly system of payments and receipts among nations. Both the banks function in different ways, have a distinct structure, receive their funding from different sources, assist different categories of members, and strive to achieve distinct goals through methods peculiar to them. The governance of the World Bank is almost similar to that of the IMF. It is directed by a board of governors composed of one representative from each member country, and the governors direct the IBRD based on weighted voting rights that are decided by each country's agreed yearly contributions to the World Bank. The largest contributor in the IMF is the US, which has the most weighted voting power, though as a practical matter, decisions are made by consensus. The World Bank also operates as a training institute for officials in development related topics. In total, the World Bank has more than 10,000 employees, spread out over 100 offices around the world and headquartered in Washington, D. C.

2.2.3 Functions of World Bank

1. The World Bank encourages and supports the poor countries to grow by providing them with technical assistance and funding for projects and policies that will realise the countries' economic potential. The bank views development as a long-term, integrated effort.

2. Two thirds of the assistance provided by the bank went to the electric power and transportation projects in the first two decades of its existence. Though the infrastructure projects remain vital, the bank has diversified its activities in recent years as it has gained experience with and gained new insights in the process of development.

3. The bank pays more attention to projects that can directly benefit the poorest people in developing countries. The direct involvement of the poorest in economic activity is being promoted through providing for agriculture and rural development, small-scale enterprises, and urban development.

4. The bank helps the poor to be more resourceful and to gain access to basic necessities like safe water and waste-disposal facilities, health care, family-planning assistance, nutrition, education, and housing.

5. In transportation projects, more attention is bestowed on constructing farm-to-market roads. Not focussing exclusively on cities, power projects increasingly provide lighting and power for villages and small farms.

6. Industrial projects place greater stress on creating employment in small enterprises. Labour-intensive construction is used where ever possible. Besides electric power, the Bank supports the development of oil, gas, coal, fuel wood, and biomass as alternative sources of energy.

7.   The bank provides financial and technical help to developing countries by assisting specific projects. Although IBRD loans and IDA credits are made on different financial terms, the two institutions use the same standards in assessing the reliability of projects.

8.   The bank does not compete with other sources of finance while giving loans to developing countries. It assists only those projects for which the required capital is not available from other sources on reasonable terms.

2.2.4 Objectives of World Bank

The World Bank was established with the aim to promote long-term foreign investment loans on reasonable terms. The objectives of the bank as set forth in the 'Articles of Agreement' are as follows:

1.   To assist in the reconstruction and expansion of territories of members by facilitating the investment of capital for productive use including

   (a)   To restore economies, damaged or disrupted by war.

   (b)   To support the development of productive facilities and resources, in less developing countries.

2.   To promote private investment by means of guarantee or participation in loans and other investments made by private investors.

3.   To increase private investment by providing on suitable finance conditions for productive purpose out of its own capital funds raised by its other resources.

4.   To endorse the long-range balanced growth of international trade and the maintenance of equilibrium in balances of payments by promoting international investment for the development of the productive resources of members, thus assisting in raising productivity, the standard of living, and conditions of labour in their territories.

5.   To arrange international loans through channels so that the most useful and urgent projects will be dealt with first.

6.   To conduct its operations with regard to the effect of international investment on business, to assist in bringing about a smooth transition from a wartime to a peacetime economy.

2.3 Global Financial Market

2.3.1 Introduction

A global financial market can be defined as a marketplace where buyers and sellers participate in the trade of assets such as equities, bonds, currencies and derivatives. Financial markets are typically defined by having transparent pricing, basic regulations on trading, costs and fees, and market forces determining the prices of securities that trade.

The importance of global financial markets has occurred on account of the developments in the area of international trade activities. Global financial markets concentrate on lending and borrowing in foreign currencies for foreign trade transactions. Global financial markets operate outside the domain of the regulations and legislative framework of a country. Euro currency market, export credit facilities, international bonds market, and institutional finance are the various constituents of global financial markets. The global financial markets are dominated by issuers and investors in bonds. The choice of a currency plays a significant role in the realm of global financial markets. The participants in the global financial markets are MNCs, corporate enterprises, governments, etc. The US dollar, sterling pound, deutsche mark, Japanese yen, etc. are the most-preferred currencies for this purpose.

2.3.2 Nature of Global Financial Markets

The crucial role that financial systems play in economic development is beyond doubt.

1. Financial markets function quite like the nervous system of the human body, gathering, processing, and disseminating information. Hence, they matter immensely both when they function well or otherwise.

2. When they work well, they channel funds to the most productive uses and allocate risks to those who can best bear them—enhancing productivity, boosting the poverty-reduction effects of growth, and spreading equality of opportunity. When they malfunction, financial markets hinder growth and accentuate inequity. In worst case scenario, they are a veritable breeding ground for irrational exuberance, waste, corruption, and crises.

3. The two-sided relevance of financial systems — the large social benefits when they perform well and the major social costs when they do not — puts a high premium on well-crafted and implemented financial sector policies and reforms, on reliable contractual and regulatory institutions, and on effective transactional and informational market infrastructures.

2.3.3 Role of IMF and World Bank in Global Financial Market

The role and functions of the IMF is to deal with 'international monetary problems' by acting as a medium for its members to 'consult' and 'collaborate' with it, in order to 'facilitate' and 'promote' 'international monetary co-operation', 'growth of international trade' and 'exchange rate stability' to attain financial and economic stability. To make sure its members continuously adhere to its underlying purposes, the IMF achieves these broad purposes through its core functions – surveillance, financial assistance and technical assistance. The three main roles that IMF and World bank has in global financial markets are surveillance, financial assistance, and technical assistance.

1.   Surveillance

The IMF sends economists to each of its member countries every year to analyse the country's economic situation. This team inspects the fiscal and monetary policy, exchange rate, general macroeconomic stability, and any other associated policies, such as labour policy, trade policy, and social policy (such as the pension system). After the section authorising it in the Articles of Agreement, this process is termed as an Article IV consultation. The goal and intention of such consultation is to give an outside check on national decisions that might influence the international economic system. The main aim of surveillance is ensuring orderly exchange arrangements' amid members. The IMF, in 'consultation' with its members by both bilateral and multilateral means, assesses individual members' economic and monetary policies against its purposes to verify if they pose a risk to the stability of the international monetary system. It provides monetary assistance to members experiencing balance of payment problems. On this basis, the individual member fulfils the conditions set for such assistance so the IMF can be assured the money will be reimbursed.

This regularly requires the member country to adjust its economic and monetary policies, giving rise to a significant level of force by the IMF to ensure changes are indeed made. The traditional functions of these banks have expanded considerably over the years, both formally through amendments of the Articles of Agreement and informally through policy pronouncements, to cover a broader set of issues that strengthen the stability of the international monetary system. The IMF's role has widened from macroeconomic policy matters of including microeconomic policy, to achieve 'inter-financial and economic stability in its broadest sense' by acting as a forum for 'international cooperation to monitor economic developments on a global scale' and specifically addressing weaknesses in the overseeing of domestic financial markets. The main concern highlighted is the risks posed by such weaknesses in the financial system, both internally and externally to others.

The conventional role of surveillance has expanded from what **Lastra** coins "macro-surveillance" to micro-surveillance" specifically focusing on financial system soundness by placing particular attention on 'weak financial institutions, inadequate bank regulation and supervision, and lack of transparency' as a result of its broad discretionary mandate articulated in the Articles of Agreement. The IMF undertakes surveillance regularly with members to 'lessen the frequency and diminish the intensity of potential financial system problems'. Members are required to cooperate with the IMF, outlining how they will attempt to deal with any issues.

2.   Financial Assistance

Another central activity undertaken by the IMF is financial assistance to national treasury departments. Member countries having balance of payments problems can get credits and loans to pay off their obligations and readjust their economic policies so that they do not face any other crisis or near-crisis However, to receive assistance, the member-country should agree, through a "letter of intent," to implement changes in its fiscal and monetary policies that IMF experts have determined. Yet, IMF assistance is considered so important to national economic health that nations generally agree even when they have strong reservations.

The loans are distributed in phases to ensure that the receiving country flourishes with the reforms. Depending on the type of loan, loans are normally granted for a relatively short period of time, for just a few months or for as long as ten years. The receiving country must pay back loans on time, on a rigorous schedule, as the loans are intended to be temporary assistance.

Countries are discouraged from becoming dependent on loans provided by IMF, and in fact, may charge extra if too much of their government funding comes from the IMF. To a certain extent, the IMF hopes to play a role of a catalyst for private banks to lend to governments, since the extension of an IMF loan is intended to express confidence that the receiving country is getting its financial house in order.

The IMF provides the assistance through several lending programs ("facilities")

(a)   Stand-by arrangements are loans granted for specific amounts over 12 to 18 months to deal with short-term problems.

(b)   The Extended IMFs Facility is used to help a member-country deal with what are called "structural" economic problems resulting from a history of poor economic planning. The IMF attaches strong conditions to loans through this facility, which are granted for three to four year terms.

(c)   The Poverty Reduction and Growth Facility are granted at low interest rates to poor countries.

(d)   The Supplemental Reserve Facility grants short-term loans during crises, but adds a surcharge to discourage too much borrowing.

(e)   Contingent Credit Lines are granted during waves of crises that can spread from one country to another, called "contagions."

(f)   Emergency Assistance is granted to countries facing military conflicts or other sudden disasters.

3.   Technical Assistance

IMF and World Bank offer technical assistance on fiscal and monetary policy, regulatory procedures, tax policy, and collection of statistics, among other issues. This program is aimed at strengthening developing countries' abilities to reform and properly manage their macroeconomic policies. The ultimate function of the IMF is to provide technical assistance to its members but without the same degree of compulsion. The IMF's technical assistance function has also advanced in the light of its broader agenda to include financial sector reform, which incorporates the FSAP, by providing technical assistance on a voluntary basis.

Primarily, the World Bank is primarily made up of two main agencies – the International Bank for Reconstruction and Development (IBRD), and the International Development Association (IDA) and affiliate agencies. The role of the IBRD aims at reducing poverty and sustainable development, although it's initial responsibility was for assistance with the reconstruction of countries affected by crisis. The World Bank operates as a mediator for its members as a facilitator for investment and technical assistance, to assist with the 'development of productive facilities and resources in less developed countries'. The loan provided comes from both private means and its own resources, but the principal objective is to give financial assistance to members on the most reasonable terms and conditions. The IBRD raises most of its funds by selling its AAA-rated bonds to financial intermediaries in the international markets.

The traditional goal it tries to 'promote' are of a long-term nature – the 'growth of international trade', 'equilibrium of balance of payments' and 'investment for the development of the productive resources of members, focusing on raising productivity, the standard of living and conditions of labour in their territories', at the same time avoiding the interference in the political affairs of the country. The main aim of the IBRD is relatively narrow in terms of its Articles of Agreement, but has obviously been interpreted from economics to health, education, environment, infrastructure and poverty alleviation. *'The articles should receive a great measure of purposive interpretation to reflect the bank's varying role as a development institution'*. The main basic functions of the World Bank as a whole are said to be to act as a financial intermediary, a development research institution and a development agency.

The World Bank also assists members by providing what are called as 'knowledge services' through assessments and technical assistance on development matters; this is one of its most important roles. The World Bank loans basically fall into two broad categories – goods and services, and adjustment loans or 'structural adjustment loans'. The latter are for policy and institutional reforms: *the 'programme of reforms . . . proposed by the country and negotiated with the World Bank to ensure the objective of the projects and the outcomes are achieved under the aegis of conditionality'*. Financial sector reform has been on the World Bank's agenda for a considerable length of time (a lot longer than it has featured at the IMF), either through financial support for structural reform projects or technical assistance to a country's authorities to expand the area of economy and develop the capacity to oversee the financial system through legislative changes and training. Structural adjustment loans have focused on a broad range of areas, including reducing government ownership and strengthening bank supervision.

Apart from these three main activities, the IMF also has established various programs to ensure the stability of financial system management on a global scale. For example, the IMF, along with the World Bank and other institutions, has sketched out voluntary standards and codes for countries and financial institutions to adapt to in order to increase accountability and transparency and to minimise corruption. The IMF also has developed two systems of collection and dissemination of statistical information to help measure the economic possibility of the domestic and international financial systems.

2.4 Emerging Markets

2.4.1 Introduction

Emerging markets are new market structures arising from digitalisation, deregulation, globalisation, and open-standards, that are shifting the balance of economic power from the sellers to the buyers. In such markets information is freely and widely available, and is almost instantly accessible. To compete in these scenarios, a firm must adopt new processes based information technologies, and must keep a close watch on the price, quality, and convenience trends. Emerging markets generally do not have the level of market efficiency and strict standards in accounting and securities regulation to be on par with advanced economies (such as the United States, Europe and Japan), but emerging markets will typically have a physical financial infrastructure including banks, a stock exchange and a unified currency.

Emerging markets, also known as emerging economies or developing countries, are nations that are investing in more productive capacity. They are moving away from their traditional economies that have relied on agriculture and the export of raw materials. Leaders of developing countries want to create a better quality of life for their people. Therefore, they are rapidly industrialising, and adopting a free market or mixed economy. Emerging markets are important because they drive growth in the global economy.

2.4.2 Characteristic of Emerging Markets

1. Markets are Fragmented

Emerging markets are highly fragmented, with few national brands that have a powerful presence. For example, pharma products saw India, China, and Russia as a huge powerful market waiting to be tapped with their global megabrands. HSBC has succeeded by making their global brands local, market by market across the world. Branding strategies and portfolios need to be tailored to the reality of fragmented, market-stall economies.

2.   Populations are Youthful and Growing

Emerging economies remain young, while Japan, Europe, and the US is concerned about pensions and the rapid aging of their populations. Peter Drucker has declared that the "youth market is over," but in the developing world, the youth market has just begun. Most of the world's population growth will take place in developing countries.

3.   Infrastructure is Weak

Almost 86 percent of the rural markets' population is unreachable by motor vehicles. They lack good sanitation and electricity. Simultaneously, the metropolitan cities are growing very rapidly, and this fast urbanisation has caused tremendous damage on the urban infrastructure. In the developing nations, infrastructure is always fragile or underdeveloped. Transportation networks are missing. Power failures are common. Clean water and sanitation are often missing. In developing nations, underdeveloped economic systems and restrictive regulations have created thriving informal or parallel economies. It is estimated that the informal economy accounts for at least 40 percent of the GNP of low-income nations.

4.   Technology is Underdeveloped

The developed nations had a longer time to build technology-intensive industries such as pharmaceuticals and biotechnology, with the support of academic institutions and supplier networks.

5.   Distribution Channels are Weak

Developing nations with emerging markets have poor distribution systems. In large cities, distribution is often through small, hole-in-the-wall shops such as the *paanwalla* shops in India, the *tiendas de la esquinas* in Mexico, and *sari-sari* stores in the Philippines. In India's villages, a market of 600 million is locked, 42 percent of which have populations of less than 500, with weak connections to the outside world. The lack of media, roadways, and electricity creates seemingly dense barriers. Some villages don't have retail outlets at all, and some distribution opportunities, such as market days or carnivals, are short-term in nature.

6.   Markets are Changing Rapidly

Although it will take decades for these emerging markets to become developed, the continuity to change rapidly is certain. These markets can shift, in a year or even a matter of months. The accurate time this development of emerging markets will take, depends on factors such as government regulations, traditional business practices and culture, and companies' actions. Rising incomes and improved economic conditions will change consumer habits and society itself, creating predictable shifts, such as the increasing empowerment of women, as these markets mature. These markets present new challenges and opportunities at each stage of their development.

7. Migration to cities

There is a clear trend that in developing countries, there is a large scale migration to cities. This is coupled with little or no infrastructure, leading to a large part of the population facing problems.

8. Finance is expensive

All developing countries have expensive funding opportunities, which makes it difficult for the businesses to sustain on large loans. Many businesses have suffered due to the big debts. The least developed countries have the highest interest rates and developing countries have comparatively lower interest rates. Many companies in developing countries thus raise finance from developed countries.

9. Standard of living is lower

The standard of living is lower than that of the developed countries. Per capita income of the developed countries is much higher as compared to the developing and least developed countries.

2.4.3 Understanding the Sources of Development Outcomes

The development community has been learning about what development means and how to achieve it. The understanding of development has evolved. It is now widely accepted that poverty reduction efforts should address poverty in all its dimensions – not only lack of income, but also the lack of health and education, vulnerability to shocks, and the lack of control over their lives that poor people face. This understanding of poverty in some cases implies different approaches than in the past, for example, an increased focus on public service delivery to vulnerable groups as well as greater attention to early disclosure of information that poor people can use. This multidimensionality of poverty is embodied in the Millennium Development Goals (MDGs) adopted by heads of states at a United Nations Summit in 2000.

Knowledge about what works and what does not has also improved. Experience has shown that neither the central planning approach followed by many countries in the 1950s and 1960s nor the minimal government free-market approach advocated by many people in the 1980s and early 1990s, will achieve these goals. Most effective approaches to development will be led by the private sector in close tandem with effective government to provide the governance framework, facilitation or provision of physical infrastructure, human capital investments, and social cohesion necessary for growth and poverty reduction. Institutional development has too often been neglected in past policy discussions, is gaining increasing attention as an essential prerequisite for achieving sustained poverty reduction. While a number of key principles for effective development are clear, there is no single road to follow. Each country must devise their own strategies and approaches, appropriate for their own country circumstances and goals.

Thus far, we have improved our understanding of the main sources of growth and poverty reduction, although there is still much to learn. Two pillars are vital for development, namely, an investment climate that encourages private sector productivity growth and job creation, and mechanisms to invest in and empower poor people so that they can participate in growth.

Promoting development requires spurring the growth of private investment and productivity. Development assistance will never be able to achieve the desired outcomes on its own, no matter how well designed and implemented the projects, simply because levels of development assistance are small relative to other financial flows and to the scale of the challenge at hand. Development aid totalled about $54 billion in 2000; this was only one-third as much as foreign direct investment in developing countries ($167 billion), which itself was only a small fraction of total investment (nearly $1.5 trillion). This underscores the point that when aid makes a major difference in the fight against poverty, it does so through demonstration effects or improvements in institutions, not simply through resource transfer. To meet the challenge of 'scaling up,' aid must help countries put in place for themselves the pillars of development that will support rapid and shared private sector-led growth. Experience and analysis show that countries reduce poverty fastest when they put in place the aforesaid two pillars of development:

1. ***Create a good investment* climate:** One that encourages firms and farms, both small and large, to invest, create jobs; and increase productivity.

2. ***Empower and invest in* poor people** by giving them access to health, education, infrastructure, financial services, social protection, and mechanisms for participating in the decisions that shape their lives. Understanding of economic growth and its causes has improved. We now understand that creating an investment climate that sustains growth requires progress in a number of areas: macroeconomic stability and trade openness; governance and institutions (including a good education system, an effective legal and judicial system, a professional bureaucracy, a strong and well-regulated financial sector, and vigorous competition); and adequate infrastructure.

2.4.4 Role of IMF and World Bank in Emerging Market

Low-Income Countries

The World Bank and IMF has a crucial role to play in working with governments to put in place good and strong governance, effective legal and judicial systems, and a robust financial system, and to assist in the fight against corruption. Without these initiatives, it will be impossible for countries to attract foreign and domestic private investment, which are as crucial as engines of growth and poverty reduction. We need to help put in place safety nets for the vulnerable, as we are doing around the world, and work with governments to focus on education, health, and nutrition. We need to step up the fight against HIV/AIDS and malaria and tuberculosis, and to work with governments to meet their basic infrastructure needs clean, potable water, sanitation, power and communications, with roads and telecommunications systems. Above all, we must recognise that debt relief is not a substitute for much-needed development assistance. It is tragic that just when many governments have begun to put in place policies to foster growth and reduce poverty, the flows of aid have begun to shrink. Aid works when governments act in a responsible and accountable manner, and we can do more to make it work for more people.

Industrial countries must also get serious on trade. Barriers to developing country exports in industrialised markets continue to severely disadvantage poor countries. Industrialised countries spend more than $300 billion a year on agricultural subsidies. That is roughly equal to the total GNP for all of Sub-Saharan Africa. And yet, even today, developed country tariffs on meat, fruits, and vegetables – all primary exports from the developing world can exceed 100 percent. Debt relief without accompanying increased market access is a sham. We must push ahead with donor coordination and harmonisation. Since that time, the development community has made some progress on donor coordination with the bilateral and the regional development banks, but not enough.

Middle-Income Countries

IMF and the world bank stresses on middle-income countries. Eighty percent of the world's poor live in middle-income countries. Although these countries are important for global financial stability, many of them have not yet put in place crucial structural and social reforms that will move them to the next stage of development. Helping these countries meet their development challenges is central to the Bank's overarching mission of tackling global poverty; it is also central to the realisation of the international development goals. Developments in these countries are also important for poverty reduction elsewhere.

The economic well-being of the middle-income countries can translate into trade opportunities for low-income countries; on the other hand, financial instability, environmental degradation, and the proliferation of communicable diseases can have deleterious effects far outside their own borders. The bank's engagement will be focused on the provision of secure long-term funding and advisory services, creating the right policy and institutional framework, and addressing weaknesses in the social, structural, and sectoral policies and institutions. With its global reach, broad sectoral knowledge, and specific engagement with the private sector through the IFC and MIGA, the bank group has a comparative advantage in advising on overall priorities and actions to improve the investment climate. Many of these countries may have a credit rating but do not have continuous access to international capital in the amount they need or on terms that are manageable for them. Moreover, as our own research and experience shows, World Bank lending has a catalytic effect – it crowds in private capital. It doesn't crowd it out. But, here again, a selective approach focusing on areas where one has a comparative advantage would be more appropriate. Also, one needs to work closely with partners.

The Global Agenda

Globalisation is an opportunity to reach global solutions to national problems. Concern for the environment is a given starting point, which is already embedded in our work. As part of our strategic framework, there are three areas in which we are sharpening our focus and capabilities. Firstly, the area of focus is on the communicable diseases. Disease respects no national boundaries, and it impoverishes and poses tremendous obstacles to development. Bank-supported programmes can provide the essential country-level framework on which effective global action can be based. One has already taken note of the bank's work on HIV/AIDS. But much needs to be done on the malaria and tuberculosis front. Every year 3 million children die from measles and hepatitis because they lack access to immunisations. Major alliances, such as, the Global Alliance for Vaccines and Immunisation (GAVI) also provide seed capital, both intellectual and financial, for new initiatives of a public goods nature. Secondly, trade expansion has been a leading factor in global integration. Over the last 30 years, several developing countries have participated in trade liberalisation; but the gains from trade have been uneven. Low-income countries, particularly in Africa, have been less able to capitalise on liberalisation and world trade growth. We see a catalytic role for the bank in increasing trading opportunities for Africa and other developing countries to boost their capacities to negotiate with the World Trade Organisation (WTO) and industrial countries. Thirdly, the bank's analytical and advisory role is essential, supporting national policies to strengthen market institutions and infrastructure. This has considerable potential for creating large gains from trade. Fourthly, the financial crises of 1997-98 have brought about broad agreement that international standards, especially, in financial systems, are a necessary foundation for robust economies. The bank continues to participate in various forums – with the Fund, with the Bank for International Settlements, and other partners, for capacity building at the institutional level.

Finally, it is important to usher in knowledge and information to developing countries, if not more important than capital as an engine of development by bridging the digital divide or establishing a Global Gateway to radically transform the development business. Here, development expertise, technical assistance and capacity-building work will come in handy. That apart, one need not neglect the importance of culture in a globalised world, namely, addressing the fear of cultural homogenisation. This is needed in order to preserve not only the cultural identity of nations but also the cultural heritage in a rapidly shrinking world.

2.4.5 Impact of World Bank and IMF on Developing Countries

Uganda, Mozambique, China, Vietnam, India, and Poland are all examples of countries where, within the past two decades, policy and institutional reforms have sparked off acceleration in development. In each of these cases, the country and its government have been the prime movers for reform, and each country mapped out its own development strategy and approach. Their experiences do have some common features - most notably an increase in market orientation and macroeconomic stability - and all have seen their growth powered by private sectors (both farms and firms) that have begun to thrive. But while these countries did act along those broad guidelines on development, none of them closely followed any external blueprint for development offered by the Bank or other donors.

Yet, in all of these cases, the development assistance from many sources has supported the transformation. In some cases, advice was more important than lending. In the case of China, for example, aid flows have been dwarfed by inflows of private capital. However, development assistance helped pave the way for private sector growth and international integration - for example, when the World Bank and others provided analysis and advice to help China open its economy to investment, unify its exchange rate, and improve its ports early in the transition period.

The examples here focus mainly on contributions made by the Bank again, in support of country-owned and country-implemented reforms - but other donors have also been influential.

China: The past 20 years of reform in China have contributed more to poverty reduction than any other growth episode in history. Unquestionably, this process of growth and development was driven by China itself. The composition, sequencing, and timing of reforms were designed at home, and built on China's existing strengths in such areas as literacy and basic health. At the same time, support from outside helped make reform happen and contributed to the structure of the reforms. In the early stages of market-oriented reform, the World Bank provided advice on laying the foundation for the private investment and productivity growth that has buoyed the country's remarkable progress. The Bank provided the government with the first in-depth overall analysis of China's economic problems, and it helped China engage with the outside world again, on the country's own schedule through advice on liberalisation, exchange-rate unification, and port modernisation. The Bank's rural development projects and analytical work complemented strongly these improvements in the overall business environment by targeting poverty where it was most prevalent, namely, in the countryside. The Bank, as both knowledge and lending institution, thereby made a significant supporting contribution to the massive reduction in rural poverty: from 34 per cent of the rural population in 1985 to just 18 per cent in 1998.

India: Throughout the 1960s and 1970s, India was weakly integrated into the international economy and relied heavily on planning and licensing. As a result, economic growth and poverty reduction were unimpressive. Growth accelerated in the 1980s but was based in large measure on unsustainable public spending and foreign borrowing. With the entry of a reformist government in 1991, the Bank provided support for trade and other reforms to stabilise and open up the economy. Over the past five years, the Bank has supported India's decentralisation process, working closely with state, local, and municipal governments committed to reform. Powerful demonstration effects are beginning to emerge.

Mozambique: Mozambique is a recent example of successful post-conflict reform. The country emerged in 1992 from a long civil war, which combined with a socialist experiment had left the country one of the poorest in the world. Since then, the World Bank has helped the government to design and implement exchange rate reform, trade liberalisation, financial liberalisation, and privatisation. In this more stable and open environment, GDP has grown at an average rate of 8.4 per cent - in part due to revitalised agricultural growth and to increasing exports, which had been stagnant for a decade. The private sector has responded: Foreign Direct Investment (FDI) grew some 500 per cent between 1992 and 2001. Today, the focus has shifted towards two areas of continued weakness: strengthening the social sectors (Mozambique is struggling against the AIDS epidemic), and reforming judicial and tax systems.

Uganda: Uganda's new government in the mid-1980s inherited a country that was devastated by years of conflict and economic mismanagement. Starting with advice, the Bank helped the government learn from the comparative experience of Ghana and other countries and helped it design and implement key measures on fiscal adjustment, exchange rate reform, and trade liberalisation. Aid and the conditionality associated with bank-supported adjustment lending helped generate policy reforms in the late 1980s and early 1990s, a period during which multilateral assistance from the bank and other lenders was particularly important. Since that period, Uganda has achieved a remarkable recovery. It has increased private investment, reversed capital flight, increased external trade, and privatised commercial public enterprises. As a result, it has made great strides in primary education, with several million additional children attending school during the first year of a bank adjustment loan. Uganda has also reversed income poverty sharply, from 56 percent in 1992-93 to 35 percent by the year 2000.

Poland: Poland was the first country to emerge from the transition recession in 1992 and has since maintained an average GDP growth rate of 3.7 percent, the highest among transition economies.

Positioned to gain access to the European Union (EU) in 2004, Poland has led the way in many reforms, often taking major risks. Outside assistance has also helped. From the early phases of Poland's economic transformation, the bank provided advisory and financial support. The activities included aiding macroeconomic reforms, supporting the creation of an institutional and regulatory framework, helping with the restructuring and privatisation of industries, upgrading infrastructure with private-sector participation, and helping to restore Poland's creditworthiness. Finally, the bank also helped to improve public understanding of the government's economic strategy.

Vietnam: Vietnam has also moved strongly to reform its economy and reduce poverty over the past dozen years, beginning when it was still politically and economically estranged from major donors and, therefore, could not receive large-scale aid. The bank began to provide advice to Vietnam in 1989, at a time when the country's disastrous economic policies had produced a crisis of hyperinflation, falling economic activity, and mass exodus of economic migrants. Although it did not provide finance until 1993, the bank advised the government on stabilising the macro economy, opening to foreign trade and investment, and reforming property rights. As reforms took hold, the bank later shifted its focus to infrastructure and primary education. The results have been remarkable – the income poverty rate was cut from 58 to 37 percent in just six years.

These six countries provide recent examples of bank-supported progress, but the past 50 years of development experience also provide examples, such as, the Republic of Korea and Botswana that illustrate how effective aid can be in supporting reform. Korea, for example, progressed from borrowing from the International Development Association (IDA), the bank's soft-loan facility for the poorest countries, to borrowing from the International Bank for Reconstruction and Development (IBRD), the lending arm for middle-income countries, and finally to borrowing solely in private markets. Korea is also an example of a country that, with donor support, built both pillars of development. It invested heavily in education and human development while also greatly improving the environment for growth and entrepreneurship.

It is important to note that impressive development results do not depend on reaching all goals simultaneously. Each of the countries listed here continues to face major development challenges, whether in governance or institution-building or capacity development. However, these examples show just how strong the returns can be seen to be moving in the right direction, and how important it is to help countries that are committed to making this movement. Of course, the World Bank has also been involved in many countries, particularly, in Sub-Saharan Africa, where results have been less impressive. There are too many countries that have received very large volumes of aid over time, with little result in terms of poverty reduction. For example, between 1960 and 2000, donors disbursed more than $10 billion in aid to the Democratic Republic of Congo (formerly Zaire) – a country that, for most of that period, showed little inclination to take the steps necessary for development. GNP per capita fell strikingly for much of that period, from $460 in 1975 to $100 in 1996. And as noted above, donor-supported progress on human development indicators has been reversed by the AIDS epidemic or by conflict in many African countries. In Botswana, which otherwise has a highly successful economy, AIDS reduced life expectancy from 57 years to 39 years in the 1990s; in Sierra Leone, conflict and chaos have kept life expectancy at around 35 years. The bank and other donors provided substantial support for governments that were not willing to take decisive action against AIDS, and other development failures have helped provide a fertile ground for civil conflict.

2.5 Poverty Aid

2.5.1 Introduction

For many, the 1980s and 1990s were decades of increasing wealth. The world's total economy grew, benefiting from new technology, liberalisation and growth of trade. But at the same time, the gap between rich and poor was growing wider, and the actual numbers of people living in poverty increased. In order to overcome that we must also recognise that debt relief by itself is not a panacea. The IMF and World Bank should play a crucial role with governments to put in place good and strong governance, effective legal and judicial systems, and a robust financial system, and to assist in the fight against corruption. Without these initiatives, it will be impossible for countries to attract foreign and domestic private investment, which are as crucial as engines of growth and poverty reduction.

We need to help put in place safety nets for the vulnerable, as we are doing around the world, and work with governments to focus on education, health, and nutrition. We need to step up the fight against HIV/AIDS and malaria and tuberculosis, and to work with governments to meet their basic infrastructure needs clean, potable water, sanitation, power and communications, with roads and telecommunications systems. Above all, we must recognise that debt relief is not a substitute for much-needed development assistance. It is tragic that just when many governments have begun to put in place policies to foster growth and reduce poverty, the flows of aid have begun to shrink. Aid works when governments act in a responsible and accountable manner, and we can do more to make it work for more people.

Industrial countries must also get serious on trade. Barriers to developing country exports in industrialised markets continue to severely disadvantage poor countries. Industrialised countries spend more than $300 billion a year on agricultural subsidies. That is roughly equal to the total GNP for all of Sub-Saharan Africa. And yet, even today, developed country tariffs on meat, fruits, and vegetables-all primary exports from the developing world can exceed 100 per cent. Debt relief without accompanying increased market access is a sham. We must push ahead with donor coordination and harmonisation. Since that time, the development community has made some progress on donor coordination with the bilateral and the regional development banks but not enough.

Poverty

We must also recognise that while there is social injustice on a global scale, both between states and within them, while the fight against poverty is barely begun in too many parts of the world; while the link between progress in development and progress toward peace is not recognised – we may win a battle against terror but we will not conclude a war that will yield enduring peace.

1. Poverty is our greatest long-term challenge. Gruelling, mind-numbing, poverty – it snatches one's hope and opportunity from young hearts and dreams just when they should take flight and soar.

2. Poverty – takes the promise of a whole life ahead and stunts it into a struggle for day-to-day survival.

3. Poverty – together with its handmaiden, hopelessness, can lead to exclusion, anger, and even conflict.

4. Poverty – does not itself necessarily lead to violence, but can provide a breeding ground for the ideas and actions of those who promote conflict and terror.

2.5.2 Factors that would help in Poverty Aid

The World Bank and its partners – United Nations agencies, bilateral donors, and governments – have committed to a common set of poverty-reduction results, including the Millennium Development Goals agreed to by governments at major conferences in the 1990s. The goals are accompanied by numerical targets expressed in terms of changes between 1990 and 2015; reducing the share of people living in poverty worldwide by half; reducing infant and child mortality by two-thirds; reducing maternal mortality by three-quarters and improving access to reproductive health services; and halting the increase in incidence of communicable diseases (AIDS, malaria, TB) and reducing malnutrition. The factors that would help in poverty aid are as follows –

1. Growth and Poverty Reduction

Economic growth is essential for sustained progress on poverty reduction. The countries that have reduced income poverty the most are those that have grown the fastest, and poverty has grown fastest in countries that have stagnated economically. Between 1992 and 1998, for example, the share of the population in poverty fell by an average of 5 to 8 percent annually in fast-growing Uganda, India, Vietnam, and China. In Nigeria, by contrast, per capita consumption fell 16 percent between 1992 and 1996, and the poverty share increased by half from 43 percent to 66 percent of the population.

2. Income Distribution and Poverty Reduction

Some have expressed fear that growth alone cannot be relied upon to provide for significant poverty reduction in developing countries. Evidence shows that income distribution has not changed on an average in periods of growth in the typical country, and that, therefore, overall growth has meant that the incomes of the poor have increased proportionately. In China, inequality did increase with reform; but the increase in inequality was an inevitable feature of the improvement in the incentive structure, which led to growth and poverty reduction. Indeed, growth was so strong that poverty fell sharply despite worsening income distribution. In other cases, Uganda, for example, income distribution improved at least modestly with reforms and growth. Nevertheless, it is the case that countries with better income distribution see growth translate into faster poverty reduction. At the same rate of GDP growth, a country with highly equal distribution (that is, one with a Gini coefficient of 0.30) will see poverty fall twice as fast as a highly unequal country (Gini of.35). In addition, the evidence suggests that greater inequality of important assets, such as, land and education, may retard society-wide growth.

It is also the case that groups of poor people will experience reform and growth differently. A large increase in the income of one group may be offset by a smaller increase or even decline in the income of another group. This underlines the importance of ensuring that there is adequate social protection in place as a complement to structural adjustment measures. Social protection helps build broader support for action, besides enabling individuals to take risks involved in entrepreneurship.

And social protection is not just an instrument for achieving growth. It also targets poverty directly, by reducing the income vulnerability that poor people identify as one of the defining elements of a life in poverty.

3. Determinants of Improved Social Indicators

Once we recognise that poverty is about more than income, we see that there are other determinants of poverty reduction beyond growth. Social indicators – health and education improved far faster in the 20th century than we would have expected, given the rate of income growth. Most countries have made major progress in increasing educational attainment and health outcomes by targeting these goals directly, and by applying new knowledge and technologies rather than just waiting for the effects of income growth to improve these indicators. At every level of income, infant mortality fell sharply during the 20th century. For example, a typical country with per capita income of $8,000 in 1950 (measured in 1995 dollars) would have had, on average, an infant mortality rate of 45 per 1,000 live births. By 1970, a country at the same real income level would typically have had an infant mortality rate of only 30 per 1,000; by 1995, only 15 per 1,000. Similar reductions have occurred all along the income spectrum, including in the poorest countries.

The improvements in social indicators are remarkable by historical standards. As noted in the preface, life expectancy in developing countries increased by 20 years over a period of only 40 years, as it shot from the mid-40s to the mid-60s. By comparison, it probably took millennia to improve life expectancy from the mid-20s to the mid-40s. Literacy improvements have also been remarkable; whereas, in 1970 nearly two out of every four adults were illiterate, now it is only one out of every four.

These advances in education and health have greatly improved the welfare of individuals and families. Not only are education and health valuable in themselves, but they also increase income-earning capacity. Where macroeconomic analyses of the growth effects of education have been somewhat ambiguous, the microeconomic evidence of the returns to education is overwhelming and robust. Each additional year of education increases the average individual worker's wages by at least 5 to 10 percent. And educating women is a particularly effective way to raise the human development levels of children. Mothers who are more educated have healthier children, even at a given level of income. They are also more productive in the labour force, which raises household incomes and thereby increases child survival rates, in part, because compared with men, women tend to spend additional income in ways that benefit children more.

4. Rich Countries Provide Aid

The aforesaid question can be answered in several ways. Here, we look at three – an ethical view, a notion of a better world, and an approach based entirely on enlightened self-interest. A fundamental and crucial ethical argument proceeds from the view that human beings have a basic responsibility to alleviate suffering and to prevent the needless deaths of other human beings. It is a notion that is central to all the major religions of the world. It is part of our understanding of being a decent citizen of the world. To accept the persistence of desperate poverty, that is, to do nothing to change a world where 1.2 billion people subsist on less than a dollar a day, where 120 million children do not attend school, and where tens of millions of people die annually from the combined effects of poor nutrition and diseases that could easily have been prevented or treated – is morally untenable. In such a world, people fortunate enough to be born into the richer societies have a moral obligation to share their good fortune with others.

Foreign aid is increasingly acting as a catalyst for change, and it is helping to create conditions in which poor people are able to raise their incomes and to live longer, healthier, and more productive lives. The past 50 years have seen remarkable successes, as well as failures, in development assistance. Better policies in developing countries, together with improved allocation of aid since the end of the Cold War, imply that aid is more effective today at reducing poverty than ever before. Yet, much of the developing world saw little progress over the past several decades, and in some places, such as, parts of Sub-Saharan Africa, living standards declined.

Moreover, huge challenges remain, such as reversing the Acquired Immune Deficiency Syndrome (AIDS) and malaria epidemics, and finding ways to spur growth and empower poor people in countries with weak institutions, governance, and policies. An estimated 1.2 billion people subsist on under $1 per day, and the majority of the developing world's population lives on less than $2 per day. (Dollar amounts in this paper are US unless otherwise noted.) Moreover, the world's population will increase by 2 billion in the next 30 years, with almost all of the growth coming in developing countries. How effective the development community is in helping poor societies respond to these challenges will depend on continued learning and on improvements in the allocation, design, and delivery of foreign aid.

Development depends on two pillars, which together support sustained growth and poverty reduction:

  (a) **Countries must build a good investment climate:** An environment in which the private sector will invest and produce efficiently, in a way that generates jobs and productivity growth. The investment climate consists of all the factors that most influence private-sector decisions – macroeconomic stability and openness, governance and institutions, and infrastructure. The private sector should be understood not only (or even primarily) to include large firms and multinationals, but also farmers and Small and Medium Enterprises (SMEs).

(b) Countries must empower and invest in poor people, so that they can participate in growth. We know that sustained growth is essential for poverty reduction, so the investment climate focus is itself a tool for poverty reduction. At the same time, governments need to target poverty more directly, notably by equipping poor people with the tools necessary to contribute to growth, such as, education and health, and by giving them access to infrastructure and financial services. People are empowered when they are given the ability to shape their own lives, whether through greater capabilities or through participation in decision-making. Direct actions by government, international organisations, and NGOs are necessary to make this happen.

Many countries have built up these two pillars in recent decades and have seen the rewards – rapid growth and poverty reduction. Although too many other countries continue to fall behind economically, a majority of the developing world's population lives in countries that have grown rapidly and are closing the gap with the rich countries. Even the countries that have stagnated economically have, for the most part, seen material improvements in social indicators, such as, health and education measures. Development assistance has helped accelerate this progress. It aims at helping countries build both pillars – improving the investment climate (through building the factors that contribute to investment and growth), and empowering people (through education, health, and social protection).

5.   The Role and Effectiveness of Development Assistance

These trends make it clear that public policy matters. Government has a role not only in ensuring delivery of good basic services in health and education but also in ensuring that technology and knowledge spread widely through the economy. The dramatic improvement in life expectancy at a given income level is attributable to environmental changes and is the result of public health actions. The control of diarrhoeal diseases, including the development of oral rehydration therapy to reduce child mortality, is one such example; the education of women was an important component of these efforts. Small pox eradication, made possible through a combination of advances in public health research and effective programme management, is another example of a successful 20th century public health effort.

We have learned much about the overall sources of growth and poverty reduction.

(a)   Understanding of economic growth and its causes has improved greatly. We now understand that sustained growth depends on broad progress in a number of areas – macroeconomic stability and trade openness; governance and institutions; including a good education system, effective legal institutions, and professional bureaucracy; vigorous competition; and adequate infrastructure, especially in countries that are landlocked or face other geographical barriers.

(b) **Poverty reduction depends heavily on sustained economic growth**. On an average, income distribution does not worsen during periods of economic growth, so the incomes of poor people rise at the same rate as those of wealthier people. The countries that grew rapidly in the 1990s such as China, India, Vietnam, and Uganda managed to reduce the share of their people in absolute poverty by 5 to 8 percent per year.

(c) But while growth is essential, countries can accelerate reduction of income poverty by acting to ensure that **poor people have the tools necessary to contribute to growth**, such as, health and education.

(d) **Policies and investments aimed directly at reducing non-income dimensions of poverty** can be highly effective. Countries can accelerate health and education progress far beyond what would result simply from economic growth.

However, the facts show that despite difficulties and setbacks, we have made important progress in the past, and will continue to do so in the future.

(a) Over the past 40 years, life expectancy at birth in developing countries has increased by 20 years – about as much as was achieved in all of human history prior to the middle of the 20th century.

(b) Over the past 30 years, illiteracy in the developing world has been cut nearly in half, from 47 percent to 25 percent in adults.

(c) Over the past 20 years, the absolute number of people living on less than $1 a day, after rising steadily for the last 200 years, has for the first time begun to fall, even as the world's population has grown by 1.6 billion people.

Driving much of this progress has been an acceleration of growth rates in the developing world – more than doubling the income of the average person living in developing countries over the past 35 years.

These are not just meaningless statistics. They indicate real progress in real people's lives.

(a) In Vietnam, where the number of people in poverty has halved over the last 15 years.

(b) In China, where the number of rural poor people fell from 250 million to 34 million in two decades of reform.

Policies must be locally owned and locally grown since any effort to fight poverty must be comprehensive. There is no single magic bullet that alone will slay poverty. But, we know too that there are conditions that foster successful development – Education and health programmes to build the human capacity of the country; good and clean government; an effective legal and justice system; and a well-organised and supervised financial system. Also, we have learned that corruption, bad policies, and weak governance will make aid ineffective, and that country-led programmes to fight corruption can succeed.

That apart, we must focus on the conditions for investment and entrepreneurship, particularly, for smaller enterprises and farms. But that is not enough for pro-poor growth. One must also promote investment in people, empowering them to make their own choices.

More than ever today, a new wind is blowing though the world of development, transforming our potential to make development happen. In this new world, development is not about aid dependence. It is more about a chance for developing countries to put in place policies that will enable their economies to grow, one that will attract private investment, and allow governments to invest in their people-promoting aid independence. It is about treating the poor not as objects of charity, but as assets on which we can build a better and safer world. It is about scaling up moving from individual projects to programmes. And it is the developing countries that are leading the way.

These leaders, and leaders and people like them through much of the developing world, are recognising what must be done to allow their countries to develop. They are committing to good governance, to improving the investment climate, to investing in their people. The resultant marked improvement in policies in much of the developing world since the 1980s shows that they are serious and are beginning to have an effect. In some countries, these improvements in policies and governance have generated growth, led by the private sector, which involves poor people. By building a more favourable environment for productivity and development, they are creating jobs, encouraging growth in domestic savings and investment, while also spurring increases in foreign direct investment flows.

They are not sitting back waiting for development to be done to them. They are helping to finance their own development; and they recognise the crucial importance of building human capacity within their countries. But they cannot do it alone. Everybody needs to join in this new partnership, both developing and developed countries. This is an urgent imperative since the need of the hour is to create a more stable and peaceful world.

2.5.3 Role of IMF and World Bank in Poverty Aid

The World Bank (WB) and the International Monetary Fund (IMF), has also devised a number of strategies to assist the poorer countries of the developing world join the global party. The IMF's structural adjustment policies, or SAPs were the most well-known which were meant to stabilise national finances and open economies for international trade. Although, SAPs did not succeed in helping the poorest to mount ahead of poverty – as techniques often included cuts in education, health and welfare that hit the poorest.

The World Bank and IMF then launched the HIPC (Highly Indebted Poor Countries) Initiative, which intended to decrease the amount of debt the poorest countries had to repay. Finally, in 1999, the World Bank, along with the IMF introduced its Poverty Reduction Strategy Papers –also known as PRSPs. PRSPs aspires to focus development efforts on poverty eradication. They are applicable to over 70 low-income countries. A PRSP begins with an analysis of poverty, and then identifies the poverty reduction outcomes a country wishes to achieve and the key actions required. The country qualifies for debt relief and concessional lending; once a country's PRSP has been completed and approved by the World Bank and IMF. The process of developing PRSPs has generated a greater awareness and focus on poverty, nature of poverty and understanding of its causes. In many countries, relations between government and civil society have improved due to this step. Governments are opening up their budgeting processes and spending on public. Non-governmental organisations (NGOs) have come together in what has been for many a new way of working. The media too is beginning to examine its role in helping the public understand and get involved in the development and monitoring of PRSPs.

What is poverty reduction strategy?

Poverty Reduction Strategy Paper (PRSP) is a national strategy created by governments of low-income countries, for aiming government expenditure on measures to reduce poverty. A PRSP begins with analysing the causes of poverty, further identifying the poverty reduction outcomes a country wishes to accomplish and the key actions – policy changes, institutional reforms, programmes and projects – essential to attain these outcomes. It must establish targets, indicators and monitoring systems. The country qualifies for debt relief and concessional loan, once a PRSP has been approved by the World Bank (WB) and International Monetary Fund (IMF). The PRSP approach was originated by the World Bank and IMF in September 1999, as part of an enhanced Highly Indebted Poor Countries (HIPC) initiative. They have also been adopted by many donor countries as a framework for their development cooperation. The WB and IMF work together to help countries develop and implement PRSPs, each concentrating on its traditional area of expertise. They collaborate on issues where they both have expertise such as fiscal management, budget transparency, and tax administration.

The process and how it works

There are two stages to the PRSP process.

Countries must first draw up an Interim PRSP. This is intended as a 'road map' for developing a full PRSP – consisting of a plan for civil society participation, which is not needed at this stage.

The Interim PRSP involves

1. Assessment by the WB/IMF in-country staff – the 'Joint Staff Review'; and recommendation to the Executive Boards of WB and IMF.

2. Endorsement of the plan by the Boards. This is known as the 'Decision Point'.

3. At this stage, the country receives Interim debt relief – funds granted from the IMF to pay a proportion of the country's debt service payments – and continuing WB/IMF assistance.

The second stage is the development of the full PRSP. This includes –

1. Understanding poverty in the country

2. Strategy design choice of policy options and strategies

3. Approval by the government and parliament

4. World Bank/IMF Joint Staff Assessment

5. Endorsement by the Executive Boards of the Bank and IMF

6. Implementation

7. Monitoring and annual progress report

Steps along the path include

1. The World Summit on Social Development, where 186 governments resolved to wipe out poverty.

2. The declaration of the first 'United Nations Decade for the Eradication of Poverty'.

3. The initiatives by the World Bank/IMF of the HIPC initiative – to lessen the debt of poor countries to multilateral institutions.

4. 1997-98 International Development Goals agreed, to divide the number living in extreme poverty by 2015.

5. 1998-1999 World Bank President James Wolfensohn introduced the Comprehensive Development Framework (CDF) approach. A precursor to PRSPs, the CDF was to be a country-led strategy involving all a country's development partners.

6. Poverty Reduction Strategies and Poverty Reduction and Growth Fund introduced.

7. The Meltzer Report to the US Congress, which was critical of the performance of the World Bank and IMF.

8. The UN Millennium Declaration – an endorsement of the International Development Goals, agreed by over 160 world leaders at the UN General Assembly.

How it helps in reducing poverty

The sheer fact of debt relief will release funds for social spending. The use of these funds – put into a special fund, targeted at poverty-reduction – is the heart of the PRSP. Assessments of the impact of PRSPs highlight not only the impact of this spending but the impact of changes in overall government policy and behaviour related with the PRSP process. The following impacts are starting to appear – optimists see signs that they will be achieved over the coming years, while sceptics are inclined to regard their absence as evidence that the whole process and concept is flawed.

1. **The consultative approach:** *'The open and participatory nature of the PRSP approach is regarded by many as its defining characteristic and its most significant achievement. 'The PRSP is believed to bring a new culture of consultation of the poor, accountability and sense of ownership of one's national development,' says the Pastoralist Forum, Ethiopia.*

2. The PRSP approach calls for strong analysis of poverty – lots of effort, including consultation with poor people themselves, has gone into identifying who they are, the reasons of poverty, their needs, etc.

3. It has highlighted the necessity for better data about poverty and inequality – for improved ongoing data collection and better analysis. Often the data that the countries have at present is unreliable and outdated. For instance, World Vision, an NGO says that much of the planning in Tanzania was based on a ten-year-old household survey.

4. It demands governments to focus on available funds on sectors that help the poor create and benefit from, such as education, health, and rural infrastructure.

5. While allocating national budgets, it demands finance departments to prioritise poverty. It also means that national projects and programmes must be monitored.

   This is recognised as important by the World Bank and by NGOs, because monitoring is one of the main ways in which civil society will be involved and will be able to hold governments accountable.

There are a number of key directions that governments are already taking, as identified by the World Bank's:

1. Good governance

- Improve Public Expenditure Management (PEM) to increase efficiency, transparency and accountability.
- Implementation must be reported annually, and each country's PRSP reviewed and amended after three years.
- Stimulate coherence of policymaking within governments, requiring different departments to work together.
- Stimulate engagement of civil society in planning and implementation.
- Address corruption.

2. Rural development is a goal, though the means to achieve it are not very defined. All mention rural credit and most rural infrastructure.

3. Access to education is a priority in all PRSPs.

4. Access to health services, especially primary, is a priority in African PRSPs.

5. Most emphasise the role of the private sector in growth, with access to markets as key.

Points to Remember

- The International Monetary Fund (IMF) is the inter-governmental organisation headquartered in Washington D. C. United States, that oversees the global financial system by following the macroeconomic policies of its member countries, in particular, those with an impact on exchange rate and the balance of payments.

- The International Monetary Fund was created in July 1944 towards the end of the Second World War. This was done to avoid another worldwide economic disaster like the Great Depression that had weakened some nations and had contributed to the rise of fascism and the war.

- The aim of international monetary fund was to stabilise exchange rates and assist the reconstruction of the world's international payment system. It started off with forty-five members.

- The objective of IMF is to facilitate the balanced growth of international trade. To contribute to the promotion and maintenance of high levels of employment and real income and to the expansion of the productive resources of all members as primary objectives of economic policy to promote exchange stability, to sustain orderly exchange arrangements between members, and to avoid competitive exchange depreciation.

- The World Bank Group (WBG) was established in 1944 to rebuild post-World War II Europe under the International Bank for Reconstruction and Development (IBRD).

- World Bank is an international financial institution that provides leveraged loans to developing countries for capital programmes. The World Bank has a stated goal of reducing poverty.

- Despite having similarities with IMF, the World Bank remains distinct. The basic difference is that the World Bank is primarily a development institution, whereas, the IMF is a cooperative institution that seeks to maintain an orderly system of payments and receipts among nations.

- The World Bank encourages and supports the poor countries to grow by providing them with technical assistance and funding for projects and policies that will realise the countries' economic potential. The Bank views development as a long-term, integrated effort.

- A global financial market can be defined as a marketplace where buyers and sellers participate in the trade of assets such as equities, bonds, currencies and derivatives.

- The role and functions of the IMF is: to deal with 'international monetary problems' by acting as a medium for its members to 'consult' and 'collaborate' with it, in order to 'facilitate' and 'promote' 'international monetary co-operation', 'growth of international trade' and 'exchange rate stability' to attain financial and economic stability.

- The World Bank also assists members by providing what are called as 'knowledge services' through assessments and technical assistance on development matters; this is one of its most important roles.

- Emerging markets are new market structures arising from digitalization, deregulation, globalization, and open-standards, that are shifting the balance of economic power from the sellers to the buyers. In such markets information is freely and widely available, and is almost instantly accessible.

- The World Bank (WB) and the International Monetary Fund (IMF), has also devised a number of strategies to assist the poorer countries of the developing world join the global party.

- Poverty Reduction Strategy Paper (PRSP) is a national strategy created by governments of low-income countries, for aiming government expenditure on measures to reduce poverty.

Questions for Discussion

1. What is IMF and its nature?
2. State the objectives of IMF.
3. Explain the functions of the World Bank.
4. Define global financial market.
5. Explain the role of IMF and World Bank in global financial market.
6. Elaborate the impact of World Bank and IMF on developing countries.
7. What is poverty eradication?
8. How do WTO and IMF help in poverty eradication?

Chapter **3**...

Global Human Resource Management

Contents ...

3.1 Introduction of Global Human Resource Management

    3.1.1 Functions of Global HRM

    3.1.2 Hofstede's Theory of the Cultural Relativity

    3.1.3 Challenges in Global Human Resources

3.2 International Labour Relations

    3.2.1 Introduction

    3.2.2 Actors in International Labour Relation

    3.2.3 Key Issues in International Labour Relation

3.3 Organised Labour

    3.3.1 Concerns of Organised Labour

    3.3.2 Strategy of Organised Labour

    3.3.3 Approaches to Organised Labour

3.4 Mobilising Talent for Global Development

    3.4.1 International Labour Migration

    3.4.2 Causes of International Migration

    3.4.3 Advantages of International Labour Migration

    3.4.4 Disadvantages of International Labour Migration

    3.4.5 Impact of Migration

    3.4.6 Policies to Improve the Developmental Impact of Remittances and Migration

    3.4.7 Low Skilled Migration

    3.4.8 High Skilled Migration

    3.4.9 Recent International Migration Trends

• Points to Remember

• Questions for Discussion

Learning Objectives ...

- To understand the concept of global human resource management
- To enlist the functions of global HRM
- To discuss the challenges of global HRM
- To describe international labour relations
- To identify the actors in international labour relations
- To define organised labour
- To summarise the concerns and strategies of organised labour
- To understand the causes of international labour migration
- To discuss the advantages and disadvantages of international labour migration
- To list the impact of migration on various factors
- To describe low skilled and high skilled migration

3.1 Introduction of Global Human Resource Management

Global Human Resource Management (GHRM) refers to the policies and practices associated to people and their management in an internationally oriented organisation. While GHRM includes the same functions as domestic HRNI, there are many distinctive aspects to global human resource management.

Today, the world is experiencing a growing workforce globally. Both, global human resource problems and opportunities are immense as well as expanding. Global Human Resource Management (GHRM) is the use of global human resources to achieve organisational goals irrespective of geographical boundaries. People dealing with global human resource management face a lot of challenges beyond that of their domestic counterpart. These challenges range from cultural barriers to political barriers to international aspects such as compensation. Before the higher authorities in an organisation decide on a global move, it is very important to consider the critical nature of human resource.

Business involved in the global economy place even greater emphasis on strategic HPR. Those engaged in the managing of global human resources develop and work through an integrated global human resource management system, although, the functional areas related to efficient global human resource management are similar to the ones they experience nationally. For a successful performance, sound global human resource management is a must. While with domestic human resources, the functional areas are not separate and distinct, but are highly interconnected.

3.1.1 Functions of Global HRM

Depending on the geographical area of operations, corporate culture and other parameters, the functions of global human resource management should be modified. HR policies and strategies help in the formation of guidelines for HR functions. The parameters of these functions grow when operations of a company become globalised. They are driven by efficiency, information exchange, international legal provisions, convergence of business processes, experience in internationalisation and adapting the company's HRM policies to local conditions. The five main functions of global human resource management are as follows:

1.   Staffing and Recruitment
2.   Salaries
3.   Training and Development
4.   Administration
5.   Human Relations
6.   Ensuring Legal Compliance

1.   Staffing and Recruitment

In HR management, staffing and recruitment rank high in priority. The ethnocentric strategy for recruiting personnel for overseas has both, advantages and disadvantages. Consideration must be given to the host country, as well as the business requirements of the home office. Companies who exercise an ethnocentric model of staffing have an advantage in staffing the host country's facility with managers who are trained in the culture of the organisation, including techniques and skills exclusive to that organisation. However, ethnocentric staffing can be problematic if the host country feels that the organisation is not utilising the local workforce.

2.   Salaries

In global human resources, compensation is a top issue. Sending domestic employees to a host country as an emigrant and awarding them for their efforts is increasingly difficult as the economy shifts. The threat of terrorism is also an issue in some host countries. Short-term assignments overseas can disturb family life. Ample compensation in these situations can help to make up for quality of life issues faced by managers as they commute long distances to be with family. Organisations must provide financial incentives to offset qualitative differences in international locations.

3.   Training and Development

According to the Society for Human Resource Management, training and offering language courses for managers and other employees is a priority. As the marketplace becomes more globalised, communication between domestic and international employees increase. Everybody from the administrative assistant who sets up meetings for international visitors to production floor members who are trained under domestic managers may have language and cultural barriers to overcome. Even cultural training has become a trend with international companies. Employees learn basic customs and cultural differences about host countries opening cultural barriers.

4. **Personnel Administration**

Working conditions vary greatly in different operating locations. Getting suitable resources for production will be quite different while establishing firms at different locations. Cultural differences may also occur in work schedules. In order to make the employees feel more comfortable, overseas managers should implement policies that strike a balance between the customs of the host country and the policies of the home office.

5. **Human Relations**

Employee relations at international facilities challenge even the most experienced managers. As workers switch to their new positions, they face family challenges, that is, the inability of spouses and children to assimilate in the host country. In this situation, absenteeism and productivity also can be a factor. Managers must recommend employees seek help through employee-assistance programs. These programmes provide counselling and resources to employees who are experiencing challenges in their personal lives.

6. **Ensuring Legal Compliance**

The final function of human resource management is ensuring legal compliance with labour and tax law. It is a vital part of ensuring an organisation's continuous existence. The federal, state as well as the local government, where the business operates, impose terms on companies regarding the working hours of employees, tax allowances, required break times, minimum wage amount, and policies on discrimination. Being aware of these laws and policies and functioning to keep the organisation completely legal all the time is an important role of human resource.

3.1.2 Hofstede's Theory of the Cultural Relativity

Nowadays, HR professionals understand that cultural differences between nations do not influence the effectiveness of HRM policies and practices. The responsibility of an HR professional is to realise these differences and make sure that workers are compatible with one another.

A number of models, of how culture persuades work behaviour exist. The most widely recognised is Hofstede's "theory of the cultural relativity of organizational practices". Hofstede's argues that national cultural differences are not varying greatly, even though more apparent work-related norms and values might be. Consequently, he feels that national culture maintains to have a strong influence on the effectiveness of various business practices.

According Hofstede, cultures differ in at least five ways that may have significant implications for understanding business. The five dimensions are as follows:

1. **Individualism versus collectivism:** Cultures vary in terms of the relationship of a person to his or her "family." In a few societies, such as Peru and Taiwan, the group's accomplishment and happiness will be emphasised over the individuals. In contrast, individualistic societies like the United States and Australia lay more stress on individual actions, achievements, and goals.

2. **Power distance:** Cultures also differ in their view of power relationships. Human inequality is nearly 'inevitable, but cultures with a high "power distance" emphasise these differences. For instance, symbols of power and authority such as large offices, titles, etc. are generally found in a culture with high power distance. In a culture with a low power distance, there is less emphasis on such displays. In German corporations, the idea of coordination and worker councils is common. Considering employees genuine input into significant decisions is an organisational practice typical of loin-power-distance cultures.

3. **Avoidance of uncertainty:** Another certainty is, being unaware of what the future holds. Cultures like Japan and Portugal with a high prevention of uncertainty try to predict, control, and influence future events, while cultures with a low avoidance of uncertainty are more keen on taking things gradually. To the extent that control lessens uncertainty, the rigid use of managerial control systems is more likely to be found in organisations in high-uncertainty-avoidance cultures.

4. **Masculinity:** This refers to the division of roles for males and females that a particular culture imposes. Male dominated cultures have strict roles and female dominated cultures have less well-defined roles. From an organisational perspective, male dominated cultures like Austria and Japan may tend to be less encouraging of efforts to amalgamate women into upper-level management than feminine cultures found in Norway and Sweden.

5. **Long-term versus Short-term orientation:** This dimension is not a part of Hofstede's original work but was added later as a result of studies concerning Chinese values. It usually refers to the extent to which cultures believe in terms of the future (the long term) or in terms of more immediate events (the short term).

Practically, every feature of HRM can be influenced by cultural disparity along one or more of these dimensions. For instance, the national differences in uncertainty avoidance and power distance can influence the range of organisational selection practices. Similarly, dissimilarities in individualism and collectivism can affect the overall success that a training program has on culturally diverse audiences.

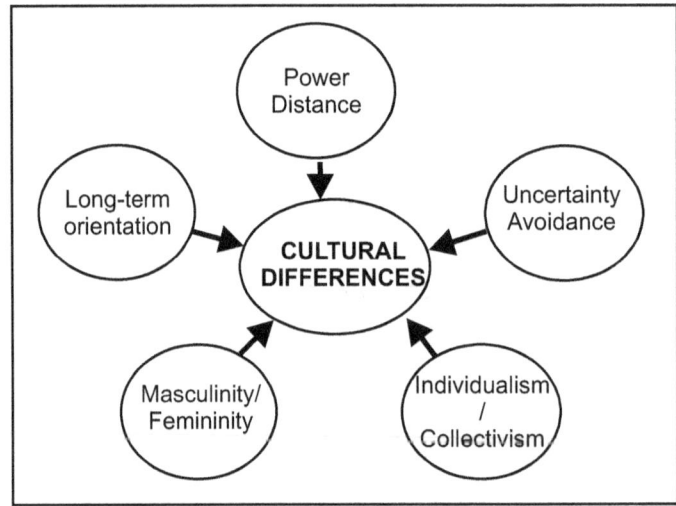

Fig. 3.1

3.1.3 Challenges in Global Human Resources

Following are a number of the most critical, and often, immediate challenges faced by human resource professionals involved in supporting the international operations, by way of

1.   Gaining acceptance as a business partner.

2.   Establishing new operations.

3.   Involvement in mergers and acquisitions.

4.   Undertaking recruitment drive for key positions.

5.   Developing compensation and benefits strategies.

6.   Establishing and maintaining global ethical standards.

1.   Gaining Acceptance as a Business Partner

As so much of international human resource management involves new business development activities, a thorough understanding of the company's business strategies, competitive challenges, and products and services is essential. Without this knowledge, human resource managers will never gain the credibility to be a key business partner and will find themselves relegated to the role of an administrator trying to implement organisation and staffing decisions that they have had no part in making.

(a) Proactivity is the key. It means orchestrating invitations to participate in international business planning meetings and then being seen as an active contributor. It means volunteering to take responsibility for developing resource plans and solutions to staffing problems. In short, it translates into being seen as a part of the solution rather than as an obstacle to progress.

(b) Dealing with the consequences of poor staffing decisions is one of the most depressing and frustrating aspects of international human resource management, especially, with the realisation that a more proactive involvement on the part of human resources could well have avoided the problem.

(c) The challenge is not an easy one. Business development executives frequently prefer to appoint their own candidates to manage international projects and operations.

(d) Human resource managers are often excluded from international mergers and acquisitions until the deal has been concluded and then left to try to resolve a myriad of cultural, organisational, and policy issues post event.

(e) However, once human resource managers have been able to prove that their contribution to the international business development process is equally valuable to those of finance and marketing executives, their 'place at the table' is generally assured.

2. Establishing New Operations

Even relatively small companies are now looking globally to source raw materials, market their products, or find cheaper methods of manufacturing. Human resource managers are finding themselves being asked to help establish new operations not only in countries such as China, India, Mexico, and Brazil, but also in newly emerging economies such as Vietnam, the Philippines, and the former Soviet Union Republic. Establishing a comprehensive staffing plan for the new operation is the critical first step –

(a) What is the timeline for establishing the new operation?

(b) What are the short and long-term staffing requirements and the timeframe?

(c) What level of expertise and skills are required?

(d) Which positions will need to be filled immediately?

(e)   What is the availability of suitable local candidates?

(f)   Which positions will require expatriates and short-term assignees either for management control purposes or to provide the necessary technical and professional support?

The recruitment of qualified local staff frequently necessitates being able to identify reliable recruitment agencies, which can be particularly challenging in lesser developed countries. As a result, being able to network and share market intelligence with other multinationals operating in the same countries is one of the essential job requirements of international human resource managers.

The timeframe for establishing new country operations is invariably short. Local recruitment efforts often are started before human resource policies and systems have been finalised. Payroll arrangements, compensation and benefits programmes, terms and conditions of employment all have to be put in place before the first local employee is hired. This is when critical errors of judgment are frequently made.

Under pressure, line managers all too often agree to provide compensation arrangements, benefits, and perquisites demanded by candidates who claim that all other major companies do likewise. These types of ad hoc initial deals set precedents that can create problems for years to come. Payroll arrangements can be especially problematic. Paying local employees offshore because the company has not yet established a local payroll is fraught with tax and legal risks. Temporary solutions can be found in almost all countries— for example, by arranging to have local employees paid through an accounting firm or one of the specialised international payroll agencies.

3.   Involvement in International Mergers and Acquisitions

International mergers and acquisitions are high-risk situations.

It is now widely recognised that clashes of management styles and organisation cultures are the most common contributors to international merger and acquisition failures. It is clearly critical to involve HR managers in the due diligence process before the merger and acquisition occurs.

However, in many cases, the executives responsible focus their attention so heavily on the financial aspects and potential business synergies of the proposed merger or acquisition that they neglect or choose to ignore the equally important human resource issues. The desire to land the deal at any cost can, at times, induce executives not only to turn a blind eye to business realities on the ground but also to other major potential obstacles.

Human resource issues that need to be addressed during the due diligence process, include:

(a) Undertaking the evaluation of the management team of the proposed merger or acquisition partner in terms of experience, skills, potential, and cultural fit. HR managers can provide objective input as to which key managers to retain and how to retain them.

(b) Identifying potential obstacles to organisational changes such as union agreements or works council regulations.

(c) Identifying any unacceptable employment practices.

(d) Assessing and comparing pay and benefits philosophies and practices and evaluating the impact of integrating those programmes.

Assessing the potential compensation and benefits issues of a proposed merger or acquisition is one of the most tangible contributions that HR managers can make to the due diligence process. Some of the critical areas that need to be reviewed are:

(a) Philosophical differences in compensation strategies that can send messages about corporate cultures. For example, a company with high base salaries and low to medium incentives that tries to merge with or acquire a company that pays below-market base salaries but with highly leveraged incentive programmes will inevitably face some major integration challenges.

(b) Trying to address differences in benefit programmes can also prove to be a massive financial undertaking. Any promises or commitments made during the merger and acquisition process can have long-term, financially disastrous implications.

(c) Highly visible policies such as perquisites are usually very sensitive problems to try to resolve. Differences, for example, in the types and level of company care programmes can easily result in ongoing bitter disputes.

(d) Underfunded pension plans can represent a significant, although easily identifiable, financial liability. This becomes a more complex issue in countries such as Germany and Austria, where pension plans are typically completely unfunded. It is also critical to try to identify any executive pension 'promises,' which may come to light only through a thorough review of individual employment agreements and offer letters.

(e) Any unusual or potentially risky compensation arrangements such as offshore payments for local managers or cash allowances that are not being declared for tax purposes need to be identified and evaluated for legal risk. Tax authorities in most countries have become highly sophisticated and, are therefore, less likely to turn a blind eye to questionable tax avoidance or tax evasion practices.

4. Undertaking recruitment drive for key positions

Being asked to recruit candidates to fill up top executive international positions is a high risk proposition for any HR manager. The task of trying to find a well-qualified local candidate to fill, for example, a general manager position for an international subsidiary can be a daunting one. Depending on the country and the industry, suitable candidates may turn out to be few and far between and potential candidates may be very reluctant to change companies.

Finding the right candidate can often require loads of patience and, of course, lots of luck.

For the HR manager, the following action steps are generally essential –

(a) Invest enough time to understand the nature and scope of the business, key challenges, as well as short and long-term objectives.

(b) Develop a comprehensive position description, candidate profile, and target compensation level with the senior executives to whom the position will report.

(c) Engage an international search firm that can demonstrate extensive experience in the country and industry involved.

(d) Require the search firm to prepare a realistic assessment of the potential availability of suitable candidates.

Once the search process is underway, the HR manager needs to engage in a proactive role in the process. It is not enough just to commission a search firm and wait for them to produce a shortlist of suitable candidates. It is important to ask the search firm to provide regular updates on the research they have carried out and the types of potential candidates they are targeting to ensure that the search is on track. It is also very valuable to get ongoing feedback from the search firm on the reaction of individuals they have contacted regarding the potential position and the company. Interviewing candidates is, of course, a key responsibility for the HR manager, both in terms of evaluating individuals as potential executives as well as acting as an ambassador for the company. After the interview process, thorough reference checks are vital, if necessary, the search firm should be asked to talk not only to individuals that the candidate has worked for, but also to former colleagues and subordinates. It can be very tempting to take short cuts with reference checks in the interest of filling a position quickly. This is one situation where the saying, "Act in haste, repent at leisure" all too often applies.

5. Developing Compensation and Benefits Strategies

After a number of discussions with agreement on the following key principles:

(a) Competitive comparisons would be made against other leading consumer goods companies in each country.

(b) Base salary policies would normally be established at the median or 50th percentile.

(c) Management incentive plans would be structured to provide total compensation (base salaries plus bonus) at the upper quartile, or 75th percentile, provided performance targets were met or exceeded.

(d) Benefit plans would be established not to exceed market median.

However, compensation and benefits challenges and the philosophies and strategies needed to address them will clearly vary considerably from company to company. Company culture, competitive pressures in different industries and markets, and financial considerations are all factors that need to be taken into consideration. However, even at the earliest stages of establishing international operations, it is important to establish an agreed compensation philosophy and strategy. It is much easier to be proactive in this regard than have to deal with a series of embarrassing precedents later.

6. Establishing and Maintaining Global Ethical Standards

One of the most difficult challenges for HR managers who have responsibilities for different countries is trying to define globally acceptable ethical standards. Much has been written on this subject and it is relatively easy to identify the extremes. Bribing officials, unsafe working conditions, and blatant race or sex discrimination are all examples of indefensible corporate behaviour. The real dilemmas come from the 'gray' areas. For example, how do you deal with a situation where local executives in a Latin-American subsidiary are receiving part of their compensation through the US payroll on the basis that this is 'normal practice' amongst multinationals in that country and essential to be able to hire and retain top executive talent? What about a situation where your company has a major new project in, say, Singapore and managers insist that they must transfer employees to start work there whether or not they have proper work permits?

As an HR manager, do you turn a blind eye to these situations to avoid being categorised by line managers as overly conservative and unwilling to take risks?

In reality, appropriate business solutions can always be found to address and resolve these types of situations. They do require creativity and determination. That is why it is important to seek advice from your company's legal and tax advisers as soon as a potential issue arises. It is also one of the benefits of developing and maintaining a network of other HR managers with international experience to share ideas with and learn from their experiences as regards similar situations. If no specific policy dealing with business ethics exists, it is crucial to develop one and to make sure it is widely communicated across the organisation, including any international operations. These are the types of issues that the policy needs to address.

(a) Prohibition on payments to public officials,

(b) Prohibition on political contributions,

(c) Guidelines regarding 'facilitating payments',

(d) Authorisation procedures for transactions and disposition of assets,

(e) Approval procedures for payments, and

(f) Maintenance and retention of records.

3.2 International Labour Relations

3.2.1 Introduction

International labour relations refers to a set of phenomena, both inside and outside the workplace, worried about identifying and managing the employment relationship. International Labour Relations handles the complicated associations between employers employing foreign nationals, employees of various nationalities, home and host country governing bodies and trade unions of the organisations functioning in different nations around the world in addition to their national and international federations. The term labour relation, also known as industrial relations, refers to a system in which employers, workers and their representatives, directly or indirectly, interact to set the ground rules for the governance of work relationships. It is also known as a study of examining the workers, employers as well as governments relationships. A labour or industrial relations system reflects the communication among the main actors, that is, the state, the employer (or employers or an employers' association), trade unions and employees (who may participate or not in unions and other bodies affording workers' representation). The term "labour relations" and "industrial relations" are also used in connection with various forms of workers' participation. It also includes individual employment relationships between an employer and a worker under a written or implied contract of employment, even though these are usually referred to as "employment relations". There is a significant difference in the use of terms, reflecting the evolving nature of the field over time and place. However, there is general agreement that the field embraces collective bargaining, various forms of workers' participation and mechanisms for resolving collective and individual disputes.

International labour relations (ILR) examines how institutional stakeholders (such as international organisations, supranational bodies, trade unions, the state, society and industry) shape the conditions, standards and relations of labour. ILR is different from domestic labour relations in the sense that it permits us to consider multiple national settings. For a proper understanding of ILR we need an appreciation of various economic, social, political and institutional arrangements (Lipietz, 1997) at the domestic level. It is essential to note that, even though ILR policies and discussions may take place internationally, labour relations practice remains firmly localised.

People are pivotal to both – for the survival of global corporations and the wealth of nations. Nothing can be mobilised and no progress can be achieved in the absence of this essential resource. The purpose of this chapter will be to review current worldwide trends and practices of leading corporations (profit and non-profit) in their management of human resources and social responsibility. An examination of the responsibilities of these global corporations will be made, and recommendations for reconciling these dual responsibilities and reshaping global HR practices will be presented. Understanding the critical and unique issues involved in managing the human resource issues of global operations is becoming an essential requirement for the career prospects of all ambitious human resource professionals.

3.2.2 Actors in International Labour Relations

International labour relations have identified three actors as parties to the labour relations system: the government, employers and trade unions. These actors are the forces that transcend categories like regional and other multilateral economic integration arrangements among states and multinational corporations.

1.   The Government

The state always has an indirect influence on all labour relations. The state, a source of legislation, exerts an inevitable influence on the emergence and development of a labour relations system. Directly or indirectly, laws can hinder or foster the establishment of organisations representing workers and employers. Legislation also sets a minimum level of worker protection and lays down "the rules of the game". With the development of its labour administration, the state also has an influence on how a labour relations system might function. Through a labour inspectorate, if effective enforcement of the law is conditioned, collective bargaining can pick up where the law lets go. If the state infrastructure that emerged between employers and workers is weak, they will be left more to their own devices to develop alternative institutions or arrangements.

The extent to which the state has built up a well-functioning court or other dispute resolution system may also have an effect on the course of labour relations. The ease with which workers, employers and their respective organisations impose their legal rights can be as important as the rights themselves. Thus, the decision by a government to establish special tribunals or administrative bodies to deal with labour disputes over individual employment issue can be an expression of the priority given to such problems in that society.

The state has a direct role to play in labour relations, in many countries. In nations that do not value freedom of association principles, this may involve outright control of employers' and workers' organisations or interference with their activities. The state may try to nullify collective bargaining agreements that it perceives as interfering with its economic policy goal.

In Belgium and Ireland, government representatives have been sitting down alongside those from employer and trade union circles to hammer out a national level agreement or pact on a wide range of labour and social issues. The state plays a constant role in any labour relations system. In addition, where the state is itself the employer, or is publicly owned, it is directly involved in labour relations with the employees and their representatives. In this situation, the state is motivated by its role as provider of public services. Lastly, the influence of regional economic integration arrangements on state policy is also felt in the labour relations field.

2. Employers

Employers are usually differentiated in industrial relations systems depending upon whether they are in private or public sector. The position of state-owned enterprises varies depending upon the country. Employers have common interests to defend and specific sources to progress. In order to organise themselves, they follow several plans which in turn determines the character of their organisation. Generally, there are three main functions common to all employers' organisations – defence and promotion of their members' interests, representation in the political structure and provision of services to their members. The first function is reflected largely in lobbying government to implement policies that are friendly to employers' interests and in influencing public opinion, chiefly through media campaigns. The representative function may take place in the political structure or in an industrial relations institution.

Along with the collective level of bargaining, the structure of employers' organisations depends on the country's size, political system and sometimes religious traditions. In developing nations, the main challenge has been to incorporate the variety of mixed membership. This includes small and medium-sized businesses, state enterprises and subsidiaries of multinational corporations. The strength of an employers' organisation is reflected in the resources its members are eager to dedicate to it, whether in the form of dues and contributions or in terms of their expertise and time. In its approach to labour relations, the size of an enterprise is a major determinant, with the employer of a small workforce being more likely to depend on informal means for dealing with its workers. Small and medium-sized enterprises sometimes fall under the threshold for legally mandated workers' participation schemes. If collective bargaining takes place at the enterprise level, it is much more likely to exist in large firms. While, if it takes place at the industry or national level, it is more likely to have an influence on areas where large firms have significantly dominated the private sector market.

However, The International Employers Organisation's (IOE's) main activity is to arrange employers, every time they have to deal with social and labour matters at the globally. The IOE is one of only two organisations that the employer community has established to represent the interests of enterprises on a global level. The other is the International Chamber of Commerce, Paris, which basically deals with economic matters. Though, structurally quite different, the two organisations complement each other. They collaborate on the basis of an agreement which defines their areas of responsibility and some good personal relations between their representatives on a common membership base.

3.   Trade Unions

Trade union is "a continuous association of wage earners for the purpose of maintaining or improving the conditions of their employment" (Webb and Webb 1920). The history of trade union goes back as far as the first attempts to organise collective action at the beginning of the industrial revolution. In short, it began when governments first began to concede the unions' legal right to exist in the modern sense. Trade unions assure that the bonding of workers can improve their situation. Trade union rights were born out of economic and political struggle which saw short-term individual sacrifice for longer-term collective gain. At regional and international levels, trade unions have often played an important role in national politics and have influenced developments in the world of work. However, in recent years, their role is under challenge after having suffered membership losses. The pattern is mixed with areas of membership growth in the public service in many countries around the world and with a new lease on life in places where trade unions were previously non-existent or active only under severe restrictions.

Another significant function of trade union is its control function – their legitimacy depends upon the ability to exert discipline over the membership, for example ending a strike. The trade unions' constant challenge is to increase their number of members as a percentage of the formal sector workforce. The members of trade unions are individuals; their dues, a contribution in some systems, support the union's activities. Trade unions financed by employers or "company unions" are not considered here, since only independent organisations of workers are true trade unions, although some unions that have been able to win closed shop or union security arrangements are considered to be the representatives of all workers covered by a particular collective bargaining agreement. Trade unions can be affiliated to umbrella organisations at the industrial, national, regional and international levels.

3.2.3 Key Issues in International Labour Relations

1.   Handling Labour Relations

The national dissimilarities in economics, political, and legal systems create varied labour-relations system across nations. MNCs assign the control of labour relations to their foreign subsidiaries. Handling labour relations is impacted by 4 key elements –

- If the level of inter-subsidiary production integration is high, the labour relations function is centralised and is coordinated by the headquarters.
- The nationality of ownership of the subsidiary has a control on who should pay attention to the employee relations.
- In addition, subsidiary character has a bearing on who should deal with employee relations.
- Ultimately, where a subsidiary is dependent more on its parent company for resources, better corporate involvement in labour relations is observed.

2.   Trade Union Tactics

In order to deal with international business, trade unions make use of a number of tactics, 'strike' being the most common. A strike is a rigorous but temporary suspension of work planned to put pressure for the fulfilment of their demands. Before resorting to a strike, unions should be cautions, as in the international scenario the bargaining power of a union could probably be threatened by the financial resources of an MNC. This is particularly obvious, where a multinational firm uses transnational sourcing and cross subsidisation of its goods across various international locations. Among the International Trade Secretariats (ITSs) there are fifteen ITSs who help in the exchange of information. The main objective of ITSs is to achieve transactional bargaining with the MNCs. For several years, trade unions have lobbied for restrictive national legislation in the US and Europe. Trade unions carry out restrictive national legislation to avoid the export of jobs via multinational investment policies and interference from global bodies like ILO, UNCTAD, EU, and OECD. ILO has issued guidelines which cover disclosure of information, competition, financing, employment, industrial relations, taxation, science and technology.

3.   Political

In the international environment, specifically social democracy, neo-liberal and authoritarian, there are 3 faces of industrial relations which the international union movement encounters. The variation in national industrial relations systems are reflected in the structure, power and status of individual actors in the system. For instance, trade unions, even if their role is a lot more limited in the US context, maintain a comparatively strong position within the Scandinavian IR model. The international labour movement usually prohibits direct access to robust intergovernmental establishments like the WTO. Thus, to represent their interests to these institutions, they have to depend on the national government. Significantly, the interests of the government might not always be directly in line with the union movement.

4. Social and Identity Differences

A major problem with the international labour movement and specifically international collective bargaining is the absence of identity that individual workers have with their international associates. Moreover, they see these peak relations to be a lot more conventional than activists at the local level. There is also a lack of unity between actors at a national level. Additionally, there are extensive cultural, social and language differences between individuals in different countries resulting in low degree of a shared identity among workers on an international level.

5. Power and Knowledge

While labour power continues to be local in scope, capital has become more global in nature and decisions effecting workers are increasingly being made at a supra-national level. The focus of multinationals decision-making stretches beyond national borders. The main reality is seldom transparent or accessible to trade unions. In addition, multinational organisations can counter the strength of local unions by threatening to move manufacturing to another place so that they can outsmart trade unions.

3.3 Organised Labour

Organised labour is an organisation of workers who have come together to achieve work related goals, such as higher pay and better conditions. Organised labour is an association of workers united as a single representative body. The main purpose of organised labour is to improve the workers' economic status and working conditions through collective bargaining with employers. It is also known as "unions". Basically, there are two types of unions – the horizontal union, in which all members share a common skill, and the vertical union, which is composed of workers from across the same industry.

3.3.1 Concerns of Organised Labour

The HRM function of an international business is accountable for international labour relations. The key issue in international labour relations is the degree to which organised labour can limit the choices of an international business.

Through collective bargaining with management, labour unions get better pay, greater job security and better working conditions for their members. The bargaining power of trade unions is derived largely from their ability to threaten or to disrupt production either by strike or work protest. This threat is quite powerful since the management has no other option but to employ union labour.

The main concerns of domestic unions in multi-national firms are as follows –

1. The company can counter its bargaining power with the choice of moving production to a new country. For example, Ford, very clearly threatened British unions with a plan to move manufacturing to Continental Europe unless British workers neglected work rules that limited productivity, showed moderation in negotiating for wage increases and curtailed strikes and other work disruptions.

2. International business will keep highly skilled tasks in its home country and outsource low-skilled tasks to foreign locations. Such practices make it comparatively easier for an international business to switch production locations from one place to another as economic conditions permit.

3. When an international business imports employment practices and contractual agreements from its home country and when these practices are new to the host country, the labour union fears that the change will decrease their influence and power.

3.3.2 Strategy of Organised Labour

Organised labour has responded to the increased bargaining power of multinational corporations by taking three actions – (1) trying to establish international labour organisations; (2) lobbying for national legislation to restrict multinationals; and (3) trying to achieve international regulations on multinationals through such organisations as the United Nations.

A further barrier to co-operation has been the wide variation in union structure. Trade unions develop independently in each country. Similar to the nature of collective bargaining, the structure and ideology of unions tend to differ significantly from country to country. The ideological gap among union leaders in different nations has made co-operation complicated. Different ideologies are reflected differently on the role of a union in society.

Organised labour has seen only limited success in its effort to get national and international bodies to regulate multinationals. Such international organisations as the International Labour Organisation (ILO) and the Organisation for Economic Co-operation and Development (OECD) have approved codes of conduct for multinational firms to follow in labour relations. However, these guidelines are not as resourceful as humans. They also do not provide any enforcement mechanism.

3.3.3 Approaches to Organised Labour

Approaches to international labour relations vary from one international business to other. The main difference is the degree to which labour relations activities are centralised or decentralised. Apparently, most international businesses have decentralised international labour relations activities to their foreign subsidiaries as labour laws, union power and the nature of collective bargaining differs too much from nation to nation.

A universal rise in competitive pressure in industry has made it important for firms to control their costs. Labour costs account for a large percentage of total costs and many firms are now using the threat to move production to a new nation in their negotiations with unions, to change work rules and limit wage hike. Since such a move would entail major new investments and plant closures, this bargaining tactic needs the input of headquarters management. Thus, the level of centralised input in labour relations is growing.

Also, the realisation of the way work is organised within a plant can be a major source of competitive advantage, is growing. Much of the competitive advantage of Japanese automakers has been credited to the use of self-managing teams, job-rotation, cross-training, etc. The Japanese firms have tried to replicate their work practices there, in order to replicate their domestic performance in foreign plants. This frequently brings them into direct conflict with traditional work practices in those countries, as sanctioned by the local labour unions, so the Japanese firms bargains openly with local unions to gain union agreement to changes in work rules before committing to an investment.

3.4 Mobilising Talent for Global Development

The generation of new ideas and their application for productive uses is a significant engine for growth and development. This is an area in which developing countries usually lag behind developed countries and is where development gaps are more obvious. Behind every generation of ideas, innovations, and new technologies there is 'human talent', an inner capacity of individuals to develop ideas and objects, some of them with a high economic value. The 'human factor' is critical to the success or failure of many endeavours. Many countries like China, India, Russia, Poland, and some Latin-American countries, are emerging as an important source of talented people. This can lead to change in the international patterns of comparative advantages and reduce development gaps. This talented lot, in developing countries, migrate to developed countries for work, typically US, UK, and other OECD nations. Simultaneously, multinational corporations are outsourcing many of their productive and service activities, including research and development, to developing countries to take advantage of the talent being developed there.

Consequently, today we notice a double movement of talent and capital across the globe; talented and able people from developing countries are migrating to seek better opportunities where people are equipped with more capital, technologies, and effective organisations. Talented individuals like students, professionals, information technology experts, entrepreneurs, cultural workers, and others are now more internationally mobile in the world economy as a response to new opportunities that are offered by globalisation. This trend has been reinforced by the information flows on economic opportunities and lifestyles in various cities and nations across the globe for lower transportation costs.

What Types of Talent Move

There are basically three broad types or groups of talent mobility in terms of their motivation and development impact –

1.   Entrepreneurs, technical talent, technology innovators, and business creators

2.   Scientific and academic talent and international students

3.   Health professionals and cultural workers.

In this era of information technology, the first group of talent has a more directly productive impact through business creation and application of new technologies on host and source countries. The second group is related to the production of science and knowledge in general, the service sector, and the government, which is more indirect. The third group is related to social service, such as health services, with some complex impacts on the source countries. The mobility of cultural talent reflects both an aesthetic value as well as the manifestation of creativity that can be highly appreciated by individuals and markets.

3.4.1 International Labour Migration

Generally, migration is defined as the movement of a person or a group of people from one geographical unit to another, across an administrative or political border, hoping to settle permanently or temporarily in a place other than their place of origin. As the movement involving two geographical units does not have to take place directly, one can further distinguish between the place of origin or sending region and the place of destination or receiving region. Movements in a country are typically defined as internal migration and movements across international borders are known as international migration.

In terms of migration motives, one can distinguish three types of migrants – those looking for economic opportunity in the destination country; migrants who plan to gather savings or human capital while being abroad; and migrants who move due to political, ethnic or religious oppression in their home country. The desire to improve their material living conditions or quality of life is the main driving force behind the migration decision for majority of migrants . Usually, it is assumed that these migrants plan their move in aspects of human capital that are necessary for a successful integration into the labour market and society of the receiving country. Migration for employment is a significant global issue, which now affects most nations globally. Two major labour market forces that result in increased migration for work are functioning today. Firstly, many people of working age either cannot find employment or cannot find employment enough to support themselves and their families in their own countries. Secondly, some countries have a shortage of workers to fill positions in various sectors of their economies. Apart from this, other factors include demographic change, socio-economic and political crises, and widening wage gaps among developed and developing countries. Consequently, now there is much movement across borders for employment, with women independently migrating for work in greater numbers than in the past and comprising about half of all migrant workers."

3.4.2 Causes of International Migration

Migration can be defined as a form of relocation diffusion (the spread of ideas, innovations, behaviours, from one place to another) including permanent move to a recent location. One of the most considerable reasons that people migrate would be due to push and pull factors. Push and pull factors are forces that can either persuade people to move to a new location or compel them to leave old residences; they can be economic, political, cultural, and environmentally based. Push factors are forceful conditions that can drive people to leave their homes. For instance, less job opportunities, desertification, famine/ drought, political fear, poor medical care, loss of wealth, natural disasters, etc. Pull factors are exactly the opposite of push factors; they are factors that attract people to a certain location. Examples of these push factors are job opportunities; better living conditions; political freedom, religious freedom; enjoyment; education; better medical care, and security. In this, people are so attracted to these luring opportunities that they are pulled towards it.

Major factors of migration are

1.   Push Factors

(a) Economic
People think about emigrating from places that have job opportunities. Due to, economic restructuring, job prospects often differ from one country to another and also within regions of the same country.

(b) Cultural
Forced international migration occurs for two main cultural reasons: slavery and political instability. In the past, millions of people were shipped to other countries as slaves or as prisoners, especially from Africa to the Western Hemisphere. Wars have also forced large-

scale migration of ethnic groups in the 20th and 21st centuries in Europe and Africa. Another push factor is the fear of prosecution, where people are refugees, that is, people who have been forced to migrate from their homes and cannot return for fear of harassment.

2. Pull Factors

(a) Economic

People immigrate to places where jobs seem to be existing. An area that has valuable natural resources, such as petroleum or uranium, may attract miners and engineers. A new industry may lure factory workers, technicians, and scientists.

(b) Cultural

Political conditions are also considered as pull factors, especially the lure of freedom. People are attracted to democratic countries that encourage individual choice in education, career, and place of residence. After Communists gained control of Eastern Europe in the late 1940s, many people in that region were pulled toward the democracies in Western Europe and North America.

(c) Environmental

Attractive environments for migrants include mountains, seaside, and warm climates. Proximity to the Rocky Mountains lures Americans to the state of Colorado, and the Alps pull French people to eastern France. England, France, and Florida attract migrants, especially retirees, who enjoy swimming and lying on the beach. Regions with warm winters attract migrants from harsher climates.

3.4.3 Advantages of International Labour Migration

1. **Economic Opportunities:** If a person is unable to find a job in his local area, the best option may be to look for a job in a new place. A migrant may have a job, but he may want to move to an area with improved living conditions and more economic activity. Some places offer more educational opportunities for career advancement and have a more flexible class structure than other societies.

2. **Cultural Freedoms:** One of the major pulls for migrations of people is the hope of freedom in various areas of life, for example, a migrant who cannot openly practice his religion in his home country. Similarly, a scholar may flee to a new country in search of academic freedom. Cultural deviants may find that their behaviour is tolerated in a different place, and they may trade some of the benefits of their home society to discover these behaviours.

3. **Reduced Labour Costs:** A major advantage of hiring immigrants is low labour costs. Immigrants often come to US to pursue economic opportunities that are not available in their native countries. As a result, they may be willing to work at a lower wage than native-Americans.

4. **Business Expansion:** Hiring immigrants can be of great value from a marketing point of view, to expand business into a foreign market. For instance, if an individual wants to reach the Hispanic market, a Latino sales representative can provide language and cultural knowledge that current staff members do not possess.

5. **Other Advantages**
    (a) Job vacancies and skills gaps can be filled.
    (b) Economic growth remains constant.
    (c) Services to an ageing population can be sustained when there are inadequate young people locally.
    (d) The pension gap can be filled by the contributions of new young workers who are also tax payers.
    (e) Immigrants bring along energy and innovation.
    (f) Host countries are enriched by cultural diversity.
    (g) Developing countries gain benefit from remittances (payments sent home by migrants).
    (h) Unemployment is reduced and young migrants enhance their life prospects.
    (i) Returning migrants bring savings, skills and international contacts.

3.4.4 Disadvantages of International Labour Migration

1. **Employee Resistance:** On the downside, hiring immigrants may meet with resistance from your current employees. If an employee base consists of people of a specific ethnicity, cultural background, it may be difficult to incorporate immigrants into your work culture.

2. **Language Barriers:** Hiring immigrants present a challenge to performing business. For instance, if an immigrant who does not have full command of English or speaks with a heavy accent, is hired, one may experience difficulties in roles such as customer service or liaising with other businesses. In a few cases, the organisation also has to pay for language training for a highly qualified applicant.

3. **Legal Issues:** All the necessary documentation, such as green cards and I-9 forms, to verify their legal right to work overseas, must be considered while hiring immigrants. If an organisation frequently prefers hiring immigrants over native-born citizens, the organisation needs to protect itself against possible charges of reverse discrimination.

4. **Environmental Differences:** Migration brings a change in geographies and climates. For a few migrants, a change of scenery can be very interesting, but many

may have trouble adjusting to major changes in climate. For example, some countries like Korea are situated at a higher altitude, where migrants may have difficulty breathing.

5. **Emotionally Disturbed:** Migrants, while migrating, leave behind family members and friends when they make their journey to a new place. Moving away from the comfort zone of a family leaves a migrant alone without a support system. Sometimes migrants must leave their immediate families at home and send money back for financial support.

6. **Culture Shock:** Migration brings different people together in an entirely new environment. Culture shock can be defined as the difficultly people have in adjusting to a new culture different from their own. The most difficult part of a culture shock for migrants is that they have no plans of going back home and are forced into accepting a new culture. Language, if it is different from their home country, remains an obvious problem for migrants, making it difficult for them to communicate. Other differences include diet, clothing, and music.

7. **Other Disadvantages:** Apart from the above stated the other drawbacks can be as follows:
   (a) Temporary depression of low wages may occur.
   (b) Having workers willing to work for relatively low pay may allow employers to ignore productivity, training and innovation.
   (c) Migrants may be subjected to exploitation.
   (d) Increases in population puts pressure on public services.
   (e) Unemployment may rise if there are unrestricted numbers of incomers.
   (f) There may be integration difficulties and friction with local people.
   (g) Large movements of people lead to more security monitoring.
   (h) Ease of movement may facilitate organised crime and people trafficking.
   (i) Economic disadvantage for origin countries through the loss of young workers.
   (j) Loss of highly trained people for the country, especially health workers.
   (k) Social problems for children left behind or growing up without a wider family circle.

3.4.5 Impact of Migration

The production and transfer of knowledge, productivity growth, international competitiveness, fiscal revenues, and the size of the middle class, among others, are all developmental effects of the international mobility of talent. Analytically, the emigration of human capital reduces the stock of human capital and output in the source country and increases it in the receiving one. In addition, there can be a loss of welfare for the remaining population in the home country because of externalities due to a loss of scarce skills. From a global perspective, world income should be higher with more mobile human capital (talent), as the marginal productivity of human capital in the world economy increases when talent moves from countries with lower marginal productivity to countries with higher marginal productivity. As a result, there is global efficiency gains associated with an increased international mobility of talent. The gains and losses from the mobility of talent for sending and receiving countries depend on whether the international flow of people is temporary or more permanent. On the other hand the impact of migration has major effects on the following:

1. Migrants
2. Destination Countries
3. Origin Countries

1. Migrants

(a) The bulk of the economic gains from migration accrue to migrants and their families, and these gains are often large.

(b) Wage levels (adjusted for purchasing power) in high-income countries are approximately five times those of low-income countries for similar occupations, generating an enormous incentive to emigrate. Moreover, to the extent that migrants devote a portion of their income to remittances, the gains are even greater.

(c) Essentially migrants can earn salaries that reflect industrial-country prices and spend the money in developing countries, where the prices of non-traded goods are much lower. Migrants, however, incur substantial costs, including psychological costs, and immigrants (particularly, irregular migrants) sometimes run high risks and many suffer from exploitation and abuse.

(d) The decision to migrate is often made with inaccurate information. Given the high costs of migration—including the risks of exploitation and the exorbitant fees paid to traffickers—the net benefit in some cases may be low or even negative.

(e) There are costs, too, for family members left behind—particularly children—although these costs must be balanced against the benefits of the extra income that migrants send back home to their families.

2. Destination Countries

(a) Destination countries can enjoy significant economic gains from migration. The increased availability of labour boosts returns to capital and reduces the cost of production.

(b)   In addition, high-income countries may benefit from increased labour-market flexibility, an increased labour force due to lower prices for services such as child care, and perhaps economies of scale and increased diversity.

(c)   Nevertheless, there are losers within destination countries. Some workers may see an erosion of wages or employment, although this effect is found to be marginal in most empirical studies. In the model-based simulation of the impact of increased migration, earlier migrants suffer significant income losses, while the impact on natives' wages is small. (The differential impact is reduced if foreign-born workers are viewed as closer substitutes for natives.)

(d)   Easing rules that limit labour-market flexibility, and strengthening institutions that provide education and training, will help workers displaced by immigration (both natives and resident migrants) to find work.

(e)   Note that the simulation results are not intended to incorporate all of the economic impacts of migration. Neither do they capture important social and political implications.

(f)   The goal is not to forecast the overall impact of increased migration but rather to give us insights into the economic gains that might be expected from changes in policy or circumstances, as well as insights into the channels through which migration affects welfare.

3.   Origin Countries

(a)   Migration also generates economic benefits for origin countries, the largest being remittances.

(b)   International remittances received by developing countries have doubled in the past five years, as a result of (a) the increased scrutiny of flows since the terrorist attacks of 9/11, (b) changes in the industry that support remittances (lower costs, expanding networks), (c) improvements in data recording, (d) the depreciation of the dollar (which raises the dollar value of remittances denominated in other currencies), and (e) growth in the migrant stock and incomes.

(c)   However, records still underestimate the full scale of remittances, because payments made through informal, unrecorded channels are not recorded.

(d)   Econometric analysis and available household surveys suggest that unrecorded flows through informal channels may conservatively add up to 50 percent (or more) of recorded flows.

(e)   Several countries with significant migrant populations do not report data on remittances at all, even those sent through formal channels, or they report remittances under other balance of payments entries.

(f) While the impact of remittances on growth is unclear, remittances do play an important role in reducing the incidence and severity of poverty (with no significant effect on income inequality).

(g) Remittances directly increase the income of the recipient and can help smooth household consumption, especially, in response to adverse events such as crop failure or a health crisis.

(h) In addition to bringing the direct benefit of higher wages earned abroad, migration helps households diversify their sources of income (and thus reduce their vulnerability to risks) while providing a much needed source of savings and capital for investment.

(i) Remittances appear to be associated with increased household investments in education, entrepreneurship, and health—all of which have a high social return in most circumstances.

(j) Measuring the poverty impact of remittances is difficult: data are scarce, and calculating the income gains from remittances requires assumptions concerning what migrants would have earned if they had stayed at home.

(k) Careful analyses of the available household survey data indicate that remittances have been associated with declines in the poverty headcount ratio in several low-income countries—by 11 percentage points in Uganda, 6 in Bangladesh, and 5 in Ghana, for example. In Guatemala, remittances may have reduced the severity of poverty by 20 percent.

(l) By generating a steady stream of foreign exchange earnings, remittances can improve a country's creditworthiness for external borrowing and, through innovative financing mechanisms (such as, securitisation of remittance flows), they can expand access to capital and lower borrowing costs.

(m) While large and sustained remittance inflows can contribute to currency appreciation, this outcome may be less severe than it is in the case of natural resource earnings, because remittances are distributed more widely thus avoiding undue strains on institutional capacity that are often associated with natural resource booms.

(n) Migration has economic implications for origin countries beyond remittances. The small size of migration flows relative to the labour force suggests that the effects of South-North migration on working conditions for low-skilled workers in the developing world, as a whole, must be small as well.

(o)   However, in some countries, low-skilled emigration can raise demand for the remaining low-skilled workers (including, poor workers) at the margin, leading to some combination of higher wages, lower unemployment, less underemployment, and greater labour force participation.

(p)   Thus, low-skilled emigration can offer a valuable safety valve for insufficient employment at home. In the long run, however, developing country policies should aim to generate adequate employment and rapid growth rather than relying on migration as an alternative to development opportunities.

3.4.6 Policies to Improve the Developmental Impact of Remittances and Migration

1.   Remittances Policies

Remittances are economic transfer payments sent by migrants to support their families or friends who still live in the source countries. Remittances are sent by all different kinds of migrants: internal and international, male and female, legal and undocumented, temporary and established, high and low-skilled. Remittances are transferred through official banking system, special agencies, with the help of fellow countrymen, or directly by the migrants, when he or she returns to the source country to visit family and friends. Non-monetary gifts sent by mail or bought personally – are considered to be remittances of a kind. Transfer payments by descendants of migrants and pensions paid to former migrants who had been migrants in the past are also considered as remittances. Remittances are not channelled through formal institutions but reach the lower income strata directly, unlike other transfer payments, such as development aid or interregional adjustment programs. *Remittances are not charity nor are they connected to certain regulators. They are money earned by the migrant families themselves and represent an important source of income (Durand et al. 1996b).*

Following are the Remittances Policies:

(a)   Governments in destination and origin countries can sharpen the developmental impact of remittances through the application of appropriate policies. Access of poor migrants and their families to formal financial services for sending and receiving remittances could be improved through public policies that encourage expansion of banking networks, allow domestic banks from origin countries to operate overseas, provide identification cards to migrants, and facilitate the participation of microfinance institutions and credit unions in providing low-cost remittance services.

(b)   Remittances, in turn, can be used to support financial products — housing and consumer loans and insurance — for poor people. Competition among providers of remittance services could be increased by lowering capital requirements on remittance services and opening up postal, banking, and retail networks to non-exclusive partnerships with remittance agencies.

(c)   Alleviating liquidity constraints by providing a credit line either to the sender or the recipient, based on past remittance activity, would enable senders to take advantage of the lower fee rates available only for larger remittances. Reducing exchange rate distortions could also lower the cost of remittance transactions. Finally, regulatory regimes need to strike a better balance between preventing financial abuse and facilitating the flow of funds through formal channels.

Several origin countries have attempted to improve the developmental impact of remittances by introducing incentives to increase flows and to channel them to more productive uses. Such policies are more problematic than efforts to expand access to financial services or reduce transaction costs, because they pose clear risks. Tax incentives to attract remittance inflows, for example, may also encourage tax evasion, while matching fund programmes to attract remittances from migrant associations may divert funds from other local funding priorities.

2. Migration Policies

The term migrant is defined as *"any person who lives temporarily or permanently in a country where he or she was not born, and has acquired some significant social ties to this country"*. According to some states' policies; *a person can be considered as a migrant even when s/he is born in the country*. International migration is a universal phenomenon that is increasing in scope, complexity, and impact. Migration is both, a cause and effect of broader development practices and an inherent feature of our global world. Migration can be a positive force for development, when supported by the right set of policies. The increase in global mobility, the rising complexity of migratory patterns and its impact on countries, migrants, families and communities have all contributed to international migration becoming a concern for the international community. In the erosion of traditional boundaries between languages, cultures, ethnic group, and nation-states, migration is an important factor. Even non-migrants are affected by movements of people and by the resulting changes. Migration is not a single act of crossing a border, but rather a lifelong process that affects all aspects of the lives of those involved.

Following are the Migration policies:

(a)   Greater emigration of low-skilled emigrants from developing to industrial countries could make a significant contribution to poverty reduction. The most feasible means of increasing such emigration would be to promote managed migration programmes between origin and destination countries that combine temporary migration of low-skilled workers with incentives for return.

(b)   Temporary programmes have several advantages, and some disadvantages, relative to permanent migration. From the perspective of the destination country, managed, temporary migration programmes ease social tensions by limiting permanent settlement; they limit the potential burden on public expenditures because immigrants are guaranteed a job and are less likely to bring dependants; and they allow for controlled variation of the number of immigrants in response to changes in labour-market conditions, thus, limiting adverse effects on low-skilled native workers.

(c)   However, temporary migration can be less efficient than permanent migration for firms in destination countries because of its attendant high training costs.

(d)   From the origin-country perspective, managed, temporary migration may be the only means of securing deliberate increases in low-skilled emigration and may raise remittances and improve the skills of returning workers. On the other hand, managed migration programmes do not guarantee future access to labour markets (and thus, to remittances), because it is easier for destination countries to suspend temporary programmes than to expel immigrants.

(e)   Overall, however, such programmes do represent a feasible approach to capturing the efficiency gains from labour migration.

(f)   Origin countries that are adversely affected by high-skilled emigration face challenges in managing it better. Service requirements for access to publicly financed education can be evaded and are likely to discourage return; and proposals for the taxation of emigrants to the benefit of the origin country have made little progress.

(g)   Origin countries can help to retain key workers by improving working conditions in public employment and by investing in research and development. Origin countries can also take steps to encourage educated emigrants to return by identifying job opportunities for them, cooperating with destination countries that have programmes to promote return, permitting dual nationality, and thereby facilitating the portability of social insurance benefits.

By providing authoritative information on migration opportunities and risks, the governments concerned could help avoid unfortunate, costly-to-reverse migration decisions and limit the abuse of vulnerable migrants. Labour recruiters too can play a valuable role in promoting migration, but emigrants' lack of information often enables recruiters to capture the lion's share of the rents generated by constraints on immigration and imperfect information. Origin countries with effective public sector institutions might consider the regulation of recruitment agents to limit rents and improve transparency.

3.4.7 Low Skilled Migration

Low-skilled labour is a section of workers associated with a low skill level or a limited economic value for the work performed. Generally, low-skilled labour is characterised by low education levels and small wages. Workers, who fall into the unskilled labour force, require no specific education or experience. Unskilled labour offers a significant part of the overall labour market, performing daily production tasks that do not depend on technical abilities or skills. Repetitive tasks are a typical characteristic of unskilled labour position. Low skilled labour does not require workers to have special training or skills. Due to technological and societal advances, jobs that require unskilled labor are continually shrinking. Jobs that previously required little or no training now require training. For example, labour that was once done manually is currently performed by computers or other technology. Examples of low skilled labor occupations generally include farm labourers, grocery clerks, hotel maids, and general cleaners and sweepers.

Improves labour market conditions for other poor workers

The stock of low-skilled emigrants who moved from developing to industrial countries, is about 0.8 percent of developing countries' low-skilled, working-age residents. The regions with countries close to the major destination countries had relatively high rates of low-skilled emigration.

Low skill emigration also may reduce underemployment or raise labour-market participation without significant wage increases. The impact of international migration may differ considerably among regions within countries of origin, depending on the degree of geographic concentration of emigration and the links with other regions through internal migration. People in regions lying close to a common border with the destination country or, with easier access to overseas markets (such as metropolitan centres or coastal areas) have a tendency to migrate. These effects can be greatly magnified through the influence of migrant networks, once initiated from a specific location.

Contributes to Poverty Alleviation

The reduced supply of low-skilled workers may help alleviate poverty, if, as a result of emigration, poor people receive higher wages or find new opportunities to work or receive remittances. Low-skilled emigration also alleviates poverty to the extent that the people emigrating are poor. It is unlikely, however, that a large proportion of migrants to industrial countries are poor according to the World Bank's definition of poverty as living on less than $2 a day—although certainly a very large share is poor compared to even the poorest in high-income countries. Individuals with very low incomes are unlikely to be able to obtain the financial resources necessary for migration. Most of the world's poor people live in countries that are far away from industrial countries (Bangladesh, Brazil, China, India, Indonesia, and most of the countries of Sub-Saharan Africa), so transportation is expensive. Moreover, many poor people lack the rudimentary skills required to obtain a job in industrial countries, as well as the social networks that would facilitate migration and provide assistance once in the destination country.

Nevertheless, the limited data indicate that the very poor do move abroad to some extent.

Migration of low-skilled workers is usually beneficial

Low-skilled workers in the home labour market gain, directly or indirectly, from additional remittance spending, whether emigration results in reduced under-employment, increased labour-market participation, or higher wages. Thus, emigration of low-skilled workers can act as a safety valve for the failure to produce suitable employment at home. Also, reliance on large-scale emigration may retard efforts to address the issue of employment expansion over the long term, as a result of either the remittance-driven exchange-rate appreciation or the concentrated pressure for policy reform. In general, however, the opportunity to send low-skilled workers abroad provides substantial profits to origin countries due to the impact on labour markets and remittances.

3.4.8 High Skilled Migration

Skilled labour can be defined as a labour that require workers having specialised training or a learned skill-set to perform the work. These workers can be either blue-collar or white-collar workers, with different levels of training or education. Professionals fall in the highly skilled workers category, while doctors and lawyers fall in the skilled labour category. Some more examples of skilled labour are electricians, law enforcement officers, computer operators, financial technicians, and administrative assistants. Some skilled labour jobs have become so specialised that there are worker shortages.

High-skilled migration is often beneficial for origin countries

The costs of high-skilled emigration should be evaluated against the beneficial effects of migration, skilled and unskilled – increased remittances, higher wages, and benefits to destination countries. Moreover, high-skilled emigration will have a limited impact if it is difficult for high-skilled workers to find productive employment in the country of origin. This may be the case for the following three reasons.

Firstly, the investment climate may be so poor because of political instability or other reasons, that many high-skilled workers cannot pursue their professions. Even under such conditions, however, high-skilled emigration may be harmful if it deprives the government of competent administrators and limits the prospects for growth once the investment climate improves.

Secondly, a significant proportion of high-skilled workers may not be trained in professions required by the economy, perhaps because of the given government's subsidy policies.

And thirdly, some of the smallest developing countries lack the economic scale to productively employ a large number of specialised professionals. These issues serve to underscore concerns over the appropriateness of state subsidisation of university education in many countries.

High-skilled emigration has had a negative impact on living standards of those left behind and on growth

There are several reasons that migration of high-skilled workers may decrease living standards and growth. Firstly, the total return to education may be greater than the private return because highly educated workers may be more productive when interacting with similar workers and they may help train other workers. One statistical measure of the beneficial impact of high-skilled immigrants is that in the United States, both international graduate students and skilled immigrants were found to be positively correlated with patent applications. Highly educated citizens may also make contributions to public goods—for example, in improving governance and strengthening the administrative capacity of the state—which may be lost through high-skilled emigration.

Secondly, the productivity of firms may increase with size. If large firms require networks of professionals with specialised skills, then, the overall productivity will be higher with the availability of many professionals.

Thirdly, emigration of high-skilled workers may impose a fiscal cost. In most developing countries, education is heavily subsidised by the state, and therefore, the permanent emigration of educated workers represents a loss of fiscal revenues.

Finally, the emigration of high-skilled workers will increase the price of services that require technical skills. It is difficult to provide comparable levels of service with low-skilled workers, and thus, greater resources devoted to training may be lost through further emigration.

3.4.9 Recent International Migration Trends

1. Employee mobility is often studied from the perspective of employers. They are regularly targeted to learn about their actions and intentions regarding their workforce.

2. Relocation is an investment in the employee and employers want them to succeed and hit the ground running. If the employee has the appropriate supports and compensation, employers will get the best return on their investment.

3. Most people will move if they are offered enough money, but the current global economic environment makes that approach less realistic than ever before. More importantly, enticing talent to consider a move abroad requires more than pay. Employers can minimise costs and maximise pay to the individual through an appealing incentive programme that takes into consideration what employees themselves are hoping for and fearing.

4. There is a core group of global employees who would be very likely to move abroad for an assignment. They would be easiest to convince if employers wish to move them. These individuals, 25% of the overall sample of employees from around the world, are the most motivated to take an international opportunity.

5. Demographically, and considering the entire sample on a global basis, several cohorts were most likely to display eagerness. These groups, who lean towards a foreign assignment statistically significantly more than the global employee average, include a senior executive/decision maker at their work (30%); those most likely under the age of 35 (28%); men (27%); those with a low income (27%); and those who are not married (27%).

6. Those working in the fields of telecommunications and information technology (28%) and construction (28%) are most inclined to say they are 'very likely' to consider the move, followed by those working in the commercial/retail (25%), education (23%) and medical (23%) sectors.

7. Participants in the survey were invited to consider which destinations they would most desire to move to for work. They were offered a randomised list of 51 countries, plus the option of 'other', and asked to select their top three picks. Employees select the United States (34%) as their combined top choice by a wide margin, followed by the UK (22%), Canada (20%), Australia (20%) and Switzerland (16%).

8.   Employee Relocation Policy Survey, conducted across 500 Canadian companies, the top international destinations that employers are sending staff to are (in order of popularity): the United States, the European Union, China, Australia and South America

9.   Essentially, employees appear ready and willing to travel to traditionally industrialised, wealthy nations but are less ready to name the emerging markets as their top pick and would likely need more convincing for these destinations.

10. Respondents from every geographic region we measured select the United States as number one (except North America, which chose Australia). This is also true among all the industries measured on this survey.

11. North Americans would most prefer to move to Australia (33%) or the UK (28%). Those from Latin America would most prefer to go to the United States (42%), Canada (25%) or Spain (24%). Employees from the Middle East and Africa would most likely choose the United States (43%), the United Kingdom (29%) or the United Arab Emirates (23%). Europeans would most prefer the United States (29%), the UK (20%), Australia (20%) or Switzerland (20%) and those from Asia-Pacific would most prefer to move for work to the US (37%), the UK (24%) or Singapore (22%).

12. The relocation of an employee in many cases must be viewed as the relocation of the family unit as 43% indicate they would want their employer to provide immigration assistance for their spouse's career development in the new country. One in six respondents (16%) strongly agrees that they "can't move abroad for any period of time because family in my home country rely on me."

13. Senior executives or decision makers at their work also favour the guarantee to come back to a similar role after two years (45%), but they are also very keen to take a trip to the country before the assignment to see what the country is like (44%), to have immigration assistance for their spouse to find employment (44%) and education courses to upgrade skills (44%).

14. Many employees might be further convinced to take the offer if they were given the guarantee to take their old job after two years (44%), immigration assistance for their spouse to obtain employment (38%), a chance to see the country first (37%), return airfare for them or their family members while in the new country (36%) and paid language training (35%).

Points to Remember

- Global Human Resource Management (GHRM) refers to the policies and practices related to managing people in an internationally oriented organisation. Although GHRM includes the same functions as domestic HRM, there are many unique aspects to human resource management in the international organisation.

- Global human resource management is driven by efficiency, information exchange, international legal provisions, convergence of business processes, experience in internationalisation and adapting the company's HRM policies to local conditions.

- Functions of global HRM is are:
  1. Staffing and Recruitment
  2. Salaries
  3. Training and Development
  4. Administration
  5. Human Relations
  6. Ensuring Legal Compliance

- Following are a number of Critical Strategic Global Human Resources challenges faced by human resource professionals involved in supporting the international operations, by way of:
  1. Gaining acceptance as a business partner.
  2. Establishing new operations.
  3. Involvement in mergers and acquisitions.
  4. Undertaking recruitment drive for key positions.
  5. Developing compensation and benefits strategies.
  6. Establishing and maintaining global ethical standards.

- International labour relations refers to a set of phenomena, both inside and outside the workplace, worried about identifying and managing the employment relationship. International Labour Relations handles the complicated associations between employers employing foreign nationals, employees of various nationalities, home and host country governing bodies and trade unions of the organisations functioning in different nations around the world in addition to their national and international federations.

- Classically, three actors have been identified as parties to the labour relations system – the government, employers and trade unions.

- Organised labour is an organisation of workers who have come together to achieve work related goals, such as higher pay and better conditions. It is the labor union movement. It is an association of workers united as a single representative entity for the purpose of improving the workers' economic status and working conditions through collective bargaining with employers.

- Today we see a double movement of talent and capital around the globe. On the one hand talent from developing countries is moving north seeking better opportunities where people are equipped with more capital, technologies, and effective organisations.

- Migration is usually defined as the movement of a person or group of persons from one geographical unit to another across an administrative or political border, and wishing to settle permanently or temporarily in a place other than their place of origin.

- The reasons that people migrate would be due to push and pull factors. Push and pull factors are forces that can either induce people to move to a new location or oblige them to leave old residences; they can be economic, political, cultural, and environmentally based. Push factors are conditions that can drive people to leave their homes, they are forceful, and relate to the country from which a person migrates.

- Destination countries can enjoy significant economic gains from migration. The increased availability of labour boosts returns to capital and reduces the cost of production.

- Low skill emigration also may reduce underemployment or raise labour-market participation without significant wage increases. The impact of international migration may differ considerably among regions within countries of origin, depending on the degree of geographic concentration of emigration and the links with other regions through internal migration.

- The reduced supply of low-skilled workers may help alleviate poverty, if, as a result of emigration, poor people receive higher wages or find new opportunities to work or receive remittances. Low-skilled emigration also alleviates poverty to the extent that the people emigrating are poor.

- Skilled labor refers to labor that requires workers who have specialised training or a learned skill-set to perform the work. These workers can be either blue-collar or white-collar workers, with varied levels of training or education.

Questions For Discussion

1. Define global HRM.
2. Explain the nature of global HRM.
3. State the functions of global HRM.
4. Enlist the actors in international labour relations.
5. Summarise the concern and strategy of organised labour.
6. State the causes of international migration.
7. Enumerate the advantages and disadvantages of international labour relations.
8. Discuss the impact of migration on:
   (a) Migrants
   (b) Origin countries
   (c) Destination countries

Chapter 4...

Challenges Confronting
the Global Economy

Contents ...

4.1 Global Economy

    4.1.1 Introduction

    4.1.2 Advantages of Global Economy

    4.1.3 Disadvantages of Global Economy

    4.1.4 Factors Influencing the Global Economy

    4.1.5 Challenges Confronting Global Economy

4.2 Energy Crisis

    4.2.1 Introduction

    4.2.2 Causes of Energy Crisis

    4.2.3 Preventive Measures for Energy Crisis

4.3 Commodity Crisis

    4.3.1 Challenges of Commodity Crises

    4.3.2 Factors Responsible for Commodity Crisis

    4.3.3 Preventive Measures for Commodity Crisis

4.4 Financial Turmoil

    4.4.1 Introduction

    4.4.2 Types of Financial Turmoil

    4.4.3 Causes of Financial Crisis

    4.4.4 Preventive Measures for Financial Turmoil

• Points to Remember

• Question for Discussion

Learning Objectives ...

- To understand global economy
- To highlight the factors influencing global economy
- To identify the challenges confronting global economy
- To discuss energy crisis
- To describe the causes of energy crisis
- To understand commodity crisis
- To enlist the challenges of commodity crisis
- To highlight the preventive measures for commodity crisis
- To define financial turmoil
- To enumerate the different types of financial turmoil
- To demonstrate the causes and preventive measures of financial turmoil

4.1 Global Economy

4.1.1 Introduction

Global economy refers to the economy of the world, comprising of different economies of individual nations, with each economy related with one another. It is a world economic activity. Globalisation, being an important factor, is the process that leads to individual economies around the world. It is interwoven in such a way that an event in one country affects the state of other world economies. Lately, the focus on globalisation has intensified a lot. More and more trade is connecting different countries. Common restrictions on movement and business, across borders have been reduced a great deal. Now, people are able to trade their goods, globally in any market. Since, customers can obtain the commodity from other location apart from their own countries; they enjoy a much wider variety of goods and services. It is the collective economic activity that takes place in each individual economy. It comprises of production, trade, financial flows, investment, technology, labour and economic behaviour in and among nations. It is the economic relations amid countries globally, where markets in individual countries are now extended and integrated beyond national boundaries.

4.1.2 Advantages of Global Economy

1. **Better use of Resources:** The producers try to control the cost by most favourable combination of factors of production to avoid the misuse of production factors.

2. **Economies of Large Scale:** The economies of production transport management, finance and advertisement are accessible to the producers.

3. **Cultural Diversity:** Due to the import and export of goods and services, the world gets to know the culture preferred by a specific nation.

4. **Monopoly:** It abolishes monopoly. At times, commodities can be imported and surplus can be exported. In both cases the seller is unable to create monopoly in the market.

5. **Employment Opportunities:** With an increase in export, the rate of manufacturing goods increases. This requires manpower and in turn increases employment opportunities.

6. **Economic Development:** Due to exports, both, the production and per capital income rises which results in economic prosperity.

7. **International Relations:** It builds friendly relations among countries which can lead to employment opportunities, educational scholarship, etc.

8. **Transfer to Technology:** With the development trade relations, nations can afford improved method machinery for inventions and innovation.

9. **Price Stability:** It is beneficial to keep prices stable as a result of supply of goods in time. The exported surplus goods, if faced with scarcity, can be imported to maintain the price level.

10. **World Peace:** In order to increase the exports and employ manpower in the world, countries indulge in international trading to keep friendly relations with each other.

4.1.3 Disadvantages of Global Economy

1. **Local Industry Suffers:** When countries import goods or services from some other countries, they willingly purchase it at cheap prices. Any local industry cannot compete with the quality or price offered by such imports, for instance, Chinese products.

2. **Excessive Use of Natural Resources:** After getting involved in the international trade market, countries are willing to export in bulk quantity. In order to do that, production of goods in bulk is required; this involves utilisation of natural resources.

3. **Shortage in the Local Market:** For capturing market share, countries undertake export; while doing so, they face shortage in the local market and hence notice hike in prices.

4. **Unemployment:** When the capitalists discover that importing goods can get them more profit than producing it in the local market, they prefer importing which leads to unemployment in the local market.

5. **Colonialism:** Sometimes independent countries become colonies of other nations. So much so, that a time comes when their whole economy is handled by corporate tycoons. They become so influential that they threaten the country economically

and politically. In today's world, many countries are following neo-colonisation by supporting other countries.

6. **Economic and Military War:** Every country wants to lead in export. This sound economic policy leads to having economic rivals. They weaken their rivals by terrorism, wars, etc. Exporting military weapons, atomic weapons (aircrafts, missiles, tanks, automatic and semi-automatic guns etc.) is another example of international trade.

7. **Dumping:** many countries are dumping products in other countries which leads to businesses going bankrupt in other countries. China is a very good example of dumping. It results in other countries levying an anti – dumping duty.

4.1.4 Factors Influencing the Global Economy

It is complex to understand global business environment. Aspects like who wins, who loses, and how the game is played is often myriad, complex, and contradictory. Moreover, over time, many of these factors change abruptly and in an unpredictable manner. Global managers should constantly be alert to challenges and changes in the environment. They should be willingly prepared to undertake decisive action when needed. In order to understand this complex global business environment conceptually it is divided into four parts.

1. **Economic environment:** The economic environment of global business consists of issues of supply and demand, impact of global economics and foreign investment decisions made by companies, and also the national trade policies and economic development strategies of different governments as they try to support their local businesses. An understanding of the emerging forces, both, for and against globalisation is also useful. An awareness of various theories of international trade and competitive advantage is the key to understand economic environment, since they affect both national and corporate success.

2. **Legal-political environment:** The legal-political environment of global business relates to how political and governmental actions affect international business. It also deals with issues like how companies and managers make ethical decisions governing business practices. Political risk also comes as a key challenge to firms trying to succeed in the global marketplace. Since, the legal environment of global business relates to doing business globally, it consists of both national laws and regulations and international laws and agreements. While some laws are aimed at facilitating international business transactions, others are not.

3. **Cultural environment:** As economic barriers to trade decline, cultural barriers increase and present new challenges and opportunities for global firms. When various cultures begin interacting more often, they unite in some aspects, but their

national peculiarity may become accentuated. This comes across as a managerial challenge. The cultural environment of global business focuses on how cultural differences across nations and regions can influence the ways in which national and international business are transacted. For instance, what is it about a particular culture that either facilitates or inhibits entrepreneurship, trade, and success in global markets? How does culture influence the ways in which companies are organised, approach strategic decisions, and manage their workforce?

4. **Global business environment:** The intersection of three forces — economic, legal-political, and cultural — forms the arena in which companies compete in the global business environment. It represents the "eye of the hurricane" in international business. This is where global managers succeed or fail and an understanding of this environment is crucial to success. It creates an organising framework for understanding how global business works and what managers can do to make it work better.

5. **Technological environment:** Today, companies and countries that have the best technology controls the business of the world. This can be achieved by having more funds and other resources allocated to research and development. USA is a very good example of a country that does this. Companies like APPLE, Microsoft, etc. Consistently allocate large funds to R & D thus providing best of products with the most advanced technology. That is one of the biggest reasons USA is the largest economy in the world.

4.1.5 Challenges Confronting Global Economy

The opportunities and challenges of international trade has been a major concern for economists and policy makers of the contemporary world. As far as the challenges facing the international trade are concerned, they differ with the economic and social set-up of the nations involved in cross border track. Some of the challenges are as follows.

1. A major challenge of global trade is to maximise the gains from trade, be it a developed or developing economy. Countries involved in international trade try to focus on the efficient utilisation of the opportunities resulting from exchange of goods and services with their trading partners. To utilise the benefits of the open market economy is another major challenge before the world trade.

2. In this era of globalisation, international trade has a crucial role to play in order to bring about economic and social harmony among the developed and developing nations of the world. With openness to trade becoming popular, the issues of trade solidarity both at the domestic and multilateral level has achieved huge importance across the globe. Globalisation and the resulting economic liberalisation have opened up a range of challenges before the developed and less developed economies involved in international trade.

3. One of the major challenges in the case of relatively backward economies is that the macroeconomic policies of these countries are in disproportion to utilise the gains from world trade. International trade can be favourable if the gains derived from it are distributed equally among the different layers of the society. This reflects the importance of "trickle-down" effect.

4. Domestic trade is the exchange of production at regional level; whereas international trade guarantees better mobility of latest technology equipped goods and services across the globe. Global trade helps the developing countries being accessible to the modern techniques of production. However, the challenge here is to use these techniques in an efficient manner.

5. The open regionalism as a guiding principle for the Asian Pacific Economic Cooperation forum was suggested as a strategy to avoid inward regionalism and further fragmentation of the global trading system (Bergsten, 1994). The industrial setup and social infrastructure must be developed as per the global standard so as to optimise the benefits from international trade.

6. Before opening up the economy, the backward nations need to safeguard the interests of the domestic entrepreneurs. The liberalisation policies should be taken up slowly so as to help the emerging small industries face the challenges of the changing economic scenario. Thus, the challenges before international trade may arise from different fronts. The countries linked in world trade should adopt balanced policy measures to make use of the gains from trade for the overall development of their economics.

7. With a boost in competition, international trade is subjected to many challenges. This can be psychological, infrastructural and physical. The challenge of international trade and other related information and guidelines are generally made aware of in the trade policies.

8. When the term competitive is used, it means competing by following a set of rules laid down for international trade and the capacity to move up to the increasing demands of the market. Trade liberalisation has to a great extent abolished the negative impacts of the challenge of international trade.

9. In addition to the trade related challenges, a new challenge which is waiting at large, and had practically confounded the United States of America, is the fight against terrorism. There was a global economic slowdown in wake of the terrorist attacks on the World Trade Centre. International trade suffered massively.

10. With regard to shipments, export, and import of commodities, if the shipment can be traced in real time, loss worth several million dollars can be prevented.

11. The fruits of economic activities must be fairly distributed with a focus on meeting the basic needs of the world's poor. The economic activities must respect the interests of future generations, preserving the integrity of ecological processes and natural systems so that the life opportunities of future people are not lessened.

4.2 Energy Crisis

4.2.1 Introduction

Energy is universal and drives everything. Our modern life, both individual and societal, depends on its abundance, convenience, and potential. It is the motivational force within our bodies, propelling our vehicles, lighting our planet. Its importance in our daily lives can be understood through a dead cell phone battery; living without energy, for even ten minutes. Simultaneously, we live in an amazing ecosystem which is flexible and fragile. Our energy comes from and returns to a global environment. These tools help us understand and solve the challenges in context to energy and climate. Technology and strategy if taken together on an intentional, practical, and coordinated manner can be a motivation for a new and far superior future.

Today, owing to an escalation in global energy demand, planet Earth is facing an energy crisis. Constant dependence on fossil-based fuels for energy generation and transportation and boost in world population, exceeding seven billion people are rising steadily. Excessive burning of fossil fuels is not only reducing natural resources, but is also resulting in a sound increase of carbon dioxide emissions, which professionals believe is responsible for increasing average global temperatures. Although, natural cyclical variations occur in regional and global climates, scientific communities and governments agree that recent climate change is increasing as a result of human intervention and that rapid and intense measures will be required to decrease harmful impacts. Concentration levels of greenhouse gases are rising gradually and are now superior than it was several years ago. Major changes to the world climate may result if concentration levels are not inverted, bringing significant effects on people, industry, and the world economy. Energy and commodity crisis is a situation where in, the nation suffers from a disruption of energy and commodity supplies accompanied by promptly increasing energy and commodity prices that pressurise economic and national security.

4.2.2 Causes of Energy Crisis

There are many causes for energy crisis. It would be simple to lay the blame for the entire energy crisis at their door, but that would be a very naive and unrealistic interpretation of the cause of the crisis.

1. Overconsumption

The energy crisis is a result of many different damages on our natural resources, not just one. Due to overconsumption, there is a strain on fossil fuels such as oil, gas and coal, which in turn puts a strain on our water and oxygen resources by causing pollution.

2.   Overpopulation

The steady increase in the world's population and its demands for fuel and products has been another cause of energy crisis. No matter what type of food or products one opts to use – from fair trade and organic to those made from petroleum products – not one of them is made or transported without a major drain on our energy resources.

3.   Poor Infrastructure

Another reason for energy shortage is aging infrastructure of power generating equipment. Many energy producing firms use outdated equipment restricting the production of energy. It is the responsibility of utilities to keep on upgrading the infrastructure and set a high standard of performance.

4.   Unexplored Renewable Energy Options

In most of the countries, renewable energy still remains unused. Most of the energy comes from non-renewable sources like coal. It still remains the top choice to produce energy. The problem of energy crisis cannot be solved unless we give renewable energy a serious thought. Renewable energy sources can lessen our dependence on fossil fuels and also helps to reduce greenhouse gas emissions.

5.   Delay in Commissioning of Power Plants

In some countries, there is a considerable delay in commissioning of new power plants that can help fill in the gap between demand and supply of energy. The result is that old plants come under huge stress to meet the daily demand for power. When supply doesn't match demand, it results in load shedding and breakdown.

6.   Wastage of Energy

In most parts of the world, the importance of conserving energy is not understood. It is only limited to books, internet, newspaper ads, and seminars. Things won't change unless a serious thought is given. Basic things like switching off fans and lights when not in use, using maximum daylight, walking instead of driving for short distances, using CFL instead of traditional bulbs, proper insulation for leakage of energy can go a long way in saving energy.

7.   Poor Distribution System

Frequent tripping and breakdown are a result of poor distribution systems.

8.   Major Accidents and Natural Calamities

Natural calamities like eruption of volcanoes, floods, earthquakes or major accidents like pipeline burst can also cause interruptions to energy supplies. The huge gap between supply and demand of energy can elevate the price of basic necessary items which can in turn give rise to inflation.

9.   Wars and Attacks

Wars among countries can also obstruct supply of energy, especially if it happens in Middle East countries like Saudi Arabia, Iraq, Iran, Kuwait, UAE or Qatar. During the 1990 Gulf war, when price of oil reached its peak, it caused global shortages and created major problems for energy consumers.

10. Miscellaneous Factors

Tax hikes, strikes, military coup, political events, severe hot summers or cold winters can cause unexpected increase in demand of energy and can block supply. A strike by unions in an oil producing firm can also cause an energy crisis.

4.2.3 Preventive Measures for Energy Crisis

Most of the possible solutions are already introduced today but they have not been widely adopted.

1. Move towards Renewable Resources

The top solution is to decrease the world's dependence on non-renewable resources and to develop overall conservation efforts. Much of the industrial age was fashioned using fossil fuels, but there is also a known technology that uses other types of renewable energies – such as steam, solar and wind. The continuous use of coal pollutes the atmosphere and destroys other natural resources in the process of mining the coal that has to be replaced as an energy source. It isn't simple, since many of the leading industries use coal, as their primary source of power for manufacturing.

2. Buy Energy Efficient Products

Replace traditional bulbs with CFLs and LEDs. They use less watts of electricity and last for a longer time. If people across the globe use LEDs and CFLs for residential and commercial purposes, the demand for energy can fall and an energy crisis can be averted.

3. Lighting Controls

There are a lot of latest technologies that make lighting controls, which help to save a lot of energy and cash in the long run. Preset lighting controls, slide lighting, touch dimmers, integrated lighting controls are few of the lighting controls that can help to preserve energy and cut overall lighting costs.

4. Easier Grid Access

People using different options to produce power should be given permission to plug into the grid and getting the credit for power one feeds into it. The hassles of getting credit of supplying surplus power back into the grid must be removed. Similarly, subsidy on solar panels must be given so as to encourage more people in exploring renewable options.

5. Energy Simulation

Energy simulation software can be used by big corporations to improve building units and decrease running business energy costs. Engineers, architects, and designers could use this design to come with most energy efficient building and lessen carbon footprint.

6. Perform Energy Audit

Energy audit is a procedure that helps you to identify the areas in your home or office that is losing energy and the steps you can take to improve energy efficiency. Energy audit, when done by a professional, can help you reduce the carbon footprint, save energy and money and avoid energy crisis.

7. Common Stand on Climate Change

Both developed and developing countries should adopt a common stand on climate change. They should focus on decreasing greenhouse gas emissions through an effective cross border mechanism. With the existing population growth and overconsumption of resources, the result of global warming and climatic change cannot be ruled out. Both developed and developing countries must focus on emission cuts to cut their emission levels to half from current levels by 2050.

4.3 Commodity Crisis

A commodity is practically standardised merchandise bought and sold freely as an article of commerce. Commodities comprise of agricultural products, fuels, and metals that are traded in bulk on a commodity exchange or spot market. The four categories of trading commodities include energy, metals, livestock, meat and agricultural. Today, the world is facing its worst commodity crisis since the 1980s. Energy and food prices have been increasing significantly in the past years. Humankind has experienced situations of rapidly growing food prices before and the current situation is exceptional as prices have gone up for nearly all food commodities and because of the simultaneous record prices in energy commodities. Dramatic hikes in global food prices are a source of concern for both developed and developing countries. They are inflating domestic prices of basic staple items, escalating the number of people suffering from poverty, malnutrition and hunger. This situation has given rise to riots in many countries, threatening political and social stability.

Majority of the population of developing countries depends on the production and exports of primary commodities for their welfare and livelihood. Thus, considering the economic and social progress of developing countries, the economic return to commodity producers is an essential element. While doing so, the importance of the commodity sector for the developed countries must not be ignored; these countries, themselves being major producers of a wide range of commodities, plus being the traditional markets for a major part of the commodity exports of developing countries. Modification in the conditions of commodity production, consumption, trade, and above all the resultant changes in commodity prices, can have important influence on the economic situation of both developed and developing countries, thus reflecting on the global economy.

Developing countries are more vulnerable in the current situation than developed countries in this regard. This is so, due to notable difference in productivity, scale and financial resources. Amongst developing countries, the impact of the crisis varies depending on their production and trade patterns. In this sense, higher food and energy prices impact most on, and thereby pose greater policy challenges for, dual importers of food and energy and countries with limited available resources, that is, Low-Income, Food-Deficit Countries (LIFDCs) and Least Developed Countries (LDCs). Within any one country, poorer population sub-groups are more vulnerable in the current context, because of the high proportion of their total expenditures which is required for food costs. This, in turn, directly impacts on their real incomes.

The commodity crisis can be understood in terms of supply and demand side analysis where supply has not been able to keep pace with growing demand. On the supply side, decreased production capacity in developing countries is the most important factor in understanding the current situation. This decreased production capacity is the result of years of inappropriate support policies and declining investment in the agricultural sector, Deregulation of agricultural markets and trade liberalisation, encouraged by international financial institutions, affected the incentives for farmers to remain engaged in agricultural production, eroding production capacity, increasing import dependence and increasing the incidence of import surges and dumping in many developing countries. Decreasing stocks have also been cited as a factor contributing to the crisis on the supply side.

4.3.1 Challenges of Commodity Crises

The rising trend in commodity prices, coupled with higher energy prices and the fact that there are large populations of urban poor, has increased hunger and, as a fall-out, triggered disturbance in dozens of countries.

1.   In the current crisis, developing countries are more vulnerable than developed countries because of a notable difference in productivity, scale and financial means to cope with increasing import bills and support to agriculture.

2.   Agricultural sectors in developed countries are equipped with advanced technologies, large financial resources and support systems to provide secure incomes to their farmers and to manage quick shifts in the market and in environmental conditions.

3.   In contrast, many developing countries are not able to – (a) provide services, infrastructure and support to their small farmers, or (b) deal effectively with volatility in agricultural markets, due to a lack of institutional and financial means.

4.   The reason for the same is that since the 1980s, most developing countries have followed recommendations from the international financial institutions, which have over-emphasised fiscal discipline. These recommendations entailed encouraging the production of export crops over food crops for domestic consumption and led to a dismantling of institutional frameworks, such as, state trading enterprises, subsidies and services to support agriculture and producers.

5.   The effect of the commodity crisis experienced globally represents a challenge for economic management in these countries. They face inflation, as well as financial constraints due to increased import bills, which add pressure to their foreign exchange reserves and widen the balance of payments.

6.   If prices remain high over the coming years, it would add to the already increasing budgetary pressures many developing country governments are facing. Current financial constraints are also derived from specific measures undertaken to stem the domestic food increase and dampen its impact on vulnerable groups in the short term. Many governments have implemented measures to avoid passing on price increases to consumers.

7.   Many analysts believe that these measures are not sustainable. They believe that cash and food transfers should be replaced, in the medium term, by policies aimed at developing the capacity of producers to take advantage of the current market conditions. For example, through improved access to credit and improved processing and storage capabilities.

8.   The high commodity prices spell double trouble, that is, at the household level, it reduces the purchasing power of the family concerned; and, at the national level, the same translates into crisis for developing countries. Lack of access to commodity can represent a threat to political stability and security.

4.3.2 Factors Responsible for Commodity Crisis

Some of the key factors which have contributed to the commodity crisis have been built up over the years. On the supply side, they include, decreased production capacity in developing countries and, on the demand side, increased requirements of food commodities for biofuel production, and greater demands from emerging countries.

1.   Reduction of Production Capacity in Developing Countries

Many agriculture-based developing countries have seen their domestic production per capita of food staples stagnate and decline, their self sufficiency rates decline and their food import bill increase since the 1970s. During the past three decades, many developing countries have moved from being net food exporters to net food importers. For instance, the African sub-continent used to be a net exporter of basic food staples. But in less than 40 years, it has to make do with imports and food aid.

Years of inappropriate support policies and declining investment in the agricultural sector are the main contributory factors to this decreased production capacity. These factors were induced by the deregulation of agricultural markets and trade liberalisation, encouraged by the international financial institutions. The policy prescriptions during the 1980s and 1990s led to:

(a)   Reduced governmental incentives to support agricultural production, such as, extension services to farmers (from access to information about market opportunities and prices, to pest and disease control and research and development).

(b)   Elimination of institutional mechanisms (for instance, marketing boards), creating a vacuum that the private sector was not able to fill in most developing countries.

(c)   Re-orienting resources to export-oriented production of cash crops, to the detriment of production of staple crops that were important for local consumption.

As production capacities weakened and markets have been forced to open, import dependence, import surges, dumping, exposure to price and supply risks, aid dependence, agriculture abandonment and migration to urban areas have increased in most developing countries.

Also, removal of tariffs in the context of low commodity prices has made it cheaper to import than to produce. These countries have even paid more per import unit than before the WTO Agreement on Agriculture (AoA) and that the impact of increased imports has been negative in terms of displacing domestic food production and increasing unemployment rates.

Persistent agricultural trade distortions, unfair competition from rich countries which subsidise their food production and exports, have been a major problem for developing countries. Subsidies provided by developed countries can –

(a)   Reduce the export-earning potential of competitive producers by displacing them as sources of imports.

(b)   Depress prices, by promoting increased production and supplies in the world market.

(c)   Displace domestic food production and increase unemployment rates.

2.   Effects of Subsidies and Protection given by Developed Countries to their Farmers

The effect of agriculture subsidies in developed countries is that their farm production levels are kept artificially high and their producers dispose off their surplus in other countries, by often dumping on world markets at less than the production cost. Farmers in developing countries incur losses in three ways –

(a)   They lose export opportunities and revenues from having their market access blocked in the developed countries using the subsidies;

(b)   They lose export opportunities in third countries, because the subsidising country is exporting to these countries at artificially low prices;

(c)   They lose their market share in their own domestic market or, in some cases, even lose their livelihoods, due to the inflow of artificially cheap subsidised imports.

High protection in developed countries and further liberalisation in developing countries have resulted in surges of imports to many developing countries across the world. In many cases, these imports were artificially cheapened by domestic and/or export subsidies. There are many cases of 'dumping' in which the developed country products' export price is below the cost of production, and where the farms or companies in developed countries are still able to make a profit because their revenues are pumped up by subsidies.

As long as the subsidies continue, the dumping of artificially cheapened agricultural products to developing countries will continue. This has serious effects on rural livelihoods and food security in developing countries. Artificially cheapened products are being imported into developing countries. Even though the poorer countries may have more efficient farmers, their livelihoods are threatened by inefficient farmers in rich countries because of subsidies.

There are several inter-related aspects in the general problems faced by many developing countries relating to global agricultural commodity trade. They include –

(a) The trend decline in export prices of many of the developing countries' agricultural commodities, instability in the markets and also in some cases the falling share of developing countries in total exports.

(b) The continued high protection of the developed countries of their agriculture sector, including the maintenance of domestic support measures and export subsidies. This prevents developing countries from having access to the agriculture markets of the North, and also facilitates export dumping into the South.

(c) The limited capacity of many developing countries to export or to derive adequate benefits in export, including climbing up the value chain of the commodities they produce. This hampers the ability of these countries to benefit from agriculture trade.

(d) The rapid liberalisation of imports in developing countries and the effects of this on the prices, incomes and livelihoods of the farmers.

(e) The global framework governing agriculture trade, which is presently imbalanced and creates disadvantages for developing countries.

3. Weather and Natural Disasters

Agricultural production is highly vulnerable to climatic conditions. Weather vagaries can devastate crops, climate change can increase crop susceptibility to pests and viruses and natural disasters can damage infrastructure necessary for the production of and access to food.

As a result of adverse weather conditions, the developing countries faced exceptional shortfalls in food production and severe localised food insecurity. In many instances, they required external assistance in order to be able to cope with food emergency situations.

Table 4.1: Countries affected by weather related phenomena

Africa	Asia	Latin America
Lesotho (drought)	Korea, DPR (floods)	Bolivia (floods)
Somalia (adverse weather)	Bangladesh (cyclone)	Dominican Republic (floods)
Zimbabwe (drought and floods)	Tajikistan (floods/landslides)	Ecuador (floods)
Mauritania (drought)	Timor-Leste (drought and floods)	Haiti (floods)
Ghana (drought and floods)	Nicaragua (floods)	
Kenya (adverse weather, insufficient rainfall)		
Ethiopia (insufficient rainfall)		

Projections state that the situation may worsen in the years to come. In many developing countries, climate change has the potential to induce increased flooding, less precipitation, drought, salinisation and desertification of agricultural land, and reduced crop yields. According to economist William Cline, a Senior Fellow at the Institute for International Economics and the Centre for Global Development in Washington, global warming is likely to cause a 16 percent decline in global agricultural gross domestic production by 2020, inducing a fall in output of 20 percent in developing countries and of six percent in industrialised nations. These prospects threaten not only to decrease national food sufficiency but also to increase the import and aid dependence of developing countries in the future.

4.   Increased Energy Prices

As explained above, high energy prices have contributed to the crisis by inducing an increase in:

(a)   The demand for agricultural feedstock for use as alternative sources of energy.

(b)   Transportation costs.

(c)   Prices of agricultural inputs, such as, fertilisers and pesticides.

Various commentators have attributed the price increases of the most recent period to a confluence of factors including rising consumption, difficulties of supply to keep up with demand growth (due to a decline in petroleum reserves, downward revisions in supply for non-organisation of the Petroleum Exporting Countries (OPEC) members, low surplus capacity in non-OPEC countries and disruptions of supply in OPEC countries, supply uncertainties in several oil exporting regions, geopolitical tensions and oil price speculation.

5. Increase in population:

Population explosion, especially in countries like India leads to crisis as the amount of production remains the same and number of people increases. The production needs to increase to counter the increase in population. India is producing marginally more commodities compared to the exponentially rise in population if you compare the past few decades.

6.   Limited technology for farming in developing countries:

Technology, especially in developed countries is not modern and thus yield per hectare is very low. Developed countries need to be kept updated with the newer practices of agriculture and also supported by the providing updated weather systems and information.

4.3.3 Preventive Measures for Commodity Crisis

1.   Placing high global priority on seeking solutions to the commodities crisis

(a)   National governments and international institutions, like the UN General Assembly and UNCTAD must give priority to seeking solutions to the crisis of commodities.

The high global priority previously given to attaining reasonable and stable prices must be restored. The commodities issue should be incorporated as a priority issue on the agenda of meetings and organisations of the South, namely in the G-77, Non-Aligned Movement, African Union, etc. of the North in the G-8 process, the European Commission, etc. apart from the international agencies, like the Millennium Development Goals process, the high-profile meetings of the UN in 2005, etc.

(b) The establishment on commodities by an eminent persons' group is a good start made by the UN General Assembly. The main points of its report and recommendations (United Nations 2003) should be followed up by the UN system, other international agencies and by the Helsinki Process.

(c) A recent major development has been the establishment of an international task force on commodities through the UNCTAD XI meeting. The work of this task force should be actively supported by governments, organisations of the South and North, international agencies, and the Helsinki Process.

(d) To lift the profile of the commodity crisis, there can be an international UN conference or convention on commodities that discusses the whole range of aspects with institutional mechanisms to follow up on the conference. The Helsinki Process initiates such a conference by creating a political condition for it. The issues below could be part of the agenda of such a conference.

(e) A review of the previous experience of joint producer-consumer commodity agreements must be conducted (for example, by UNCTAD and the Common Fund for Commodities), including examining the possibility and appeal of stimulating such agreements.

(f) Although reviving international cooperation is an ideal method of improving the commodity situation, this may not be possible at present. In the absence of joint producer-consumer cooperation, producers of export commodities can make their own scheme to rationalise their global supply so as to better match global demand. Such initiatives by developing supplier countries must be welcomed. Studies should be carried out on emerging producer supply arrangements to observe their function and whether the same principles and operations can be applied to other cases.

(g) The oversupply problem can also be tackled by regional groupings of developing countries, as well as by countries on an individual basis. During periods of glut the production levels can be reduced. Arrangements like financing, compensation to affected producers and crop substitution, should be examined and good practices should be benchmarked.

(h) UNCTAD, the UN Industrial Development Organisation (UNIDO) and other agencies can help commodity-producing developing countries to develop their capacity for growing the value of their commodities by going up the value chain through processing, manufacturing, and marketing. At the same time, the developed countries should decrease tariff growth and permit improved market access for developing countries' processed and commodity-based manufactured products, so as to help commodity producers obtain better profits from the trading system.

(i) In case of commodities, developed countries are also producing and exporting unfair competition from the latter in the form of export and domestic subsidies. This should be phased out as soon as possible.

(j) Debt-relief measures should be extended taking into account the financial problems faced by commodity-producing countries. Due to the decline in commodity prices and earnings, shortfalls faced by developing countries should be offset through debt relief.

(k) Compensatory finance schemes to protect developing countries from the effects of price instability should be examined and its feasibility and execution must be worked upon.

(l) A review can be made of the policy advice of the international financial institutions and donor agencies for encouraging developing countries to produce export commodities, which could contribute to the oversupply situation and the resulting fading of prices. More practical projections of demand and prices, and better planning of supply, should be introduced.

(m) The elimination of marketing boards and institutions and other support mechanisms in many developing countries led to an institutional vacuum and weakened the bargaining power of developing countries' producers. This institutional vacuum must be filled. Ample and appropriate methodologies need to be evolved to conquer the same.

(n) To help developing countries overcome excessive dependence on a few commodities and to add value to their commodities through processing and manufacturing, an international export diversification fund can be established.

2. **Reviewing the global framework which influences agricultural trade as well as developing countries' agriculture**

A thorough and comprehensive review of agricultural trade within the global framework needs to be undertaken to incorporate the loan conditionalities of the international financial institutions. This is so, since they relate to and have an effect on trade, the rules of the WTO and the new proposals tabled in the WTO negotiations, and the workings of commodity markets. A system of monitoring trends and developments in these areas could be set up.

3. Addressing the issues of Northern subsidies and import liberalisation in the South in WTO negotiations

The issue of continued high subsidies, protection in developed-country agriculture, and the problems caused by extreme import liberalisation in developing countries, should be concentrated on in the WTO negotiations on agriculture.

The capacity of policy makers and negotiators must be strengthened by developing countries. Besides, in the WTO, there should be regular monitoring and analysis of the on-going negotiations on agriculture. This can be done by international agencies with an interest in the conditions of rural producers, by independent organisations and also by the producer organisations themselves. Information must be provided to the farmers' organisations and ways should be found to enable them to partake at least in having their voices heard and their inputs considered. Also, information in the Agriculture Ministries and agencies dealing with agriculture and farmers should be provided to policy makers in developing countries.

In the negotiations on agriculture, modalities should be evolved to give maximum priority to the interests of the small farmers in developing countries. The main beliefs for the modalities should be the removal and reduction of protection in the developed countries as soon as possible and special and differential treatment for developing countries, for guarantying the maintenance enabling the feasibility of small farmers' livelihoods. A more detailed proposal would be that:

(a)   The export subsidies (and concessional export credits) of the developed countries should be abolished in a definite time frame.

(b)   In the developed countries, on the domestic support front, the Amber Box subsidies should be reduced to a large extent; the Blue Box subsidies should be re-categorised as Amber Box subsidies and subjected to decreased disciplines; while a re-examination of the Green Box subsidies can be made to tighten the criteria, cap the applicable subsidies and cut them.

(c)   Developed countries must extensively reduce their high agricultural tariffs and tariff peaks and to ensure this, an approach on market access should be adopted.

(d)   The inequity in the WTO Agriculture Agreement that currently curb or limit the ability of developing countries to supply subsidies to their farmers must be rectified. For food products and the products of small farmers, domestic subsidies should not be restricted, so as to consider the food security and the rural development needs of developing countries.

(e)   In the area of market access commitments, special and differential treatment should be created and applied to developing countries. Additionally, the developing countries should not be subjected to further tariff reductions for food products and products of small farmers as long as the high subsidy in developed countries continues.

(f) A Special Safeguard Mechanism (SSM) and the designation of Special Products (SPs) must be established for developing countries, to help them deal with the incidence and problems of import surges effectively. The SSM and SP mechanisms should be devised in a simple and effective way to operationalise and to serve their objectives.

4. Reviewing the trade conditionalities linked to the loans of the international financial institutions

An ongoing review can be made of the aptness of the policies attached to loans of the international financial institutions, in the structural adjustment programmes and other latest forms, like the Poverty Reduction Strategy Papers (PRSPs). The recommendations of a report by the Structural Adjustment Participatory Review International Network (SAPRIN) as it pertains to the agriculture sector can be considered. For example:

(a) Policy should be reoriented to give priority to production for the domestic market and ensuring food security;

(b) Trade policy in the sector should be different and distinct, allowing countries to pursue some degree of self-reliance while stimulating production by marginalised farmers to maintain the rural poor in accessing affordable food; and

(c) The execution of effective steps to support small producers and attain food security should precede and then be integrated with, the opening of the sector and promotion of exports.

Additionally, there should also be an independent on-going review of the trade aspects of the present and proposed conditional ties of present and future loans. Developing countries currently have flexibilities in the WTO rules to regulate their applied tariffs up to their bound rates and in some situation even beyond the bound rates. Loan conditionality should not be a constraining factor for the developing countries for making use of these flexibilities.

5. Improving supply capacity in developing countries

Some international and regional agencies already have programmes to assist developing countries enhance their productive and trade capacity, including the International Trade Centre (ITC), UNCTAD, UNIDO and the multilateral and regional development banks. However, these efforts are insufficient, given the continuing weaknesses and deficiencies of many developing countries. It would be worthwhile for developing countries to recognise and assess the impact of programmes being conducted by various agencies. These should include schemes that help the poor and small producers to boost their production, storage and marketing capacity, and diversification schemes to promote production of primary commodities to enhancing value-added through processing and manufacturing based on the commodities.

6. Divergent and Convergent Perspectives on Solutions to the Problem

Although, there is a broad agreement in terms of the causes of the problem, differences are clear with respect to possible solutions. The disagreements comprise of the following issues: (a) the usefulness of biofuels to guarantee energy security and to reduce climate change effects, (b) whether a 'green revolution' is the appropriate response in order to increase productivity in the South, and (c) the place of trade liberalisation as a solution.

7. Divergent Perspectives on Solutions to the Problem

Biofuel Production: Biofuels are being extensively promoted as an alternative source of energy to offer greater energy security to lesser greenhouse gas emissions, to deal with increased prices of fossil fuels and also to boost rural incomes. According to some studies conducted by the International Institute for Sustainable Development (IISD), the contribution of biofuels to the policy objectives it intends to attain is uncertain. Biofuels are still far from being a source of energy that could afford a real alternative to the global dependence on fossil fuels. Presently, the contribution of biofuels to total global energy is very little.

Biofuels are not necessarily helpful to environmental benefits. For example, they would contribute to the reduction of greenhouse emissions only if the quantity of energy put into their production is lower than the quantity of energy released when they were burned. It depends on the type of feedstock used. Studies imply that biofuel derived from sugar cane originating in tropical countries would be more useful than biofuels produced from maize in the US or grain in the EU. In addition, if biofuels are not produced in a sustainable manner, they can contribute to deforestation, soil degradation, erosion, and water depletion. This would be determined by land use and management systems and technology.

Biofuels not necessarily entail reducing the costs of energy, since their costs depends on the price of feedstock's used for their production and on prices of energy. There are some developing countries that can efficiently produce biofuels. Exploiting these advantages can tackle energy needs, climate change challenges, and support rural development and poverty reduction.

Developing countries have increased the production of biofuels rapidly. The European Union (EU) has set targets for biofuel production and consumption. By 2030, this target shall replace one fourth of liquid fuel with biofuel and puts in place several programmes for developing and increasing investment in new technologies. In 2003, the EU established targets with respect to the proportion of biofuel in petrol and diesel consumption (two percent in 2005 and 5.75 percent in 2010) and introduced some incentives such as tax reductions or exemptions.

The solution to the current crisis lies in increased productivity and another green revolution. In Asia, between 1970 and 1995, the green revolution led to –

(a) A doubling of cereal production.

(b) A 30 percent increase in calorie availability.

(c) Higher yields and profitability reduced prices, increased farmers' incomes and increased employment.

Today, the green revolution is needed to sustain the ever increasing population. For example, in India, the population has increased manifold since the 1970s but the agricultural output has not kept pace with it. Therefore, another green revolution is essential. The green revolution was also criticised in terms of its effects on environmental degradation, as (a) the improved use of fertilisers and pesticides resulted in the failure of soil fertility, (b) increased irrigation led to salinisation, water logging and lowering of water levels, and (c) the promotion of monocultures of high-yielding crops reduced biodiversity.

The followers of green revolution cite increasing yields to provide food for the hungry as their major reason. In 2002, the Inter Academy Council (IAC) was conducted under the command of the UN Secretary-General to develop a strategic plan to aid Africa substantially increase its agricultural productivity and develop its food security. It concluded that –

➢ Using traditional ecological knowledge, that is, using local plants and seed, would be more helpful to food security than the high-tech varieties and high-cost approaches of the green revolution of the 1970s.

➢ Improving agricultural productivity and sustainability would require the taking into account of the heterogeneity of the farming systems and various ecological systems in Africa, through initiatives like intercropping or permaculture (as opposed to monocultures).

The world is also facing its worst food crisis since the 1970s. Food prices have been rising since 2002 but have sharply increased since 2006. However, the present situation is exceptional since prices have gone up for nearly all food commodities due to the immediate record price hikes for energy commodities and also because of an increased link between energy and food prices. The growing trend of food prices, coupled with higher energy prices, is a source of global concern as it carries serious implications for international security, economic growth and social progress.

When probing the underlying causes and possible solutions, there seems to be a broad agreement with respect to the decrease in production capacity in developing countries, to climatic changes, natural disasters, increased energy prices, financial speculation and in declining stocks. The existing crisis calls for urgent coordinated action among governments, international organisations, development institutions, donors, and civil society to put in place adequate policies for overcoming the challenges posed by the current situation and to respond effectively to the complex problem faced by developing countries.

4.4 Financial Turmoil

4.4.1 Introduction

The term '**financial turmoil**' or '**financial crisis,**' is applied broadly to a variety of situations wherein some financial institutions or assets suddenly lose a large part of their value. Earlier, there have been many crises in the financial sector which were associated with banks which led to many recessions. Other situations that are often called financial crises include stock market crashes and the bursting of other financial bubbles, currency crises, and defaults by countries in payments. Financial crises directly result in a loss of paper wealth; they do not directly result in changes in the real economy unless a recession or depression follows. Many economists have offered theories about how financial crises develop and how they could be prevented. These theories are not accepted everywhere and thus, financial crises are still a regular occurrence around the world.

Financial crisis is a state in which the value of financial institutions or assets drops quickly. It is frequently associated with a fright or a run on the banks, in which investors sell off assets or extract money from savings accounts with the expectation that the value of those assets will go down if they remain a financial institution. A financial crisis can occur due to institutions or assets being overvalued and can be aggravated by investor behaviour. A rapid string of sell-offs can further result in lower asset prices or more savings withdrawals. If not checked, the crisis can give rise to a recession or depression in the economy. A lack of necessary liquidity in financial institutions can also be a cause of economic recession or depression. A financial crisis can also be caused due to natural disasters, negative economic news or an event with a significant financial impact. Financial crises tend to be a source of decrease in business activities, leading to a self-reinforcing intensification of the crisis.

In short, the term financial crisis is widely used to refer to a situation where an institution or institutions lose a huge part of their value. Nowadays, financial crises are a common occurrence in specific sectors of the economy. It has to be noted, that though a financial crisis affects the entire economy, it can hit a single sector of an economy and not necessarily affect the other sectors.

4.4.2 Types of Financial Turmoil

The reasons of a financial crisis differ with the type of crisis. Even though many economists have come up with causes of financial crises, there is barely a consensus between economists on these causes. This is because of the different perspectives of economics and perhaps because every financial crisis is peculiar to itself. Recently, financial crises have stopped the momentum of economic development of many countries around the globe. In some cases, they have almost completely destroyed financial systems. The purpose of this study is to analyse the types of financial crisis and the impact caused in the countries that have experienced them. This study reveals **five types of financial crises:**

1. Banking crisis
2. Speculative bubbles and crashes
3. Market failures
4. International financial crises
5. Wider economic crisis

1.   Banking Crisis

Banks usually provide deposit accounts where people deposit their savings and can withdraw them anytime. The banks then use these deposits to provide loans which are paid over a long period of time. When a bank suffers a sudden rush of withdrawals by depositors, this is called a bank run. Since banks lend out most of the cash they receive in deposits, it is difficult for them to quickly pay back all deposits if these are suddenly demanded, so a run may leave the bank in bankruptcy, causing many depositors to lose their savings unless they are covered by deposit insurance. This happens when the country or region is in a panic situation, when there is a large outflow of money, etc. A situation in which bank runs are widespread is called a systemic banking crisis or just a banking panic. A situation without widespread bank runs, but in which banks are reluctant to lend, because they worry that they have insufficient funds available, serves to deepen the crisis. In this way, the banks themselves end up becoming a trigger of a financial crisis. Alternatively, banks may see this situation coming, and in trying to avoid this situation, banks will then be reluctant to provide credit and loans to people because of fears that it may not have enough cash to lend out. Such a situation is usually referred to as a credit crunch and it also accelerates a financial crisis.

Financial and corporate sectors in a country experience financial difficulties in their payments due to systematic banking crisis. As a result, loan related problems arise and most of the capital of the banking system declines. This situation is generally accompanied by increased interest rates, slowdown or reversal of capital flows, and the depressed prices of assets including capital and real estate. A similar situation prevents banks to pay back deposits if they are needed suddenly by their customers. Banking crises that have appeared in the past decades have presented many challenges and problems before bankers, policy-makers, researchers and analysts in different countries across the globe to manage banking activities more effectively. This has happened since financial stability is crucial to support economic development of individual countries to be more competitive in regional and global markets. Banks are considered to be essential in any business activity in a given market. Consequently, during the financial distress, banks are supported by their respective governments through emergent liquidity or other related forms to ensure protection of the economic unity.

2.   Speculative Bubbles and Crashes

People in a stock exchange buy stocks to achieve from the income it generates. However, some people buy stock by guessing the price and hoping to see it a higher price afterwards. If majority of people in a stock market buy speculatively, then chances are high that the price of that stock will be very high. While, when they all want to sell at the same time, the prices are likely to fall too. While buying, when the price of a stock is more than its current price plus dividends and interest, then the stock is said to be exhibiting a bubble.

Economists say that a financial asset (stocks, for example) exhibits a bubble when its price exceeds the present value of the future income (such as, interest or dividends) that would be received by owning it to maturity. If most market participants buy the asset primarily in hopes of selling it later at a higher price, instead of buying it for the income it will generate, this could be evidence that a bubble is present. If there is a bubble, there is also a risk of a crash in asset prices: market participants will go on buying only as long as they expect others to buy, and when many decide to sell, the price will fall. However, since it is difficult to tell in practice whether an asset's price actually equals its fundamental value, it becomes hard to detect bubbles reliably. However, there are some economists who insist that bubbles never or almost never occur.

A speculative bubble alludes to a situation in which the price of securities or stocks rises above its real value. Such trend continues until potential investors believe that the prices are not correlated with the market value. Until then, they usually buy shares as they believe the share prices will continue to rise to the extent that they implement profit when you decide to sell them out. The presence of speculative bubbles increases the opportunity of the market failure given the investors commitment to buy shares while share prices rise constantly. In situations where most traders decide to sell their shares at the same time, there will be no buyers in the market. As a result, believed market prices will fail and the value of stocks and shares will go down severely.

(a)   Banking crisis
(b)   Speculative bubbles and crashes
(c)   Market failures
(d)   International financial crises
(e)   Wider economic crisis

3.   Market failures:

This occurs when there is an inefficient allocation of resources in a free market. Market failure can occur due to a variety of reasons, such as monopoly (higher prices and less output), negative externalities (over-consumed) and public goods (usually not provided in a free market). There are two types of market failure:

Complete and partial market failure

(a)   Complete market failure occurs when the market simply does not supply products at all - we see "missing markets"

(b)   Partial market failure occurs when the market does actually function but it produces either the wrong quantity of a product or at the wrong price.

Reasons of market failure:

(a)   **Positive externalities:** Goods / services which give benefit to a third party, e.g. less congestion from cycling

(b) **Negative externalities:** Goods / services which impose cost on a third party, e.g. cancer from passive smoking

(c) **Merit goods:** People underestimate the benefit of good, e.g. education

(d) **Demerit goods:** People underestimate the costs of good, e.g. smoking

(e) **Public Goods:** Goods which are non-rival and non-excludable – e.g. police, national defence.

(f) **Monopoly Power:** when a firm controls the market and can set higher prices.

(g) **Inequality:** unfair distribution of resources in free market

(h) **Factor Immobility:** E.g. geographical / occupational immobility

(i) **Agriculture:** Agriculture is often subject to market failure – due to volatile prices and externalities.

(j) **Information failure:** where there is lack of information to make an informed choice.

4. **International Financial Crisis**

This type of crisis takes place when a country is forced to devalue its currency, either because of a speculative attack or because it is not in a position to pay its debts. When a country is not able to pay its debts, that situation is called as a default. When this takes place, all the countries that were trading with this particular country will be adversely affected. The investors will also lose the value of their investments due to the reality that the currency they are using will have a much lower value. Countries that faced international financial crises, have caused chaos within the respective economies. Such crises have created social dissatisfaction, reduction in employment rate, credit rating cuts by various agencies, the fall of shares in stock exchanges, decline in foreign direct investments, and privatisation of public assets and industries. Measures taken by governments which have fallen into financial crisis intended to stabilise markets and to rebuild their economies. A monetary crisis because of devaluation of currencies and failure to pay sovereign debt has resulted in state bankruptcy. As such, these are very common crises that affect the international financial system.

In the recent decades, the issue of preferred currency exchange regime has evolved considerably for developing economies. During the early 1990s, a change of fixed exchange rate system attached to a strong international currency was familiar, especially for countries that had gone through transitional phases from centralised economies to liberal ones. Impacts of speculators have led many countries to devalue their currency due to consecutive attacks. Decreased foreign capital inflows has affected the balance of the payment system, and leading to a monetary collapse. Subsequently, such a system of monetary exchange has highlighted the weakness of the system and the inability to protect against speculation

5. **Wider Economic Crisis**

Economic crises with wider dimensions have sent a shock wave through different countries of the world. This has been a source for many large businesses, even those with international and transatlantic activity, to suffer severe blow and failures due to economic crisis with broader implication. Crises with such proportions that influence individual countries or in block if they are under the single umbrella of economic union are known as recession and depression. Negative economic growth of the GDP for more than two consecutive quarters generally in a single economy is defined as recession. If economic growth continues with such negative rates for longer period it will result in depression (David Begg and Damian Ward, 2009). Countries that fall under recession or economic depression have also experienced increased unemployment rate in all of its economic sectors. Alternatively, economic stagnation is defined by economists as a state when the pace of economic development slows down. Some of the well known crises globally with larger dimensions are the great depression of the 1930s and the mortgage crisis.

4.4.3 Causes of Financial Crisis

1. Strategic Complementarities in Financial Markets

It is often observed that successful investment requires each investor in a financial market to guess what other investors will do. Therefore, a fall in one market has a cascading effect on the other markets.

Furthermore, in many cases, investors have incentives to coordinate their choices. For example, someone who thinks other investors want to buy lots of Japanese yen may expect the yen to rise in value, and therefore, has an incentive to buy yen too.

2. Leverage

Leverage means borrowing to finance investments, and is frequently cited as a contributor to financial crises. When a financial institution (or an individual) only invests its own money, it can, in the very worst case, lose its own money. But, when it borrows in order to invest more, it can potentially earn more from its investment, but it can also lose more than all it has. Though leverage magnifies the potential returns from investment, it also carries with it an inherent risk of bankruptcy. Since bankruptcy means that a firm fails to honour all its promised payments to other firms, it may spread financial troubles from one firm to another. Thus, the virus of bankruptcy spreads very quickly.

3. Asset-liability Mismatch

Another factor believed to contribute to financial crises is asset-liability mismatch, a situation in which the risks associated with an institution's debts and assets are not appropriately aligned. For example, commercial banks offer deposit accounts which can be withdrawn at any time and they use the proceeds to make long-term loans to businesses and home owners. The mismatch between the banks' short-term liabilities (its deposits) and its long-term assets (its loans) is seen as one of the reasons why bank runs occur when depositors panic and decide to withdraw their funds more quickly than the bank can get back the proceeds of its loans.

In an international context, many emerging market governments are unable to sell bonds denominated in their own currencies, and therefore, sell bonds denominated in US dollars instead. This generates a mismatch between the currency denomination of their liabilities (their bonds) and their assets (their local tax revenues), and thus, they run a risk of sovereign default due to fluctuations in exchange rates.

4.   Uncertainty and Herd Behaviour

Historians have pointed out that crises often appear soon after major financial or technical innovations that present investors with new types of financial opportunities.

Unfamiliarity with recent technical and financial innovations may help explain as to why investors sometimes grossly overestimate asset values. Also, if the first investors in a new class of assets (for example, stock in 'dot com' companies) profit from rising asset values as other investors learn about the innovation (in our example, as others learn about the potential of the Internet), then, still more others may follow their example, driving the price even higher as they rush to buy in hopes of similar profits. If such herd behaviour causes prices to spiral up far above the true value of the assets, a crash may become inevitable. If for any reason the price briefly falls, and that investors realise that further gains are not assured, then, the spiral may go into reverse, with price decreases causing a rush of sales, reinforcing the decrease in prices.

5.   Regulatory Failures

Governments worldwide have attempted to eliminate or mitigate financial crises by regulating the financial sector. One major goal of regulation is transparency – making institutions' financial status publicly known by requiring regular reporting under standardised accounting procedures. Another goal of regulation is making sure institutions have sufficient assets to meet their contractual obligations, through reserve requirements, capital requirements, and other limits on leverage.

As insufficient regulation has been found to be the root cause of some financial crises; it, willy-nilly has served to make a case for changes in regulation in order to avoid such recurrence of crisis.

However, excessive regulation has also been cited as a possible cause of financial crises. In particular, the Basel II Accord has been criticised for requiring banks to increase their capital when risks rise, which might cause them to decrease lending precisely when capital is scarce, potentially aggravating a financial crisis.

6.   Fraud

Fraud has played a role in the collapse of some financial institutions, when companies have attracted depositors with misleading claims about their investment strategies, or have embezzled the resulting income.

Many rogue traders who have caused large losses to financial institutions have been accused of acting fraudulently in order to hide their trades. Fraud in mortgage financing has also been cited as one possible cause of the 2008 subprime mortgage crisis.

7.   Contagion

Contagion refers to the idea that financial crises may spread from one institution to another, as when a bank run spreads from a few banks to many others or, from one country to another, as when currency crises, sovereign defaults, or stock market crashes spread across countries. When the failure of one particular financial institution threatens the stability of many other institutions, this is called systemic risk.

8.   Recessionary effects

Some financial crises have little effect outside of the financial sector, like the Wall Street crash of 1987, but other crises are believed to have played a role in decreasing growth in the rest of the economy. There are many theories why a financial crisis could have a recessionary effect on the rest of the economy.

4.4.4 Preventive Measures for Financial Turmoil

Governments and central banks, in response to the global financial crisis, took different measures to resolve the problems and put the financial markets and the economies back on track. The most important of these measures are −

1.   Government fiscal policies

Government fiscal spending and stimulus packages are significant during recession periods. However, public spending should focus on infrastructure and construction activities that can lead to economic development. Extreme spending on bailouts, unemployment benefits, and subsidy programs, to boost spending will not have a long-term impact. Short-term objectives and spending will only aggravate future growth.

2.   Market regulation and supervision

Governments and Central Banks around the globe must be active in supervising and monitoring the activities of financial firms locally and internationally. In the short run, efforts must be focussed on cleaning the balance sheet of financial firms from toxic assets. Credit lines should be offered for companies with good practices. A better process of monitoring the tax reports of financial companies is required. It must be noted that the existing financial system is very complicated to understand and control. Hence, the proficiency of financial specialists and central banks must be considered to plan new policies and regulations.

3.   New global financial system

International Monetary Fund (IMF) should play a major role in regulating and auditing the global financial system. The IMF should possess both resources and playing a broader role in the world economy as compared to the past. To insure the prevention of future collapses, newer measures and regulations should be adopted. Investment companies should be penalised for conducting unfair practices. Financial practices must be constant globally. The creation of new global currency to replace dollars should be considered since the dependency of the world on the dollar is a major cause of the crisis.

4.   Financial rescue plans

The intention of the financial rescue plan is to save important investment banks and insurance companies from bankruptcies to avoid further financial deterioration. Many central banks across the globe presented similar rescue plans with different measure.

5. Central bank's monetary policies

Central banks around the globe have resorted to all monetary policies to control financial crisis. The most significant of these policies was to lower the interest rate considerably. The objective is to minimise the cost of borrowing for private businesses and consumers to encourage commercial activities.

6. Public stimulus packages

Huge stimulus packages were launched by the government, to pull their economies out of recession. While the financial crisis pushed the economies into deep recession, consumer spending declined sharply owing to fear and lack of confidence. As a result, industrial output declined and unemployment has grown sharply. Thus, the stimulus packages aim to increase public spending on infrastructure projects. Public spending should produce more jobs and stabilise consumer spending patterns. However, recovery from the current recession could be very slow. Production idle capacity and unemployment are on the rise. This makes it difficult for companies to employ workers that will keep demand at low levels and increase idle capacity.

Points to Remember

- Global economy refers to the economy of the world, comprising of different economies of individual countries, with each economy related with the other in one way or another. A key concept in the global economy is globalisation, which is the process that leads to individual economies around the world being closely interwoven such that an event in one country is bound to affect the state of other world economies.
- Planet Earth is facing an energy crisis owing to an escalation in global energy demand, continued dependence on fossil-based fuels for energy generation and transportation, and an increase in world population, exceeding seven billion people and rising steadily.
- If concentration levels are not reversed, major changes to the world climate may result, bringing significant effects on people, industry, and the world economy.
- Energy and commodity crisis is a situation wherein the nation suffers from a disruption of energy and commodity supplies accompanied by rapidly increasing energy and commodity prices that threaten economic and national security.
- Tax hikes, strikes, military coup, political events, severe hot summers or cold winters can cause sudden increase in demand of energy and can choke supply. A strike by unions in an oil producing firm can definitely cause an energy crisis.
- A commodity is a reasonably homogeneous good or material, bought and sold freely as an article of commerce. Commodities include agricultural products, fuels, and metals and are traded in bulk on a commodity exchange or spot market.
- The commodity crisis can be understood in terms of supply and demand side analysis where supply has not been able to keep pace with growing demand.

- The rising trend in commodity prices, coupled with higher energy prices and the fact that there are large populations of urban poor, has increased hunger and as a fall-out, triggered disturbance in dozens of countries.

- Biofuels are being increasingly promoted as an alternative source of energy to provide greater energy security, to lower greenhouse gas emissions, to cope with increased prices of fossil fuels and to increase rural incomes.

- The term 'financial turmoil' or 'financial crisis,' is applied broadly to a variety of situations wherein some financial institutions or assets suddenly lose a large part of their value.

- Financial crises directly result in a loss of paper wealth; they do not directly result in changes in the real economy unless a recession or depression follows.

- The term financial crisis is used in a wide variety of contexts to refer to a situation where, for some reason or other, an institution or institutions lose a huge part of their value. Financial crises are a common occurrence in the world today especially in specific sectors of the economy.

- The four types of financial crisis are:
  1. Banking crisis
  2. Speculative bubbles and crashes
  3. Market failures
  4. International financial crises
  5. Wider economic crisis

Question for Discussion

1. Define global economy.
2. Contrast the advantages and disadvantages of global economy.
3. State the factors influencing the global economy.
4. Explain energy crisis.
5. List the causes of energy crisis.
6. What is commodity crisis?
7. Enumerate the factors responsible for commodity crisis.
8. What are the preventive measures taken for commodity crisis?
9. Write a short note on biofuels.
10. Explain financial turmoil.
11. List the types of financial turmoil.
12. Summarise the causes and measures of financial turmoil.

Chapter 5...

India in the Global Setting

Contents ...

5.1 Introduction

5.2 India's Growth Story

    5.2.1 Industrial Growth

    5.2.2 Infrastructure

    5.2.3 Trade

5.3 Challenges faced by the Indian Economy

5.4 India – An Emerging Market

    5.4.1 An Emerging Market

    5.4.2 Indian Market – The Exploding Number

5.5 India in Global Trade

    5.5.1 Export Growth

    5.5.2 Imports

    5.5.4 Challenges in India's Trade Sector

5.5 Liberalisation and Integration with the Global Economy

    5.5.1 Meaning of Liberalisation

    5.5.2 Measures Taken for Liberalisation

    5.5.3 Advantages of Liberalisation

    5.5.4 Disadvantages of Liberalisation

5.6 Globalisation of Indian Economy

    5.6.1 Measures Adopted for Globalisation

    5.6.2 Advantages of Globalisation

    5.6.3 Disadvantages of Globalisation

    5.6.4 Impact of Globalisation on Indian Economy

5.7 Regional Integration

    5.7.1 Types of Regional Integration

    5.7.2 Major Areas of Regional Economic Integration and Cooperation

•   Points to Remember

•   Questions for Discussion

Learning Objectives ...

- To understand the recent economic growth
- To highlight India's growth story
- To list the trade, infrastructure and industrial growth of the Indian economy
- To describe the challenges faced by the Indian economy
- To discuss India as an emerging market
- To understand trade growth of India globally
- To illustrate the challenges in trade growth
- To define liberalisation of Indian economy
- To enumerate globalisation of Indian economy
- To differentiate the advantages and disadvantages of globalisation
- To identify the measures taken for liberalisation
- To define regional integration
- To understand the different types of regional integration

5.1 Introduction

Since the past few years, India has been consistently proving itself by clocking a plus six percent growth year by year. India is turning out to be an attractive investment destination due to its stability, democracy, strong governance, and improving infrastructure. India has progressively been establishing and maintaining good bilateral treaties with more and more countries like USA, Japan, EU, ASEAN, etc., and thereby increasing its trade and commerce and investment to and from these countries. Today, India has become the second most sought after Foreign Direct Investment (FDI) destination surpassing even the USA. A decade back, it was not even in the reckoning for the top ten spots.

5.2 India's Growth Story

There is an under-appreciated side to India's growth story. India saves a little more than one-third of its output and invests that much and little bit more, drawing on global savings, to squeeze out 9 percent growth. Per unit of capital, India produces far more output, thanks to two things: capital is unsubsidised and costly and this forces Indian companies to constantly innovate production processes and business models. India's pharmaceutical industry's cost efficiency might have its origins in the erstwhile process patent regime (now superseded by a TRIPS compliant product patent regime), but its culture of constantly improving its own process continues to pay dividends.

India depends again, for the most part, on domestic savings for capital formation. Yet, foreign capital inflows do play a significant role in the Indian economy insofar as they stimulate the stock market, reduce the cost of debt for large firms with access to global sources, feed off a veritable crop of entrepreneurship by taking good advantage of venture capital and private equity. This, in general, meets the gap between investment and domestic financial savings (a large part of domestic household savings are in a physical form and not available for investment to anyone other than the saver concerned). India's fast growth attracts a lot of foreign capital. As significantly Indian industry's overseas investment is also growing proportionately, with India, for example, emerging as the second largest foreign investor in London, UK.

India maintains control on foreign debt (total debt stock is roughly equal to total foreign currency assets), its debt service ratio is low (at a healthy 5 percent), the share of short-term debt in total debt is about 18 percent, even as the share of concessional debt in the total has come down by half to about 18 percent from the early years of the decade. So, foreign creditors have little reason to be concerned by the recent widening of India's current account deficit, stubbornly below 2 percent of GDP and even negative in the early part of the decade.

India also regulates foreign investment in some crucial sectors of the economy – banking, insurance, retail, the media, telecom, and so on. The historic record is that most such caps are gradually raised and finally abandoned, over time. Such caution has served India well and it is highly unlikely that India would be swept off its feet by any foreign wooer of its domestic opportunities.

Like any other fast developing major economy, India has to further accelerate its growth rate while, at the same time, conscious of environmental aspect. India's carbon footprint is small in terms of total footprint per capita. The country has also committed to reduce the emission intensity of its growth – units of emissions per unit of additional output – by more than a fifth over the next one and a half decades. Green energy, green buildings, green habitats, greater energy-efficient factories, offices and commercial places – although seems to be daunting challenges, yet are simultaneously goldmines of opportunity for high-tech firms around the world.

As India grows in size and clout, it will inevitably have an impact on the correlation of forces in the world. Although India does not harbour any aggressive designs on foreign lands, it yet needs to upgrade its defence capabilities to become more sophisticated and stronger to ward off any threats to its security. Larger procurement of advanced equipment leads on to offsets, joint ventures, domestic manufacture and eventually, India-based research and development, drawing on the tens of thousands of engineers who come out of India's colleges every year, the best among them being world class.

Visitors to India are astounded at the manner in which the physical landscape keeps changing, from one visit to the next. The change that is even more striking than the new airports, roads, metro rail and high-rises that keep getting added is the new mood of optimism that India's young people, the largest pool of youth in the world, have about themselves and the future. Trade liberalisation, financial liberalisation, tax reforms and opening up to foreign investments were some of the important steps, which helped Indian economy to gain momentum.

5.2.1 Industrial Growth

The high growth in the overall industrial output was solely on account of the heavyweight manufacturing sector. The other two sectors also remained in the positive zone. However, the growth in output was lower than the growth seen in the corresponding period of the previous year. The Index of Industrial Production (IIP) growth numbers released in September for July 2012 showed that the overall industry posted 13.8 percent growth, which is much higher than the growth of 7.2 percent posted in the corresponding month of previous year.

1. The three constituents of the overall industry, namely, the mining, manufacturing and electricity were seen to grow positively. However, what mainly led to the sizable increase in the overall growth was a high growth of 15 percent in the manufacturing sector in contrast to the increase of 7.2 percent in the previous year.

2. The use-based classification shows that production of basic goods, capital goods, intermediate goods grew at 5.1 percent, 63 percent and 9.1 percent as compared to 4.7 percent, 1.7 percent and 9.1 percent. The growth in the consumer goods decelerated slightly from 9.7 percent previously to 6.7 percent in the current year.

3. The industry sectors which among the 17 industry sectors saw an increase were the food products that increased by 9.1 percent (-0.1 percent), cotton textiles by 12.1 percent (0.5 percent), jute products by 19.3 percent (−28.1 percent), paper products by 7.3 percent (1.7 percent), rubber, plastic, petroleum and coal products by 19.4 percent (12.5 percent), metal products rose by 14.8 percent (12.6 percent), machinery and equipment and transport by 49.4 percent (12.0 percent) and transport equipment by 24.9 percent (10.9 percent).

The industry segments that registered a sizable increase in output were food products, cotton textiles, jute products, paper products, rubber and plastic products, petroleum, coal and tar, metal products and among the capital goods were the machinery and equipment, transport equipment and parts.

1. The growth momentum of the six core infrastructure industries was maintained thanks to the increase in petroleum products (crude petroleum and petroleum refinery). Production in coal and power remained positive. However, the growth numbers were not higher than the previous year.

2. The broad money supply rose by 3.4 percent over the period from April to July 2010-11, which was lower than the supply recorded in the same period of previous year. The aggregate deposits was also seen to expand slowly by 3.3 percent during the period from April to July of the current fiscal as compared to the expansion of 6.2 percent during the same period of 2009-10. The bank credit rose by 3.5 percent calculated in July over April 2010.

3. The total revenue of the government stepped up sharply this year with more than a two-fold increase, from ₹ 1,05,378 crores up to July 2010-11 to ₹ 2,38,524 crores up to the month of July of current fiscal. Consequently, the magnitude of fiscal deficit has contracted by almost 43 percent during this period of 2010-11 over the previous year.

4. According to RBI, the government acquired higher than anticipated revenue in July from the auction of 3G band spectrum and revenue from taxes helped the holding back of fiscal deficit within the targeted level of 5.5 percent. The disinvestment policy too reaped rewards for the government by fetching an additional amount of money to make infrastructural projects and assist poorer people.

5. Impressive collection in the direct and indirect taxes front in July has rendered the overall tax scenario buoyant. However, in growth terms, the indirect tax was observed to be much higher as compared to the growth in direct taxes.

6. The indices continue to stay close to the all time highs and it seems only a matter of time before they hit all time highs. It is mainly driven by the Foreign Institutional Investors (FIIs) who seems to have taken a liking for India and is investing a lot of money in the Indian markets.

7. Further increase in the forex reserves has been witnessed; this has been observed to rise from less than USD 250 billion a year back to more than USD 300 billion and enough to cover 12 months of imports.

Industrial Services

1. These days India is not merely confined to its traditional sector, that is, agriculture. With no dearth of sharp entrepreneurial minds, the Indian economy is poised to enter and conquer newer and newer fields. Indian minds are respected all over the world and this is the reason why Indians occupy top positions in various sectors outside India.

2. The emergence of Indian economy as the second fastest growing economy has opened various gates for India to start global trading. Indian economy is now engaged in agriculture, handicrafts, manufacturing, IT, BPO, aviation, textile, petroleum and mining etc.

3. More recently, Indian economy has grown very fast, thanks mainly to foreign investment. India is serving major new fields and, in some sectors, it enjoys leadership position. That apart, India is also providing business and services to various other major economies.

4. The recent sectors that have shown strong potential with high growth rates are BPO, telecommunication, IT, finance, biotechnology, nanotechnology, aviation, travel and tourism, media and entertainment, retailing and many more.

5. Today, major corporate and other government departments have come up with new financial plans to accelerate the growth of Indian economy. India has also experienced infrastructural growth more recently.

6. Various industrial giants in the world are collaborating with Indian companies to get the growth of the business. All these economic activities are forming a ground affirmation for India to make it the biggest economy in the world.

7. The Indian economy is now poised to resume its fast pace of growth, recovering double-quick from the crisis-induced slowdown. Population growth having come down to 1.5 percent a year, India's per capita income is growing at close to 7.5 percent a year, a rate that will allow it to more than double in ten years. This would be a remarkable achievement in human history, with China's example as the only precedent.

8. Industry accounts for 28 percent of the GDP and employs 14 percent of the total workforce. However, about one-third of the industrial labour force is engaged in simple household manufacturing only. In absolute terms, India is 16th in the world in terms of nominal factory output.

9. Economic reforms brought foreign competition, led to privatisation of certain public sector industries, opened up sectors hitherto reserved for the public sector and led to an expansion in the production of fast-moving consumer goods.

10. Post-liberalisation, the Indian private sector, which was usually run by oligopolies of old family firms and required political connections to prosper was faced with foreign competition, including the threat of cheaper Chinese imports. It has since handled the change by squeezing costs, revamping management, focusing on designing new products and relying on low labour costs and technology.

11. Textile manufacturing is the second largest source for employment after agriculture and accounts for 26 percent of manufacturing output. Tata Motors' embarked on a venture to produce the world's cheapest car – Nano.

12. India is fifteenth in services output. It provides employment to 23 percent of work force, and it is growing fast, growth rate 7.5 percent from 4.5 percent. It has the largest share in the GDP, accounting for 55 percent from 15 percent.

13. Business services (IT), information technology-enabled services (ITes), business process outsourcing (BPO) are among the fastest growing sectors contributing to one-third of the total output of services.

14. The growth in the IT sector is attributed to increased specialisation, and an availability of a large pool of low cost, but highly skilled, educated and fluent English-speaking workers, on the supply side, which is matched on the demand side by an increased demand from foreign consumers interested in India's service exports or those looking to outsource their operations.

15. In 2009, seven Indian firms were listed among the top 15 technology outsourcing companies in the world. In March 2009, the annual revenues from outsourcing operations in India amounted to US $60 billion and this is expected to increase to US $225 billion by 2020.

16. Regulations prevent most foreign investment in retailing. Moreover, over thirty regulations, such as 'signboard licences' and 'anti-hoarding measures' may have to be complied with before a store can open its doors. There are taxes for moving goods to states, from states, and even within states.

17. Tourism in India is relatively undeveloped, but growing at double digits. But there is a booming tourism known as 'medical tourism' wherein overseas patients visit India for undergoing medical treatment – one, which is, not only cheaper but world class.

18. Yields per unit area of all crops have grown due to the special emphasis placed on agriculture in the five-year plans and steady improvements in irrigation, technology, application of modern agricultural practices and provision of agricultural credit and subsidies since the Green revolution in India. However, international comparisons reveal the average yield in India is generally 30 percent to 50 percent of the highest average yield in the world.

19. India is the world's largest producer of milk, cashew nuts, coconuts, tea, ginger, turmeric and black pepper. It also has the world's largest cattle population at 193 million; second largest producer of wheat, rice, sugar, cotton, silk, peanuts and inland fish; third largest producer of tobacco. That apart, India is the largest fruit producer, accounting for 10 percent of the world fruit production. It is the leading producer of bananas, chickoos and mangoes.

20. India is the second largest producer and the largest consumer of silk in the world, with the majority of the 77 million production taking place in Karnataka State, particularly in Mysore and the North Bangalore regions of Muddenahalli, Kanivenarayanapura, and Doddaballapura, the upcoming sites of a INR 700-million 'Silk City'.

5.2.2 Infrastructure

India's emergence as a fast-growing trillion-plus dollar economy has enormous significance for the rest of the world. The remarkable thing about India's rise is that it is mostly benign and perceived as such by much of the world. It is also true that India faces numerous economic challenges. But India's new prosperity is indeed trickling down to the bottom of the pyramid. The government's redistributive policies play a major role – direct tax collections (essentially, tax on personal and corporate incomes) have been growing at close to 30 percent a year, thanks to lower rates and better tax administration and the government has initiated sizable rural development and employment schemes.

1. Considerable emphasis is being given on infrastructure development and urban renewal. New national highways are being built across India, and this road building activity also drives growth in the rural areas. Indeed, highway projects have been a trigger for a state like Bihar, (one of India's 28 states), to register growth in excess of 11 percent a year for five recent years.

2. The Planning Commission pegs investment in physical infrastructure to be a cumulative $542 billion during the Eleventh Five Year Plan period of 2007/08-2011/12. And this is expected to go up further to $1,000 billion over the 12th Five Year Plan 2012/13-2016/17.

No economy can sustain such fast growth without undergoing accelerated urbanisation.

1. The 2001 Census put India's urban population at 28 percent of the total. It probably has already moved past 31 percent. It is a safe bet to expect half of India to live in towns by 2030, which means that over 230 million additional town-dwellers.

2. The urban space that is required to accommodate these many additional people would be upwards of 20,000 sq. km. While this is a great policy challenge, there is little alternative but to build this required space, to house the fast growing sectors of industry and services.

3. Building new energy-efficient, climate-friendly towns and habitats, using mixed land use to minimise commute, extensive public transport, green building codes and green energy would be both, at the same time, a policy challenge and a great investment opportunity. India allows 100 percent FDI in building new townships.

The UN estimates that India would contribute fully a quarter of the addition to the world's workforce over the next 10 years.

1. India would produce 136 million workers, while China would contribute just 23 million.

2. The main challenge for India would be to ensure that these young people are educated, skilled and productively employed.

3. While school retention rates have gone up over the last five years, raising the quality of education and increasing the proportion of students who go on to college would be major challenges. India's education sector offers huge growth opportunities.

The government has been extremely keen to use **Public Private Partnership** (PPP) to **build infrastructure.**

1. Thus, national highways, power plants and airports are being built under PPP at great speed. New Delhi's latest international airport terminal, T-3, one of the largest in the world built within a record time, stands as a gleaming testimony to the efficacy of the PPP framework.

2. A national skill development programme is underway, with extensive collaboration between the government and the private sector.

3. Thanks essentially to a sustained rise in the demand for food, especially, for superior food from rural households due to their additional purchasing power arising from enhanced transfers and new economic activity, India is also facing the challenge of food inflation, in recent times.

This is both a problem and an opportunity to raise farm output and boost farmer incomes. While agriculture now contributes less than 18 percent of gross domestic output, it still employs a little more than half the workforce.

5.2.3 Trade

- The total merchandise trade (including the imports and exports) during the first four months of the 2010-11 stood at USD 180 billion as against USD 136 billion.

- Merchandise exports neared USD 70 billion in the fourth month of the present fiscal, and imports were seen to rise to the level of USD 112 billion.

- The high imports have increased the deficits to USD 43 billion from USD 31 billion in the same period of previous year.

- The fiscal deficit continues to stay high. Persistent fiscal deficits play a role in shaping expectations over the currency rate as well.

- Trade deficit has expanded by ₹ 40,000 crores in the last quarter. This has resulted in increased imports and spike in dollar demand.

5.3 Challenges Faced by the Indian Economy

1. **Population Explosion:** This is eating up into the success of India. Such a vast population puts a lot of stress on economic infrastructure of the nation. Thus, India has to control its growing population.

2. **Poverty:** As per records of National Planning Commission, 36 percent of the Indian population was living Below Poverty Line (BPL). Though, of late, this figure has decreased, there is still a long way to go. In this regard, some major steps are needed to be taken for eliminating poverty from India.

3. **Poverty:** The increasing population is pressing hard on economic resources as well as job opportunities. Indian government has started various schemes such as Jawahar Rozgar Yojana, and Self Employment Scheme for Educated Unemployed Youth (SEEUY). But these are akin to a drop in the ocean.

4. **Rural Urban Divide:** It is often said that India resides in its villages. Even today, when there is lots of talk going about migration to cities, 70 percent of the Indian population still lives in villages. There is a very stark difference in pace of rural and urban growth. Unless this anomaly is remedied, Indian economy cannot grow further in a real sense.

5. **Inflation:** Inflation in India, fuelled by rising wages, property prices and food prices is an increasing problem. Inflation is at present between 8-10 percent. Despite periods of economic slowdown inflation has always been a problem. For instance, in late 2013, in spite of growth falling to 4.8 percent, Indian inflation reached 11 percent. Inflation is related to cost push inflationary factors and not just excess demand. For instance, supply limitation in agriculture has caused growing food prices. This gives rise to inflation which is a major factor in reducing living standards of the poor who are sensitive to food prices. The Central Bank of India has made reducing inflation a top priority and is ready to raise interest rates. But cost push inflation is more difficult to solve as it may cause a fall in growth.

6. **Inequality has risen rather than decreased:** It is assumed that a growth in economy would drag the Indian poor beyond the poverty line. However, until now economic growth has been extremely uneven benefiting only the skilled and wealthy excessively. Majority of the poor rural India is yet to receive any substantial benefit from the India's economic growth. Even today, more than 78 million homes do not have electricity. 33 percent (268 million) of the population lives on less than $1 per day. In addition, with the spread of television in Indian villages the poor are increasingly aware of the inequality between rich and poor.

These challenges can be overcome by following sustained and planned economic reforms. These include:

1. Maintaining fiscal discipline. To reduce the difference between exports and imports.
2. Orientation of public expenditure towards sectors in which India is faring badly such as health and education.
3. Introduction of reforms in labour laws to generate more employment opportunities for the growing population of India.
4. Reorganisation of agricultural sector, introduction of new technology, reducing agriculture's dependence on monsoon by developing means of irrigation.
5. Introduction of financial reforms including privatisation of some public sector banks.

5.4 India – An Emerging Market

In the global economic setting, India ranks among the well-known emerging markets. With the introduction of emerging market in 1990, India has prospered and the Indian economy has enhanced to a greater extent. In short, in terms of the growth of the market and industrial development, emerging market is used to evaluate the socio-economic scenario of the country. As per a recent survey, there are around 28 emerging markets in the world out of which India ranks the second. A perfect competition market, a high standard of living and per capita income, the development of medical facilities and infrastructure, the increase in foreign investments, etc. are the main factors behind this booming emerging market.

Over the past few years, there has been a considerable growth of the Indian market resulting in the high Gross Domestic Product (GDP). An average annual growth rate ranges between 6 to 7 percent. The Indian government is taking some favourable steps, in order to boost the emerging market. The main aim is to increase the growth rate to around 9 percent. More and more industries and customer base are flourishing with positive existence of emerging markets. In terms of the purchasing power parity, India is the 4th largest economic system in the world. This recent economic development has put a positive impact on different sectors. There has been a noticeable development in the agricultural, service and industrial sector in the country. To match the rapid pace of economic growth, the service sector contributes around 54 percent of the annual GDP. In India, the increase in foreign investment has also casted a favourable effect on the emerging market. Well-known global companies are now investing in the Indian market, due to the increase in demand. The foreign institutional investments (FII) amount has reached around US $10 billion mark. In case of the foreign direct investments (FDI, there has been a significant increase of around 85.1 percent from US $25.1 billion to US $46.5 billion.

5.4.1 An Emerging Market: Factors and Indicators

India is emerging as one of the biggest markets in the world. It is certainly one of the growth markets of the future.

While the market for a number of products in the developed countries are saturating or fading, India comes across as an expanding market due to the following factors:

1. Availability of a large backlog of unfulfilled desires, like those for consumer durables.
2. Ever-increasing population.
3. Increasing wages.
4. The revolutionary changes in communication and change in social attitude has given rise to a revolution of rising expectations and demand.

The Indian economy presents a mixed picture of problems and opportunities. India is the second most crowded country in the world. Even though today China's population is about 30 percent higher than that of India, in future, the population of India may overtake that of China, since the population of India is growing faster than China. Considering the geographical size, the population problem is severe in India as China has nearly three times the land area of India.

India is among the poorest countries of the world in terms of per capita income. India produces only about 1.6 percent of the world GDP with almost 17 percent of the world population. It is nearly 5.5 percent, in purchasing power parity terms. The per capita income of India is less than half of the average per capita income of the developing countries. Even if the per capita income of India is relatively low, the size of its Gross National Income (GNI) is big. Among the developing countries, only China had a GNI larger than that of India. While the GNI of many developed economies is less than that of India, India is the fourth largest economy in the world, in purchasing power parity terms. It is estimated that by the year 2030, it will be the third largest (after China and USA). The growth rate of the Indian economy, however, has been very poor as compared to that of several East Asian countries.

Table 5.1: Some Indicators of India's Position in the Global Economy

	Share (Percentage)	Rank
Area	2.47	7
Arable land	11.24	2
Population (2006)	17.00	2
GNI (2006)	1.9	10
GNI measured at purchasing power parity (PPP) (2006)	6.3	4
Human Development Index (2005)	–	128
Export of goods (2007)	1.0	26
Import of goods (2007)	1.5	18
Export of services (2007)	2.7	9
Import of services (2007)	2.5	13
Net Foreign Direct Investment Inflow (2003)	0.8	–

Table 5.2: India's Global Ranking

Factor	Rank	Factor	Rank
Population	2	Milk production	1
Area	7	Butter and Ghee production	1
Arable land	2	Sugar production	2
Irrigated area	1	Merchandise exports	31
Tractors in use	2	Merchandise imports	24
Nitro fertilizer consumption	2	Services exports	20
Rice production	2	Services imports	23
Wheat production	2	GNI	12
Tobacco production	2	GNI at purchasing power parity	4
Tea production	1		

India is one of the largest producers of a number of primary and manufactured products. While the productivity is very low for agricultural commodities, by using productive methods, the output can substantially be increased. Some of the Indian companies are among the largest ones. Today, India has the second largest economy in Asia.

Considering countries with GDP of 100 billion and above to be in the Big League, India was already in this League in the 1980s. Although India's share in the combined GDP of this League declined in the 1980s and 1990s, it is expected to rise.

Table 5.3: Big League of World Economy

Countries		Collective GDP US $ million	Share of India (Percentage)
1980 (Total 19) India, China, Brazil, Mexico, Argentina, Saudi Arabia, Spain, Italy, UK, Australia, Japan, Canada, US, Netherlands, France, Belgium, Sweden, Germany, Switzerland		86,68,190	1.74
1990 (Total 24) *New Entrants* Indonesia, Iran, Denmark, Austria, Korea, Norway, Finland, Argentina, Saudi Arabia		1,76,24,570	1.44

Countries		Collective GDP US $ million	Share of India (Percentage)
1994 (Total 28) *New Entrants* Thailand, South Africa, Saudi Arabia, Argentina, Turkey		2,23,47,726	1.31
2000 (Total 33) *New Entrants* Poland, Malaysia, Portugal, Israel, Finland		2,59,43,552.7	1.68
2010 (Total 38) *New Entrants* Philippines, Colombia, Pakistan, Iran, Chile		3,48,31,636.5	2.62
2020 (Total 42) (expected) *New Entrants* Peru, Hungary, Venezuela, Greece		5,24,88,568.2	4.07

Note: Countries with GDP of $100 billion and above are considered countries in the Big League.

Courtesy: T. K. Bhaurnik, Senior Advisor, CII (Reproduced here from A. P. J. Abdul Kalam and Y. S. Rajan, India 2020: A Vision for the New Millennium).

India is considered as a very important emerging stock market. Robert Lloyd George, a Hong Kong investor, argues that India is the most promising among the large emerging markets, making it more promising than China. This belief is supported by the maturity of India's stock market. The enormous growth potential is indicated by the fact that the penetration level of many consumer items in India now is very low.

5.4.2 Indian Market - The Exploding Number

India ranks second in terms of the size of the population and ranks seventh in terms of area. With around 2.4 percent of the total area, India shelters about 17 percent of the population of the world. By 2045, the size of the Indian population is estimated to surpass China.

Though, the population growth rate in India has significantly come down, the addition to the Indian population every year is more than or nearly equal to the total population of a number of countries. The annual Indian population is nearly equal to the combined total population of three developed nations, Sweden, Norway and Denmark. In short, in regards to the number of consumers, annually, India is adding by itself a market as large as the above three developed markets put together.

This rapidly ever-growing population has given rise to a number of serious problems. Almost 29.5 percent of the Indian population lies below the poverty line and almost 8.6 percent is unemployed. The number of families in India with inadequate basic necessities is larger than the total number of households in most of the nations. In order to eradicate these problems, the additional employment appointment to be created, the additional houses to be built, the additional number of people to be provided with health and sanitation facilities, water supply, etc. during any Five Year Plan in India is more than what many nations have done over centuries. While all these emphasise on the gigantic challenges that a poor nation faces, they also point out the enormous investment and business potentials.

Although, it is true that the number of Indians below the poverty line is larger than the total population of most nations, it is also true that the total number of wealthy Indians is larger than the total population of many nations. India has millions of income tax payers. Besides this, India also has quite a good number of people with middle or high income who are not tax payers.

5.5 India in Global Trade

World trade volume growth, which slowed down in 2012 showed signs of recovery later. With the advanced economies, there was a reversal of roles, showing better signs of recovery than the emerging market and developing economies (EMDEs). With a lift in exports and moderation in imports, trade deficit contracted considerably during the year as compared to that in the previous year. It was during 2013-14 that India's external sector witnessed important progress. Pick-up in growth of trade partner economies and decline of the rupee helped India's exports to progress in 2013-14. India's exports began recovering in July 2013 though the uptrend in exports was temporarily decreased in February and March 2014. Imports also moderated since June 2013, largely driven by fall in gold imports and lower non-oil, non-gold imports clearly showing a decrease in domestic economic activities and in international prices of some commodities (metal) too. This resulted in narrowing of India's trade deficit by about 28 percent in 2013-14. With the share in world exports and imports increasing, India's merchandise trade has been flourishing over the years, from 0.7 percent and 0.8 percent respectively in 2000 to 1.7 percent and 2.5 percent respectively in 2013. As per the World Trade Organisation (WTO), India's ranking in the top merchandise exporters and importers in the world has also improved from 31st in 2000 to 19th in 2013 in exports and from 26th to 12th for imports in the same years. There has also been a marked development in India's total merchandise trade to GDP ratio from 21.8 percent in 2000-01 to 44.1 percent in 2013-14.

5.5.1 Export Growth

In the last five years, India's export growth has seen ups and downs, being in the downbeat field twice: in 2009-10 as an aftershock of the 2008 crisis and in 2012-13 as a result of the euro zone crisis and global slowdown. During 2013-14, India's exports were US $312.6 billion against a target of US $325 billion, though they grew by a positive

4.1 percent as compared to the negative growth of 1.8 percent during the earlier year. 2013-14 has seen many ups and downs in monthly export growth rates. The export growth was in double digits from July to October 2013, but they decelerated to single digit from November 2013 to January 2014, stayed in the negative territory for the next two months and finally ended with a positive but low growth of 4.1 percent for the following year. In April 2014, export growth was to some extent better at 5.3 percent and with the 12.4 percent growth in May 2014.

Although the pace of export growth was largely uneven, India's merchandise exports improved in 2013-14. After declining in Q_1, exports recovered in Q_2 and grew continuously in Q_3 though at a slower pace finally declining in Q_4 in 2013-14. On cumulative basis, India's exports grew by 4.1 percent to US \$312.6 billion in 2013-14 as against a decline of 1.8 percent at US \$300.4 billion in 2012-13 (5.4).

Table 5.4: India's Merchandise Trade

(US \$ Billion)

Item	2012-13 R	2013-14 P
Exports	300.4	312.6
	(−1.8)	(4.1)
of which Oil	60.9	62.7
	(8.6)	(3.0)
Non-oil	239.5	249.9
	(−4.2)	(4.3)
Gold	6.5	6.2
	(−3.2)	(−5.4)
Non-oil Non-gold	233.0	243.8
	(−4.2)	(4.6)
Imports	490.7	450.1
	(0.3)	(−8.3)
of which Oil	164.0	165.2
	(5.9)	(0.7)
Non-oil	326.7	284.9
	(−2.3)	(−12.8)
Gold	53.8	28.9
	(−4.7)	(−46.3)
Non-oil Non-gold	272.9	256.0
Trade Deficit	−190.3	−137.5
of which Oil	−103.2	−102.5
Non-oil	−87.2	−35.0
Non-oil Non-gold	−39.8	−12.3

Commodity-wise and Destination-wise Exports

In 2013-14, segregated commodity-wise data demonstrated rise in total exports. This can largely be credited to the turnaround in the exports of manufactured engineering goods and textile products. Among other categories, exports of petroleum products grew at a reasonable pace than in the corresponding period of 2012-13. At the same time, growth in exports of agricultural goods moderated due to a decline in almost all the principal goods excluding rice, tobacco and marine products (Table 5.5).

In 2013-14, the manufacturing sector exports of major product groups like 'engineering goods', 'leather and manufacture', 'chemicals and related products', 'textile and textile products' and 'handicrafts' improved drastically. Turnaround in engineering goods sector was primarily reflected in the strong export performance of 'transport equipments' and 'iron and steel' which registered a growth of 16.8 percent and 20.6 percent, respectively during 2013-14. In 2013-14 a sharp rise in 'textile and textile products' by 15 percent against a decline of 2.4 percent in 2012-13, is credited primarily to the growth in exports of readymade garments, cotton yarn, and manmade fibre. Apart from better external demand, recovery in the garment segment can be attributed to the depreciation of rupee and enhanced competitiveness. Decline in exports of 'gems & jewellery' by 5.4 percent in 2013-14 could somewhat be due to the softening of global prices of precious metals (for example, gold) which are used as basic input in gems and jewellery sector. It may be noted that gold prices declined by about 20 percent during 2013-14.

Table 5.5: India's Exports of Principal Commodities

(Percent)

	Commodity Group	Percentage Shares			Percent Change	
		2011-12	2012-13	2013-14	2012-13	2013-14
I.	Primary Products	15.0	15.5	15.4	1.4	3.5
	Agriculture and Allied Products	12.2	13.6	13.6	9.2	4.0
	Ores and Minerals	2.8	1.9	1.8	−33.5	−0.4
II.	Manufactured Goods	60.6	60.9	61.5	−1.3	5.0
	Leather and Manufactures	1.6	1.6	1.8	2.0	16.7
	Chemicals and Related Products	12.1	13.0	13.2	5.3	5.9
	Engineering Goods	22.2	21.8	22.2	−3.6	6.4
	Textiles and Textile Products	9.2	9.1	10.1	−2.4	15.0
	Gems and Jewellery	14.7	14.4	13.1	−3.2	−5.4
III.	Petroleum Products	18.3	20.3	20.1	8.6	3.0
IV.	Others	6.1	3.3	3.1	−46.0	−3.9
	Total Exports	100	100	100	−1.8	4.1

Destination-wise, improved export performance in 2013-14 could be due to a transformed export demand from the major trade partners like Belgium, Germany, Italy, UK, USA, Japan, China and Hong Kong. The share of China and US in India's exports increased during this year (Table 5.6). However, there was significant moderation in exports to UAE, Netherlands, Malaysia, Thailand, African and Latin American countries. Followed by a rise in exports by 8.2 percent in 2013-14 compared to a growth of 4.1 percent in 2012-13, the US became the top export destination for India with an improved share of 12.5 percent in total exports. In spite of a considerable decline in exports by 16 percent in 2013-14, exports to UAE continued to be the second largest export destination constituting 9.8 percent of total exports followed by China (4.8 percent) and Hong Kong (4.1 percent). Pick-up in demand from major trade partners seems to have been maintained by growth recovery in these economies in recent quarters.

Table 5.6: India's Exports to Principal Regions

(Percentage Shares)

Region/Country	2011-12	2012-13	2013-14
I. OECD Countries	33.8	34.2	34.8
EU	17.2	16.8	16.5
North America	12.0	12.7	13.2
US	11.4	12.0	12.5
Asia and Oceania	3.0	2.9	3.0
Other OECD Countries	1.6	1.8	2.1
II. OPEC	19.0	20.9	19.4
III. Eastern Europe	1.1	1.3	1.2
IV. Developing Countries	40.8	41.6	41.5
Asia	29.7	28.7	29.0
SAARC	4.4	5.0	5.6
Other Asian Developing Countries	25.3	23.6	23.4
People's Republic of China	6.0	4.5	4.8
Africa	6.7	8.1	8.4
Latin America	4.4	4.9	4.1
V. Others / Unspecified	5.4	1.9	3.2
Total Exports	100	100	100

Higher rise in exports to EU, North America, and developing Asia was reflected in the increase in their relative contribution in 2013-14 which, on the other hand, turned negative, in case of OPEC, Eastern Europe and Latin America (Table 5.7).

Table 5.7: Region-wise Relative Weighted Variation in India's Export Growth

(Percent)

Region/country	2011-12	2012-13	2013-14
EU	2.6	−0.7	0.4
North America	4.1	0.5	1.0
Other OECD	0.5	0.1	0.4
OPEC	1.8	1.6	−0.8
Eastern Europe	0.2	0.2	−0.1
Developing Asia	8.3	−1.5	1.5
of which			
People's Republic of China	1.1	−1.5	0.5
Africa	1.8	1.3	0.6
Latin America	1.3	0.4	−0.6
Others	-3.0	−3.7	1.1
Total Exports	21.8	−1.8	4.1

The recent sectoral performance of exports shows that though many sectors were in the negative growth zone in 2012-13, in 2013-14, all other major sectors apart from gems and jewellery and electronic goods have moved to positive growth territory. In the initial first two months of 2014-15 (P), there was added improvement in the performance of engineering goods (21.7 percent), petroleum products (14.0 percent), marine products (40.1 percent), and textiles (13.2 percent). One remarkable feature of the sectoral performance is that many labour-intensive export sectors have performed comparatively fine in 2013-14. Textile exports grew by 14.6 percent in 2013-14. The EU and USA accounted for nearly half of India's total textile exports. Growth of our textile exports to these markets was 13.5 percent and 7.0 percent respectively in 2013-14. Another development is India's growing textile exports to China with China's share growing from around 2 percent in 2010-11 to 5 percent in 2012-13 and further to 7 percent in 2013-14. Export growth of another labour-intensive sector, leather and leather manufactures, was soaring at 16.7 percent. Nearly 72 percent of total leather exports were to the EU and USA in 2013-14 with a growth of 15.4 percent and 27.2 percent respectively. Growth of exports of handicrafts including carpets was also in double digits at 10.9 percent, although its share in total exports was only 0.4 percent in 2013-14. One development in India's export sector is the growing foreign value addition and declining domestic value addition. The method of fragmentation of the production process among countries and continents is gradually becoming an important feature of economic globalisation, especially for developing economies like India. Particularly, more and more intermediate parts and components are created in subsequent stages or processes across different countries and then exported to other countries for further production. While analysing trade performance and the contribution of trade to domestic employment and income generation, this development needs to be taken note of.

5.5.2 Imports

Moderation in goods imports which began in June 2013 increased further in Q$_3$ of 2013-14 but the pace of decline moderated marginally in Q$_4$ of 2013-14. On cumulative basis, India's merchandise imports at US $450.1 billion recorded a decline of 8.3 percent in 2013-14 as compared with a marginal increase of 0.3 percent in 2012-13 (Table 5.1). In India, policy measures aimed at restricting gold imports, as well as weaker domestic demand for non-oil non-gold imports, caused a fall in merchandise imports during the period. Import growth slowed down sharply from 32.3 percent in 2011-12 to 0.3 percent in 2012-13 and fell to a negative −8.3 percent in 2013-14, owing to fall in non-oil imports by 12.8 percent. Among the major items of import, the value of petroleum, oil, and lubricants (POL), which constituted 36.7 percent of total imports in 2013-14, grew marginally by 0.7 percent. This marginal growth was on account of moderate quantity growth of POL (2.6 percent) despite the moderation in crude oil prices with the average price of crude oil (Indian basket) falling to US $105.5/bbl in 2013-14 from US $108.0/bbl in 2012-13. Gold, remains the other major item of import, the import of which declined from 1078 tonnes in 2011-12 to 1037 tonnes in 2012-13 and further to 664 tonnes in 2013-14, despite several measures taken by the government. In value terms, gold and silver imports fell by 40.1 percent to US $33.4 billion in 2013-14. Capital goods are the other major import category. As in 2012-13, capital goods imports had negative growth in 2013-14 also of −14.7 percent, which is a cause of worry. Within capital goods, import growth of machinery except electrical and machine tools and transport equipment fell by more than 10 percent in 2013-14. However, the quantum of capital goods imports has actually increased in 2012-13 as specified previously.

Commodity-wise and Destination-wise Imports

Commodity-wise, gold and silver accounted for 58 percent of decline in merchandise imports. Following the various gold import measures undertaken during the year, the downward trend in gold imports began in July 2013. On cumulative basis, imports of gold and silver contracted by 42.3 percent (only gold by 46.3 percent) during 2013-14. Quantity of gold imported also moderated sharply by about 34 percent in 2013-14 compared to a decline of 6 percent in 2012-13. Among other major components of imports, decline in imports of capital goods pronounced more in 2013-14 indicating slower investment activity. In contrast, imports of export-related items (particularly pearl, precious and semi-precious stone), witnessed a growth of 4.3 percent in 2013-14 as against a decline of 9.6 percent in 2012-13 (Table 5.8). POL import growth sharply decelerated to 0.7 percent in 2013-14 as compared with 5.9 percent in 2012-13. Moderation in import growth of POL products mostly reflects fall in international crude oil prices by about 2 percent and a marginal increase in quantum of POL imports during 2013-14 (y-o-y) (Fig. 5.1). Growth in consumption of POL products also moderated to 0.7 percent in 2013-14 from 6 percent in 2012-13.

(US $/barrel)

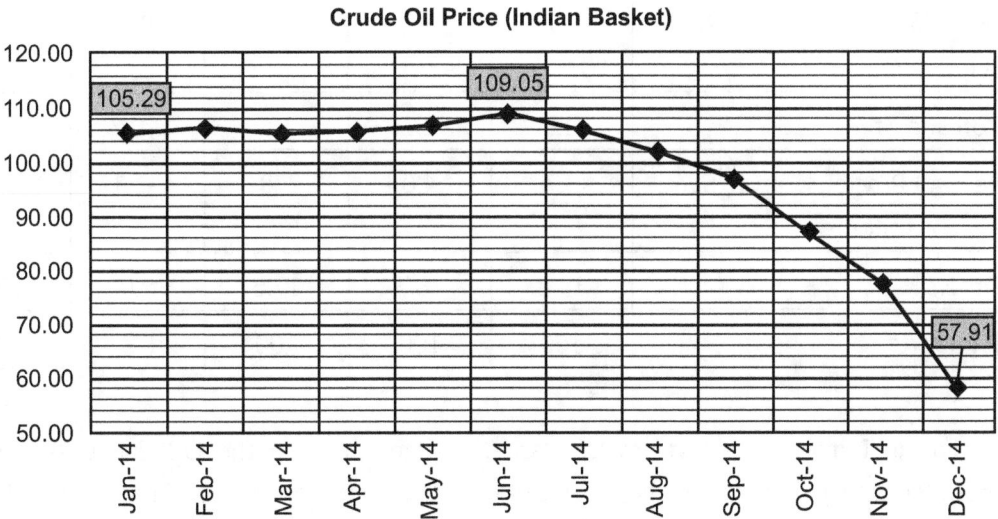

Fig. 5.1: Trends in Crude Oil Prices

Currently crude price is ranging between US $ 40 to 50 per barrel. This rate is expected to continue for the next some time. This is great news for countries like India that are major importers of oil and related products.

Table 5.8: Imports of Principal Commodities

(Percent)

Commodity/Group	Percentage Share			Relative Weighted Variation	
	2011-12	2012-13	2013-14	2012-13	2013-14
1. Petroleum, Crude and Products	31.7	33.4	36.7	1.9	0.2
2. Capital Goods	20.3	19.3	18.9	−0.9	−2.0
3. Gold and Silver	12.5	11.3	7.1	−1.2	−4.8
4. Organic and Inorganic Chemicals	3.9	3.9	4.5	0.1	0.2
5. Coal, Coke and Briquettes, etc.	3.6	3.5	3.6	−0.1	−0.1
6. Fertilisers	2.4	1.9	1.4	−0.5	−0.5
7. Metalliferous Ores, Metal Scrap, etc.	2.7	3.1	3.0	0.3	−0.3
8. Iron and Steel	2.5	2.2	1.8	−0.2	−0.6
9. Pearls, Precious and Semi-Precious Stones	5.7	4.6	5.3	−1.1	0.3
10. Others	14.8	16.7	17.6	2.0	−0.6
Total Imports	100	100	100	0.3	−8.3

Decline in India's imports from US, Japan, Switzerland and the OPEC countries were further outstanding. For other major trading partners, for example, China, Hong Kong, Singapore, EU, the decline in imports continued though at a slower pace (Table 5.9). Imports from Switzerland declined by 41.8 percent in 2013-14 compared to a marginal decline of 0.9 percent in 2012-13 primarily on account of a sharp decline gold and silver imports. Switzerland accounted for about 52 percent of India's total imports of gold and silver in 2013-14. Decline in imports from the US was chiefly attributed to the decline in gold and silver imports along with a moderation in imports of machinery in 2013-14.

Table 5.9: Shares of Groups/Countries in India's Imports

(Percentage Shares)

Region/Country	2011-12	2012-13	2013-14
I. OECD Countries	30.2	28.8	25.6
EU	11.9	10.6	11.0
France	0.9	0.9	0.8
Germany	3.3	2.9	2.8
UK	1.6	1.3	1.3
North America	5.6	5.7	5.7
US	5.0	5.1	4.9
Asia and Oceania	5.7	5.3	4.5
Other OECD Countries	7.0	7.1	4.5
II. OPEC	35.5	38.3	39.5
III. Eastern Europe	1.7	1.6	1.7
IV. Developing Countries	32.3	30.8	32.2
Asia	25.9	23.5	24.8
SAARC	0.5	0.5	0.5
Other Asian Developing Countries	25.3	23.0	24.2
People's Republic of China	11.8	10.7	11.3
Africa	4.0	3.9	3.3
Latin America	2.4	3.4	4.1
V. Others/Unspecified	0.3	0.5	1.0
Total Imports	100	100	100

Trade Deficit

The sharp fall in imports and moderate export growth in 2013-14 resulted in a sharp fall in India's trade deficit by 27.8 percent. In absolute terms, trade deficit fell to US $137.5 billion from US $190.3 billion during 2012-13. However, there was not much change in the POL deficit which was hovering at around US $100 billion in the last two years. With the fall in imports of both gold and capital goods, non-POL deficit fell sharply to US $35 billion in 2013-14 from US $87.2 billion in 2012-13.

5.5.3 Direction of Trade

In 2013-14, there was fine growth of exports to North America (9.1 percent) and Africa (7.2 percent), low growth to Europe (4 percent) and Asia (1.7 percent), and negative growth to Latin America (−20 percent) and the CIS and Baltics (−4.7 percent). While export growth to the US was 8.3 percent, it was just 2.2 percent to the EU 27 due to the slowdown in the EU. Exports to the UAE fell to a negative −16 percent. Exports to Asia still cover around

50 percent of India's exports. While India's exports to ASEAN (Association of South East Asian Nations) grew by a small 0.5 percent, exports to South Asia grew vigorously with high growths to all the four major SAARC (South Asian Association for Regional Cooperation) countries, Sri Lanka, Bangladesh, Nepal and Pakistan, as well as Bhutan. There was also good export growth to China and Japan at 9.5 percent and 11.7 percent respectively. Region-wise, imports from all five regions declined, with the highest decline of −19.3 percent in imports from Europe.

The share of the top 15 trading partners of India in India's trade at 58 percent in 2013-14 was more or less the same as in earlier years. The top three trading partners of India are China, USA, and UAE, with the top slot shifting between the three. Export import ratios reflecting bilateral trade balance show that among its top 15 trading partners, India had bilateral trade surplus with four countries, that is, the USA, UAE, Singapore, and Hong Kong, in 2013-14 with high increase in the export-import ratio with the USA. India's bilateral trade deficit with Switzerland declined sharply from US $31.1 billion in 2012-13 to US $17.6 billion in 2013-14 due to a fall in gold imports. India has high and rising bilateral trade deficit with China, which however fell by 6.6 percent in 2013-14. Given the growing importance of these two Asian giants, keeping in view India's export potential in China, India needs to formulate a comprehensive trade strategy for China (Table 5.10).

Table 5.10

Rank	Country	Share in Total Trade				Export/Import Ratio*			
		2010-11	2011-12	2012-13	2013-14 (P)	2010-11	2011-12	2012-13	2013-14 (P)
1	China	9.50	9.15	8.32	8.63	0.36	0.33	0.26	0.29
2	USA	7.30	7.31	7.76	8.06	1.26	1.49	1.43	1.76
3	UAE	10.72	9.14	9.54	8.82	1.03	0.98	0.93	1.05
4	Saudi Arabia	4.04	4.75	5.53	6.39	0.23	0.18	0.29	0.33
5	Switzerland	4.11	4.57	4.21	2.78	0.03	0.03	0.03	0.09
6	Germany	3.0	2.95	2.73	2.66	0.57	0.51	0.51	0.59
7	Hong Kong	3.18	2.94	2.55	2.63	1.10	1.24	1.55	1.74
8	Indonesia	2.52	2.71	2.55	2.60	0.57	0.45	0.36	0.33
9	Iraq	1.56	2.48	2.59	2.55	0.08	0.04	0.07	0.05
10	Singapore	2.73	3.17	2.67	2.53	1.38	2.02	1.82	1.75
11	Kuwait	1.96	2.20	2.23	2.39	0.18	0.07	0.06	0.06
12	Belgium	2.32	2.20	1.97	2.24	0.67	0.69	0.55	0.59
13	Nigeria	2.08	2.20	1.87	2.23	0.19	0.18	0.23	0.19
14	Qatar	1.16	1.73	2.07	2.19	0.06	0.06	0.04	0.06
15	Korea	2.29	2.16	2.19	2.18	0.36	0.34	0.32	0.34
	Total of 15 countries	58.46	59.65	58.78	57.89	0.54	0.49	0.48	0.53
	Total	**100.00**	**100.00**	**100.00**	**100.00**	**0.68**	**0.63**	**0.61**	**0.69**

Trade Credit: Indian Scenario

Trade credit is a crucial component of trade. According to a WTO study, a 1 percent increase in trade credit of a country leads to a 0.4 percent increase in real imports of that country. During end March 2014, the gross inflow of short-term trade credit (up to one year) of India reached ₹ 6,02,400 crores which represented a year-on-year decline of 9.7 percent. Inflow of trade credit during 2013-14 at US $100.2 billion was 18.4 percent lower than in 2012-13, while growth in outflow of trade credit was at 4.0 percent. As a result, there was a net outflow of US $5 billion under trade credit in 2013-14 as compared to a net inflow of US $21.7 billion in 2012-13.

After a low growth in 2012, export credit grew to 14.2 percent in 2012-13. In 2013-14 it declined to 10.5 percent. Export credit as a percentage of net bank credit, which has been declining continuously over the years, fell from more than 9 percent from 23 March 2001 to 3.8 percent on 21 March 2014. The government and the RBI have taken some measures to assist availability of trade credit to exporters.

5.5.4 Challenges in India's Trade Sector

India's merchandise exports share in world exports improved from 0.5 percent in 1990 to only 1.7 percent in 2013, whereas China's share increased from 1.8 percent to 11.8 percent during the same period. Thus, in the share of world merchandise exports, there is a wide gap between India and China. The gap is narrower in service exports. India must aspire to boost its share in world merchandise exports from 1.7 percent in 2013 to a respectable ballpark figure of at least 4 percent in the next five years for which exports should grow by a CAGR of around 30 percent. During 2003-04 to 2007-08, India's exports grew constantly by above 20 percent annually with 29 and 31 percent growth in two years. Achieving this in the medium term is the big challenge for which some basic steps need to be taken like product diversification, building export infrastructure, focusing on useful FTAs/regional trade agreements (RTAs)/CECAs, addressing the inverted duty structure, rationalising export promotion schemes, and taking steps for trade facilitation. In terms of share in world exports, India's export sector is yet to take off, though it has had bouts of high growth at different stretches of time.

Some important issues in this sector are the following:

1. Product diversification: Although, there has been market diversification and compositional changes in India's export basket, not much of demand-based product diversification has taken place. India has only five items with a share of 5 percent and above in the top 100 imports of the world at four-digit HS level in 2013. Even in this, except for diamonds (21.0 percent) and articles of jewellery (11.2 percent), with double-digit shares, the other three items have only around 6-7 percent share. Many items in the top 100 world imports consist of the three Es—electronic, electrical, and engineering items—and some textile items. Although, the gain in shares of engineering goods in recent years is a positive sign, India lags behind many other competing countries. The electronics hardware sector needs special attention which virtually collapsed with the signing of the Information Technology Agreement (ITA)-1 by India, when India's semiconductor sector was at a promising stage of development, while that of newly industrialised countries (NICs) and developed countries had already taken off. Focus should be shifted from export to items for which there is world demand and we also have basic competence. A demand-based export basket diversification approach with a perceptible shift to the three Es could lead to greater dividends for India.

2. **Export infrastructure:** Export infrastructure, mainly ports-related infrastructure, which affects trade, needs instant attention. Even the finest of our ports do not have state-of-the-art technology as in Singapore, Rotterdam and Shanghai. Poor port infrastructure include poor road conditions, port connectivity, congestions, vessel berthing delays, poor cargo handling techniques and equipment, lack of access for containerised cargo, and frequent EDI server down or maintenance, resulting in multiple handlings, increased lead time, high transaction costs, and thus loss of market competitiveness. Export infrastructure should be built on a war footing. Just as drastic changes have been brought about in India's airports and metro rail, sea ports should be the main concern.

3. **Focus on useful regional trading blocs**: Some FTAs/RTAs/CECAs of India have led to an inverted duty structure-like situation with import duty on some finished wares being nil or lower than the duty on raw materials imported from other countries. Besides, the domestic sector relating livelihood concerns has also been affected by some of them. India's push towards regional and bilateral agreements should end up in meaningful and result-oriented FTAs /RTAs/CECAs. So, a reality check of existing RTAs/FTAs/CECAs is required by assessing the performance of the items for which duty concessions have been given along with the impact on domestic production. India must prepare itself to face new pressures like the Transatlantic Free Trade Agreement (TAFTA), between the US and EU, which aims to produce the world's largest free trade area, protects investment, and removes preventable regulatory barriers. Besides, there is also need to have some new useful RTAs/FTAs/CECAs, for some of which negotiations have already started. More involvement of stakeholders could also help in ironing out differences.

4. **Inverted duty structure:** An inverted duty structure is making Indian manufactured goods uncompetitive against finished product imports in the domestic market since finished

goods are taxed at lower rates than raw materials or intermediate products. This hampers domestic value addition. This inversion is not only because of basic customs duty but also other additional duties. The regional/bilateral FTAs along with countries like Japan and South Korea and ASEAN, have added to a new inverted duty-like situation with some final products of these partner countries having nil or low duty while materials for these items from other countries have higher duty. Inverted duties are found in different sectors. This must be avoided and there should be stability among different stakeholders.

5. **Export promotion schemes:** There are many overlapping export promotion schemes with many focus markets and focus products with items and markets getting added each year in the foreign trade policy. One thing that is visible even from the short select list of trade policy measures is the variety of schemes and concessions that are extended at regular intervals. The export promotion schemes should be reduced to a bare minimum which can also lessen transaction costs and trade legal actions. Also many rates of concession should be avoided. Even for duty drawback schemes, there must be limited rates instead of having different rates even for similar items. This will make things simpler and evade discretionary decisions. Every time tariffs are low or can be reduced, export incentives must be withdrawn as the transaction costs would be higher than the benefits owing to duty concessions.

6. **SEZs:** A clear signal should be given for Indian SEZs as fresh investments are slowing down in recent years and the Greenfield SEZs have not really flourished in full swing. While the new manufacturing zones (NMZs) are being designed, a lot of investment has already been made in SEZs waiting to be tapped to the full potential. There are also areas where SEZs are worse off than domestic tariff area (DTA) units as in the case of non-applicability of FTA concessions when SEZs sell in DTAs.

7. **Trade facilitation:** Another major challenge is to promote greater trade facilitation by removing the delays and high costs on account of procedural and documentation factors, besides infrastructure bottlenecks. As per the World Bank and International Finance Corporation (IFC) publication Doing Business 2014, India ranks 134 in ease of doing business with Singapore at first place and China at 96. Across borders, India ranks 132, Singapore 1, and China 74 in trading. India needs 9 export documents compared to 3 in Singapore and 8 in China. The number of import documents needed is 20 for India and 4 for Singapore. Cost of exports per container is US $1170 in India, US $460 in Singapore, and US $620 in China and cost of imports per container is US $1250 in India, US $440 in Singapore, and US $615 in China. There are also inter-ministerial delays. The present move towards integration of related ministries is a step in the right direction. Simultaneously, policy announcement and issue of notification should take place.

8. Intertwining of domestic and external-sector policy: While a steady agro-export policy is required, any domestic shortage or excess influences exports. Similarly, external shortages affect the domestic sector. As a result, a smooth intertwining of domestic and external-sector policies particularly for agriculture is essential. Advanced economic and market intelligence to avoid major mismatches is also needed. These issues, if concentrated on, could lead to exponential gains for India's exports.

5.5 Liberalisation and Integration with the Global Economy

The growing integration of economies and societies around the world has been one of the most hotly-debated topics in international economics circles over the past few years. Rapid growth and poverty reduction in China, India, and other countries that were poor twenty years ago, has been a positive aspect of Liberalisation, Privatisation and Globalisation (LPG). But globalisation has also generated significant international opposition over concerns that it has increased inequality and environmental degradation. There is a need to study the impact of globalisation on developing countries from the viewpoint of inward foreign direct investment. Attention should also be focused on the role which some developing countries, particularly, from parts of Asia and Latin America, are playing as initiators of globalisation through their own MNCs.

India opened up the economy in the early nineties following a major crisis that led by a foreign exchange crunch that dragged the economy close to defaulting on loans. The response was a slew of rigorous domestic and external sector policy measures partly prompted by the immediate needs and partly by the demand of the multilateral organisations. The new policy regime radically pushed forward in favour of a more open and market-oriented economy.

To a large extent, the amount of trade and capital accounts of any country reflects the level or integration of that country into the world economy.

The wave of change which accelerated in the last two decades has put pressures on countries/governments to liberalise their trade, open up their capital accounts and deregulate their markets by removing restrictions on competition. In fact, this tide is reshaping the division of labour among the economies of the world. As this reshaping method is under way, the potential gains to be derived from it by individual countries depend on the right sequencing of liberalising trade and capital accounts and designing the basic institutional framework.

The integration of national economies into the world economy through trade and capital account liberalisation brings about new dynamics and interrelations with several new agents, many of which have varied backgrounds and varying jurisdiction. Hence, the opening up of those economies calls for evolving the traditional structural framework to persuade the needs and requirements of the interested parties.

Integration into the world economy should be regarded as a means and a course of development. Although, in some developing countries like South East Asia, during the last two decades in assuring faster growth rates, a large number of them made slow economic growth and some others, especially in Africa, even lost ground and were trapped in the process of marginalisation and faced increasing problems of human poverty and deprivation.

The integration of individual economies into the world economic system simply means finding a place for those economies in the global network with resource endowments, specialisation capacities, and potentials. The degree of openness in economy's integration has diverse implications in regards to the expected total benefits, the potential costs of the process, and the institutional structure it involves. As opening up introduces new relations, contracts, agents and forms of association and requires additional restructuring, failure to meet the liabilities incurred bears the potential of increasing the system's costs. In this situation, free movement of money and capital acts as a factor that supplements domestic firms' investment needs.

With a diverse background of knowledge, business habits and jurisdictions, those newly-formed relations require an objective treatment and approach on the part of national authorities and produce the need to share the available information with other actors on an equal footing. In short, successful integration into the world economy requires a restructuring in the institutional set-up of the market economy.

5.5.1 Meaning of Liberalisation

Liberalisation signifies reducing unnecessary restrictions and controls on business units forced by government. It basically means procedural simplification and comforting trade industry from unnecessary bureaucratic hurdles. By 1991, government had imposed several types of controls on Indian economy, for instance, industrial licensing system, price control, financial control on goods, import licence, foreign exchange control, restrictions on investment by big business houses, etc. It was noted that these controls gave way to several shortcomings into the economy and reduced the enthusiasm of the entrepreneurs to set up new industries. These controls also gave rise to corruption, undue delays and inefficiency. Rate of economic growth fell sharply and high-cost economic system came into existence. Hence, economic reforms were made to reduce restrictions imposed on the economy. It was based on the assumptions that market forces are capable of channelising the economy in a more efficient way than government control. Examples of other underdeveloped nations like Korea, Thailand, Singapore, etc. that saw rapid economic development due to liberalisation, were worth praising.

5.5.2 Measures Taken for Liberalisation

1.   Liberalisation of Industrial Licensing: The main feature of the New Industrial Policy is to adopt a policy of liberalisation instead of controlled economy. Until now, the execution of the private sector of the economy was functioning under a rigid licensing system. Under The New Economic Policy, the private sector has been to a large extent, freed from licences and other restrictions. As per the amendment in the new economic policy 2006, industrial licensing has been eliminated for all other industries with the exception of 5 industries. They are (i) liquor, (ii) cigarette, (iii) defence equipments, (iv) industrial explosives, (v) dangerous chemicals. A new entrepreneur can easily float in any new business except in the above-mentioned five industries, without any restriction.

2.   Concessions from Monopolies Act: According to the provisions of Monopolies and Restrictive Trade Practices Act (MRTP Act) companies having assets worth more than ₹ 100 crores were declared MRTP firm and also, were subjected to several restrictions. Currently, the concept of MRTP act has faded. These firms are now no longer required to gain prior approval of the government for investment decisions. They are free to expand themselves. Companies failing under MRTP Act are given large concessions. The capital investment limit that was fixed earlier has been removed. Thus, there would be no restriction on dominant companies and industrial houses for their expansion, taking over or amalgamation. However, in order to safeguard the interests of the consumers, more emphasis is laid on checking unfair trade practices. The newly empowered Monopoly Board is authorised to look into any matter *suo motu* (at its own) or on complaints received from individual consumers. In year 2002, MRTP Act has been abolished and in its place a much liberal Competition Act 2002 has been established.

3.   Freedom for Expansion and Production to Industries: Under the policy of liberalisation, industries (which are not covered under industrial licensing) are free to expand and produce. They do not need any prior official approval. Under liberalisation policy industries have been given the following freedom –

(i)   Prior to liberalisation, under the provisions of the old policy, at the time of granting licence, government used to fix maximum limit of production capacity. No industry can manufacture beyond this limit. Now, with liberalisation, this limit has been removed so as to enable the industry to take full advantage of large-scale production.

(ii)   Producers are now free to produce anything in the market, considering the demand. Previously, only those goods could be produced which were mentioned in the licence.

4. **Increase in the Investment Limit of Small Industries:** Investment limit of the small industries has been raised to ₹ 5 crores in order to facilitate modernisation. Investment limit of tiny industries or micro enterprises have been increased to ₹ 25 lakhs.

5. **Freedom to Import Capital Goods and Raw Materials:** Under the policy of liberalisation, for expansion and modernisation, industries are free to buy machines and raw materials from abroad.

6. **Freedom to Import Technology:** New economic policy or economic reforms have laid emphasis on the usage of new technology to promote modernisation. Government has allowed agreements to import high technology to promote technological dynamism in Indian industries. There is a provision in the new industrial policy that high priority industries relating to high technology need not seek permission to enter into agreements.

7. **Replacing FERA with FEMA:** Earlier, for regulating foreign exchange transactions, government had enacted Foreign Exchange Regulation Act – FERA. This act is very restrictive in nature. It involved several checks and controls on transactions involving foreign exchange. Following the economic liberalisation and changed attitude of government towards foreign capital, FERA was replaced with Foreign Exchange Management Act – FEMA in the year 1999, the provisions of FEMA are quite liberal.

8. **Liberalisation of Export and Import Transactions:** Government has liberalised its import and export policy. It has made the import of capital goods, raw materials, technology very simple. Quantitative restrictions on import have been withdrawn. Provisions regarding import quota, import-permit, and import-licence have been simplified. The procedures and documents associated to import and export has been simplified.

9. **Liberalisation in Taxation Policy:** Previously, tax rates were very high. This proved as a hindrance in the path of rapid economic development. High tax rates de-motivate the entrepreneurs in setting up new enterprises or expanding the existing enterprise. Following major changes have been made in taxation policy –

(i)   Peak income tax rates have been reduced to 30 percent.

(ii) Custom-duty rates have been drastically reduced from 250 percent to 10 percent.

(iii) Excise-duty rates have been reduced.

(iv) Complex sales tax structure has been replaced with a simple value-added tax.

10. **Liberalisation in Capital Market:** Previously, provisions regarding public issue of shares, debentures of companies were extremely restrictive. Only big companies could implement these conditions. But now, these provisions have been liberalised. At present, companies are given the liberty to fix the price of their public issue and to raise funds from foreign capital markets.

11. Liberalisation in Banking Sector: Banks play a vital role in the economic development of any nation. Earlier, monetary policy was very restrictive which hindered development of banking sector. Now following main liberalisations have been made in the banking sector –

(i)   Statutory Liquidity Ratio – SLR has been reduced to 25 percent.

(ii)   Bank Rate has been reduced to 6 percent.

(iii)   Cash Re-serve Ratio (CRR) has been reduced to 6 percent.

(iv)   Repo Rate and Reverse Repo Rate have been reduced to 5.25 percent and 3.75 percent respectively.

(v)   Banks have been given freedom to determine their interest rates within certain limits.

(vi)   Banks have been given freedom to recruit their employees.

(vii)   Norms for setting up private sector banks have been liberalised.

5.5.3 Advantages of Liberalisation

1. **Increase in Foreign Investment:** Liberalisation has encouraged globalisation. The inflow of foreign investment has increased with liberalisation. Now foreign investors consider India as a favourable destination. There has been a vast inflow of foreign investment in the form of foreign direct investment and portfolio investment in the past few years.

2. **Increase in Foreign Exchange Reserves:** India was facing acute shortage of foreign exchange prior to new economic policy of 1991. After the liberalisation wave, foreign exchange reserves of India have improved. Due to the huge inflow of foreign investment and increase in exports, India's foreign exchange reserves were 27,971 billion US dollars, in March 2010.

3. **Increase in Industrial Production:** Due to liberalisation several checks and controls have been removed. Companies Act, MRTP Act, Licensing Act have been liberalised. This has encouraged entrepreneurs to set up more industrial units. Due to liberalisation, many foreign entrepreneurs have also set up industrial units in India. All this has boosted industrial production.

4. **Increase in Competition:** Due to liberalisation, many domestic and foreign enterprises have started business operations in India. It has increased the competition in the market. For instance, in case of telecommunication, competition has increased since many foreign and domestic units like Reliance, Tata, Vodafone, Airtel, etc. have entered this business. Due to this sudden boost in competition, the prices have declined and quality improved. Eventually, it has benefitted the customers by improving their standard of living.

5. **Control over Price:** The inflation rate was very high in our economy before liberalisation. Competition and production have increased with liberalisation. It has helped in keeping a check on the rising prices. In the year 2009-10, inflation rate was only 3.6 percent per annum while this rate was 12.1 percent in the year 1990-91. In March 2010, inflation rate again increased to 9.9 percent per annum.

6. **Check on Corruption:** Before liberalisation, different licences, quotas, permits, approvals were required to be taken from government officials for business units. These officials used to demand bribe for granting these licences, permits, etc. With liberalisation the restrictions have been liberalised. It has helped to check corruption.

7. **Reduction in Dependence on External Commercial Borrowings:** Earlier our government had to elevate external commercial loans to meet balance of payments deficit. Liberalisation has helped to increase the inflow of foreign funds, which has consequently reduced the need of external commercial borrowings. It has also condensed the debt burden of government.

8. **Technology coming to the Country:** Due to liberalisation, technology reaches to other countries which do not have large research and development facilities and funds. This leads to a big advantage for the country as in due course of time, they start producing their own products. E.g. When Hero Motors tied with Honda, Hero Motors started developing their own scooters after a few years.

5.5.4 Disadvantages of Liberalisation

1. **Increase in Unemployment:** Liberalisation has encouraged the import of capital intensive technology. It has promoted automation, computerisation and mechanisation of industrial activities in the economy, which has in result, highlighted the problem of unemployment.

2. **Loss to Domestic Units:** Liberalisation has promoted competition in the economy. It has badly affected domestic business units which are adequately weak to compete with multinational corporations. Many small domestic units have become sick and have been closed.

3. **Increased Dependence on Foreign Nations:** Indian customers have gradually started using foreign goods due to the liberal import of foreign goods. Nowadays, a common man also uses imported TV, fridge, AC, washing machine, mobile phone, etc. With liberal import of technology, Indian business units also have stopped using and developing original technology. This can adversely affect the nation in the long run. Increased dependence on foreign goods has hampered the self-sufficiency of our nation.

4. **Unbalanced Development:** Many MNCs have entered the premium product segments and have targeted the upper income group. Foreign enterprises give less importance to mass consumption goods or goods meant for lower income group. Liberalisation has thus not been much beneficial for lower income group. It has further increased income discrimination.

5. **Increase in Regional Imbalances:** Private sector units and foreign enterprises do not set up their business units in backward regions. They prefer to establish their units in areas which are already developed and have good quality infrastructure. It has given rise to regional imbalances.

6. **Natural Resources Over-utilised:** Natural resources like water, oil, etc are being utilised which depletes the environment. E.g. Some areas have stopped manufacturing of colas as the water level was reducing drastically near the manufacturing facilities.

7. **MNCs not Interested in other Countries' Development:** MNCs typically enter countries with the intention of making profits. They are mostly not interested in the economic, social or other conditions of the countries. They therefore do not adhere to the norms of the society and try to find loopholes in the legal system, which leads to chaos.

5.6 Globalisation of Indian Economy

Globalisation is connecting the economy of a nation with the economies of other nations through free trade, free mobility of capital and labour, etc. It also involves attracting multinational corporations to invest in India. Economic reforms presume that Indian economy should have close association with the world economy. This can result in unrestricted flow of goods and services, capital, people, technology and expertise between different countries of the world. There will be an increased collaboration of Indian economy and the other economies of the world. Capital and technology will flow from the developed countries of the world towards India. Eventually, the aim of globalisation is to look upon the world as a 'global village'.

The term globalisation means international integration. It consists of an array of social, political, and economic changes. Incredible progress in modes of communications, transportation, and computer technology has given globalisation a new lease of life. The world is more interdependent now than ever before. Multinational companies manufacture products across countries and sell it to consumers across the globe. Money, technology, and raw materials have broken the international hurdle. Not only products and finances, but also ideas and cultures have violated the national boundaries. Laws, economies, and social movements have become international in nature. Along with the globalisation of the economy, globalisation of politics, culture and law is the order of the day. The formation of General Agreement on Tariffs and Trade (GATT), International Monetary Fund and the concept of free trade has improved globalisation.

The Indian economy had witnessed dramatic policy changes. The thought behind the new economic model known as Liberalisation, Privatisation and Globalisation in India (LPG), was to make the Indian economy one of the best growing economies in the world. An array of reforms began for industrial, trade, and social sectors to make the economy more competitive. This has had dramatic effect on the overall growth of the economy. It also heralded the integration of the Indian economy into the global economy.

5.6.1 Measures Adopted for Globalisation

1. **Increase in Foreign Investment:** Under economic reforms, limit of foreign capital investment has been raised. In many industries foreign direct investment up to 100 percent are allowed without any restriction and red tape hassles. Even export trading houses are allowed foreign capital investment up to 100 percent. In this regard, Foreign Exchange Management Act (FEMA) is enforced.

2. **Partial Convertibility of Indian Rupee:** To achieve the purpose of globalisation, partial convertibility of Indian rupee was authorised. It was in accord with economic reforms. Partial convertibility is to buy or sell foreign currency like dollar or pound sterling, for foreign transactions at a price determined by the market. This convertibility is applicable for the following transactions – (i) Import and export of goods and services; (ii) Payment of interest or dividend on investment; (iii) Remittances to meet family expenses. It is known as partial convertibility as it does not cover capital transactions.

3. **Foreign Trade Policy:** In conformity with economic reforms, foreign trade policy was enforced for a long duration. Now India's current foreign trade policy is quite moderate. Under this policy, all restrictions and controls on foreign trade have been removed. Open competition is encouraged and all facilities are provided to this end. Administrative controls have also been minimised.

4. **Reduction in Tariffs:** To provide Indian economy benefits internationally, custom duties and tariffs imposed on imports and exports are being condensed gradually.

5. **Export Promotion:** Various measures have been taken to meet the deficit of balance of payments. Exports have been encouraged. In order to boost the share of Indian exports in world trade, special facilities have been provided to the exporters.

6. **Freedom to Repatriate:** Prior to new economic policy, foreign investments were permitted in India on non-repatriation-basis, that is, foreign investors could not take

their income back to their country without the prior approval of the Reserve Bank of India. RBI allows this repatriation on a very restrictive basis. This provision proved as a great hindrance in the inflow of foreign investment. However, foreign investors are now free to repatriate their investment as well as income on investment. It has attracted more foreign investors to invest in India.

7. **Devaluation:** The first step towards globalisation was taken with the announcement of the devaluation of the Indian currency by 18-19 percent against major currencies in the international foreign exchange market. In fact, this measure was taken in order to resolve the BoP crisis.

8. **Disinvestment:** In order to make the process of globalisation smooth, privatisation and liberalisation policies are moving along as well. Under the privatisation drive, most public sector undertakings have been, or, are being sold to the private sector.

9. **Dismantling of the Industrial Licensing Regime:** Only six industries are under compulsory licensing, mainly on accounting of environmental safety and strategic considerations. A significantly amended locational policy in tune with the liberalised licensing policy is in place. No industrial approval is required from the government for locations not falling within 25 kms of the periphery of cities having a population of more than one million.

10. **Allowing Foreign Direct Investment** (FDI) across a wide spectrum of industries and encouraging non-debt flows. The Department has put in place a liberal and transparent foreign investment regime where most activities are opened to foreign investment on automatic route without any limit on the extent of foreign ownership. Some of the recent initiatives taken to further liberalise the FDI regime, inter alia, include opening up of sectors, such as insurance (up to 26 percent); development of integrated townships (up to 100 percent); defence industry (up to 26 percent); tea plantation (up to 100 percent subject to divestment of 26 percent within five years to FDI); enhancement of FDI limits in private sector banking, allowing FDI up to 100 percent under the automatic route for most manufacturing activities in SEZs; opening up B2B e-commerce; Internet Service Providers (ISPs) without gateways; electronic mail and voice mail to 100 percent foreign investment subject to 26 percent divestment condition etc. The Department has also strengthened investment facilitation measures through Foreign Investment Implementation Authority (FIIA).

(a) Non-Resident Indian Scheme: The general policy and facilities for foreign direct investment as available to foreign investors/companies are fully applicable to

NRIs as well. In addition, the Government has extended some concessions especially for NRIs and overseas corporate bodies having more than 60 percent stake by NRIs.

(b) Throwing open industries reserved for the public sector to private participation: At present, there are only three industries reserved for the public sector.

(c) Abolition of the Monopolies and Restrictive Trade Practices Act (MRTP Act) which necessitated prior approval for capacity expansion.

(d) The removal of quantitative restrictions on imports.

(e) The reduction of the peak customs tariff from over 300 percent prior to the 30 percent rate that is applicable now.

(f) Severe restrictions on short-term debt and allowing external commercial borrowings based on external debt sustainability.

(g) Wide-ranging financial sector reforms in the banking, capital markets, and insurance sectors, including the deregulation of interest rates, strong regulation and supervisory systems, and the introduction of foreign/private sector competition.

5.6.2 Advantages of Globalisation

1. **Increase in Foreign Collaborations:** Globalisation has encouraged collaboration of foreign companies with many Indian companies. These collaboration agreements can be technical collaboration, financial collaboration or both. In financial collaboration, foreign companies supply financial resources, while in technical collaboration modern foreign technology is provided by foreign companies. Foreign companies are setting up many enterprises in India in collaboration with Indian companies.

2. **Expansion of Market:** Globalisation has helped in the expansion of the market. It has permitted Indian business units to develop their business in the world. At present, multinational corporations have no national boundaries. Indian companies like Infosys, Tata Consultancy, Wipro, Tata Steel, Reliance etc. are undertaking their business in many countries.

3. **Technological Development:** Globalisation facilitates the inflow of foreign technology, which is very superior and advanced. Indian business units now use this modern technology.

4. **Brand Development:** Globalisation has promoted the usage of branded goods. Along with durable goods, products like garments, juices, snacks, food grains etc. are also branded. Foreign brands are very popular among Indian customers. Brand-expansion has led to quality up-gradation.

5. **Development of Capital Market:** Globalisation has helped in the development of Indian capital market. Many foreign investors invested in Indian Capital market. Lately, there has been considerable increase in inflow of foreign direct investment and portfolio investment.

6. **Development of Service Sector:** Globalisation has helped in the development of the service sector. With the entry of foreign companies, remarkable progress has been witnessed in various services like telecommunication, insurance, banking etc.

7. **Increase in Employment:** Globalisation has promoted employment opportunities. Foreign companies are setting up their production and trading units in India. It has improved employment opportunities for Indians, for example, many Indians are currently employed in foreign insurance companies, mobile companies etc.

8. **Reduction in Brain Drain:** Many multinational corporations have established their business units in India as a result of globalisation. These MNCs grant attractive salary packages and high-quality working conditions to efficient, skilled Indian engineers, managers, professionals etc. Now Indians get good employment opportunities in India itself which has resulted in reduction in brain drain.

9. **Improvement in Standard of Living:** Globalisation has improved the standard of living of the Indian population. Indians now get better quality goods at low prices. Globalisation has resulted in reduction of prices of several products chiefly electronic items like television, AC, mobile phones, refrigerator etc. Now the middle-income group also uses these luxury products, which were earlier used by the rich only.

10. **Real Income Increasing as Cost of Goods Coming Down:** Due to competition, the manufacturers need to keep profits and thus, prices of the products low. This will lead to more savings to the consumers. Thus, their real income will increase, which will lead to their standard of living.

5.6.3 Disadvantages of Globalisation

1. **Loss to Domestic Industries:** As a result of globalisation, overseas competition has increased in India. Now, Indian industrial units have to compete with foreign industrial units. Many Indian industrial units are forced to shut down after being unsuccessful in facing competition, due to availability of better quality and low cost of foreign goods. Small cottage industries are most affected by this increased competition.

2. **Unemployment:** Foreign companies functioning in India apply capital intensive technology. Even some Indian companies use imported capital intensive technology. Employment opportunities are reduced, due to the increase in use of new technology.

3. **Exploitation of Labour:** Unskilled workers are given low wages, less job security, long working hours due to globalisation. Labourers are forced to work even in such conditions as a bad job with fewer wages is better than being jobless.

4. **Demonstration Effect:** Demonstration effect has increased among Indians with the easy availability of foreign goods. Many consumers are now using luxury products by imitating others. It has encouraged a tendency of wasteful consumption in India. This growing wasteful expenditure has consecutively reduced saving and capital formation.

5. **Increase in Inequalities:** Globalisation has also given rise to inequalities in our economy. MNCs and big industrial units have flourished due to globalisation but small cottage industries are badly hit by it. It has also increased income inequalities in India.

6. **Dominance of Foreign Institutions:** Along with globalisation, governance of foreign institutions has increased in India. Globalisation has facilitated foreign companies in enlarging their market share. For example, in India, a large share of the cold drink market is controlled by Pepsi and Coca-Cola, which are foreign companies.

Thus, new economic policies are, to some extent, successful in achieving their objectives, although, in sectors like poverty alleviation, employment generation, reduction in inequalities etc. they have failed completely.

5.6.4 Impact of Globalisation on Indian Economy

The implications of globalisation for a national economy are many. Globalisation has intensified interdependence and competition between economies in the world market. Globalisation in India had a favourable impact on the overall growth rate of the economy. This is a major improvement given that India's growth rate in the 1970s was very low at 3 percent and GDP growth in countries like Brazil, Indonesia, Korea, and Mexico was more than twice that of India. Though India's average annual growth rate almost doubled in the eighties to 5.9 percent, it was still lower than the growth rate in China, Korea and Indonesia. The pickup in GDP growth has helped improve India's global position. Consequently, India's position in the global economy has improved from the 8th position to 4th, when GDP is calculated on a purchasing power parity basis. Today, India is poised to occupy the 3rd position by overtaking Japan.

1. **Structure of the Economy**

Due to globalisation not only the GDP has increased but also the direction of growth in the sectors has also been changed. Earlier the maximum part of the GDP in the economy was generated from the primary sector but now the service industry is devoting the maximum part of the GDP. The services sector remains the growth driver of the economy with a contribution of more than 57 percent of GDP.

India is ranked 18th among the world's leading exporters of services with a share of 1.3 percent in world exports. The services sector is expected to benefit from the ongoing liberalisation of the foreign investment regime into the sector. Software and the ITeS-BPO sectors have recorded an exponential growth in recent years.

2. Foreign Direct investment inflows

FDI increased from around US $100 million to US $5536 million. The details of the foreign investment inflow can be seen from the following table.

(a) The current account deficit has hovered at less than 1 percent of GDP in recent years.

(b) The strength of the external sector was reflected in a sizable accumulation of India's foreign exchange reserves comprising foreign currency assets, gold, SDRs and the reserve position with the IMF which touched US $141.5 billion.

(c) The composition of debt is also favourable. Short-term debt amounts to 3.5 percent of external debt and concessional debt amounts to 36.5 percent of total debt.

(d) The external debt burden looks sustainable according to a range of measures of indebtedness. Both debt service payments as a proportion of current receipts, and the external debt-to-GDP ratio have been falling steadily during the 1990s, and currently stand at around 17 percent and 22 percent, respectively.

3. Foreign Trade (Export-Import)

India's imports in 2004-05 stood at US $107 billion recording an increase of 35.62 percent compared with US $79 billion in the previous fiscal. Export also increased by 24 percent as compared to the previous year. Oil imports zoomed by 19 percent with the import bill being US $29.08 billion against US $20.59 billion in the corresponding period last year. Thus, we find that the economic reforms in the Indian economy initiated since July 1991 have led to fiscal consolidation, control of inflation to some extent, increase in foreign exchange reserve and greater foreign investment and technology towards India. This has helped the Indian economy to grow at a faster rate. Presently, more than 100 of the 500 fortune companies have a presence in India as compared to 33 in China.

A Comparison with Other Developing Countries

(a) Consider global trade – India's share of world merchandise exports increased from 0.05 percent to 0.07 percent over the past 20 years. Over the same period, China's share has tripled to almost 4 percent.

(b) India's share of global trade is similar to that of the Philippines, which is an economy six times smaller, according to IMF estimates.

(c) Over the past decade, the FDI flows into India have averaged around 0.5 percent of GDP against 5 percent for China and 5.5 percent for Brazil. FDI inflows to China now exceed US $50 billion annually. Currently, though, India has the second best inflows at US $6 billion.

5.7 Regional Integration

Regional integration is a multidimensional process which not only includes coordination, cooperation, convergence, deep integration initiatives, economic and trade but also political, social, cultural and environmental issues as well. Regional integration can also be defined as a process by which two or more nation-states agree to co-operate and work closely together to achieve peace, stability and wealth. Generally, integration involves one or more written agreements that describe the areas of cooperation in detail, as well as some coordinating bodies representing the countries involved. This co-operation normally begins with economic integration and continues to include political integration.

In regional integration, states enter into a regional agreement to improve regional cooperation through regional institutions and rules. Regional integration as an association of states is based upon location, in a given geographical area, for preserving or promoting. It is an association whose terms are fixed by a treaty or other arrangements. Regional integration makes solving existing conflicts, preventing new ones, enhancing administration, and economic development simpler. It generates larger and stronger markets that incorporate into the world market smoothly. It also helps the countries involved to tackle common challenges effectively. Regional integration is a process by which groups of countries liberalise trade by developing free trade areas or customs unions, which ultimately creates a common market for goods, services, human resources, and capital.

5.7.1 Types of Regional Integration

Regional economic integration has enabled countries to focus on issues that are applicable for development as well as to encourage trade among countries.

There are four main types of regional economic integration –

1. Free trade area

2. Customs union

3. Common market

4. Economic union

5. Political union

1. **Free trade area:** This is the most essential form of economic cooperation. Member countries eliminate all barriers to trade among themselves. They are also free to independently determine trade policies with non-member nations. North American Free Trade Agreement (NAFTA) is an example of it.

2. **Customs union:** This type of regional integration offers economic cooperation in a free-trade zone. Barriers to trade are removed among member countries. The main difference from the free trade area is that members agree to treat trade with non-member countries in the same way. The Gulf Cooperation Council (GCC) is an example.

3. **Common market:** This type allows for the establishment of economically integrated markets among member countries. Trade barriers and restrictions on the movement of labour are eradicated. Similar to customs unions, there is a common trade policy for trade with non-member countries. The main benefit to workers is that they no longer need a visa or work permit to work in another member country of a common market. An example is the Common Market for Eastern and Southern Africa (COMESA).

4. **Economic union:** This type is created when countries enter into an economic agreement to eliminate barriers to trade and implement common economic policies. An example is the European Union (EU).

5. **Political union:** This type is created when two areas or countries come together and form a new country. E.g. In the year 1989, West Germany and East Germany came together to form one country called Germany. The country has become bigger and stronger as a result of the same.

In the past decade, trading blocs with more than one hundred agreements in place have increased. A trade bloc is basically a free-trade zone, formed by one or more tax, tariff, and trade agreements among two or more countries. Some trading blocs have resulted in agreements that have been more substantive than others in creating economic cooperation.

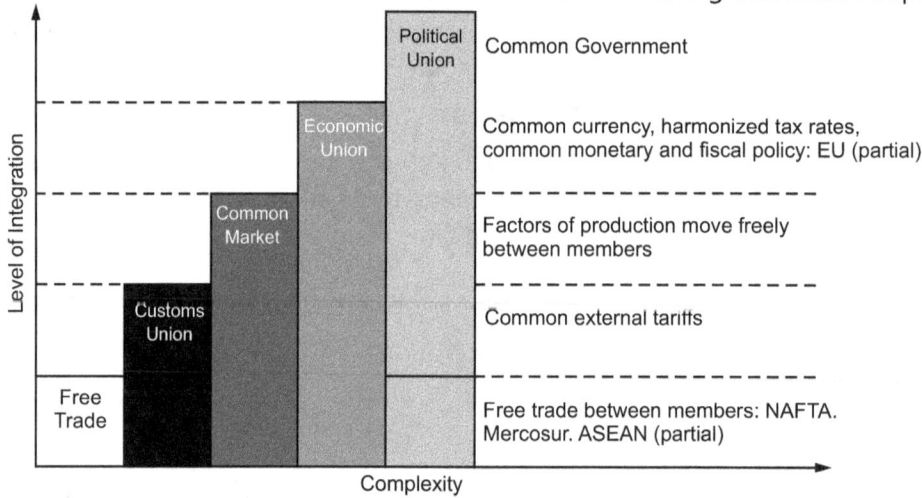

Fig. 5.2

5.7.2 Major Areas of Regional Economic Integration and Cooperation

There are more than one hundred regional trade agreements in place, a figure that is constantly growing, as countries reconfigure their economic and political interests and priorities. With the expansion of the World Trade Organisation (WTO), smaller regional agreements have become outdated. Some of the regional blocs also created side agreements with other regional groups leading to a network of trade agreements and understandings. Free trade is a form of trade policy that permits traders to operate with no intervention from government. The policy allows mutual gains of trading partners from trade of goods and services. Under a free trade policy, prices are a sign of true supply and demand and are the only determinant of resource allocation. Free trade varies from other forms of trade policy, where the allocation of goods and services between trading countries are determined by artificial prices that do not reveal the true nature of supply and demand.

Many states conduct trade policies that are to a lesser or greater degree protectionist. One ubiquitous protectionist policy employed by states comes in the form agricultural subsidies whereby countries try to protect their agricultural industries from outer competition by creating artificial low prices for their agricultural goods.

Some Free Trade Agreements are –

- North American Free Trade Agreement or NAFTA
- European Union or EU
- Association of South East Asian Nations or ASEAN
- Latin American Free Trade Association or LAFTA
- South Asian Free Trade Area or SAFTA

1. NAFTA

The North American Free Trade Agreement (NAFTA) is a RTA for the United States, Canada, and Mexico. It was signed on 17 December 1992 and took effect on 1st January 1994. It aims to abolish barriers to trade within the region and set up a framework for international cooperation. To achieve this, in addition to ordinary rules, it creates some unique rules for investment, intellectual property rights, and competition policy on the trade in goods and services (elimination of tariffs and quantitative restrictions within the region, harmonised rules of origin etc.).

In December 1994, the three NAFTA members reached an agreement with Chile to commence negotiations on its membership in the RTA (a FTA between Canada and Chile took effect in June 1997). During the summit held at roughly the same time, with participation from all thirty-four countries, the agreement was reached to conclude negotiations on the Free Trade Area of the Americas (FTAA). The North American Free Trade Agreement (NAFTA) came into being during a period when free trade and trading blocs were accepted and positively perceived. In 1988, the United States and Canada signed the Canada-United States Free Trade Agreement. Soon, after it was agreed upon and implemented, the United States went ahead to negotiate a similar agreement with Mexico. When Canada asked to be party to any negotiations to preserve its rights under the most-favoured-nation clause (MFN), the negotiations began for NAFTA, which was finally signed in 1992 and implemented in 1994.

The main aim of NAFTA is to encourage trade between Canada, the United States, and Mexico. By reducing tariffs and trade barriers, the countries hope to create a free-trade zone where companies can gain from the transfer of goods. In the 1980s, Mexico had tariffs as high as 100 percent on selective merchandise. Almost all tariffs between Mexico, Canada, and the United States were phased out, over the first decade of the agreement. The rules governing the origin of content are a key to NAFTA. As a free trade agreement, the member countries can set up their own trading rules for non member countries. NAFTA's rules make sure that a foreign exporter cannot sail to the NAFTA country with the lowest tariff for non member countries. NAFTA rules demand that at least 50 percent of the net cost of most products should come from or be incurred in the NAFTA region.

2. EU

The European Union (EU) is an economic and political union of 27 member states, situated primarily in Europe. The EU was established by the Treaty of Maastricht on 1st

November, 1993 on the fundamentals of the pre-existing European Economic Community. With about 500 million citizens, the EU combined produces an estimated 30 percent share of the nominal gross world product. Through a standardised system of laws, the EU has developed a single market which applies in all member states, making sure of the freedom of movement of people, goods, services, and capital. It maintains universal policies on trade, agriculture, fisheries and regional development. 16 member states have already accepted the euro, as a common currency and are known as the Euro zone. Having representation at the WTO, G8 summits, and at the UN, the EU has a restricted role in foreign policy. It has passed legislation in justice and home affairs, including the abolition of passport controls among member states. The EU functions through a hybrid system of supranationalism and intergovernmentalism. In some areas, it relies upon agreement between the member states; otherwise, supranational bodies are allowed to decide without agreement.

The Council of the European Union, the European Council, the European Court of Justice, and the European Central Bank are important institutions and bodies of the EU that creates the European Commission. The European Parliament is elected every five years by member states' citizens, to whom the citizenship of the European Union is guaranteed.

3. ASEAN

The Association of Southeast Asian Nations or ASEAN was established on 8 August 1967 in Bangkok by five original member countries, Indonesia, Malaysia, Philippines, Singapore, and Thailand. Brunei Darussalam joined in 1984, Vietnam in 1995, Lao PDR and Myanmar in 1997, and Cambodia in 1999. Today, the ASEAN region has a population of about 560 million, a total area of 4.5 million square kilometres, a combined gross domestic product of almost US$ 1,100 billion, and a total trade of about US$ 1,400 billion.

According to the ASEAN Declaration states the aims and purposes of the Association are:

(1) To boost economic growth, social progress and cultural development in the region.

(2) To encourage regional peace and stability through enduring respect for justice and the rule of law in the relationship between countries in the region and being loyal to the principles of the United Nations Charter. The ASEAN Community is consists of three pillars, the Political-Security Community, Economic Community and Socio-Cultural Community. Each pillar has its own plan approved at the summit level, and together with the Initiative for ASEAN Integration (IAI) Strategic Framework and IAI Work Plan Phase II (2009-2015), they form the roadmap for and ASEAN Community 2009-2015.

ASEAN demands far greater influence on Asia-Pacific trade, political, and security issues than its members could accomplish individually. This has driven ASEAN's community building efforts. Their work is based mainly on consultation, consensus, and cooperation.

4. LAFTA

The Latin American Free Trade Association (LAFTA), by the 1960 Treaty of Montevideo by Argentina, Brazil, Chile, Mexico, Paraguay, Peru and Uruguay. The aim was to create a common market in Latin America that offered tariff rebates between member nations. LAFTA came into effect on January 2, 1962. When the trade association began, it had seven members with the urge to eliminate all duties and restrictions on the majority of their trade within a twelve year period. By the late 1960s the area of LAFTA had a population of 220 million and manufactured about $90 billion of goods and services yearly. By the same time, it had an average per capita gross national product of $440. The main objective of the LAFTA is to create a free trade zone in Latin America. It should foster mutual regional trade between the member states, as well as with the United States (US) and the European Union. The LAFTA agreement has some limitations too –

(i)   It only refers to goods, not to services.

(ii) It does not include a coordination of policies.

With LAFTA in position, existing productive capacity can be used more productively to supply regional needs. As a result of potential economies, industries could reduce costs through expanded output and regional specialisation and attract new investment that took place due to the emerging regional market area.

5.   SAFTA

South Asian Free Trade Area is an agreement reached at the 12th SAARC summit at Islamabad on 6st January 2004. SAFTA came into existence on 1st January 2006. It generated a framework for the creation of a free trade area covering India, Pakistan, Nepal, Sri Lanka, Bangladesh, Bhutan and the Maldives. The seven foreign ministers of the region signed a framework agreement on SAFTA with zero customs duty on the trade of all goods by end 2016. SAFTA requires the developing countries in South Asia, to bring their duties down to zero in a series of yearly cuts. The least developed nations in South Asia consisting of Nepal, Bhutan, Bangladesh and Maldives have an additional three years to decrease tariffs to zero.

SAFTA is governed by the provisions of this agreement and also by the rules, regulations, decisions, understandings and protocols to be agreed upon within its framework by the Contracting States. The contracting states confirm their existing rights and obligations with respect to each other under Marrakesh Agreement Establishing the World Trade Organisation and other Treaties/Agreements to which such contracting states are signatories. SAFTA is based and applied on the principles of overall reciprocity and mutuality of advantages so as to fairly benefit all contracting states, considering their respective levels of economic and industrial development, the pattern of their external trade and tariff policies and systems. SAFTA involves the free movement of goods, among countries through, the elimination of tariffs, para tariffs and non-tariff restrictions on the movement of goods. SAFTA involves adoption of trade facilitation and the progressive harmonisation of legislations by the contracting states in the relevant areas. The special needs of the Least Developed Contracting States are clearly recognised by adopting concrete preferential measures in their favour on a non-reciprocal basis.

6.   There are many other agreements like MERCOSUR, SACU, Arab Maghreb Union, GCC, etc. which are also operational and working for the betterment of their respective countries.

Points to Remember

- India has progressively established and maintained good bilateral treaties with more and more countries like, USA, Japan, EU, ASEAN, etc., and thereby increasing its trade and commerce and investment to and from these countries.

- India's emergence as a fast-growing trillion-plus dollar economy has enormous significance for the rest of the world.

- Population Explosion
  1. Poverty
  2. Rural Urban Divide
  3. Inflation
  4. Inequality

- Inflation in India, fuelled by rising wages, property prices and food prices is an increasing problem.

- In the global economic setting, India ranks among the well-known emerging markets. With the introduction of emerging market in 1990, India has prospered and the Indian economy has enhanced to a greater extent.

- The Indian economy presents a mixed picture of problems and opportunities.

- India is among the poorest countries of the world in terms of per capita income. India produces only about 1.6 percent of the world GDP with almost 17 percent of the world population.

- India ranks second in terms of the size of the population and ranks seventh in terms of area. With around 2.4 percent of the total area, India shelters about 17 percent of the population of the world.

- With a lift in exports and moderation in imports, trade deficit contracted considerably during the year as compared to that in the previous year. It was during 2013-14 that India's external sector witnessed important progress.

- In 2013-14, the manufacturing sector exports of major product groups like 'engineering goods', 'leather and manufacture', 'chemicals and related products', 'textile and textile products' and 'handicrafts' improved drastically.

- Decline in India's imports from US, Japan, Switzerland, and the OPEC countries were further outstanding.

- Trade credit is a crucial component of trade. According to a WTO study, a 1 percent increase in trade credit of a country leads to a 0.4 percent increase in real imports of that country.

- India's merchandise exports share in world exports improved from 0.5 percent in 1990 to only 1.7 percent in 2013, whereas China's share increased from 1.8 percent to 11.8 percent during the same period.

- There are many overlapping export promotion schemes with many focus markets and focus products with items and markets getting added each year in the foreign trade policy.

- Another major challenge is to promote greater trade facilitation by removing the delays and high costs on account of procedural and documentation factors, besides infrastructure bottlenecks.
- Rapid growth and poverty reduction in China, India, and other countries that were poor twenty years ago, has been a positive aspect of Liberalisation, Privatisation and Globalisation (LPG).
- Liberalisation signifies reducing unnecessary restrictions and controls on business units forced by government. It basically means procedural simplification and comforting trade industry from unnecessary bureaucratic hurdles.
- Prior to liberalisation, under the provisions of old policy, at the time of granting licence, government used to fix maximum limit of production capacity. No industry can manufacture beyond this limit. Now, with liberalisation, this limit has been removed so as to enable the industry to take full advantage of large-scale production.
- FERA act involves several checks and controls on transactions involving foreign exchange. Following the economic liberalisation and changed attitude of government towards foreign capital, FERA was replaced with Foreign Exchange Management Act – FEMA.
- Liberalisation has encouraged globalisation. The inflow of foreign investment has increased with liberalisation.
- Due to liberalisation, many domestic and foreign enterprises have started business operations in India. It has increased the competition in the market.
- Liberalisation has encouraged the import of capital intensive technology. It has promoted automation, computerisation and mechanisation of industrial activities in the economy, which has in result, highlighted the problem of unemployment.
- Globalisation is connecting the economy of a nation with the economies of other nations through free trade, free mobility of capital and labour, etc. It also involves attracting multinational corporations to invest in India.
- Globalisation has encouraged collaboration of foreign companies with many Indian companies. Globalisation has intensified interdependence and competition between economies in the world market.
- Regional integration is a multidimensional process which not only includes coordination, cooperation, convergence, deep integration initiatives, economic and trade but also political, social, cultural and environmental issues as well.
- There are four main types of regional economic integration. They are as follows –
  1. Free trade area
  2. Customs union
  3. Common market
  4. Economic union
- The North American Free Trade Agreement (NAFTA) is a RTA for the United States, Canada, and Mexico. It was signed on 17th December 1992 and took effect on

1st January 1994. It aims to abolish barriers to trade within the region and set up a framework for international cooperation.

- The Association of Southeast Asian Nations or ASEAN was established on 8th August 1967 in Bangkok by five original member countries, Indonesia, Malaysia, Philippines, Singapore, and Thailand.
- The European Union (EU) is an economic and political union of 27 member states, situated primarily in Europe. The EU was established by the Treaty of Maastricht on 1st November, 1993 on the fundamentals of the pre-existing European Economic Community.
- Some Free Trade Agreements:
  1. North American Free Trade Agreement or NAFTA
  2. European Union or EU
  3. Association of South East Asian Nations or ASEAN
  4. Latin American Free Trade Association or LAFTA
  5. South Asian Free Trade Area or SAFTA
  6. MERCOSUR
  7. SACU
  8. Arab Maghreb Union
  9. GCC, etc.

Questions for Discussion

1. Define the challenges faced by the Indian economy.
2. Elaborate on India as an emerging market.
3. Explain the place of India in the global trade.
4. Write short notes on:
   (a) Import
   (b) Export
   (c) Direction of trade
5. List the challenges faced by India in the trade sector.
6. Define liberalisation.
7. State the measures taken for liberalisation.
8. Contrast the advantages and disadvantages of liberalisation.
9. Summarise the measures adopted for globalisation of Indian economy.
10. Explain the advantages and disadvantages of globalisation.
11. Highlight the impact of globalisation on the Indian economy.
12. Define regional integration.
13. What are the main types of regional integration?
14. Define free trade agreement and its types.

Chapter 6...

Case Studies in Economic and Business Environment in the Global Economy

Contents ...

6.1   India and Europe

    6.1.1 Introduction

    6.1.2 Political Exchange

    6.1.3 Parliamentary Interaction

    6.1.4 Economic and Commercial Relations

    6.1.5 Cultural Cooperation

    6.1.6 India's Agricultural Trade Relations with Europe

    6.1.5 Bilateral Trade Relations

    6.1.6 Trade with India

    6.1.7 Foreign Investment

6.2 India and Association of Southeast Asian Nations [ASEAN]

    6.2.1 Introduction

    6.2.3 Political Relations and Security

    6.2.4 Economic Cooperation

    6.2.5 Social and Cultural Cooperation

    6.2.6 Major Commodities of Export and Import – ASEAN

    6.2.7 ASEAN Free Trade

6.3 India and North America

    6.3.1 Introduction

    6.3.2 India-North America Bilateral Relation

    6.3.3 Trade and Economic Relations

    6.3.4 Country Synopsis

    6.3.5 Science and Technology (S & T)

6.3.6 Energy and Climate Change

6.3.7 Defence Cooperation

6.3.8 India and North America Multi-Fibre Agreement

6.3.9 Prospect for further India-U.S. Economic Cooperation

- Points to Remember
- Questions for Discussion

Learning Objectives ...

- To understand the economic relation between India and Europe
- To describe the trade relations between India and Europe
- To discuss the social and cultural cooperation between India and Southeast Asian nations
- To highlight the export and import commodities between India and ASEAN
- To define ASEAN free trade
- To illustrate the bilateral relation between India and North America
- To understand the trade and economic relation between India and North America
- To describe the India and North America Multi Fibre Agreement

6.1 India and Europe

6.1.1 Introduction

India-EU relations date to the early 1960s, with India being amongst the first countries to establish diplomatic relations with the European Economic Community. A cooperation agreement signed in 1994 took the bilateral relationship beyond trade and economic cooperation. At the 5th India-EU Summit at The Hague in 2004, the relationship was upgraded to a 'Strategic Partnership'. The two sides adopted a Joint Action Plan in 2005 provided for strengthening dialogue and consultation mechanisms in the political and economic spheres, enhancing trade and investment, and bringing people and cultures together. The EU and India are committed to further increase their trade flows in goods and services as well as bilateral investment and access to public procurement through the Free Trade Agreement negotiations that were launched in 2007. Substantial progress has been made so far, and key areas that need to be further discussed include improved market access for some goods and services, government procurement and geographical indications, and sustainable development.

The European countries have been important trade partners with India over the years. The volume of total trade between the two regions has grown exponentially over the years, even during the adverse global economic conditions at some points in time. In addition to historically strong growth in the last decade, it is believed that there is still a huge potential for further growth. It is aimed at strengthening India's engagement with Europe through two-way trade and investment and to develop brand India in the European region. A critical analysis of economies reveals that the region has significant expertise in industries like chemicals, pharmaceuticals, automobile, machinery, construction and mechanical and engineering goods. The European economies can certainly benefit from the rising demand for manufactured goods in India which can translate into increased trade and investment in the industrial sector. Similarly, with a wide agricultural base, India can focus on manufacturing agricultural and primary goods including raw materials for manufacturing businesses. The European region offers a host of incentives in the form of tax exemptions, greater market access as well as opening up of sectors for foreign investments. These incentives focus on priority sectors such as R&D, infrastructure, construction, transport, communication, energy and in general, aim at improving services sector and attract more Greenfield investments in the future. India can definitely benefit directly and indirectly from these developments. The requirement of a well-structured IT industry as a base for various European industries can only increase its demand in the future, and this is where India's expertise in the services sector might be helpful.

Our industry specific analysis focuses on determining the relative comparative advantage enjoyed by the Indian industry vis-a-vis that of the European trading partners. The basis for this analysis stems from the fundamentals of trade theory, which concludes that free trade will result in specialisation in certain products/industries in which the country enjoys a comparative advantage and will end up producing and exporting more products from these industries. The following Indian industries enjoy a greater competitive advantage relative to their counterparts in the European countries:

- Agricultural products like sugar, coffee, spices etc.
- Pearls and precious stones
- Textiles
- Minerals
- Computer and information industry

On the other hand, the following industries in Europe enjoy a larger competitive advantage than the counterparts in India:

- Machinery
- Automobile
- Pharmaceuticals
- Insurance and Financial services
- Travel and Transport of certain industries like Chemicals, Metallic manufacturing of iron/steel.

A more fruitful partnership can evolve between the two regions with India exporting agricultural goods and importing machinery and technical know-how in mechanised farming, a well-established practice in the European economies, to increase its own productivity. Similarly, despite at a comparative disadvantage in manufacturing industry, India can still gain from increased association with European economies in these industries by gaining in terms of intangible benefits, particularly, technical know-how. In the services sector, computer and information industry is central to any set-up and with most of the European economies trying to invest in heavy industries such as infrastructure, communications, retail and R&D, there are many opportunities for Indian exporters. The overall analysis broadly depicts the fact that the Indian economy as a whole has a strong hold on the primary sector industries and the services industry, with the European economies more dominant in the industrial and manufacturing sectors. A closer look at the economic structure, government policies and future plans of these economies, however, show that both the regions have tremendous opportunities to enhance their trade and investment relations and benefit significantly from enhanced trade and investment activity.

6.1.2 Political Exchange

The first India-EU Summit took place in Lisbon in June 2000 and marked a watershed in the evolution of the relationship. Since then, twelve annual summits have been held, the last one in New Delhi on 10 February 2012. The 12th summit was the first summit to be held in India after the entry into force of the Lisbon Treaty. Ex-Prime Minister, Shri. Manmohan Singh led the Indian delegation while the EU was represented by Mr. Herman Van Rompuy, President of the European Council and Mr. Jose Manuel Barroso, President of the European Commission. The two sides reviewed bilateral relations as well as exchanged views on regional and global issues. The leaders expressed satisfaction at the intensification of negotiations on the Bilateral Trade and Investment Agreement, welcomed the enhanced cooperation in the field of security, and called for finalisation of an agreement on R&D cooperation in the peaceful use of nuclear energy. The two sides also signed a Memorandum of Understanding on Statistics and issued Joint Declarations on Research and Innovation Cooperation and Enhanced Cooperation in Energy. The 13th summit is expected to be held in Brussels in 2013.

India and the EU also interact regularly at the Foreign Ministers level. The 23rd India-EU Ministerial Meeting took place in Brussels on 30 January 2013. External Affairs Minister, Shri. Salman Khurshid led the Indian delegation while the EU side was led by High Representative for Foreign Affairs and Security Policy, Baroness Catherine Ashton. Bilateral relations as well as international and regional issues of mutual interest were discussed at the meeting. Both sides have recently instituted Foreign Policy Consultations at the level of Secretaries. The first meeting took place in New Delhi on 15th November 2011, followed by a second round in Brussels on 20th July 2012. A Security Dialogue envisaged under the Joint Action Plan is held annually since May 2006. The sixth round was held in Brussels on

25th October 2012. A bilateral Joint Working Group on Counter-Terrorism reports to the Security Dialogue, as do the dialogues on Cyber-Security and Counter-Piracy. Both sides have recently agreed to the institution of a dialogue on nuclear proliferation and disarmament as well under the umbrella of the Security Dialogue. An annual India-EU Ad-hoc Dialogue on Human Rights is held in New Delhi and there is also a Delhi-based Joint Working Group on Consular Issues. In addition, a high-level dialogue on Migration and Mobility has been instituted at Secretary level between the Ministry of Overseas Indian Affairs and DG Home Affairs, the third round of which took place in New Delhi on 2nd July 2012.

6.1.3 Parliamentary Interaction

A delegation for relations with India (D-IN) was officially constituted in the European Parliament (EP) in 2007. This was done to pursue relations with India. The ambassador of India, on 19th March 2014, exchanged views with MEPs on issues of mutual interest. Selected members also pay an orientation visit to India once a year. Such a visit last took place from 29th April to 3rd May in 2013. In May 2014, a new D-IN consisting of 43 members drawn from different political groups in accordance with their numerical strength in the EP has been formed.

6.1.4 Economic and Commercial Relations

The EU as a bloc of 28 countries is India's largest regional trading partner, while India was the EU's 10th largest trading partner in 2013. Bilateral trade in goods recorded a decline of −4.09 percent in 2013, being valued at €72.70 billion as compared to €75.80 billion in 2012. In 2013, Indian exports to the EU amounted to €36.8 billion as compared to €37.33 billion in 2012, showing a decline of 1.42 percent. India's imports from EU stood at €35.9 billion in 2013 as compared to €38.47 billion in 2012, showing a decline of 6.68 percent.

Bilateral trade in services was €23.9 billion in 2013 as compared to €22.5 billion in 2012. Consequently, reflecting a yearly growth of 6.22 percent. India's services exports to the EU were valued at €1.22 billion and Indian services imports from the EU were valued at €12.70 billion, reflecting a trade balance which continues to be vaguely in favour of the EU by €1.48 billion in 2013 as against €5 billion in 2012.

The EU is one of the major sources of Foreign Direct Investment (FDI) for India. In 2013, FDI inflows from the EU to India were €5.48 billion in 2012 and €3.2 billion. Indian investments in the EU 28 were €0.4 billion in 2013. In 2013, the most significant EU countries for FDI inflows into India were the UK and Germany (with both investing €0.9 billion each), followed by Italy (€0.6 billion) and Belgium (€0.2 billion).

India and the EU are in the process of negotiating a bilateral broad-based Trade and Investment Agreement (BTIA) that will significantly improve the commercial relationship once applied.

The India-EU Joint Commission, dealing with economic and commercial issues meets yearly for Economic and Development Cooperation. The last Joint Commission meeting at the level of Secretaries was held in June 2014 in New Delhi and the last meetings of the Sub-Commissions on Economic Cooperation and Trade were held in Brussels in March 2014, while the Sub Commission on Development Cooperation met in June 2014, in New Delhi.

Additionally, there are Joint Workings Groups on textiles and clothing, agriculture and marine products, sanitary and phytosanitary issues, pharmaceuticals and biotechnology (SPS/TBT) and finally food processing industries, which meet frequently to improve sector-specific cooperation.

A macroeconomic dialogue at secretary level along with a dialogue on financial services regulations has also been introduced and takes place yearly. The 7th India-EU macro-economic dialogue was held in June 2014 in New Delhi.

Collaboration in the field of Science and Technology is also moving rapidly. The India-EU Science and Technology Steering Committee meet yearly in order to discuss cooperation in this field. It was last held in October 2013 in Brussels. A meeting of the Co-chairs of the India-EU/Member-States Group of Senior Officials (GSO) took place in Brussels in June 2013, followed by the opening meeting of the GSO in Brussels in October 2013. A dialogue on Information and Communications Technology has also been introduced, with the last meeting taking place in September 2013 in Brussels, which incorporated a business dialogue.

An Energy Panel was set up by India and the EU in 2005 to enhance cooperation in the critical sector of energy and energy security. The last meeting of the panel was held in Brussels in 27th March 2014 where the Secretary (West) led the Indian delegation. Separate sub-groups have been formed under the panel dealing with coal and clean coal conversion technologies, energy efficiency and renewable energy, etc. The Joint Working Group on Clean Coal Technologies last met in June 2013 in Brussels and the India-EU Coal Working Group had its eighth meeting in November 2013 in Chennai.

As envisioned in the Joint Action Plan, a Joint Working Group on environment dealing with prevention of pollution, waste minimisation, protection of biological diversity, sustainable forest management, environmental education, etc. has been formed and held its eighth meeting in Brussels in April 2014. An Environmental Forum bringing together academia, business, and civil society for an exchange of views on specific environmental issues also meets yearly.

6.1.5 Cultural Cooperation

The India-EU forum has surfaced as an important Track II forum for a conversation among policy analysts on both sides. It is led by the Paris-based European Union Institute for Security Studies and the Indian Council of World Affairs that includes contribution from academics, think-tanks and even policy makers on the EU side. The fifth India-EU Forum was together organised by ICVIVA and EUISS in collaboration with the Spanish think-tank FRIDE in April 2014 in New Delhi.

The framework of India-EU cooperation in the fields of education and culture is granted by three Joint Declarations signed in latest years covering cooperation in the fields of Education and Training, Multilingualism and Culture. The first Senior Officials Meetings on Education and Multilingualism took place at Secretary Level in May 2011 in Brussels, followed by a second round in April 2013 in New Delhi. The Policy Dialogue on Culture was further launched at Secretary Level in April 2013 in New Delhi.

The EU leadership also participated enthusiastically in the Europalia-India festival inaugurated in Brussels in October 2013 by President Pranab Mukherjee and King Philippe of Belgium. The President of the European Council, Herman Van Rompuy attended the introductory ceremony of the festival and addressed the crowd. Commission President Jose Manuel Barosso inaugurated the second major exhibition of the festival called 'Indomania' on 15th October 2013.

6.1.6 India's Agricultural Trade Relations with Europe

In the year 2013-2014, India's total export of agricultural commodities to EU was of the order of U.S. $4197.4 million. During this period, India's major agricultural exports were shrimps and prawns, cashew nuts, grapes, coffee, rice, castor oil, and soya oil meals. During the same period, the agricultural import from EU was of the order of U.S. $608.52 million. India's major imports were whiskies, ethyl alcohol, food preparations and grounding used in animal feeding.

The issues relating to trade in agriculture and marine products are discussed under the support of India – EU Joint Working Group (JWG) on Agriculture and Marine products. The 7th Meeting of India – EU JWG on Agriculture and Marine Products was held on 17th October 2013.

The following important issues were discussed in the last meeting of JGW –

- Certification of organic products by EU.
- Revocation of equivalence for Indian processed food products (organic).
- Varieties of basmati rice in India.
- Tuna fish harvesting in India.

Percent share of top commodity in agri export and import between two countries

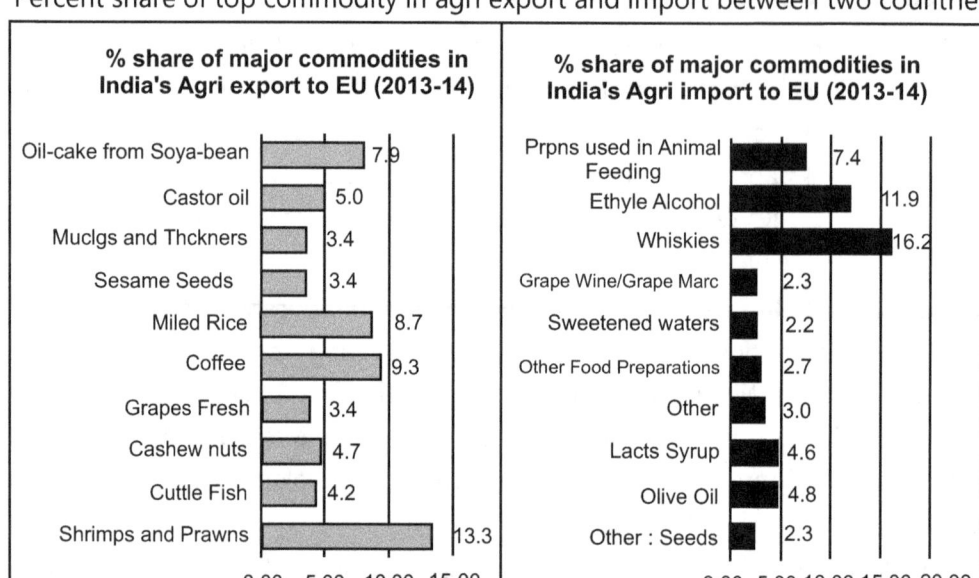

Fig 6.1

India-EU Agriculture Trade Trend

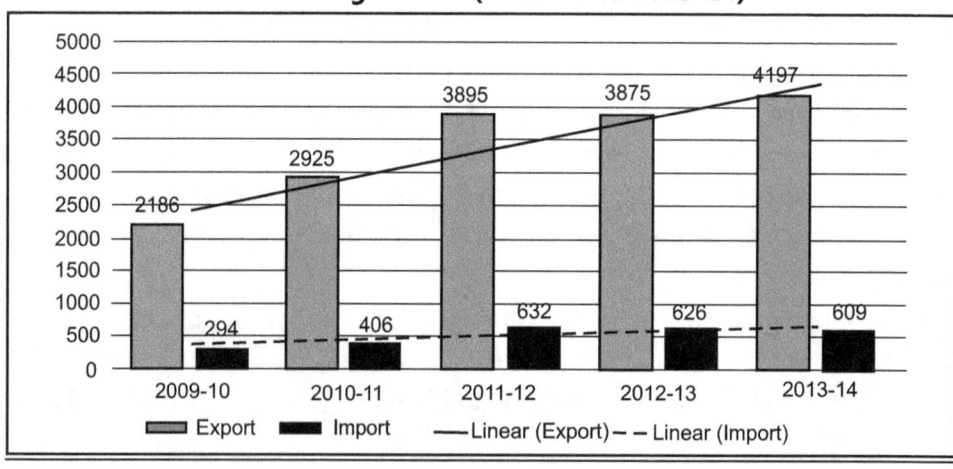

Fig 6.2

India's agriculture export to EU showed a growing trend from 2009-10 to 2013-14, while, EU's share in India's total global agriculture import is 3.60 percent in 2013-14.

Percent share of global agri export and import

- India's share in EU total agriculture import is 0.76 percent (2013). While, EU's share in India's total global agriculture import is 3.60 percent in 2013-14.

Average agriculture tariff

- Average agriculture tariff rate of India and EU are 33.5 percent and 13.2 percent respectively.

Table 6.1: India's top agri exports to EU

(U.S. $ Million)

Sr. No.	HS Code	Commodity	2012-2013	2013-2014
1	30617	OTHER SHRIMPS AND PRAWNS: FROZEN		559.39
2	30749	CUTTLE FISH AND SQUIDS LIVE/ FRESH/CHILLED	181.93	176.82
3	80132	CASHEW NUTS FRESH/DRIED SHELLED	178.8	196.88
4	80610	GRAPES FRESH	102.76	144.2
5	90111	COFFEE NEITHER ROASTED FOR DECAFFEINATED	431.2	389.83
6	100630	SEMI-WHOLLY MILLED RICE WHEN POLISHED/GLAZED	385.77	363.27
7	120740	SESAME SEEDS WHEN BROKEN	118.74	142.62
8	130232	MUCILAGES AND THICKENERS WHEN MODIFIED DERIVED FROM LOCUSTS BEAN SEEDS/GUAR SEEDS	177.16	144.51
9	151530	CASTOR OIL AND ITS FRACTIONS	212.45	211.45
10	230400	OIL-CAKE AND OTHER SOLID RESIDUE WHEN GRINDED IN PELLET FORM OBTAINED FROM SOYA-BEAN OIL EXTRACTION	262.95	332.6
		India's total agri exports to EU	**3875.11**	**4197.1**

Table 6.2: India's top agri exports to EU

(U.S. $ Million)

Sr. No.	HS Code	Commodity	2012-2013	2013-2014
1	121190	Other seeds	9.81	14.01
2	150990	Other olive oil and its fractions (excluding virgin)	25.36	29.03
3	170211	Lactulose and Lactulose syrup containing 99 percent or more lactulose calculated on the dry matter	23.19	28.09
4	180690	Other	20.32	28.09
5	210690	Other food preparations	16.63	16.54
6	220290	Other sweetened flavoured waters	10.35	13.57
7	220820	Sprites obtained by distilling grape wine/grape marc	10.8	14.08
8	220830	Whiskies	82.26	98.72
9	220890	Other undenatured ethyl alcohol	66.81	72.42
10	230990	Other preparations of a kind used in animal feeding	43.02	45.23
		India's total agri imports from EU	**625.73**	**608.52**

6.1.5 Bilateral Trade Relations

The EU and India are important trading partners and founding members of the World Trade Organisation (WTO) multilateral trading system. The Commission is facilitating EU trade with India by seeking to ensure that progress is made in the Doha Development Agenda (DDA) and by co-operating at expert level in order to remove existing trade barriers between the two trading partners and preventing new ones from emerging. During their Summit of 7th September 2005, the EU and India adopted the India-EU Strategic Partnership Joint Action Plan and agreed to take positive steps to further increase bilateral trade and economic cooperation and to tackle barriers to trade and investment. Specifically, they agreed to set up a High Level Trade Group to study and explore ways and means to deepen and widen their bilateral trade and investment relationship and agreed to cooperate on a number of other trade-related issues.

The High Level Trade Group reported to the 7th EU-India Summit in Helsinki on 13th October 2006, in recommending that an expanded trade partnership be developed through the negotiation of a broad-based trade and investment agreement. The EU-India

Summit endorsed the recommendations of the High Level Trade Group in agreeing that both sides move towards negotiations for such an agreement.

Following that agreement, the Council adopted a negotiating Directive for a Free Trade Agreement (FTA) with India on 23rd April 2007 (together with negotiating Directives for an EU-ASEAN and an EU-Korea FTA). Negotiations for this EU-India FTA were launched on 28th/29th June 2007 in Brussels. Further negotiating rounds are planned to take place later this year in both Delhi and Brussels. We expect the FTA to be fully WTO compatible, ambitious and comprehensive covering not only trade in goods and services, but also investment and paying special attention to non-tariff barriers, and to rules and regulations such as Intellectual Property Rights, competition, government procurement, and transparency.

The policy of moving towards an FTA with India reflects the EU's Global Europe strategy, which suggests a new generation of competitiveness-driven FTAs based primarily on economic criteria (market potential, protection against EU interests, FTAs/ongoing negotiations with EU competitors). India meets all these criteria. It constitutes a sizeable market, its GDP growth rate is between 8 percent and 10 percent and substantial tariff and non-tariff barriers hinder trade with the EU.

6.1.6 Trade with India

The graph in figure 6.3 represents the total trade between the two regions, which has grown exponentially through the years. The last decade saw a steep growth in trade activities with trade rising from U.S. $3.6 billion in 2000-01 to $37.75 billion in 2012-13. There has been a steady rise in trade activities involving the two regions, which was not interrupted even during the financial crisis, when global trade became unpleasant. On the other hand, the rise in trade has been irregular with Indian imports greatly outweighing its exports. Imports as compared to the exports by India have grown at a much higher pace, particularly in the last three years (2008-09 to 2012-13) with imports growing at a CAGR of 25.8 percent as compared to an export CAGR growth of 11.2 percent. Consequently, trade in the post-crisis era has seen a distinctive trend among the two regions with Indian imports greatly dominating trade.

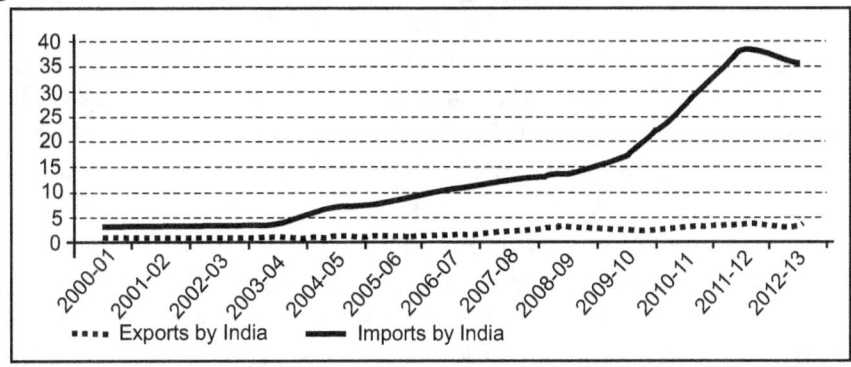

Fig. 6.3

The below figure 6.4 represents a detailed picture of the trade between the two regions. It is clear that Switzerland followed by Austria dominates the Indian imports, whereas, Croatia and Slovenia are at the other end of the spectrum being favourable Indian export destinations among the CE10 economies. Nations like Bulgaria, Hungary, Poland and Slovakia fall in the middle crust with balanced exports and imports. Many fiscal policies of the CE10 economies are in agreement with the EU policies with a higher degree of trade liberalisation and liberal investment policies. This has significantly helped the region to improve trade and investment activities with India.

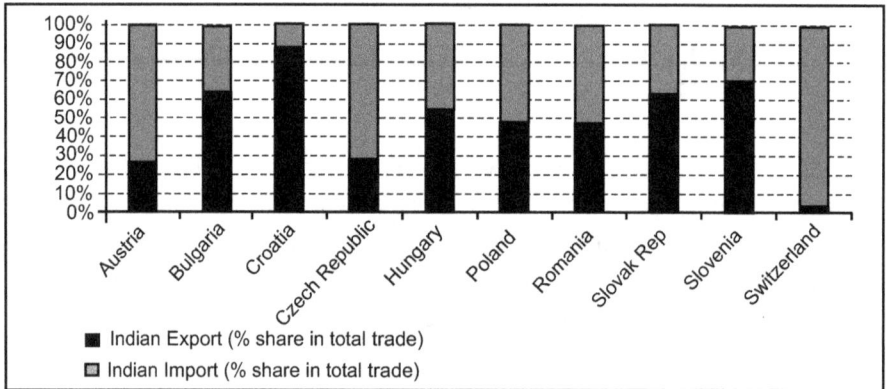

Fig. 6.4

6.1.7 Foreign Investment

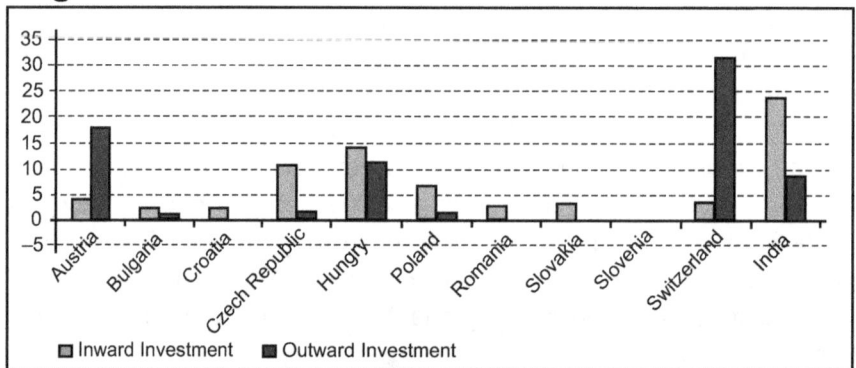

Fig. 6.5

The above figure 6.5 elaborates the investment activity in the two regions in 2011-12. As it is clearly evident in the graph, Switzerland and Austria lead the pack along with India, as far as total FDI investment are considered. Foreign investments of Switzerland and Austria are dominated by the outflow of direct investments, while, Indian foreign investments are dominated by inflow of direct investments. With comparatively stable growth rates, durable economic structure and future growth opportunities, India has always been a striking destination of FDI in varied sectors like services, construction, telecommunication, pharmaceuticals, and consumer goods. With the recent slew of measures taken, more sectors were opened up for foreign investment; India is likely to remain an important destination for global investments.

In recent years, India has also witnessed a considerable uptrend in outward FDI with equity investment resting at U.S. $7.1 billion in 2012-13. India showed a steady performance even in the toughest of times and thus, is looked upon as a strategic international player and an important source of funds for other economies. By 2024, India is expected to be the principal source of emerging market. FDI activity in the CE10 region, other than Switzerland and Austria, has been low, with the dominance of Poland. However, when compared to the rest of Europe, the FDI activity in Europe is relatively high and more essentially consistent and stable. Their capability to remain an attractive destination for FDI even during the Euro crisis, with a constant inflow of investors, sets the Europe region apart from the rest of Europe. The common perception of high yields and abating risk due to moderately stable financial institutions has been luring foreign investment into the region. The region has some investment-friendly policies, which are in accord with the larger policy framework of the EU. This has helped in increasing investment activities in the region. With extra focus on sectors like infrastructure, Greenfield investments, energy, automotive industry, manufacturing and research and development (R&D) projects, the Europe economies are expected to constantly attract FDI in future.

Central European Investments into India from India

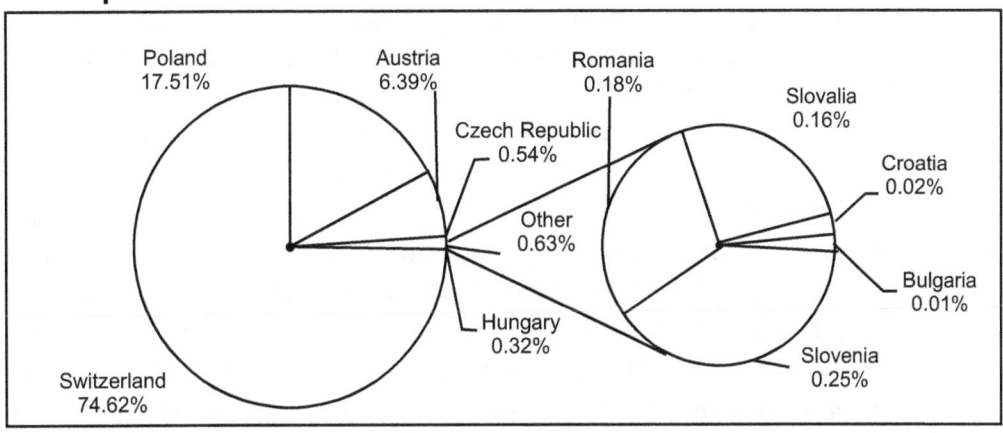

Fig. 6.6: Central European Investment into India (Country-wise percent)

The above figure 6.6 describes the cumulative inflow of FDI into India from April 2000 to October 2013. As is visible in the figure, a huge portion of the FDI inflow is from Switzerland with a contribution close to 75 percent followed by Poland with an input of close to 18 percent – India and Switzerland share close ties, with more than 150 companies investing in India to the tune of 172 billion Swiss Francs and employing over 60,000 workers. Investment from Switzerland crosses over a wide range of sectors such as engineering, chemicals, pharmaceuticals, tourism, financial and logistics services, plus industrial equipment.

Among the other CE10 economies, both Austria and Poland share a favourable atmosphere for investments with India. In India, there are about 500 Austrian companies belonging to various different sectors such as infrastructure, engineering, automotive, and energy. On the whole, since 2000, the inflow of investments from CE10 economies comprise less than 2 percent of the total FDI attracted by India. This indicates that there is further possibility of investments into India from Central European countries.

During the financial year 2012-13, India had invested U.S. $231 million in the Central European countries with major Indian companies investing in Europe including Arcelor Mittal, Videocon, Escorts Ltd., Strides Arcolab, Reliance Industries, Ranbaxy, Essel Propack, Zensar Technologies Ltd., Tata Consultancy Services, HCL Technologies and Infosys. Out of these investments, Switzerland has landed equity investments of U.S. $228 million.

6.2 India and Association of Southeast Asian Nations [ASEAN]

6.2.1 Introduction

ASEAN was founded on August 8th, 1967. ASEAN or Association of Southeast Asian Nations was formed with Malaysia, Philippines, Indonesia, Thailand and Singapore. These five countries were the original members. Several other countries followed suit and became members of ASEAN. They were Brunei Darussalam (January 8th, 1984), Cambodia (April 30th 1999), Myanmar (July, 23rd 1997), Lao PDR (July, 23rd 1997) and Vietnam (July, 28th, 1995). India-ASEAN relations, as they exist today, are in some ways, a reconfiguration of age old ties which is 2,000 years old. Only the modes of trade have changed. Now, countries are using tech-oriented routes instead of the silk route which was used in older days. ASEAN, the latest version of what was the Asian trade network ages ago, is an effort to establish cooperation in the economic, social, cultural, technical, educational and other fields among its member countries, namely Indonesia, Malaysia, Philippines, Singapore, Thailand, Brunei Darussalam, Vietnam, Laos, Myanmar and Cambodia.

Since independence, India has shared a close and a mutual relationship with ASEAN countries. Mutual interest led ASEAN to invite India in becoming its full dialogue partner during the fifth ASEAN summit in 1995 in Bangkok. Also, in 1996, India became a member of the ASEAN Regional Forum (ARF). The relationship was further elevated with the organising of the ASEAN-India Summit in 2002 in Phnom Penh. All these happened in a decade that signifies the importance of the dialogue partnership to ASEAN and India and the growth made in the cooperation. In October 2009, India signed a Free Trade Agreement (FTA) with the ASEAN members in Thailand. Under the ASEAN-India FTA, the ASEAN member countries and India will lift import tariffs on more than 80 percent of traded goods between 2013 and 2016. Moreover, in 2016, tariffs on sensitive goods will be reduced to 5 percent, while maintaining tariffs up to 489 items of very sensitive products.

Presently, India and ASEAN countries are negotiating Agreements on Trade in Services and Investment. The services negotiations are being conducted on a request-offer basis, where both sides make requests for the openings they hunt for and offers, based on the requests, are made by the receiving country. India has made requests in areas like teaching, nursing, architecture, chartered accountancy, and medicine. India is also keen on increasing its telecom, IT, tourism, and banking network in the ASEAN countries.

6.2.3 Political Relations and Security

The collaboration has exceeded the sphere of functional cooperation to cover political and security dimensions, since the time India became a Dialogue Partner of ASEAN. Under the ASEAN-India Dialogue Relations, India participates in a series of consultative meetings with ASEAN that include summit, ministerial meetings, senior officials meetings, meetings at experts level, and through dialogue and cooperation frameworks initiated by ASEAN, like the ASEAN Regional Forum (ARF), the Post Ministerial Conference (PMC) 10+1, the East Asia Summit (EAS), Mekong-Ganga Cooperation and Bengal Initiative for Multisectoral Technical and Economic Cooperation (BIMSTEC) that help contribute to the enhancement of the regional dialogue, increasing regional integration. In indicating its commitment and shared interest to assure peace, security, stability, and development in Southeast Asia, India agreed to the Treaty of Amity and Cooperation in Southeast Asia (TAC) on 8th October, 2003 during the 2nd ASEAN-India Summit in Bali, Indonesia. Simultaneously, ASEAN and India signed a Joint Declaration for Cooperation in combating international terrorism, symbolising concrete plan in setting up cooperation in the struggle against terrorism.

As a sign of the interest of ASEAN and India to strengthen their engagement, the ASEAN-India Partnership for peace, progress and shared prosperity, which sets out the roadmap for long-term ASEAN-India engagement, was signed at the 3rd ASEAN-India Summit on 30th November 2004 in Vientiane, Lao PDR. To execute partnership, a plan of action (2004-2010) was also developed. The summit also agreed on a new and more improved phase of the plan of action in order to implement the said partnership to grab the opportunities and overcome the challenges arising from global financial crisis and developing political and economic landscape. Consequently, the new ASEAN-India Plan of Action for 2010-2015 was developed and accepted by the leaders at the 8th ASEAN-India Summit in October 2010 in Hanoi. Following the access into force of the ASEAN Charter and based on the strong foundation of the ASEAN-India Dialogue Relations, India has accredited its Ambassador to ASEAN based in Jakarta, mainly to work personally with the Committee of Permanent Representatives to ASEAN (CPR) and the ASEAN Secretariat. At the 10th ASEAN-India Summit in Bandar Seri Begawan on 9th October 2012, India announced its aim to set up a separate Diplomatic Mission to ASEAN with a Resident Ambassador as an illustration of the intensification of the ASEAN-India Strategic Partnership.

On 20th December 2012, ASEAN and India marked the 20th anniversary of their Dialogue Relations with a Commemorative Summit held in India. Many commemorative activities were carried out to signify the growth and extent of the Dialogue Partnership. In this relation, the ASEAN-India Eminent Persons group (EPG) was established to consider ASEAN-India associations over the past 20 years, explore ways to broaden and deepen existing cooperation among ASEAN and India, plus recommend measures to further support ASEAN-India relations in the future, taking into account existing documents adopted by both sides, as well as key ASEAN documents, particularly the ASEAN Charter, roadmap for an ASEAN community, the three blueprints of the ASEAN Community and other related documents. The report of the AIEPG was submitted to the 10th ASEAN-India Summit in November 2012 in Phnom Penh, Cambodia. In this view, the leaders tasked the ministers to judge the report carefully and to apply the key recommendations wherever apt.

6.2.4 Economic Cooperation

The amount of trade and investment flows among ASEAN and India remained moderately low as compared to other dialogue partners of ASEAN. Between 1993 and 2003, ASEAN-India bilateral trade grew at an annual rate of 11.2 percent, from U.S. $2.9 billion in 1993 to U.S. $12.1 billion in 2003. The total trade between ASEAN and India declined by 5.4 percent, from U.S. $71.8 billion in 2012 to U.S. $67.9 billion in 2013. At the 10th ASEAN-India Summit in November 2012, the leaders put the target of U.S. $100 billion by 2015 for ASEAN-India trade. Foreign direct investments (FDI) from India fell by 41 percent from U.S. $2.2 billion in 2012 to a slightly more than U.S. $1.3 billion in 2013, rebounding from negative U.S. $1.7 billion in the previous years. Acknowledging and recognising the trend and the economic prospective of closer linkages, both sides recognised the opportunities for deepening trade and investments and settled to negotiate a framework agreement to give way for the establishment of an ASEAN-India Free Trade Area. In 2003, at the 2nd ASEAN-India Summit, the leaders signed the ASEAN-India Framework Agreement on Comprehensive Economic Cooperation. The Framework Agreement laid a perfect basis for the establishment of an ASEAN-India Free Trade Area (FTA) that includes FTA in goods, services, and investment.

After six years of negotiations, ASEAN and India signed the ASEAN-India Trade in Goods (TIG) Agreement in Bangkok on 13th August 2009. The signing of the ASEAN-India Trade in Goods Agreement gives way to the establishment of one of the world's biggest free trade areas (FTA) – market of almost 1.8 billion people with a combined GDP of U.S. $2.8 trillion. The ASEAN-India FTA will see tariff liberalisation of over 90 percent of products traded amid the two dynamic regions. Tariffs on over 4,000 product lines will be eradicated by 2016. The ASEAN-India TIG Agreement entered into force on 1st January 2010.

During the 10th ASEAN-India Summit in November 2012, the ASEAN-India leaders tasked their ministers to intensify their efforts and flexibility to conclude the ASEAN-India Trade in Services and Investment Agreement at the earliest. Consequently, an announcement on the conclusion of the negotiations on both agreements on ASEAN-India Trade in Services and Investment was prepared at the ASEAN-India Commemorative Summit on 20th December 2012. The Agreement has been signed by all ASEAN Member States and India in January 2015. ASEAN and India are also working on improving private sector engagement, including the re-activation of the ASEAN-India Business Council (AIBC), the holding of the first ASEAN-India Business Summit (AIBS) and an ASEAN-India Business Fair and Conclave (AIBFC) held in New Delhi in March, 2011, along with the participation of an estimated 500 trade exhibitors, business leaders, practitioners and entrepreneurs from ASEAN and India to display their products and services. The 2nd AIBF took place at the sidelines of the ASEAN-India Commemorative Summit, in New Delhi in December 2012. In order to encourage trade and business-to-business interaction, the events were part of the efforts.

The 14th ASEAN Transport Ministers (ATM) Meeting in November 2008 in Makati Metro, Manila, Philippines adopted the ASEAN-India Aviation Cooperation Framework that will lay the foundation for quicker aviation cooperation among ASEAN and India. In 2012, for the first time, India participated in the 21st ASEAN Land Transport Working Group (LTWG) Meeting. Throughout the meet, India presented its initiatives for better cooperation on ASEAN Action Plan, covering a range of sectors like land transport, maritime transport, border management, customs, immigration, logistics and safety, and Public Private Partnership (PPP). The India-Myanmar-Thailand Trilateral Highway Project and its extension to Laos and Cambodia is one of the examples of ASEAN-India physical connectivity. The project was planned in a way to connect the ASEAN Highway Network with the highway system in eastern India.

In tourism, the number of visitor arrivals from India to ASEAN in 2012 was 2.84 million, an increase from 2.711 million 2011. The 2nd Meeting of ASEAN and India Tourism Ministers (ATM + India) held in January 2010 in Bandar Seri Begawan supported the establishment of the ASEAN Promotional Chapter for Tourism (APCT). It was done as an essential collaborative platform for ASEAN National Tourism Organisations (NTOs) to market Southeast Asia to the Indian consumers and to generate mutual awareness amid ASEAN member states and India. During the 3rd ATM + India held in January 2012, in Manado, Indonesia, the ASEAN and India Tourism Ministers signed the Memorandum of Understanding (MoU) between ASEAN and India on Strengthening Tourism Cooperation, to boost tourism collaboration between ASEAN and India through concrete activities, which would serve as the key instrument for more action-oriented cooperation, motivating both parties to cooperate in facilitating travel and tourist visits to strengthen the close tourism partnership. The Ministers also received the ASEAN-India Car Rally. This rally marked another significant step in ASEAN-India tourism cooperation and simultaneously reflected the existence of land route connectivity that would assist tourism exchange among ASEAN and India.

Furthermore, the 10th ASEAN-India Summit welcomed the establishment of India's Inter-Ministerial Group on connectivity and supported regular exchanges among the Group and the ASEAN Connectivity Coordinating Committee (ACCC) to discover concrete ways and ways to support the MPAC, in areas where India has strong expertise and interest. The 1st ASEAN-India ACCC meeting was held in Balikpapan, Indonesia. The meeting served in providing a format for expeditious exchange of information to assist easy decision making on broad project proposals and ideas mentioned in the various studies on ASEAN-India connectivity. Major noteworthy developments can also be witnessed in the field of agriculture and forestry sector, since ASEAN and India have successfully held the first and second ASEAN-India Ministerial meeting on Agriculture and Forestry. The ministers adopted the Medium Term Plan of Action for ASEAN-India Cooperation in Agriculture (2011-2015) for promoting and intensifying cooperation in the agriculture and forestry sector between ASEAN and India, to meet the challenges of food security, to exchange information and technology, to cooperate on research and development projects, to persuade agriculture and forestry-related industries, and to support human resources development. A lot of cooperative activities have been carried out in these areas, most notably the ASEAN-India Agri-Expo and the Symposium on Indo-ASEAN Export Potential of Agriculture Products, which were organised in October 2012.

6.2.5 Social and Cultural Cooperation

Since its evolution, ASEAN-India socio-cultural cooperation has been extended to incorporate human resource development, science and technology (S&T), people-to-people contacts, health and pharmaceuticals, transport and infrastructure, small and medium enterprises (SMEs), tourism, information and communication technology (ICT), agriculture, energy and initiative for ASEAN Integration (IAI). All cooperation projects are sponsored by the ASEAN-India Fund (AIF). Support in these areas are carried out through the implementation of the Plan of Action (PoA) to implement the ASEAN-India Partnership for peace, progress and shared prosperity that was adopted by the leaders at the 3rd ASEAN-India Summit in November 2004 in Vientiane. The PoA is carried out through activities under several existing ASEAN sectoral work plans, declarations concluded among ASEAN and India, plus priority activities under the roadmap for an ASEAN Community 2009-2015, which can be implemented with India.

Furthermore, India is actively contributing to the execution of the IAI Work Plan with the help of some IAI projects like the Entrepreneurship Development Centres (EDC) and the Centres for the English Language Training (CELT) in Cambodia, Lao PDR, Myanmar and Viet Nam. Also, India is optimistically considering the establishment of a CELT in Indonesia. In order to promote people-to-people contact for fostering ASEAN-India relations at individual level, ASEAN and India continue to organise programme/activities that have been on-going yearly, namely ASEAN-India Students Exchange Programme, Special Course for ASEAN Diplomats, Delhi Dialogue, ASEAN-India Media Exchange Programme, ASEAN-India Young Farmers Exchange Programme, and the ASEAN-India Network of Think-Tanks.

In 2010, pursuant to the announcement by the Prime Minister of India during the 6th ASEAN-India Summit held in November 2007, the ASEAN-India Green Fund with an initial contribution of U.S. $5 million was established to maintain cooperative pilot projects among ASEAN and India for the promotion of technologies intended at encouraging adaptation to and mitigation of climate change. In addition, the ASEAN-India Science and Technology development fund was set up to encourage collaborative Research and Development and technological growth between ASEAN and India. In 2007, India made a contribution of U.S. $1 million to the ASEAN Development Fund (ADF).The ASEAN leaders also received the declaration made by Ex-Prime Minister Manmohan Singh to distribute, during the period of ASEAN Work Plan, U.S. $50 million to the ASEAN-India Cooperation Fund and the ASEAN Development Fund in support of the above initiatives, as well as IAI programme and projects in the areas of education, energy, agriculture and forestry, SMEs and implementation of the ASEAN ICT Master Plan.

Based on the ASEAN-India Vision Statement taken up by the Commemorative Summit in November 2012, ASEAN and India launched the ASEAN-India Research and Information System for Developing Countries (RIS) in New Delhi to endorse, trade, investment, tourism and cultural exchanges. ASEAN and India are at present discussing the modalities of the Centre.

6.2.6 Major Commodities of Export and Import – ASEAN

The major commodities of export include refined petroleum (crude and products), transport equipments, machinery and instruments, meat and preparations, gem and jewellery, dyes/intermediates and coal tar chemical, electronic goods, ground nuts, drugs, pharmaceuticals and fine chemicals, marine products, etc. The major commodities of import include vegetable oils fixed (edible), coal, coke and briquettes, crude petroleum (crude and products), electronic goods, organic chemicals, machinery, metalliferous ores, metal scrap, transport equipments, wood and wood products, etc.

Table 6.3 L: India-ASEAN Trade data

(Values in U.S. $ Millions)

S. No	Country	2010-2011			2011-2012 (P)			2012-13 (P) (April-Dec)		
		Exports	Imports	Total Trade	Exports	Imports	Total Trade	Exports	Imports	Total Trade
1	Brunei	23.07	234.17	257.23	895.49	751.68	1,647.17	27.03	803.27	830.3
2	Cambodia	66.94	8.01	74.95	99.45	7.62	107.07	81.02	8.82	89.84
3	Indonesia	5,700.87	9,918.63	15,619.50	6,666.51	14,650.11	21,316.61	3,849.22	10,816.28	14,665.51
4	Lao PDR	13.11	0.22	13.33	14.97	89.53	104.5	19.34	117.88	137.22
5	Malaysia	3,871.18	6,523.58	10,394.76	3,977.30	9,555.70	13,533.00	2,663.81	8,031.64	10,695.45
6	Myanmar	320.62	1,017.67	1,338.29	543.57	1,324.74	1,868.31	343.01	1,044.64	1,387.65
7	Philippines	881.1	429.39	1,310.49	991.81	455.65	1,447.46	858.03	395.08	1,253.11
8	Singapore	9,825.44	7,139.31	16,964.75	16,794.88	8,576.94	25,371.81	9,445.60	5,774.02	15,219.63
9	Thailand	2,274.21	4,272.09	6,546.31	2,951.71	5,418.23	8,369.94	2,589.09	4,071.42	6,660.51
10	Vietnam Soc Rep	2,651.44	1,064.90	3,716.34	3,713.81	1,733.44	5,447.25	2,614.98	1,505.35	4,120.33
	Total of ASEAN	25,627.99	30,607.96	56,235.95	36,649.51	42,563.63	79,213.13	22,491.13	32,568.40	55,059.53
	percent Share in India's total	10.2	8.28	9.06	12.03	8.7	9.98	10.63	8.92	
	India's total	2,51,136.19	3,69,769.13	6,20,905.32	3,04,623.53	4,89,181.28	7,93,804.81	2,11,597.60	3,65,003.90	576,601.50

Source: DGCI&S, Kolkata

ASEAN is a geopolitical and economic organisation consisting of the following member states – Brunei, Cambodia, Indonesia, Laos, Malaysia, Myanmar, Philippines, Singapore, Thailand, and Vietnam. It covers a land area of 4.46 million kilometres and has approximately 600 million inhabitants. In 2011, its combined nominal GDP amounted to U.S. $2.2 trillion, which would rank it as the world's 10th largest economy if measured as a single entity. The six largest economies in ASEAN are known as the ASEAN six majors. They are as follows (including nominal 2011 GDP):

- Indonesia (U.S. $846.83 billion)
- Thailand (U.S. $345.65 billion)
- Malaysia (U.S. $278.67 billion)
- Singapore (U.S. $239.7 billion)
- Philippines (U.S. $224.75 billion)
- Vietnam (U.S. $123.96 billion)

Statistics for the remaining four countries are as follows –

- Myanmar (U.S. $51.93 billion)
- Cambodia (U.S. $12.88 billion)
- Brunei (U.S. $12.37 billion)
- Laos (U.S. $8.3 billion)

Area wise, India is the seventh largest country in the world, covering 3.3 million kilometres with a population of approximately 1.2 billion people. Meanwhile, in 2011, India's economy was actually the 10th largest in the world with a nominal GDP of U.S. $1.85 trillion. In 2011, India imported U.S. $461.4 billion worth of goods, including crude oil, raw precious stones, machinery, fertiliser, iron and steel, and chemicals. In contrast, India exported U.S. $299.4 billion worth of goods at the same time, including petroleum products, precious stones, machinery, iron and steel, chemicals, vehicles and apparel. India's trade with ASEAN is largely concentrated in Singapore, Malaysia, and Thailand.

India's main exports to ASEAN include:

- Petroleum products
- Oil meals
- Gems and jewellery
- Electronic goods
- Cotton yarn and wool
- Machinery and instruments
- Primary/semi-finished iron and steel
- Transport equipment
- Marine products
- Drugs and pharmaceuticals

- Inorganic, organic, and agro chemicals
- Dyes and intermediates
  ASEAN's main exports to India include:
- Coal, coke, briquettes
- Vegetable and petroleum oils
- Electronic goods
- Organic chemicals
- Non-electrical machinery
- Wood and wood products
- Non-ferrous metals, metalliferous ores and metal scrap

6.2.7 ASEAN Free Trade

The major commodities of export include refined petroleum (crude and products), transport equipments, machinery and instruments, meat and preparations, gem and jewellery, dyes/intermediates and coal tar chemicals, electronic goods, ground nuts, drugs, pharmaceuticals and fine chemicals, marine products, etc. The first framework agreement was signed in Bali, Indonesia, on October 8, 2003, and the last agreement was signed on August 13, 2009. The free trade area came into effect on January 1, 2010.

As a result of the recent ASEAN-India Commemorative Summit in New Delhi on December 20th-21st, 2012, and the successive passing of the free trade agreement (FTA) on services and investments, economic ties and prosperity are certain to flourish among the two regions. FTAs among the two regions appear to be operating efficiently and economically, the FTA in goods concluded in 2010, has helped trade to grow by 41 percent in 2011-12. The implementation of the 2012 FTA on services and investments has set annual India-ASEAN trade to grow to U.S. $100 billion by 2015. Trade connecting India and ASEAN currently stands around nearly U.S. $80 billion.

After the European Union, United States and China, ASEAN is India's fourth-largest trading partner. The trade between India and ASEAN is expected to receive a significant increase with the finalisation of the services and investment FTA.

The trade-in-goods FTA abolished tariffs of about 4,000 products (including electronics, chemicals, machinery and textiles) between the regions. Duties for 3,200 products were reduced by December 2013, and duties on the remaining 800 products are to be brought down to zero or near zero by December 2016.

There are in all 489 items excluded from the list of tariff concessions and 590 items excluded from the list of tariff eliminations relating to farm products, automobiles, certain auto-parts, machinery, chemicals, and crude and textile products. ASEAN and India have agreed to permit tariff lines or products, between 7 percent and 9 percent to be excluded from tariff reduction commitments.

(i)   Indonesia, Vietnam and Myanmar

Indonesia and Vietnam constitute two of the major six economies in ASEAN, while Myanmar is one of the fourth smallest economies in the region (alongside Cambodia, Brunei and Laos). Collectively, these three countries unite for a total GDP of U.S. $1.07 trillion, a population of 378.5 million, and exports to India amounting to U.S. $13.37 billion (or, about 2.7 percent of India's total imports). In combination with ASEAN's constant emergence as a regional economic powerhouse, these figures are on the brink of growing due to the free trade agreements (FTAs) signed between India and ASEAN.

Indonesia-India Trade

The first President of Indonesia, Sukarno, recognised the significance of the Indonesian-Indian relationship and called for greater trade ties. In November 2005, Indonesia and India signed a bilateral strategic partnership agreement in which the two countries agreed to boost bilateral trade to $10 billion by 2010. This target was surpassed that year with total trade amounting to approximately $12 billion, tripling the $4 billion amount set in 2005. In 2012, bilateral trade involving India and Indonesia topped out at $20 billion and grew up to $25 billion in 2015. In addition, to establish a Joint Study Group (JSG), Indonesia and India in 2005, signed a Memorandum of Understanding (MoU) to examine the constructive aspects that would occur by signing a Comprehensive Economic Cooperation Agreement (CECA). The CECA agreement covers economic cooperation and trade in goods and services and investments which would lead to a higher level of mutually beneficial economic cooperation among the two countries. The JSG projected that CECA would increase total exports between India and Indonesia to $17.5 billion by 2020, with exports from India increasing to $7.8 billion and exports from Indonesia reaching $9.7 billion.

Over the years, CECA discussions have progressed with talks covering tariff reductions and the lifting of non-trade barriers on various goods of interest, including palm oil products from Indonesia and pharmaceuticals and buffalo meat from India. In 2010, India implemented a FTA with Indonesia which cut import duties on products like seafood, chemicals, and apparel. Indonesia cut import duties on Indian goods, in return. By 2011, India and Indonesia had signed 18 agreements in the mining, infrastructure, and manufacturing sectors worth total of $15.1 billion, in addition to a FTA on goods.

Vietnam-India Trade

Ever since India granted Vietnam "Most Favoured Nation" status in 1975, trade relations have been robust. In 1978, the two countries signed a bilateral trade agreement, followed by the Bilateral Investment Promotion and Protection Agreement (BIPPA) in March 1997. Subsequently, both nations promulgated a Joint Declaration on Comprehensive Cooperation in addition to negotiating a free trade agreement in 2003. Bilateral trade has improved since then and India is among the ten largest exporters to Vietnam. In 2012, two-way trade achieved $4 billion, with Indian exports accounting for $2.34 billion while Vietnam's exports accounted for $1.56 billion. The two sides have set a target of $7 billion for bilateral trade by 2015. With the signing of the India-ASEAN FTA on trade in goods, bilateral trade is poised to grow at an even rapid rate. Vietnam maintains to be an attractive investment destination for Indian companies in sectors like oil and gas, steel, minerals, tea, coffee, sugar and food processing. India and Vietnam have also extended cooperation in information technology and education and are join forces on their respective national space programs. In 2010, India implemented a FTA with Vietnam to slash import duties on products like seafood, chemicals and apparel. In return, Vietnam slashed import duties on Indian goods.

Myanmar-India Trade

The Indian government has been cultivating ties with Myanmar since a long time, as part of a broader foreign policy to boost India's participation and influence in Southeast Asia. Since then, India has developed to become one of the biggest markets for Burmese exports. India is Burma's fourth largest trading partner and its second largest export market taking in 25 percent of total exports. Further, the Indian government has taken effort to expand air, land, and sea routes to strengthen trade links with Myanmar. The countries also signed a bilateral border trade agreement for border trade to be executed from designated points in Manipur, Mizoram, and Nagaland. The two countries have primarily cooperated in agriculture, health, education, pharmaceuticals, telecommunications, information technology, steel, oil, natural gas, hydrocarbons, and food processing. In 2012, India and Myanmar signed 12 MoUs extending cooperation on border development, defence and analysis and joint trade and investment. Bilateral trade amid India and Burma is expected to double by 2015, growing from $1.28 billion in 2011 to $3 billion.

(ii) Cambodia, Brunei, Laos and the Philippines

As the Philippines is a part of the ASEAN, other six majors Cambodia, Brunei, and Laos are the three smallest economies in the region. Together, these four countries combine for a GDP of U.S. $258.30 billion, a population of 115.85 million and exports to India amounting to U.S. $1.33 billion (or, about 0.27 percent of India's total imports).

Cambodia-India Trade

When India officially recognised Cambodia's new government it opened an embassy in Phnom Penh. Currently, there has been an effort to increase their cooperation through institutional capacity building, human resource development, infrastructure development, security and defence. Besides, India and Cambodia have improved bilateral cooperation through increased interactions at regional and international meetings. Optimistic relations were established during the first India-Cambodia Trade and Investment Business Forum, Exhibition and Buyer/Seller Meet which required enhancing economic engagement between the two countries. That same year, India introduced wide-ranging duty free tariff preference schemes to Cambodia. Indian businessmen in Cambodia have also set up an Indian Chamber of Commerce to encourage bilateral trade and investment ties. India and Cambodia ties were further strengthened in 2011 when they held the first round of Foreign Office Consultations (FOC). These consultations were in regard to trade and bilateral cooperation, with a focus on policy, economy, security, education and vocational training, culture, IT and agriculture.

Brunei-India Trade

The sighting of oil in 1929 brought a substantial number of Indians seeking their fortune to Brunei. However, bilateral diplomatic relations among India and Brunei were not formally established until 1984. India-Brunei relations were improved in areas ranging from agriculture and defence during the Sultan of Brunei's visit to India in 2008. During his visit, five agreements, such as the Bilateral Investment and Protection Agreement (BIPA) and the Memorandum of Understanding (MoU) on Cooperation in Information and Communication Technology were signed. In 2010, India also signed a free trade agreement (FTA) on goods with Brunei, which successfully slashed import duties on products varying from seafood to chemicals to apparel. In return, Brunei also condensed import duties on several Indian goods. The major export from Brunei to India has been crude oil, while Brunei predominately imports textile products and vehicle parts from India. Conversely, with comparatively high shipping costs between the two countries and restricted connections between Indian and Brunei business communities, attached with the narrow needs of Brunei's lesser population, bilateral trade has been a bit inhibited. Strategies to further strengthen bilateral and economic ties have lead India and Brunei to investigate the possibilities of joint ventures in hospitality and infrastructural development in addition to joint ventures in the energy sector.

Laos-India Trade

Having a lot of common views on major international issues, a mutually beneficial bilateral trade relationship has built up between India and the Lao People's Democratic Republic. Considering the close ties amid the two countries, the Lao Government established the Lao-India Friendship Association in 1997. An FTA has also been put into action, which has seen both nations cut import duties on many products. In 2010, trade relations were further boosted since the Indian Chamber of Commerce in Laos signed multiple agreements and MoUs along with organisations like the Lao Chamber of Commerce, the Confederation of Indian Industry, and the Federation of Indian Chambers of Commerce and Industry. Metals, ores, machinery, and electronic equipment account for many products imported and exported amid India and Laos. In 2011, Indian entrepreneurs committed a combined U.S. $950 million in plantation, iron ore and agarwood project, which skyrocketed India from 22nd to 6th in terms of foreign direct investment in Laos. India, in the past, has invested in Laos' hydro-power, IT, human resource development and mining sectors.

The Philippines-India Trade

Business relations among India and the Philippines began to flourish with a trade agreement signed in May 1979. In addition to this, the first Philippine Trade Mission to India, a Joint Working Group and a Joint Business Council were set up to assess and identify potential avenues for trade and to identify new areas for cooperation. The agreement to set up a Joint Commission on Bilateral Cooperation was signed in October 2007, during President Gloria Macapagal-Arroyo's state visit to India, with an aim to support and develop cooperation in areas of trade, economic, science, and technology. Its inaugural session was held in March 2011, in New Delhi, during which both sides settled to carry on with the expansion on cooperative initiatives in various fields like trade, agriculture, and defence.

India and the Philippines are also negotiating to modify and explain certain features of their double taxation avoidance agreement (DTAA), with regard to the taxation of income derived from expert skilled services. Indian business interests in the Philippines mainly lies in mining, information and communication technology, as well as business process outsourcing sectors.

6.3 India and North America

6.3.1 Introduction

Economic ties between India and North America have strengthened over the years. India-North America bilateral trade and investment is likely to grow rapidly. The region is the third largest destination of India's exports stressing the importance of the region in India's export basket. Exports to the region report for almost 15.3 percent of our global exports with a CAGR of 9.2 percent in the last three years. However, it needs no recurrence, that the days ahead will be hard as the international trade situation remains irregular, with respect to the surplus of FTAs that are being signed by the U.S., EU, and India trying to defy these mega pacts by aligning itself with the RCEP countries. Relations among India and North America, mainly the U.S., in the political, strategic and economic spheres have improved drastically. The two countries also signed essential cooperation agreements in sectors of trade and economy, defence and security, counter-terrorism, high technology, space technology, clean energy and civil nuclear energy, etc. The India-U.S. Strategic Dialogue launched in 2009 has experienced further enhancement ties between the two countries.

India-U.S. bilateral relations have developed into a "global strategic partnership", based on shared democratic values and growing convergence of interests on bilateral, regional, and global issues. The stress placed on development and goods has formed new opportunity to strengthen bilateral ties and enhance cooperation. Regular exchange of high level political visits has granted sustained force to bilateral cooperation, while the extensive and ever-expanding dialogue architecture has set up a long-term framework for India-U.S. engagement. Today, the India-U.S. bilateral cooperation is international and multi-sectoral, covering trade and investment, defence and security, education, science and technology, cyber security, high-technology, civil nuclear energy, space technology and applications, clean energy, environment, agriculture and health.

6.3.2 India-North America Bilateral Relations

The bilateral relations among India and North America have established over the years in a considerable way. India's dynamic abilities can influence global growth and provide new growth opportunities for North America. When exports are concerned, the region is the third largest destination for Indian goods, following the European Union (EU) and West Asian (GCC) countries. Exports to the region account for almost 15.3 percent of our exports globally. Exports to North America signify a diversified trend as it includes different trade patterns with the countries U.S.A., Mexico, and Canada. The following table depicts India's merchandised trade pattern with North America.

Table 6.4: India-North America Overall Trade Figures

U.S. $ Billion

Year	2012-2013	2013-2014	2014-2015
India's Export to North America	39.82	43.41	47.51
India's Total Export to World	300.40	314.41	310.57
India's Export Share to North America with regard to World	**13.26**	**13.81**	**15.30**
India's Import from North America	32.04	29.33	28.96
India's Total from World	490.74	450.20	448.04
India's Import Share from North America with regard to World	**6.53**	**6.51**	**6.46**
Total Trade with North America	**71.86**	**72.73**	**76.47**

Source: DGCI&S, Kolkata

Engineering exports, our biggest market to North America, registered a slow growth post 2012-13 but resumed massively enjoying 29 percent growth in 2014-2015.

North America ranks second, where countries like Canada and U.S.A. have registered significant growth rates particularly for items like industrial machinery, IC engines and parts, electric machinery and equipments, and auto components, etc. during the fiscal 2014-15. The engineering trade pattern and pictorial distribution to the North American countries are depicted in the figures below.

Table 6.5: India-North America Engineering Trade Pattern

U.S. $ Billion

Engineering Principal Commodities	2012-2013	2013-2014	2014-2015
Iron and steel products	2582.67	2366.65	2879.88
Non-ferrous metal and products	499.43	690.89	1102.82
Industrial machinery	1634.19	1608.53	2163.75
Electrical machinery and equipment	587.37	526.69	579.11
Auto and auto components	1115.61	1504.16	1952.85
Aircraft and spacecraft	339.8	434.01	556.52
Ship and boats	51.62	0.6	0.49
Miscellaneous	911.39	850.22	1037.96
Grand Total	**7722.08**	**7981.75**	**10273.38**

Source: DGCI&S, Kolkata

The following pie chart displays highest engineering export share to U.S.A. followed by Mexico and Canada during 2014-15.

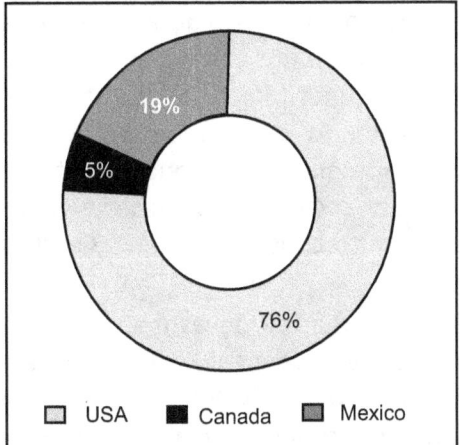

Fig. 6.7: India's Engineering Export Share to North American Countries (percent) in 2014-15

6.3.3 Trade and Economic Relations

Bilateral trade between India and the U.S. attained U.S. $63.7 billion in 2013, registering an increase of about 1.7 percent over the previous year. Indian exports accounted for U.S. $41.8 billion; whereas, U.S. exports stood at U.S. $21.9 billion. India-U.S. bilateral merchandise trade during January-October 2014 amounted to $55.86 billion with a trade excess of $20.97 million in support of India. During this period, India's merchandise exports to the U.S. increased by 6.8 percent from $35.97 billion in the corresponding period in 2013 to $38.42 billion, while U.S. exports of merchandise to India cut down by 5.36 percent from $18.43 billion to $17.44 billion. In 2012, bilateral trade in services totalled $58.76 billion, of which U.S. exports of services to India amounted to $30.17 billion and India's exports of services to the U.S. added up to $28.59 billion. During Prime Minister's visit to the U.S. in September 2014, the two sides lay a target to enhance bilateral trade in goods and services to $500 billion.

According to the U.S. Bureau of Economic Analysis, an U.S. direct investment in India is approximated at $24 billion. The cumulative FDI inflows, as per Indian official statistics from the U.S., April 2000 to September 2014, amounted to about U.S. $13.19 billion composing almost 6 percent of the total FDI into India, making U.S. the sixth largest source of foreign direct investments into India. Presently, growing Indian investments into the U.S. has been a noteworthy feature of bilateral ties. More than 65 large Indian corporations, including Reliance Industries Limited, Essar America, Tata Consultancy Services, Wipro and Piramal, have collectively invested about U.S. $17 billion in the U.S.

There are a number of dialogue mechanisms to reinforce bilateral engagement on economic and trade issues, including a Ministerial level Economic and Financial Partnership (last met in Washington in October 2013) and a Ministerial Trade Policy Forum (last met in

New Delhi in November 2014). India and U.S. are negotiating a Bilateral Investment Treaty (BIT). Both countries have dedicated to work through Trade Policy Forum to endorse jointly attractive business/investment environment. A high-level IP Working Group has been set up as a part of Trade Policy Forum to promote innovation led economic growth. There exists a Commercial Dialogue (with tenure until March 2016) that grants the framework for both Governments and the private sector to work together on trade and commercial issues of mutual interest for facilitating trade and investment opportunities across different sectors. For better involvement of private sector on issues involving trade and investment, the bilateral India-U.S. CEO's Forum was reconstituted in 2009 and had its last round of meeting in July 2013 in Washington D.C.

It was decided to create an India-U.S. Investment initiative, with particular focus on facilitating FDI, portfolio investment, capital market development and financing of infrastructure. The newly established U.S.-India Infrastructure Collaboration Platform seeks to install cutting edge U.S. technologies to meet India's infrastructure needs. U.S. firms will play chief role in developing Allahabad, Ajmer and Vishakhapatnam as smart cities. U.S. aid will serve as knowledge partner for the urban Indian population. Water, sanitation and hygiene (WASH project) to help leverage business and civil society (Gates Foundation) to facilitate access to clean water, hygiene and sanitation in 500 Indian cities.

India-U.S. Trade

Trade and commerce structure a crucial component of the quickly expanding versatile relations connecting India and U.S. From a meek $5.6 billion in 1990, the bilateral trade in merchandise goods has improved to $66.9 billion in 2014 signifying a striking 1094.6 percent growth in a span of 24 years. India's merchandise exports to the U.S. increased by 2.64 percent from $22.40 billion during the period January-June 2014 to $23 billion during the period January-June 2015. U.S. exports of merchandise to India grew by 14.33 percent from $9.68 billion during the period January-June 2014 to $11.07 billion during the period January-June 2015. India-U.S. bilateral merchandise trade during the period January-June 2015 was $34.07 billion.

Trade during the year the period January-June 2015

(i)   Major items of export from India to U.S.

Select major items with their percentage shares are given below.

   (a)   Textiles (17.2 percent)
   (b)   Precious stones and metals (20.1 percent)
   (c)   Pharmaceutical products (12.4 percent)
   (d)   Mineral fuel, oil (7.2 percent)
   (e)   Machinery (5.6 percent)
   (f)   Organic chemicals (4.7 percent)
   (g)   Articles of iron and steel (3.1 percent)
   (h)   Vehicles, excluding railways (3 percent)

(ii) Major items of export from U.S. to India

Select major items with their percentage shares, are given below.

(a) Precious stones and metals (30.7 percent)

(b) Machinery (9.7 percent)

(c) Aircraft, spacecraft, parts (7 percent)

(d) Mineral fuel, oil etc. (6.8 percent)

(e) Electrical machinery (6.4 percent)

(f) Optical instruments and equipment (5.9 percent)

(g) Organic chemicals (3.6 percent)

(h) Edible fruits and nuts (3 percent)

6.3.4 Country Synopsis

India-Canada Bilateral relation

India continues having diplomatic relations with Canada. India and Canada have enduring bilateral relationship based on democratic values, pluralistic societies, and strong people-to-people contacts. In the past years, both countries are working to improve bilateral cooperation in a number of areas of mutual importance. Several high level visits, have taken place during recent years. India and Canada have signed quite a lot of agreements until recently. Both the countries have launched the Comprehensive Economic Partnership Agreement (CEPA) negotiations in November 2010. The CEPA deal would boost Indian gross domestic product as well as promote the Canadian economy. The ninth round of negotiations toward a Canada-India CEPA was held in March 2015, New Delhi. The negotiation, where the progress continues to be made, was focused on goods and services. Canada remains committed in concluding an ambitious agreement with India.

India's engineering trade with Canada stressing the top principal commodities are given under.

Table 6.6: India-Canada Engineering Trade

Engineering Principal Commodities	2012-2013	2013-2014	2014-2015
Iron and steel products	267.02	246.95	316.34
Non-ferrous metal and products	22.62	24.21	29.33
Industrial machinery	85.25	77.87	91.71
Auto and auto components	24.15	19.54	24.97
Aircraft and spacecraft	30.11	14.08	11.2
Ship and boats	0.01	0.02	0.03
Miscellaneous	39.51	39.1	47.52
Grand Total	**482.69**	**453.04**	**556.12**

Source: DGCI&S

India-U.S.A. Bilateral Relations

India-U.S. bilateral relations have developed into a global strategic partnership, based on growing convergence of interests on bilateral, regional, and global issues. The bilateral cooperation is at present broad-based and multi-sectoral, covering trade and investment, defence and security, education and technology. However, there are four definite bilateral relationships that have influenced or are likely to influence trade relations among India and the United States.

1. Civil Nuclear Cooperation

India's position as a non-signatory to the 1968 Nuclear Non-proliferation Treaty (NPT) has kept it from accessing most nuclear related materials and fuels in the international market since many years. New Delhi's 1974 "peaceful nuclear explosion" stimulated the U.S.-led creation of the Nuclear Suppliers Group (NSC) – an international export control regime for nuclear-related trade. The U.S. government further constricted its own export laws with the Nuclear Non-proliferation Act of 1978.

2. Verified End User Program

A verified end user (VEU) program was intended in India in March 2006. The VEU program, also called as the "Trusted Customer" program, facilitates the license-free sale of otherwise controlled U.S. exports to approved Indian end users. The VEU program grants qualified Indian companies "*access to U.S. technology products in a faster, more efficient, and more transparent manner.*" As mentioned in the Wassenaar Arrangement, if India does not tighten its export controls, it was indicated that certain chemicals would likely be excluded.

3. U.S. Generalized System of Preferences

The U.S. Generalized System of Preferences (GSP) is a program designed to encourage economic growth in this growing world by providing privileged duty free access into the United States for up to 4800 products from 131 designated recipient countries and territories.

The products exported from India to U.S.A. get competitive benefit over products of other countries, due to import duty and the waiver granted to such products under the U.S. GSP program. The eligibility of the product under the U.S. GSP program is dynamic and is reviewed yearly by the U.S Trade Representative. Under the CSP program, one of the criteria under which a product is deprived of benefits is the Competitive Needs Limitations (CNL) criteria. According to the USTR, a product is considered adequately competitive, if the export value of a product exceeds 50 percent of U.S. imports or if the export of the product crosses the CNL value threshold.

India is beneficiary of the U.S. Generalized System of Preferences (GSP) Program, which "*provides duty free tariff treatment to certain products imported from designated developing countries.*" In 2006, India received GSP preferential treatment for $5.7 billion of its exports to the United States, of which $2.4 billion, or 42 percent, was jewellery or jewellery-related products.

4.   U.S.-India Economic Dialogue

The Economic Dialogue has four major tracks – The U.S. India Trade Policy Forum, the Financial and Economic Forum, the Environmental Dialogue, and the Commercial Dialogue. The main objective of the Economic Dialogue is to seek ways to resolve economic and trade issues, widen administrative capacity, and provide technical assistance.

The trade patterns of principal engineering commodities are represented in the table below:

Table 6.7: India-U.S.A. Engineering Trade

U.S. $ Million

Engineering Principal Commodities	2012-2013	2013-2014	2014-2015
Iron and steel products	2206.46	1906.46	2405.12
Non-ferrous metal and products	340.34	382.62	528.86
Industrial machinery	1429.27	1401.04	1926.78
Electrical machinery and equipment	555.27	473.64	511.63
Auto and auto components	734.08	808.34	957.43
Aircraft and spacecraft	296.17	419.94	538.2
Ship and boats	51.61	0.59	0.44
Miscellaneous	830.68	766.52	935.09
Grand Total	**6443.88**	**6159.15**	**7803.54**

Source: DGCI&S, Kolkata

India-Mexico Bilateral Relations

India-Mexico relations have always been friendly, warm, cordial, characterised by mutual understanding of increasing bilateral trade and an all-round cooperation. Antipodes, as they are on the globe, have striking similarities and commonalities' of geography, history, physiognomy, culture, and civilisation. Even factors like attitudes, mindsets, and values of people are fairly related. India and Mexico, both, are large emerging economies, with similar socio-economic development priorities and limitation, and have democratic, secular, and pluralistic systems, as well as convergent worldviews. Both to some extent, have comparable levels of economic and technological development, and are members of the important G-20.

Some of the bilateral trade agreements involving India and Mexico include Bilateral Investment Promotion and Protection Agreement (2007), Double Taxation Avoidance Agreement (2007), MoU on Cooperation in the Field of New and Renewable Energy (2008), Memorandum of Understanding Cooperation in SMEs (2006), etc.

The engineering figures are depicted below:

Table 6.8: India-Mexico Engineering Trade

U.S. $ Million

Engineering Principal Commodities	2012-2013	2013-2014	2014-2015
Iron and steel products	109.27	213.18	158.32
Non-ferrous metal and products	136.4	284.02	544.66
Industrial machinery	119.49	129.52	145.16
Electrical machinery and equipment	18.11	21.69	32.28
Auto and auto components	357.37	676.24	970.57
Aircraft and spacecraft	13.53	0	7.02
Ship and boats	0	0	0.02
Miscellaneous	41.16	44.46	55.15
Grand Total	**795.33**	**1369.11**	**1913.18**

Source: DGCI&S, Kolkata

6.3.5 Science and Technology (S&T)

The India-U.S. Science and Technology (S&T) collaboration has been gradually growing under the framework of U.S.-India Science and Technology Cooperation Agreement signed in October 2005. There is an Indo-U.S. Science and Technology Joint Commission, co-chaired by the Science Advisor to U.S. President and Indian Minister of S&T. The Joint Commission had set up an action plan for 2012-2014 that included joint projects, joint workshops, exchange of visits, and virtual networking in various disciplines.

In 2000, both the governments endowed the India-U.S. Science and Technology Forum (IUSSTF) to aid mutually favourable bilateral cooperation in science, engineering, and health. Over the years, the IUSSTF has facilitated more than 12,000 interactions between Indian and U.S. scientists, supported over 250 bilateral workshops and launched over 30 joint research centres. The U.S.-India Science and Technology Endowment Fund, created in 2009, under the Science and Technology Endowment Board promote commercialisation of mutually developed modern technologies with the potential for a positive societal impact.

Collaboration between the Ministry of Earth Sciences and U.S. National Oceanographic and Atmospheric Administration has been supported under the 2008 MoU on Earth Observations and Earth Sciences. A "monsoon desk" has been set up at the U.S. National Centres for Environmental Prediction. India's contribution of $250 million towards Thirty-Meter Telescope Project and Indian Initiative in Gravitational Observations (IndiGO) with U.S. LIGO Laboratory are examples of joint collaboration to generate outstanding research facilities.

6.3.6 Energy and Climate Change

The U.S.-India Energy Dialogue was established in May 2005 in order to promote trade and investment in the energy sector. In addition to five existing working groups in oil and gas, coal, power and energy efficiency, new technologies, renewable energy, civil nuclear co-operation, another working group on 'sustainable development' was added lately to the Energy Dialogue. Investment by Indian companies like Reliance, Essar and GAIL in the U.S. natural gas market is ushering in a new era of India-U.S. energy partnership. The U.S. Department of Energy has so far given its approval for export of LNG from seven liquefaction terminals in the U.S., to countries with which the U.S. does not have a free trade agreement. The Indian public sector entity and Gas Authority of India Limited (GAIL) have off taken agreements, totalling nearly 6 million metric tonnes per annum (MTPA). These terminals are expected to be absolute and in a position to export cargos by late 2016/early 2017.

As a priority initiative under the PACE (Partnership to Advance Clean Energy), the U.S. Department of Energy (DOE) and the Government of India have launched the Joint Clean Energy Research and Development Centre (JCERDC) planned to encourage clean energy innovations by teams of scientists from India and the United States, with a total joint committed funding from both Governments of U.S. $50 million. The Centre has funded three research projects in the areas of solar energy, second generation biofuels, and energy efficiency of buildings.

India and the U.S. are progressing in their cooperation and dialogue on climate change through a high-level Climate Change Working Group, which had its first meeting in July 2014. In November 2014, a MoU between U.S. EXIM Bank and Indian Renewable Energy Development Agency (IREDA) has been concluded to supply U.S. $1 billion in financing for India's transition to a low-carbon economy. A new U.S.-India partnership for Climate Resilience has been granted to advance capacity for climate adaptation planning, as also as a new U.S.-India Climate Fellowship Program to build long-term capacity to tackle climate change-related issues.

6.3.7 Defence Cooperation

Defence relationship has emerged as a major pillar of India-U.S. strategic partnership with the signing of 'New Framework for India-U.S. Defence Relations' and the resulting intensification in defence trade, joint exercises, personnel exchanges, collaboration and cooperation in maritime security and counter-piracy, and exchanges between each of the three services. A Joint Declaration on Defence Cooperation issued in 2013 highlighted the expansion of bilateral defence relations. The two countries now carry out more bilateral exercises with each other than they do with any other country. An Indian Navy ship took part in Rim of the Pacific (RIMPAC) exercise in 2014 for the first time. Bilateral dialogue mechanisms in the field of defence include Defence Policy Group (DPG), Defence Joint Working Group (DJWG), Defence Procurement and Production Group (DPPG), Senior Technology Security Group (STSG), Joint Technical Group (JTG), Military Cooperation Group

(MCG), and Service-to-Service Executive Steering Groups (ESGs). During Prime Minister Modi's visit to the U.S. in September 2014, it was decided to renew the 2005 'New Framework for India-U.S. Defence Relationship' in 2015.

Aggregate worth of defence acquisition from U.S. defence has crossed over U.S. $10 billion. India and the United States have set up a Defence Trade and Technology Initiative (DTTI) designed at simplifying technology transfer policies and discovering possibilities of co-development and co-production to invest in the defence relationship with strategic value. The Working Group of the DTTI had its first meeting in September 2014. The two sides, under the DTTI, have formed a Task Force to expeditiously assess and choose unique projects and technologies which would have a transformative impact on bilateral defence relations and improve India's defence industry and military capabilities.

6.3.9 Prospect for further India-U.S. Economic Cooperation

1. There are several areas where economic cooperation between India and the U.S. can grow further. These include infrastructure, IT, telecom sector, energy and other knowledge industries like pharmaceuticals and biotechnology.

2. Closer economic ties in infrastructure sector can yield mutual benefits to both the countries. The Government of India is constantly reviewing its policies to form an investor friendly environment in sectors like roads, ports, and airports. Private sector participation in management, BOT projects, greenfield airports, terminals and shipping berths, and capacity augmentation has been initiated.

3. At present, nearly two in five of the Fortune 500 companies outsource their software requirements to India.

4. Rich investment opportunities exist for further strengthening Indo-U.S. economic ties in the IT sector, especially, in areas like communication infrastructure, optic fibre cable, gateways, satellite-based communication, wireless, IT-enabled services, IT-enabled education, data centres and server farms, and software development.

5. India's telecommunication sector, already a major recipient of U.S. investment, is likely to carry on providing substantial opportunities to U.S. investors. India's telecom sector has been rising at a rate of about 20 percent per annum for the past few years.

6. The teledensity has increased from 1.94 percent in 1999 to 30.64 percent. The percentage of households moving towards richer and well to do group is escalating in India. There also exists vast untapped rural potential. India is the second largest wireless market in the world.

7. Government of India is devoted on foreign investment in manufacturing telecom equipment and handsets. India would require telecom equipment to the order of $84 billion to achieve the projected target of 650 million subscribers by 2012. Most of these investments are expected to come from foreign investment.

8. Some of the key changes include increase in foreign ownership limit, reduction of regulatory charges, moving to integrated licensing and spectrum policy, bringing

about comprehensive broad band policy, and restoring of national telecom policy. Observing the comparative advantages of the two countries, there is a great scope for further strengthening the business ties among the two countries in this sphere.

9. India's energy sector has been an important destination for U.S. investment. The sector offers for exploitation a vast untapped potential to investors in hydro electricity, oil and natural gas and coal. Even though several U.S. companies have been looking at the Indian energy market closely, progress has so far been inadequate.

10. With the introduction of Central Electricity Act 2003, the government of India has now liberalised the power sector. Private sector participation is now sanctioned in generation, distribution, and transmission. Considering the huge present and project demand supply gap, there is remarkable potential for economic cooperation among the two countries in this area.

11. Pharmaceuticals, biotechnology, and chemical industries also offer great opportunities for closer cooperation. India is one of the largest manufacturers and exporters of pharmaceuticals. It also holds the key for genotype drug design and is broadly acclaimed for its large pool of trained doctors and cost effective research and development (R&D) activities.

12. To facilitate bilateral trade and investment in the knowledge-based industries, the U.S. India Business Council (USIBC), along with FICCI, has established a Knowledge Trade Initiative (KTI). The KTI is a bilateral forum between India and the U.S. to consider key issues affecting the trade of knowledge-based products and services among the two countries. The main objective of KTI is to solidify Indo-U.S. leadership in the knowledge economy by harmonising bilateral positions on key issues affecting knowledge trade.

13. At present, the U.S. investor community is gradually sharing confidence in the future of the Indian economy. The increasing synergy between the two countries in the technology sectors and mutually shared respect for democracy, rule of law and well established business practices make the two countries natural business partners.

Points to Remember

- India-EU relations date to the early 1960s, with India being amongst the first countries to establish diplomatic relations with the European Economic Community.

- The European countries have been important trade partners with India over the years. The volume of total trade between the two regions has grown exponentially over the years, even during the adverse global economic conditions at some points in time.

- The EU as a bloc of 28 countries is India's largest regional trading partner, while India was the EU's 10th largest trading partner in 2013.

- India and the EU are in the process of negotiating a bilateral broad-based Trade and Investment Agreement (BTIA) that will significantly improve the commercial relationship once applied.

- There are Joint Workings Groups on textiles and clothing, agriculture and marine products, sanitary and phytosanitary issues, pharmaceuticals and biotechnology (SPS/TBT) and finally food processing industries, which meet frequently to improve sector-specific cooperation.

- An Energy Panel was set up by India and the EU in 2005 to enhance cooperation in the critical sector of energy and energy security.

- As envisioned in the Joint Action Plan, a Joint Working Group on environment dealing with prevention of pollution, waste minimisation, protection of biological diversity, sustainable forest management, environmental education, etc. has been formed and held its eighth meeting in Brussels in April 2014.

- India has always been a striking destination of FDI in varied sectors like services, construction, telecommunication, pharmaceuticals, and consumer goods.

- Europe is relatively high and more essentially consistent and stable. Their capability to remain an attractive destination for FDI even during the Euro crisis, with a constant inflow of investors, sets the Europe region apart from the rest of Europe.

- Among the other CE10 economies, both Austria and Poland share a favourable atmosphere for investments with India. In India, there are about 500 Austrian companies belonging to various different sectors such as infrastructure, engineering, automotive, and energy.

- India has shared a close and a mutual relationship with ASEAN countries. Mutual interest led ASEAN to invite India in becoming its full dialogue partner during the fifth ASEAN summit in 1995 in Bangkok.

- ASEAN and India signed the ASEAN-India Trade in Goods (TIG) Agreement in Bangkok on 13th August 2009. The signing of the ASEAN-India Trade in Goods Agreement gives way to the establishment of one of the world's biggest free trade areas.

- The major commodities of export to ASEAN includes refined petroleum (crude and products), transport equipments, machinery and instruments, meat and preparations, gem and jewellery, dyes/intermediates and coal tar chemical, electronic goods, ground nuts, drugs, pharmaceuticals and fine chemicals; marine products, etc.

- After the European Union, United States and China, ASEAN is India's fourth-largest trading partner. The trade between India and ASEAN is expected to receive a significant increase with the finalisation of the services and investment FTA.

- The Indian government has been cultivating ties with Myanmar since a long time, as part of a broader foreign policy to boost India's participation and influence in Southeast Asia. Since then, India has developed to become one of the biggest markets for Burmese exports.

- India-U.S. bilateral relations have developed into a "global strategic partnership", based on shared democratic values and growing convergence of interests on bilateral, regional, and global issues.
- Bilateral trade between India and the U.S. attained U.S. $63.7 billion in 2013, registering an increase of about 1.7 percent over the previous year.
- India and U.S. are negotiating a Bilateral Investment Treaty (BIT). Both countries have dedicated to work through Trade Policy Forum to endorse jointly attractive business/investment environment.
- India and Canada have enduring bilateral relationship based on democratic values, pluralistic societies, and strong people-to-people contacts. In the past years, both countries are working to improve bilateral cooperation in a number of areas of mutual importance.
- The U.S. Generalized System of Preferences (GSP) is a program designed to encourage economic growth in this growing world by providing privileged duty free access into the United States for up to 4800 products from 131 designated recipient countries and territories.
- The Economic Dialogue has four major tracks – The U.S. India Trade Policy Forum, the Financial and Economic Forum, the Environmental Dialogue, and the Commercial Dialogue. The main objective of the Economic Dialogue is to seek ways to resolve economic and trade issues, widen administrative capacity, and provide technical assistance.
- India-Mexico relations have always been friendly, warm, cordial, characterised by mutual understanding of increasing bilateral trade and an all-round cooperation. They also have striking similarities and commonalities' of geography, history, physiognomy, culture, and civilisation. Even factors like attitudes, mindsets, and values of people are fairly related.
- The Multi-Fibre Agreement was set up in 1974 as a set of formal quota agreements and restrictions, governing textiles and the clothing trade between developing countries and the developed world.
- There are several areas where economic cooperation between India and the U.S. can grow further. These include infrastructure, IT, Telecom sector, energy and other knowledge industries like pharmaceuticals and biotechnology.
- At present, nearly two in five of the Fortune 500 companies outsource their software requirements to India.
- Pharmaceuticals, biotechnology, and chemical industries also offer great opportunities for closer cooperation. India is one of the largest manufacturers and exporters of pharmaceuticals.
- At present, the U.S. investor community is gradually sharing confidence in the future of the Indian economy. The increasing synergy between the two countries in the technology sectors and mutually shared respect for democracy, rule of law and well established business practices make the two countries natural business partners.

Questions for Discussion

1. Define the economic relation between India and Europe.
2. Explain the trade relation between India and Europe.
3. Summarise the social and cultural cooperation between India and Southeast Asian nations.
4. Highlight the export and import commodities between India and ASEAN.
5. Define ASEAN free trade.
6. Illustrate the bilateral relation between India and North America.
7. Enumerate the trade and economic relation between India and North America.
8. Describe the India and North America Multi-Fibre Agreement.

April 2016

Study of Global Economics

Time: 3 Hours   **Max. Marks: 80**

N.B.:

1. Q. No. 7 is compulsory.

2. Attempt any four questions from remaining.

Q. 1   What is the meaning of globalisation? Explain arguments in favour and against globalisation. **[15]**

Q. 2   What are objectives of IMF? Explain role played by IMF and World Bank in global financial markets. **[15]**

Q. 3   What is global HRM? What are the challenges in global HR. **[15]**

Q. 4   What is commodity crisis? What are the preventive measures for commodity crisis?

[15]

Q. 5   What is regional integration? What are the major areas of regional economic integration and co-operations? **[15]**

Q. 6   Highlight the export-import commodity between India and ASEAN. **[15]**

Q. 7   Write short notes (any *four*): **[20]**

    (a)   Challenges of globalisation

    (b)   Changing world order

    (c)   SDRs

    (d)   India and infrastructure

    (e)   Mobilisation of global talent

***